PARIS TO DIE FOR

Maxine Kenneth

GRAND CENTRAL
PUBLISHING

NEW YORK   BOSTON

W9-ASK-861

Copyright © 2011 by Ken Salikof and Maxine Schnall

Grand Central Publishing
Hachette Book Group
237 Park Avenue
New York, NY 10017

www.HachetteBookGroup.com

Printed in the United States of America

First Edition: July 2011
10 9 8 7 6 5 4 3 2 1

Grand Central Publishing is a division of Hachette Book Group, Inc. The Grand Central Publishing name and logo are trademarks of Hachette Book Group, Inc.

Library of Congress Cataloging-in-Publication Data
Kenneth, Maxine.
    Paris to die for / by Maxine Kenneth. —1st ed.
        p. cm.
    ISBN 978-0-446-56741-1
    1. Onassis, Jacqueline Kennedy, 1929–1994—Fiction. 2. Women spies—Fiction. 3. Americans—France—Paris—Fiction. I. Title.
    PS3611.E667P37 2011
    813'.6—dc22
                                                                2010049218

Praise for
PARIS TO DIE FOR

"Great fun! Makes you want to buy big sunglasses and fly to Paris."

> —Rita Mae Brown, *New York Times* bestselling
> author of the Mrs. Murphy mysteries

"JFK loved Ian Fleming's creation of James Bond, so this intriguing novel may not be as far-fetched as you think."

> —Kitty Kelley, *New York Times* bestselling
> author of *Jackie Oh!*

"A bold book that makes you rethink one of our most beloved twentieth-century American icons."

> —Mark Medoff, Tony Award-winning
> playwright of *Children of a Lesser God*

"In her last year as an editor, Jacqueline Onassis was actually working on an espionage story that intersected with her own life at key points. I can imagine her paging through PARIS TO DIE FOR with a wicked smile."

> —William Kuhn, author of *Reading Jackie:*
> *Her Autobiography in Books*

"PARIS TO DIE FOR is a frothy romp through the City of Love with a determined young Jackie Bouvier. It goes down with a tickle, like a fine champagne."

> —Rebecca Cantrell, award-winning
> author of *A Game of Lies*

"Jackie. Oh! Like never before. If you like suspense, romance, Paris, and Dior you'll love this book."

—Laurie Graff, author of *You Have to Kiss a Lot of Frogs* and *The Shiksa Syndrome*

"Having known the real Jackie, I can say that she loved adventure—and had a fantastic sense of curiosity—and our imagined heroine here is likewise enterprising, brave, and fun to follow."

—Glenn Plaskin, interviewer and author of *Katie Up and Down the Hall: The True Story of How One Dog Turned Five Neighbors into a Family*

"Interesting and insightful... explores the early adventures of our thirty-fifth first lady as Jackie struggles to find herself pre–John F. Kennedy. Leaving behind the privileged life of her wealthy parents to serve her country in clandestine, death-defying adventures, Jackie never has a dull moment in PARIS TO DIE FOR."

—Diane Dimond, journalist, author, and columnist

"A ravishing romp through post-war Paris with our most elegant of icons. C'est un livre extraordinaire!"

—Shari Shattuck, author of the Callaway Wilde mysteries

*To the woman whose transcendent beauty,
intelligence, class, and courage made her
an enduring inspiration to the world*

May 7, 1951. Jacqueline Lee Bouvier, twenty-one years old and about to graduate from college, wrote a letter to Mary Campbell, personnel director of Condé Nast, sadly declining first prize in *Vogue* magazine's prestigious Prix de Paris competition. In the letter, on file in the John F. Kennedy Presidential Library, Jacqueline states that she cannot accept a position at *Vogue* because she has been offered a "special job on a certain project" with the newly formed Central Intelligence Agency. What happened next has never been revealed...until now.

PARIS TO DIE FOR

PROLOGUE

Republic of Balazistan, November 1939

She heard the *pop-pop-pop* of small-arms fire coming from beyond the palace walls and knew the revolution had begun.

Alert but strangely calm, the girl sat upright in her canopied bed just as the door to her bedroom opened, and Dexter, her personal bodyguard, stood framed in the doorway. His massive form almost completely eclipsed the hallway behind him. "The time has come, your Highness," he said to his young charge.

"Yes, I know." The girl slipped out of bed, ducked behind a filigreed screen gilded with silvery moons and stars, and began to put on her traveling clothes. Dexter didn't need to be told to turn around and give her privacy. He did it routinely as part of a well-rehearsed and often-repeated practice.

She dressed quickly, slipping on woolen leggings, a cable-knit turtleneck sweater, and a sherpa-lined hooded jacket in a blur, not even stopping to run a brush through her thick mass of russet curls, one of her few vanities.

"Where are my parents?" she asked as she finished preparing for her journey.

"They are already on their way to the airport. We will meet them in Paris."

The princess's mother was of French origin so the royal family would be granted sanctuary there. The girl took one last look around her room, fixing it in her memory and summoning all the warm emotions this beloved sanctuary encompassed. Then she composed herself and turned to Dexter.

"I'm ready," she said. Dexter took note of the moisture glistening in the little princess's eyes and remarked to himself on what a brave soul she was at such a tender age.

Dexter led her down the grand staircase and out through the hammered-brass main doors of the palace into the biting cold of the early-morning air. An old Bugatti touring car, its top up for concealment of its royal passenger and protection against incoming fire, waited in front of the entrance. Its motor was running, and a khaki-uniformed soldier—not the usual royal chauffeur—sat behind the wheel. Dexter opened the car door and ushered the princess into the backseat. She was just about to sit down when she suddenly bolted out of the touring car and headed back up the steps to the main doors.

"Where are you going?" Dexter wanted to know.

"I forgot something," the princess called back to him.

"There is no time, your Highness."

"I'll be right back." The haughty tone the princess had learned from her mother was very effective, he had to admit.

Dexter watched with a feverish sensation churning in the pit of his stomach as the princess disappeared back into the palace. The Palace of Shadows, it was called. And with good reason. Even now, with the morning sun glimmering behind the foothills of the Trans-Asian mountain chain, he had a difficult time seeing across the shadows still blanketing the courtyard. Beyond the gate, the military revolution was just now getting under way, and he could hear the stutter of machine-gun fire as a counterpoint to the percussive pop of small arms. It wouldn't be long before the violence would erupt in full fury, dragging them into a maelstrom from which any escape would be impossible.

He stared at his watch, each second that ticked by sending a fresh twinge of anxiety rippling through him. A distant rumble that grew into a loud drone drew his eyes skyward, and he watched in alarm as the low-hanging gray clouds parted to reveal the nose of a plane. A wing emerged next, and the noise steadily mounted to a low roar as the plane drew nearer to the palace.

Dexter was assailed by an ominous feeling. Why was a military plane circling overhead? Had it been hijacked by the rebels? Was it up to some harm? He glanced again at his watch and shook his head impatiently. What was keeping the princess? They needed to leave *now*. Silently, he implored her to hasten back to him like a precious turtledove completing its flight and landing safely at home.

And then, almost as though responding to his prayers, the princess reappeared, clutching to her side the one belonging he realized that she could not leave behind and had gone back in the palace to get. He could only hope it was worth it as he urged the driver to head for the airport without a moment to waste.

No sooner had the Bugatti sped through the palace gate than the deafening sound of a volcanic explosion rocketed through the air and reverberated in their ears. The plane had indeed been hijacked by the rebels, just as Dexter suspected. The palace symbolized all that the revolutionaries both envied and despised, and they had come on a mission to obliterate it, bombing it into a wild fountain of fire shooting flames into the sky.

Dexter pasted his hands over the back window, attempting to shut out the hideous sight from the princess's eyes, but he was too late. The cry she let out expressed a jumble of raw emotions—shock, terror, grief, rage, and the horrified relief of a survivor who narrowly missed being incinerated alive. Dexter put his arm around her to comfort her, but her sobs soon subsided and she grew quiet, falling into a reverie that lasted for the remainder of the ride.

The airport was located on the opposite side of the capital from the palace. Dexter told the driver to detour around the town and take the Ring, the elevated mountain road, instead. Going through town, a maze of narrow streets heavily trafficked even at this hour, was an obstacle course, at best. But today, there was always the chance that they might encounter an impromptu barricade thrown up by the rebels to snare some fleeing member of the royal family.

The Bugatti safely entered the gates of the airport and approached the one-story brick building that served as both arrival and departure terminal. Next to it, a raised wooden platform on stilts acted as the control tower. It looked abandoned, a lonely wind sock fluttering from its roof.

The Bugatti pulled up in front of the terminal. Dexter noticed that the airfield was bathed in an unnatural orange light. He looked out and saw a DC-3 engulfed in flames on runway 101. A sudden awareness surfaced inside him with a sick thrust as he realized who the passengers on that plane had to be. His first instinct was to shield the princess from the sight of the fiery remains of the plane, obviously the victim of a precision mortar attack, but he did not.

A soldier approached the Bugatti. He saluted and said, "The perimeter's been re-established. The mortar's been silenced."

Dexter nodded in response. He told the princess to duck down, then ordered the driver to make for runway 102, where a second DC-3 configured for passenger transport was waiting.

Miraculously, it was in one piece. The perimeter guard, Dexter surmised, had taken out the rebel mortar squad before it could destroy the second plane.

Dexter hustled the princess from the touring car to the plane, shielding her body with his and whisking her past the shot-down DC-3 too quickly for her to wonder who might have been in it.

Once on board the plane, he belted the princess in place, then did the same for himself. He looked down at her to make sure she was all right. Dexter had been a soldier and a mercenary before joining the royal family's personal guard and ultimately becoming the princess's private bodyguard. He had fought bravely and well in many wars and border skirmishes. But he knew that what he had to do tonight—the tragic news he had to break to the princess once they arrived in Paris, the terrible truth he would not be able to hide from her any longer—called for a different type of bravery entirely.

There was no one else on board the plane. The princess was tired and slept for most of the flight. The DC-3, a real workhorse of the air, put down only twice to refuel. Both times, Dexter unbuckled his seat belt and sat there, hand never straying far from the .45 he carried in a holster at his waist.

Finally, the plane touched down at its ultimate destination, Le Bourget. Dexter looked out of the window and saw, to his dismay, that a press contingent was waiting for them on the tarmac, notepads and Speed Graphics at the ready. At first, he thought he would wait for them to get tired and leave. But he saw that the princess, who had just awakened, was restless. It was probably best—and safest—to get her to the royal residence outside Paris as soon as possible.

Dexter stepped down from the door of the DC-3, then took hold of the princess and lowered her carefully to the tarmac.

The herd of reporters rushed forward. At first the princess cowered in front of them. But then she looked up at Dexter and grabbed his meaty hand with her tiny one.

"Don't worry," he said, "everything is going to be all right." And the amazing thing was, he believed it, every word.

One photographer on the tarmac that day won the Pulitzer Prize for his picture of the princess. It ran on the cover of *Life* magazine later in that fateful year of 1939. It shows Her Royal Highness, the eight-year-old Princess Nureen, last surviving member of the House of Mansour, clutching Dexter with her right hand and in her left holding the possession she went back into the palace to get—her teddy bear. It is the teddy bear that makes her look so young and vulnerable. But her eyes are implacable and fierce. And in the aching chasm between these two emotional states, the photographer froze the moment, and Princess Nureen Mansour entered immortality.

1

Paris, May 8, 1951

Jacqueline Lee Bouvier wasn't exactly dressed for discovering a corpse. A black Givenchy evening ensemble was no substitute for a white lab coat or whatever those people who examined dead bodies were supposed to wear. Nor was she dressed appropriately for this place—a cramped garret in a rundown apartment building in one of Paris's less fashionable arrondissements.

Jackie found to her surprise that she could handle stumbling over the dead man on the floor of the garret, even though this was the very first corpse she had ever encountered.

She could handle it when she saw the obscenely gaping wound in his chest with the blood still dripping down, although the sight of blood, even in films, usually made her sick.

She could even handle it when she watched as a scrawny rat scurried across the scarred wooden floor and tentatively began to taste the blood that had pooled beside the corpse's torso.

What she couldn't handle was the "dead" man reaching out with his hand to grab her by the ankle.

Jackie jerked her knee up—a knee-jerk reaction if ever there was one—to get away from the apparently not-so-lifeless hand, trying to stifle the scream that was fast rising up in her throat, and asked herself what she, *une fille américaine,* was doing here.

Born to wealth and privilege, crowned Queen Deb of the Year when she was presented to society at eighteen, schooled at Vassar and the Sorbonne, and recently graduated from George Washington University with a degree in French literature, how on earth had she wound up in this improbable apartment, babysitting a corpse?

Why, just twenty-four hours ago, she had been dining with this same dead man, the Russian, Petrov, at Maxim's. Of course, he hadn't been dead at the time.

And just twelve hours before that, she had been cocooned in the plush belly of a four-propeller Lockheed Constellation, curled up with a good book while flying across the Atlantic from National Airport to Le Bourget in Paris on her way to meet the Russian.

And just twelve hours before that, she had been at a party at her parents' estate in a suburb of Washington, D.C., where a chance encounter with a family friend, Allen Dulles, had set these events in motion like a rogue gene or a wayward train barreling toward an unforeseeable destination. But Jackie was forced to put all thoughts of this surreal chain of circumstances out of her head as she jumped back several steps to avoid the dead man's hand.

The Russian convulsed on the floor, and his hand opened spasmodically. Something fell out and floated across the floor to her. She leaned down to pick it up, mindful to keep a safe distance.

She looked fleetingly at what she had retrieved. It was a single ticket for the opera. She stuffed the ticket in her evening bag, then looked once more at the Russian. This time, he appeared to be well and truly dead, lifeless as the end of time. The convulsions had stopped, and he lay still. She could detect no rising and falling of his chest. She knew that she should do something. Listen for a pulse. Hold a mirror over his mouth and check it for condensation. But somehow, she couldn't bring herself to do any of those things. The fey thought nibbled at the edges of her mind that Death might be something contagious, and if she weren't careful, she could catch it too.

Incongruously, an old line from Oscar Wilde came to her: "Dying in Paris is a terribly expensive business for a foreigner."

For the first time, Jackie became aware of her surroundings. She had discovered the corpse almost as soon as she entered the garret. Now, looking around, she took in the room's few furnishings. A bed with an iron bedstead and a sagging mattress. A threadbare Algerian rug on the floor, its rucked-up condition showing that a struggle had definitely taken place here. A wooden chair and desk, both heavily pockmarked and worn with age. In the two open windows overlooking a cityscape of low rooftops, twin moth-eaten curtains fluttered in the breeze. From outside, a recording of Edith Piaf singing "La Vie en Rose" wafted through the steamy air of a Parisian summer night. The poignant music and the sultry night air created an alluring mood. And if it hadn't been for the corpse on the floor, Jackie could have seen the romantic possibilities of even such an impoverished garret. She could imagine Rodolfo and Mimi and their bohemian friends feeling right at home in this seedily seductive attic setting.

The room was illuminated by a single bare lightbulb set in an uncovered fixture in the low-hanging ceiling. The light from the lone bulb was dim, but not so dim that she couldn't see it shining off the tips of a pair of men's shoes peeking out from the bottom of the hanging sheet that served as a closet. And when one of those shoes moved ever so slightly, she knew, with a chill that froze her breath, that she was not alone in the garret.

Suddenly, the shock-induced aplomb that had carried her along like a robot until now shattered, and her numbed senses jangled alive. Every nerve in Jackie's body screamed for her feet to make for the exit. But that closet stood between Jackie and the door leading to the hallway. She was afraid of being seized as soon as she attempted to move past it. There was no other way out of the garret except through the window. But she was saving that as a last resort.

The only thing left was to stay and defend herself against an almost certain assault. But she wasn't armed. Dulles hadn't allowed for that eventuality. So Jackie looked around the room and inventoried it as quickly as possible. She saw nothing obvious that she could use as a weapon. No lamp. No heavy ashtray. Even the modest kitchenette looked bare of utensils. Where was a steak knife or a meat cleaver when you really needed one? Not that she had any expectation she could ever use one to defend herself. That kind of self-defense had not been part of her finishing-school education.

And then a lightning flash of inspiration struck, divinely, and she realized there was something in her evening bag that she could use as a weapon. Not for killing certainly, but for causing a distraction. She flicked open the clip on her beaded evening bag with her French-manicured thumbnail and fumbled around until she found what she was searching for.

With one hand in her bag and the other left free, palms sweating and her heart thumping insanely in her chest, Jackie approached the sheet-covered closet. It was only a few steps, but it felt like the longest journey of her life. With the warped floorboards creaking shrilly with each movement of her feet, there was no chance of her sneaking up on whoever was hiding in the closet. But Jackie came from a long line of storied military heroes—it was well-known among her relatives that twenty-four of her ancestors came over to America from France to fight in the Revolutionary War. As a young girl growing up in a household with a proud history, she listened in on many fascinating accounts of relatives' exploits on the battlefield. And she knew that a good general didn't wait to be attacked, but always took the attack to the enemy.

Arriving at the closet, Jackie took a deep, deep breath and flung back the sheet. A beefy, sinister-looking man was standing there inside the empty closet, and it was difficult to judge which of them was more surprised. The man recovered first and abruptly brought up a wicked-looking knife. It gave off a deadly gleam, even in this dim light.

As the knife began its swift downward plunge toward Jackie's chest, she grasped the object of her search in her handbag and held it up in front of him. She dropped her purse so she could squeeze the bulb, and the atomizer jetted a pungent spray of Chanel No. 5 smack into his face. The man screamed, pawing at his burning eyeballs, and was forced to drop the knife.

Jackie kicked the weapon across the room—it skidded under the bed—and tried to make it to the door. But the man reached out blindly, caught her by the arm, and flung her back across the cramped room. Fortunately, Jackie landed on the sagging mattress, and it broke her fall. With no other way out, she knew she had no choice but to go with the dead Russian's original plan.

She levered herself off the bed, then quick-stepped over to the nearest window and went through it, first one leg over the sill, then the other, cursing Givenchy for making this season's skirts so tight. Holding on to the windowsill with both hands, she felt around below until her feet came in contact with the narrow ledge that, according to the Russian, would be there. Jackie looked down and saw that it was six dizzying stories to the courtyard below. The Russian said to follow the ledge around the building and escape to the roof of a neighboring building in the next *rue*. As forbidding as it looked, she would take this dangerous route to avoid the killer, who looked much too big to follow her onto the ledge. Before moving any farther, she kicked off her shoes—there was no way she could negotiate this narrow ledge in black satin peep-toe stiletto heels—and heard them land with a clatter in the courtyard below.

Just then, the ledge beneath her feet crumbled away, and she lost her grip on the windowsill. So much for the Russian's plan. Jackie could feel herself falling and closed her eyes, her panic mercifully turning into stoicism. She braced herself, hoping that the impact wouldn't hurt too much or make a grisly mess in the courtyard.

Something unexpectedly arrested her fall. She opened her eyes, looked up, and saw that the man, blinking rapidly from the sting of the perfume spray, was gripping her by her right hand. He had the iron clasp of a catcher in a trapeze act, and it was this steadfast grip that had saved her life. Jackie's body swung like a pendulum from her one outstretched arm. But she was wearing silk evening gloves. Her hand began to slip ever so slowly but inexorably out of its glove, and she knew that her salvation was only temporary. This is what happens when you're a slave to fashion, she told herself as she felt her hand slip even farther.

As she dangled six stories above the courtyard, alone except for a dead body in the room above her and a killer providing a lifeline just so he could do her in himself, Jacqueline Lee Bouvier asked herself, *for God's sake, how did I get into this mess?*

II

McLean, Virginia, forty eight hours earlier

Jackie came down the elegantly winding staircase, one white-gloved hand on the curved balustrade, to a familiar scene of tasteful festivity. Her mother and stepfather were having a party at Merrywood, their magnificent forty-six acre estate, to celebrate her graduation from college. Their baronial mansion was ensconced like a giant mythical bird atop a high, luxuriant bluff overlooking the Potomac. The entire first floor was crammed with the usual crowd of friends, neighbors, and relatives, all of whom had known Jackie since her childhood. Everyone greeted her with affection and good wishes for what they were sure would be a brilliant future, meaning a successful marriage to one of their own.

Jackie thanked them as graciously as possible, wending her way politely but purposefully through the crowd of guests and black-uniformed butlers weaving in and out like shadows across the deep burgundy carpets. Her goal was the French doors that led to the terrace. She had some serious thinking to do, and this vantage point over an endless sea of emerald trees was the only place that afforded the peace and quiet she needed.

Outside, the air was thickly perfumed with the sweet scent coming off the lilac and honeysuckle bushes bordering the terrace. It was a typical summer night here in Virginia, hot as a furnace, and the air was leaden with humidity. Ordinarily, Jackie loved being home at Merrywood—riding her favorite jumper horse, Sagebrush, over the sprawling grounds, reading a book by the sun-dappled river, swimming in the pool, playing tennis or badminton in the enclosed courts, and in the winter, watching the snow fall like a benediction on those great steep hills. But tonight, she desperately wanted to be somewhere else—far away from the inescapable sound of her mother's angry voice still reverberating in her brain after the fight they'd had while getting dressed for the party.

An hour ago, her mother had been sitting at her dressing table applying her makeup when Jackie knocked on the door. "Mummy, can I come in?"

"Certainly, Jacks, what is it?" her mother asked, peering at her face in the lighted cosmetics mirror as she brushed mascara onto her eyelashes with brisk upward strokes.

Trying to control the fluttering in her gut, Jackie padded into the room in her slippers and sat down on the bed. "There's something I have to tell you. Mummy, I...I..." She faltered, her last ounce of courage leaching out of her just when she needed it most. *God, why was this so hard?*

"Come on, Jacks, what is it? We haven't got all night," her mother prompted, without turning her head. "You know how long it takes you to get dressed."

Ah, good, that verbal nettle was all she needed to get her nerve back up again. "Mummy, I can't go through with my engagement to John. I can't marry him. We have to break up."

Jackie said it in a rush, and when the words were out, she felt as if a wrecking ball had been lifted off her.

Her mother dropped her mascara brush, leaving a dark brown smear on the glass tabletop, and whirled around, glaring at Jackie with eyes as menacing as storm clouds. "What do you mean you can't go through with it? John's parents are friends of ours. His family is in the *Social Register*. They're the Husteds; they're Old Guard. John is a Yale graduate, and he's already a stockbroker on Wall Street." She took a breath and conceded, "I'm not happy that he's making only seventeen thousand dollars a year, but he has his whole life ahead of him. Is that what's bothering you?"

Jackie shook her head in frustration. Now it was her turn to get angry. "No, that's not what's bothering me," she said through clenched teeth. "You're the one who's obsessed with wealth...the *Social Register*...the Old Guard. I'm not concerned about what he does for a living or how much money he's making." She knew this would get her mother, so she tossed it at her like a quick javelin thrust. "After all, Daddy is a stockbroker too."

She watched her mother wince, resentful of how much Jackie idolized her father, drawing the purse strings of her mouth into a pinched *O*. "All right then, what is it? What's so wrong with John Husted that you can't marry him?"

Jackie thought of what her life would be like if she became Mrs. John G. W. Husted Jr., another name on the society page, whose days and nights would be bound up in a relentless round of parties, teas, dances, charity balls, and banquets. She would be walking into a one-way entrance to a lobster trap, lured into a tunnel of netting by a piece of bait—in this case, social status. She wanted no part of it.

She tried to make her mother understand. "Look, there's nothing wrong with John. It's the kind of life I would have as a society matron. It's not what I want."

"What *do* you want? Do you have any idea?" her mother shouted at her, stung by this repudiation of her highest ambition for herself and for her daughters.

"I want to become my own person, do something on my own, not just be somebody's wife. Can't you understand that?"

A fleeting look of sympathy crossed her mother's face before it hardened again. "What I understand is that this is a phase you're going through. We've all gone through it, dreaming big dreams of fame and success, but as women, we have to be realistic, know our place. And believe me, marriage to a wealthy man who loves you and will take care of you and provide the best for you and your children is no small accomplishment."

"But things are changing for women—"

Her mother cut her off impatiently. "Then think about taking a temporary job of some sort to get this out of your system. Right now, we have to finish getting dressed before the guests start arriving." She picked up her mascara brush and turned back to her mirror. Case closed. Final decree: "We'll announce the engagement in the *Washington Times-Herald* and have the wedding next June."

Tears sprang into Jackie's eyes, and she flinched as if she'd been slapped hard in the face—an indignity Jackie knew her mother was capable of when her redoubtable temper raged out of control—but she recovered quickly. "Fine, have the wedding in June if you want, but don't expect me to be there," she retorted vehemently, amazed at her own bravado, and stormed out of the room.

Jackie blotted her perspiring forehead with the palm of her hand as she stood on the terrace staring at the vast expanse of greenery. She wasn't used to this sweltering heat because usually she was away for the summer—either at her stepfather's waterfront estate in Newport, Rhode Island, or traveling Europe with school friends—but she shook off all thoughts of the outside weather and tried to contend with her own internal storm.

As long as she could remember, Jackie had been caught in the middle of a marital tug-of-war between her two mismatched parents. Pulling her on one side was her materialistic, controlling, propriety-driven mother, and on the other, the dashing, free-spirited father she adored, a glamorous sex symbol who seemed to have sprung to life from the pages of an F. Scott Fitzgerald novel. He was the epitome of the jazz age playboy, always dressed in high-style sartorial splendor and sporting a rakish pencil-thin mustache, a signal to the ladies that he was a dangerous man. Over time her mother grew disgusted with his drinking, gambling, and womanizing, but he could do no wrong as far as Jackie was concerned. It was magical growing up in her family's Park Avenue apartment when her parents were married. Who else but the man whose gorgeous dark hair and year-round tan had earned him the nickname "Black Jack" would have bought her a pony when she was six or let her keep a pet rabbit in the bathtub?

Her parents' divorce when she was eleven tore her world apart. But the moments she spent with her father took some of the terrible sting out of the divorce: every Sunday, half of every school vacation, and six weeks each summer. On Sundays, he would take Jackie and her younger sister, Lee, to baseball games or to the racetrack (places her mother abhorred) or to the movies, the zoo, or just Central Park. They would end each outing by consuming enormous ice cream sundaes at Rumplemayer's in the St. Moritz Hotel.

One of the best parts of dating John Husted during her senior year of college was that she got to stay at her father's apartment on East 74th Street. If she got engaged to John, she realized now, the real reason would be that she was afraid that no one else would ever marry her and she'd end up a housemother at Miss Porter's, her old finishing school. Oh, John was sweet and fun and affectionate, but he wasn't worldly enough for her, too *tame*. Yes, he was a stockbroker like her father, but there the resemblance ended. She took pains to keep it hidden, but there was a side of her that was very much her father's daughter. An adventurous, passionate side that her upbringing and high social status forced her to keep concealed under her straitlaced debutante's facade, like a butterfly trapped in a bell jar. But she was ready to let it out. And she was not going to let her mother stop her.

Although they had their differences, Jackie was happy for her mother when she found someone she deemed wealthy and prominent enough to remarry. Hugh Auchincloss was not only one of the most affluent and influential bankers in D.C., he was also a wonderful stepfather, protective and generous to a fault. Jackie relished being at Merrywood from the time she moved here at thirteen with her mother and Lee, but as grand as this life was, she hungered for something more.

But what? "What *do* you want? Do you have any idea?" She could still hear her mother's voice railing at her, both irritated and perplexed. At the age of nearly twenty-two, when most of her friends were already married and starting to have children of their own, Jackie Lee Bouvier had no idea what she wanted to do with her life. But she knew what she *didn't* want. No matter how hard her mother pushed, she was not going to settle for, in her father's words, "some funny-looking 'gink' who you think is wonderful because he is so romantic-looking in the evening and wears his mother's pearl earrings for dress-shirt buttons, because he loves her so."

Jackie couldn't ignore the part of her that wanted something else for herself. Something that had to do with expressing herself and being more than just a helpmeet to a man of accomplishment.

Her mother didn't want to hear that roles for women were not as rigid as they once were, but it was true. World War II had shown that women could compete with men at typical men's jobs—working on assembly lines, flying planes, and even playing on baseball teams. These days, women by the score were going to college for more than just a chance to snag a husband. They were using their college educations as a springboard for going on to law school or medical school or into business. Jackie couldn't quite see herself working on an anesthetized patient in an operating room or pleading a case before a jury of twelve inscrutable citizens or standing with a pointer in front of a graph of projected annual earnings. But she did want to do something worthwhile with her life beyond the usual charity work that women of her class did according to the unstated rules of noblesse oblige.

Sometimes Jackie thought about moving back to New York and getting a job in book publishing. Maybe, while going through the slush pile, she could discover the next *From Here to Eternity.*

Or maybe she could make her mark in magazine publishing, covering runway shows and writing about the latest fashion trends. She already had her foot in the door at *Vogue* after beating out more than a thousand other contestants to win the magazine's Prix de Paris writing contest with her essay "People I Wish I Had Known." Her passion for Oscar Wilde, Charles Baudelaire, and Sergey Diaghilev—something she never would have revealed to her peers for fear of being branded an intellectual snob—so impressed the judges that they offered her a year-long position as a trainee, dividing the time between their offices in New York and Paris. But she'd entered the contest at her mother's urging, never expecting to win, and now her mother was afraid that if her unsettled daughter spent six months in Paris, her favorite city on earth, she'd never come home. Even if her mother hadn't about-faced and wasn't urging her to decline the position, Jackie suspected that writing about hemlines and hairstyles was not her true calling. The great American novel was more her speed.

Sometimes she thought about making the clean break her mother most feared—moving to Paris altogether and leading a bohemian existence on La Rive Gauche. She could just picture it. She would dress all in black complete with beret, smoke Gitanes, work all day in a used bookstore (where occasionally Gertrude Stein or Ernest Hemingway would stop in), and stay out all night listening to hot jazz or arguing with friends about existentialism.

Then there was her ability as an equestrian that she might parlay into something. She'd been riding in horse shows from the time she was twelve. Of course, riding professionally was out. Even if female jockeys were allowed, she couldn't see showering dung on her parents by working in a demimonde of Runyonesque disreputable types. But maybe she could breed horses and might even end up producing the next Seabiscuit. And then what would her parents say?

A polite *ah-hem* from somewhere nearby interrupted Jackie's thoughts. She looked around and saw that an old family friend was staring at her through his wire-rim eyeglasses. He seemed to be studying her appreciatively as if he were standing in an art gallery admiring a painting on the wall. She was grateful that people found her so attractive, but when she read how one society columnist described her "classic features, high cheekbones, wide-set luminous brown eyes, and voluptuous mouth, all set in a frame of thick, glossy black-brown hair," she could only think, is he writing about *me*? Personally, she thought her hair was too unruly, her face too square, and her eyes too far apart—so far apart, in fact, that it took three weeks to have a pair of glasses made with a bridge wide enough to fit over her nose.

"Oh, hello, Mr. Dulles," she said, feeling somewhat embarrassed at being caught in such a state of extended wool-gathering.

"Hello, Jacqueline," Allen Dulles said. In all the years she had known him, he had never once called her Jackie. She had always pegged Dulles and his brother, John Foster, as the ultimate Washington straight arrows. Despite the oppressive summer heat, he was wearing his customary uniform of dark gray banker's suit, starched white dress shirt, and dignified tie. "I'm sorry to interrupt you," he continued.

"That's all right," she said, hoping to put him at ease. "I was just enjoying the night air." What a ridiculous thing to say, she chided herself. The only form of life capable of enjoying this night air was a mosquito from a malarial swamp.

He took a sip of his drink, and his lips widened into the hint of a disarming smile. "What I just said before was not quite true. Actually, I was hoping I could interrupt you."

Dulles seemed to be stalling for time. Jackie prayed that he wasn't going to ask what everyone asked when they knew a girl of her age was "going steady"—have you set a date for the wedding yet?—and mentally started drafting a face-saving answer.

But instead Dulles asked, "Jacqueline, now that you've just graduated from college, what are your plans for the future?"

Jackie tried not to show her surprise. Was he reading her mind? Could he tell just by looking at her how she was floundering, thrashing about at sea without a life raft? "I'm mulling over a couple of options," she told him.

"Well, that's good," Dulles responded blandly. He took another sip of his drink before asking point blank, "Did you ever think of coming to work for me?"

Jackie blinked as if blinded by a headlight. Since Allen Dulles was the deputy director of the newly formed Central Intelligence Agency, her silent answer was an astonished no. The only female spy she knew of was Mata Hari, and she couldn't see herself seducing spies in order to wheedle secrets out of them in bed.

"I didn't know the CIA accepted female candidates," she said finally.

"Normally, we don't, except for the usual secretarial pool and translation mill." Dulles twirled the stem of his glass between his fingers, carefully considering what he was about to say next. "But I have a special assignment that calls for a woman's touch. Someone attractive and intelligent in equal measure. Are you interested?"

Jackie was flattered but embarrassed to be complimented that way by an older man, even one who was an old family friend. Too flustered to speak, she just shook her head no.

"That's too bad," Dulles said, "because the assignment's location is Paris."

Paris. He had said the magic word. The city where she was dying to go. But now, instead of working there as a drone in *Vogue* magazine's office for six months, she had the once-in-a-lifetime opportunity to carry out a mission of high-level intrigue in the city of her dreams. Maybe she would get to wear that black beret after all. A chance to prove herself and justify breaking off with John Husted was being offered to her, ironically, on one of her mother's own canapé-laden silver platters.

But how to do a 180-degree turn without looking like a flighty little fool to Allen Dulles? Jackie's training in the social graces of a debutante came to the fore. "Mr. Dulles, why don't you let me freshen your drink?" she asked. "And then you can tell me all about that special assignment of yours in Paris."

"Fine; it's a dry martini with ice, Beefeater gin, just a whisper of vermouth, no fruit or vegetables," Dulles said as he drained his drink and handed her the empty glass.

Doesn't leave much to chance, does he? Jackie thought, as she went off to fetch his drink, wondering what it would be like to work for a man who operated with such clockwork precision, even in his personal life.

"He's a potential walk-in," Dulles told Jackie when she returned.

No other sounds could be heard on the terrace save for the pulsating song of the cicadas and the clinking of the ice in Dulles's glass, but Jackie leaned toward him, listening intently to every word he spoke.

"What's a walk-in?" she asked.

"A walk-in is a defector," Dulles explained in a pedantic style that went along with his scholarly look and demeanor. His wire rims, patrician nose, and high forehead topped with strands of thinning gray hair reminded Jackie of one of her college professors at George Washington U. One would never guess that during World War II, from his headquarters in Bern, Switzerland, this mild-mannered man was the very OSS station chief who had boldly penetrated to the heart of the German intelligence network and arranged for the surrender of the German war machine.

Jackie nodded, anxious to hear more.

"In recent days, it has come to our attention through circuitous means that the third cultural attaché at the Russian embassy in Paris is giving serious thought to defecting to us."

"Cultural attaché?" It was a term Jackie had heard of, but wasn't sure what it meant.

"Cultural attaché is just the usual embassy cover for SMERSH—the Soviet counterintelligence agency. It means

'Death to Spies.' Typical Russian understatement. Getting the third cultural attaché to defect would be something of a coup. Of course, we always ask that any prospective walk-in come bearing a gift."

"Really?" Jackie was well versed in the basic rules of upper-class hospitality, but she was surprised to find that the same rules applied to the world of international espionage.

"To establish his bona fides—a relatively new idea for us. You see, Jackie, like any young government entity, the CIA is making itself up as it goes along, improvising its codes, its rules, and its protocols on a daily basis."

"Ah, yes," Jackie said knowingly, just to show that she was still with him.

"And we think this third cultural attaché really has something we want to see."

"I see." Jackie hoped Dulles wouldn't think she was parroting him. "But where do I come in?"

Dulles took a swig of his drink and cleared his throat, dropping his voice to a confidential pitch that made Jackie lean in even closer to hear him. "The name of the third cultural attaché is Mikhail Petrov. We keep dossiers on all Soviet agents, and Petrov's says that he thinks of himself as a real ladies' man. Apparently, he's on the fence about defecting. But we think a female agent could provide the right incentive to convince him to make the leap to our side of the fence, if you know what I mean? There's only one problem."

Jackie waited while the answer hung suspended in the pause.

"We don't have any female agents."

Now Jackie understood where she fit into this particular scenario.

"Oh, I guess I could ask my secretary," Dulles went on, "but she's fifty-three and a grandmother three times over. I don't think our Mr. Petrov would be attracted to her. Do you?"

Jackie wanted to chide Dulles for his ungallant assumption that an older woman couldn't be sexually appealing, but she dutifully smiled at his little joke.

"You, on the other hand," he said, looking her straight in the eye, "are the perfect person for this assignment. You're attractive, speak French like a native, and are smart enough to ascertain his intentions and report back to me with your impressions of Comrade Petrov."

"Thank you." How did this man know so much about her? Jackie wondered. He was an old family friend, true, but not close with her parents the way other relatives and friends were. And then it struck her—the CIA must have a dossier on her too. The very thought of some stranger knowing all about her life made her feel distinctly uncomfortable. Despite the sodden heat, she felt a shiver inside.

"Unfortunately, our communication with Comrade Petrov is only one way. He calls the shots. He says he wants someone to meet him at Maxim's for dinner. We propose that person be you."

Once again, Dulles fixed Jackie with that direct stare. She found it impossible to turn away from it after having locked eyes with him.

"All you have to do is have dinner with him, find out what his intentions are, then report back to me. I'll give you a secure telephone number. Under no circumstances are you to go to the American embassy. Nobody there will know who you are. Nobody there knows about Petrov's intentions. The fewer people who know anything about this, the better off we'll all be."

"But who does he think he's meeting?"

"We have all that arranged. He's going to be meeting with a journalist from an American dance magazine. An interview about the Bolshoi's upcoming visit to Paris. Don't worry, she's a real person. But she's on assignment in Argentina, and her editor, a friend of a friend, owes me a little favor. So you'll be borrowing this journalist's identity for a few days. We just don't have the time to craft you a whole new legend starting from scratch."

"Craft?" "Legend?" This was all going a bit too fast for her. "Mr. Dulles, don't I need training for this?"

"For dinner and some conversation? I assume you already know which fork goes with which course."

This time, Jackie didn't feel duty-bound to laugh at his little joke. "But what about the conversation? I don't speak Russian."

"He speaks French, at least as well as you do. So I don't think communication represents any kind of challenge."

Jackie was stumped. She couldn't think of any more objections.

But Dulles seemed compelled to further persuade her, letting her know that the Cold War had escalated to a point of white-hot intensity. "I'm sure you can understand the pressure the CIA is under now that Julius and Ethel Rosenberg have been convicted of passing our country's nuclear secrets to the Soviets. They'll be the first civilians executed for espionage in United States history, but their trial unveiled a nest of other Communist spies within our scientific community we never suspected were there." Dulles shook his head, nonplussed by this conundrum. "Then there are those two British secret agents you must have read about, Sir Guy Burgess and Donald Maclean. The ones who were both working in America and suddenly disappeared a few months ago? Well, the CIA and MI6, our British cousins, are just waiting for word that they've turned up in Russia as guests of Moscow Center."

He was starting to sound exasperated. "To make matters worse, now Kim Philby, MI6's official liaison with our agency, is rumored to be somehow implicated in the twin disappearances. He's highly placed and highly respected. But also highly suspect. And of course, we have Senator Joe McCarthy in the news almost every day accusing the State Department of being riddled with hundreds of secret Communist agents."

Dulles downed the rest of his drink in a single gulp and gave Jackie a questioning look. "Do you see what we're up against and why I'm placing such a high priority on the success of my proposed operation in Paris?"

"You have a lot on your plate," Jackie had to concede. Although she wasn't a political person—her interests lay more in the arts—Jackie knew enough about the Rosenberg case to be bothered by doubts about the fairness of the trial. She had to find out if Dulles shared her reservations about Ethel Rosenberg, the thirty-six-year-old mother of two young sons, a petite sparrow of a woman who looked like Edith Piaf with a pinched bow-shaped mouth, going to the electric chair.

"This might be beside the point, but I'm just curious," she began tentatively. "Do you really think Ethel Rosenberg deserves to die?" She saw his eyebrows shoot up, and she hurried on. "I mean, throughout the trial, the only conspiracy attributed to her was typing up the information from the spy meetings. If that's all she did, the death penalty seems far too harsh a sentence."

Dulles looked at her as if he were seeing her for the first time. Jackie sensed that he hadn't expected her to know enough about the espionage trial to question the media's unanimity about the couple's guilt. The talk she'd heard about from her stepfather of a protest movement forming here and in Europe hadn't gathered much steam so far.

"Well, their lawyers are appealing, so I'm sure justice will be served in the end," Dulles assured her.

The mention of Senator McCarthy had also given Jackie pause. He gave her a creepy feeling when she saw him on television—something about his anticommunist ferocity smacked of a witch hunt. She was afraid that the net he was casting to catch disloyal subversives might be too wide and that many innocent left-leaning members of the intellectual community might be trapped in it as well. But she trusted Dulles to keep a cool head when many around him were losing theirs in an age of anticommunist hysteria.

Dulles patted her shoulder. "If you're worried about your parents' not approving of your undertaking this mission, you needn't be. I've already cleared it with them. Your stepfather's gung-ho about it, and your mother thinks it might be good for you to get away for a few days."

Oh, sure, and come back ready to fall in line with her wedding plans, Jackie thought.

"But there's just one catch," Dulles said to her, almost as an afterthought. "The dinner will take place in less than twenty-four hours. You have to be in Paris no later than tomorrow. If you are going to say yes, you have to do so now." He tried to placate her with assurances that she had a bright future with the CIA. "Look, when you come back from Paris we'll have you undergo intensive training before we send you out on another project in October. But right now, I need your commitment to have dinner with Petrov tomorrow. Otherwise, I'll have to find someone else to take your place."

"How long do I have?"

"You have the next five minutes." He turned away from her to give her a little privacy.

Jackie thought about it, weighing excitement against possible danger. But this wasn't going to be a dangerous assignment. This old family friend wasn't going to do anything that would risk getting the stepdaughter of a man as rich, powerful, and connected as Hugh Auchincloss killed. Still, there was always the unexpected, wasn't there? She was born, she knew with certitude, for a more contemplative kind of life. But hadn't she just said to herself that she wanted to make a difference?

And it was Paris, the city she loved more than any other in the whole world. Yes, she would have to write a letter to Miss Campbell, the editor at *Vogue,* declining the magazine's kind offer of a trainee position, but she could handle that with aplomb and a little judicious bending of the truth. She wouldn't tell Miss Campbell anything about the Petrov project—Dulles had made it clear that secrecy was of the utmost importance, and *Vogue* had an office in Paris. But Jackie would say that the CIA had come through with a project she'd lobbied for before she entered the Prix contest, never thinking she'd make the finals, and the CIA had invested too much in her for her to refuse now.

Jackie's veins pulsed with the bluest of blood, her genetic inheritance from a lineage of staunch, rock-ribbed conservatives who worshipped the god of gentility. Her forebears were, above all else, *sensible* people. Every fiber of her being, every particle of her existence, every trace memory of her heritage, cried out for her to say no to Allen Dulles's outlandish proposal.

Jackie said, "Yes."

III

Maxim's was Lutèce in New York City, La Caravelle in Washington, D.C., and Perino's in Los Angeles all rolled into one. It was the grande dame of all sumptuous French dining. To dine there was a singular experience, and that feeling never left you no matter how many Maxim's meals you allowed to threaten your waspish waistline. Every time at Maxim's was the first time, just as falling in love with a new lover always felt like the first time.

Unwittingly, Jackie became part of this rarefied allure as she entered the restaurant on the arm of Mikhail Petrov. Always uncomfortable in crowds, she kept her eyes straight ahead as she walked through the dining room filled with some of the most beautiful women in Paris, many of them mistresses of the city's most wealthy and powerful men. Jackie wanted only to get to her seat, but her combination of uncommon beauty, youth, and natural elegance made all heads subtly turn to follow her as though helpless to do otherwise.

The maitre d' led Jackie and Petrov to the center of the Belle Epoque–style room and pulled out an elegant dining chair for her at a glass-topped table for two decorated with a fluted velvet apron edged in scalloped satin. Jackie's eyes swept over the colorful art nouveau scrollwork, plush red banquettes, gleaming inlays of brass and stained glass, and polished mahogany woods before coming back to rest on Mikhail Petrov seated across from her. He looked to be in his late thirties and was even more handsome than the photograph Dulles had shown her. The grainy surveillance picture in his dossier didn't do justice to his suave manliness. Jackie took it all in with a visceral flurry of excitement: the square jaw, insouciant dimple in his chin, and crest of wheat-colored hair that brought out the crystalline blue of his eyes, sparkling with a playful expression as he caught her surveying him with obvious approval.

"I trust mademoiselle is finding the ambience to her liking?" he asked teasingly, smiling as Jackie blushed and nodded yes.

"The décor is even lovelier than I imagined it would be when I read about Maxim's in Colette's *Gigi*," Jackie said, quickly recovering and playfully assuming the magazine writer's role that Dulles had assigned her. "On a journalist's salary, the swankiest place I ever get to in Paris is the Ritz bar."

"Ah, the Ritz bar," Petrov said familiarly. "I've spent many a pleasant cocktail hour there myself, socializing with diplomats and people interested in cultural affairs. That and the Jeu de Paume museum are two of my favorite places in Paris." He spoke French with just the slightest trace of a Russian accent. He was as fluent in the language as she was, although Jackie doubted that, like her, he had come by his conversational skills at the Sorbonne. Petrov was every bit as charming as she had expected him to be, and in his expensively tailored Savile Row suit, he appeared to be far more worldly than most of his fellow countrymen.

Two of those countrymen had accompanied Jackie and Petrov from the hotel to the restaurant, following behind at a discreet distance. Dressed in poorly fitting suits stretched out of shape by their muscle-bound bodies, these two henchmen looked more like wrestlers than embassy officials. They reminded Jackie of characters out of some comic opera or parodies of stereotypical American gangsters dressed in black-and-white pinstriped zoot suits. And suddenly, the wisdom of Petrov having made plans to meet Jackie here at Maxim's occurred to her. His two shadows had to remain outside because they would never be permitted inside such a bastion of refinement, and he could dine with Jackie in privacy.

For the sake of verisimilitude, Jackie opened up her purse and took out a notepad and a Mont Blanc pen. If her cover was that of a journalist, it would be a good idea, she thought, to act like one. That was elementary tradecraft. But before she could launch into her first question, Petrov drew back his chair and stood up.

"I'll be delighted to provide you with any information that might assist you with your assignment," he offered pleasantly, "but first there is a small matter that requires my attention. I'll only be a moment."

"Of course."

Jackie guessed he was going to the bathroom as an excuse to make sure that his shadows were still in position across the street from the restaurant. Actually, she was relieved to see him go. She had lived in such a whirlwind state for the last twenty-four hours that it was a pleasure just to sit quietly by herself for a few moments and enjoy the amuse-bouche and Evian water that had already been brought to the table.

She quickly thought back on what had transpired between her conversation with Dulles on the terrace of her parents' house and now. Dulles had a cover story arranged with her parents to account for her movements over the next forty-eight hours. The following morning, a package had arrived with her new identity papers (passport, driver's license, American

Express travelers' checks) and a round-trip airline ticket in her new name with a Paris destination. She had packed as quickly as possible, fighting her usual habit of taking more clothes than were needed, and rushed to the airport. She had tried to rest on the plane, but found herself too keyed up to close her eyes for more than a few minutes at a time. Arriving in Paris feeling slightly sleep deprived, she had checked into a businessman's hotel located in the shadow of the avenue Daumesnil viaduct in the 12th arrondissement. It wasn't the four-star French hotel she'd been hoping for, but in her role of a mere working journalist, there was no way she could afford to stay at the Georges V or the Ritz. She barely had time to change into her evening clothes before the concierge called up to her room to say that a man named Mikhail Petrov was waiting in the lobby for her.

At the end of her conversation with Dulles, the deputy director had taken out a piece of paper and written two phone numbers on it. The first was the secure telephone number she was to call after having dinner with the Russian. The second was a number to be used in case of emergency only. Dulles explained that the number belonged to a casual, a civilian who, in the course of his daily occupation, was occasionally called on to do some contract work for the agency. This particular casual was a French photographer working as a stringer for an American wire service. It was called the Allied Press Service, and the name of the casual was Jacques Rivage. Dulles said he seriously doubted Jackie would need to contact him, and Jackie seriously hoped he was right.

Petrov returned to the table.

"Where were we?" he asked in his lightly accented French.

She looked at the first blank page of her notepad and said, "The ballet."

"Ah, yes, the ballet," he echoed, continuing with the charade.

Jackie unscrewed her Mont Blanc pen and held it poised to take down his every word.

"Well, as you know, the Bolshoi will be coming to Paris this fall. It's the same old program, I'm afraid. *Sleeping Beauty. Swan Lake.* All those Russian masterpieces have been done to death." He paused and looked up at her. "Please don't quote me on that. But there is one new thing happening…"

Jackie waited for Petrov to continue.

"A thirteen-year-old child prodigy has been accepted by the Bolshoi. His name is Rudolph Nureyev. He's incredibly talented for one so young, probably the best Russian male ballet dancer to come along since Nijinsky. I know that's heretical. But you mark my words if that doesn't turn out to be true."

Jackie dutifully jotted down everything Petrov said, intrigued by this name she'd never heard of before.

"Nureyev?" she asked him. For once, her look of wide-eyed innocence wasn't the usual schoolgirl pose that she adopted to mask the intelligence she was afraid that others would find intimidating. Occasionally, one of her Yale dates would get wise to her at a football game when she would bat her eyelashes and ask why they were kicking the ball at fourth down near their own goalpost and say, "Oh, stop it, Jackie, you know better than that." It was embarrassing that she was so transparent and a little degrading that she felt the need to dissemble in the first place.

But with Petrov she had no reason to hide how knowledgeable she was about ballet. In fact, as a writer for an American dance magazine, she was expected to be an expert on the subject. Borrowing someone else's identity made Jackie feel like an actress, but ironically, the role she was performing was more like who she really was than the person she often pretended to be in real life.

"N-U-R-E-Y-E-V." Petrov allowed himself a smug little smile, apparently pleased with himself for being able to give Jackie some inside information about the Bolshoi. He seemed eager to impress her with whatever means he had at his command.

"Thank you," Jackie said, smiling back at him appreciatively.

He put his hand over hers, and she felt a tingling sensation dance up her arm. The man was irresistibly, irredeemably romantic. There was a long pause. Jackie looked up from her notepad, all thoughts of Nureyev and Nijinsky instantly forgotten. She could tell that the Russian was about to launch into their real reason for this dinner together.

"You know, of course, why we are here," he said.

"Yes."

"I am to be a walk-in."

A shadow fell over the table. Petrov abruptly stopped speaking. He and Jackie looked up together. The sommelier hovered over them. He had a long nose, all the better to look down on patrons who thought they knew wine better than he did. He proffered the wine list to the Russian like a knight of old hurling down his gauntlet in challenge. Petrov surprised him by looking it over in cursory fashion before authoritatively ordering a '37 Mouton Rothschild.

With a condescending "Very good choice, monsieur," the sommelier retreated to the wine cellar, and Petrov turned back to Jackie. "When in doubt," he said, "always order the Mouton Rothschild."

They made small talk until the sommelier returned, not wanting to have their covert conversation interrupted again.

As they spoke, Jackie looked around the dining room and took note of one man having dinner *seul*. Although he was well dressed, he had the extravagantly overmuscled bulk of a circus strongman, a persona enhanced by his florid mustache and completely bald head. He looked like he could single-handedly lift up his table complete with the mountainous *plat de fruits de mer* he was so intently enjoying. Jackie stared at him a second longer than was considered polite while she tried to remember where she had seen this man before. Where could it have been? The hotel lobby when she first arrived? Standing under the viaduct as she and Petrov left the hotel? Or perhaps this was just her imagination running away with itself.

The sommelier returned, and Jackie dismissed her unsettling feeling of déjà vu and turned her attention back to Petrov. With a flourish, the sommelier uncorked the bottle, and Petrov went through the usual ritual of tasting the wine, pronouncing it perfection, and waiting while the sommelier poured two glasses for them. The sommelier left the bottle and returned to his station on the other side of the dining room.

Alone again, Petrov took a sip of wine before continuing. "As I was saying, you know why we're here, don't you?"

Jackie pretended to look at her notebook. "The walk-in."

"Yes, the walk-in. It must be accomplished *vitement.*"

Jackie wasn't prepared for any kind of immediate deadline and dreaded to hear what was coming next.

"I need your help," Petrov said, all business now, the blue eyes steely, purpose hardening the creamy charm. There was an urgency in his tone, a chilling gravity, and his grip tightened on her hand. "You must help me."

"I'm just the messenger," Jackie demurred.

"No messages, please. I can't afford to risk any leaks. My life is in jeopardy as it is. They already suspect me."

"Who suspects you?"

"The Organyi."

"The organza?" Jackie asked, not sure she had heard him correctly. What could a silk fabric have to do with his safety?

"The Organyi," he repeated, this time with added emphasis. "The organs of state security, the secret police."

Organyi. Organza. If she heard one more espionage term, she was going to have to start compiling a dictionary.

"But I'm not an agent," Jackie protested to the Russian. She could feel the panic rising within her. She was about to get into something over her head. This was quite beyond the scope of her brief from Dulles.

"All I need is for you to be my liaison with the American embassy."

"But I don't know anyone there," Jackie protested.

"I do."

"Why can't *you* contact him?"

"Because no one in authority must know until the walk-in is a fait accompli."

"And when is this supposed to take place?"

"Tomorrow night."

"Tomorrow night!" Jackie's voice went up an octave, and several nearby diners looked her way. She lowered her voice again. "Why tomorrow night?"

"Because tomorrow night is the one night of the week I spend with my mistress. We meet at a small apartment near the Pont d'Ivry. Do you know it?"

His mistress? Jackie was surprised at the small stab of disappointment that the word aroused in her and hoped it didn't show in her eyes. Oh well, she thought, so much for a *liaison dangereuse*.

"Yes, I know it," she said evenly. The Pont d'Ivry was also known as the *quartier chinois* and was Paris's answer to New York's Chinatown. A European would stick out there like the proverbial sore thumb, making it easy for Petrov to catch sight of anyone who was following him.

"Tomorrow night, my mistress will not be there, but my shadows don't know that. I have been planning this for the last six months. My shadows, they stay outside the building while they think I have my fun. One hour and a half only. One minute past that, and they will be at the door."

Petrov leaned over the table and spoke to Jackie in a desperate whisper.

"You will meet me there tomorrow night. At eight o'clock precisely. I have an escape route all planned out. The room is on the top floor, the sixth. One can exit the window and follow a narrow ledge outside the building that eventually overlooks the roof of a neighboring building. A small jump is all it takes. Don't worry, I have already tried it. The door there is always open. You take the stairs down and come out one street away. My shadows will be none the wiser. We will have a ninety-minute head start on them. More than enough time for us to make our way to your embassy."

Jackie started another demurral, but was cut short by Petrov's raised hand. "Do not worry. I have timed it out. There is not one element of this plan that I have not gone over and over again. It will work. Trust me."

Jackie couldn't believe what she was hearing. The audacity of the plan was impressive to her. But what was this business about going through windows and jumping to adjacent roofs? She didn't like the sound of that at all. She was beginning to worry that Allen Dulles had hired the wrong girl for the job. Besides, she was a bit miffed that instead of an exotic Mata Hari–esque seductress, Petrov saw her only as a convenient decoy to fool the two fat goons who were tailing him and as an escort into the embassy rather than the bedroom.

But Petrov had something more to tell her. He leaned over the table even farther and said in a voice so low that Jackie had to tilt her head down to hear him, "I am bringing something with me. It is of vital importance that your people see it as soon as possible. There is an expiration date attached to this material. You must help to make sure it gets into the right hands."

This is what Jackie was waiting to hear. The gift mentioned by Dulles in his brief. Now she would be hard put to turn down the Russian.

"Miss Bouvier," Petrov said, using Jackie's real name instead of the dance journalist's whose identity she had usurped. "I need you. Will you help me?"

For the second time in twenty-four hours, every fiber of Jackie's being, every particle of her existence, every trace memory of her heritage, cried out for her to say no to Mikhail Petrov's foolhardy scheme.

And for the second time in twenty-four hours, heaven help her, she said yes.

IV

Still dangling from the killer's hand, her glove slipping out of his grasp with each passing second, Jackie shuffled through the sequence of events of the past night and day. She was searching, with the slimmest glimmer of hope, for some piece of information that would get her out of the dire fix she currently found herself in.

She began with the return to the hotel. Petrov, ever the gallant Russian diplomat, escorted her to the door of her room and said that he would see Jackie tomorrow at eight p.m. sharp. The address of the apartment building was in her purse. Back in the hotel room, Jackie debated whether or not to call the secure number Dulles had given her. She had promised Petrov that she would tell no one about his future plans. In the end, though, duty won out, and Jackie called the number. Just to be on the safe side, she used the public telephone kiosk in the hotel lobby. To her surprise, an operator told her that the number was out of service, and that she had no idea when it would be fixed. Jackie put down the phone with a distinct feeling of unease. What had started as a fairly straightforward assignment was developing complications the way a hydra generated new heads. It was getting increasingly difficult to know what was the right thing to do.

Jackie spent a sleepless night, wound up from her meeting with Petrov and what she had promised to do for him. In the morning, she had *le petit dejeuner* in her room, then set out to do a little shopping and sightseeing. The hotel on avenue Daumesnil turned out to be not nearly so inconvenient a location as she had originally thought. A quick Metro ride took her to the Faubourg Saint-Honoré district, the center of haute couture in the 8th arrondissement, wedged between the Louvre and the Opéra. Having already been entranced by the *Mona Lisa*'s timelessly enigmatic smile on previous visits to the Louvre, she spent this one admiring the works of some of her favorite French artists—Fouquet, Watteau, Boucher, and Delacroix.

Window-shopping on Place Vendôme, she was drawn into Dior's by the eye-catching figure of a mannequin modeling the "New Look" style of dress that she recognized from a spread in *Harper's Bazaar*. When she tried on the dress and saw in the mirror how curvaceous the line flaring out from the waist made her look, she couldn't resist buying it, despite the exorbitant price tag. To assuage her guilt, she bought gifts for her family. At Charvet, the menswear shop that was a symbol of upper-class taste, she found two summery bold-patterned neckties for her father and stepfather, and at Hermès on rue du Faubourg Saint-Honoré, she picked up magnificent silk scarves for her mother and Lee.

Back at her hotel, she had a light supper by herself in the dining room—she was so on edge anticipating her rendezvous with Petrov, she could barely finish her meal—and took a taxi to the apartment near the Pont d'Ivry. She climbed up the four flights of stairs to the attic garret, walked in on Petrov's dead body, and now here she was, almost literally at the end of her rope.

When the last quarter-inch of Jackie's hand slid out of the glove, she could feel the hot night air on her naked hand as she began to fall. Time seemed to decelerate to an exaggerated slow-motion tempo as she plummeted floor by floor to the cobble-stone courtyard below. Vignettes from her life, a life she feared would be cut short all too soon, whipped through her mind like flashcards: at sixteen, arriving with her mare, Danseuse, at Miss Porter's School in Farmington, Connecticut... her father, movie-star handsome in a wide-lapeled, double-breasted suit, coming to visit her, and all her adoring classmates lining up to join them for dinner... at seventeen, making the grand tour of Europe with three other seniors from Holton-Arms and their chaperone and staying up all night washing their drip-dry clothes... the heady excitement of her first day at Vassar, feel-ing like Henry Hudson entering New York Harbor. She passed a lighted window in a third-story apartment and caught sight of an elderly man and woman gyrating wildly to Merv Griffin's rendition of "I've Got a Lovely Bunch of Coconuts." Please, God, Jackie prayed, don't let that be the last song I ever hear.

Choosing not to look down, she stared straight up at the decreasing figure of the killer, still framed in the window. He wore an indecipherable look on his face. Was there a hint of sadness at ending such a young life? She liked to think there was. Or was that a flash of disappointment in not actually being able to accomplish his mission with his own murderous two hands and leave nothing to chance?

He stood there for an extended moment. Then, in a sur-prisingly poetic gesture, he let go of Jackie's long black glove. Caught by an errant breeze, it wafted up and over the roof of the apartment building. Jackie could imagine the glove being handed off from one breeze to the next and sailing over the rooftops of Paris, finally coming in for a gentle landing miles from here in another arrondissement entirely. Wouldn't that be something?

But unlike that glove, there was no breeze capable of lifting Jackie up and over the rooftops of Paris. She continued to fall. And as she fell, she closed her eyes and gritted her teeth and hoped that her impact with the cobbles wouldn't hurt too much or go on too agonizingly long.

The impact, when it came, was not at all what Jackie expected. She seemed to be caught in some kind of net that collapsed in on her as it simultaneously held her in place.

Dazed, and more than a little bit grateful to find herself alive, Jackie opened her eyes and looked around at her surroundings. She appeared to be in some kind of man-sized spider's web. For a second, she tried to conjure up exactly which size spider could produce such an enormous web, and she knew that she didn't really want to discover the answer. Then she realized that she was just being silly, perhaps was hallucinating as a by-product of the sudden jolt of euphoria that came with the knowledge that her family wouldn't have to read of her untimely demise in the *International Herald-Tribune*.

When her head cleared, she saw that her fall had been arrested by a large clothesline that radiated up and out in concentric squares from a single pole set in the cobblestone floor of the courtyard. And Jackie gave a silent thanks to whomever had taken down the wash while still leaving the pole standing in place.

The pole gave way and slowly careened over on its side. Fortunately for Jackie, its fall was slow enough that she could easily roll out of the clothesline netting and onto the ground without getting hurt.

She lay there for a minute, trying to get her bearings and figuring out what to do next. First things first. Jackie spotted her shoes lying a short distance away and rose to retrieve them. She was just about to put the second one on when she saw the killer framed in the doorway of the courtyard entrance to the apartment building. Knife in hand, he was here to find out if he would get to finish the job.

Jackie could see the surprised look on his face. Yes, I'm still alive, she thought to herself, no thanks to you. As he closed in on her, she looked around for something she could use as a weapon. Her second high heel still in hand, Jackie automatically snapped out her wrist and flung the stiletto in his direction. It missed his head, but not by much, so he still had to duck to avoid it.

Jackie reached for the clothesline pole on the ground. It was heavy, but her heightened adrenaline enabled her to lift up the pole and use it to fend off the killer, who was once again trying to close in on her with the knife. Jackie knew she couldn't ward him off forever, and the pole was getting heavier by the second. Having no other recourse, she pitched the pole in his direction and hoped for the best. It flew across the courtyard like a missile, and its tip struck the killer square in the chest, knocking him backward. The clothesline itself snagged at his hands and made him struggle to extricate himself.

Jackie quickly made for the wooden door that led to the street. Once through it, she began to run down the *rue*, hoping to find a passing taxi or bus or anything that would get her the hell away from here *très rapide*. Running in a lopsided gait with one shoe off and one shoe on was slowing her down, so she abandoned her other shoe and continued fleeing down the street in her stockinged feet.

Turning her head momentarily, Jackie looked over her shoulder and saw that the killer had just exited the courtyard door to the street. He was coming after her, although he didn't seem as fleet as she expected him to be. Maybe he was out of shape. Or maybe the pole to the chest had knocked the wind out of him. Whatever the case, inspired by a mental image of Roger Bannister breaking away from the pack in the Penn Relays, Jackie put on an extra burst of speed.

She turned her head forward again, but wasn't in time to catch sight of a car's headlights rapidly bearing down on her from the front. The closer the headlights got, the more they dazzled her and made it difficult to see where she was going. Without looking back, she could hear the killer gaining on her and knew it was only a matter of moments before she was within range of his deadly-looking knife again.

Jackie kept running, and the car headlights kept coming. At the last possible second, the driver slammed on the brakes. The car began to fishtail, and as it swung around, Jackie got a good look at its silhouette. To her surprise, it was a Rolls-Royce Silver Wraith. She had never seen any vehicle that large skid before, and it was a little like watching a landlocked battleship go unnervingly out of control. Now it was the passenger's side of the car that was in danger of slamming into her. But the driver must have had Grand Prix training because the skid turned out to be a controlled one, and the car stopped short scant inches from a terrorized Jackie.

She looked back and saw that the killer had gotten his second wind and was rapidly closing the distance between them. Frantically, she looked for a way around the car. Nothing. She felt hopelessly trapped in an ending suitable only for a diehard nihilist, a cornered insect about to be smashed into oblivion for no discernible reason. Poor Mummy, she said to herself, as she thought of her hysterical mother keening over her loss.

Then, all of a sudden, the driver's-side window lowered, and a familiar face appeared. From the egg-bald head and the florid mustache, Jackie recognized the driver as the circus strongman dining alone in Maxim's last night. But his presence confused her more than clarified things in her mind. What was he doing here? Wasn't this a little too much of a coincidence?

The driver looked at her, then past her to the oncoming killer, then back to Jackie.

"Get in," he said to her, "if you want to live."

Jackie didn't have to be asked twice. She opened the rear door just as the killer caught up with her. She heard the swish of the knife blade coming down and felt it snag on the material of her jacket. But before she knew it, she was inside the car, thrown sideways across the backseat, the door closing automatically as the driver swung sharply around to make a U-turn back down the *rue*. Straightening herself, Jackie had one last look at the killer through the rear window, watching as he grew smaller. Then she settled back, trying hard to get her breathing under control, while the car disappeared into the blue darkness of the Parisian night.

V

Jackie sat tensely in the back of the Rolls-Royce Silver Wraith, not knowing whether she was passenger or prisoner—or both. She tried to think of something to say to establish a rapport with the driver, but the last couple of hours had been so taxing that her normal fluency in French failed her.

"*Merci beaucoup*," she managed. Well, that was lame, she thought to herself.

If the driver heard her, he failed to respond. He just kept driving. Mostly what Jackie saw of him through the glass partition that separated the driver and passenger compartments was a wedge-shaped slice of his thick bull neck from which his carotid artery bulged like a knotty section of rope. The collar of his shirt just barely concealed some faded pink scar tissue running around his neck like a barbed-wire choker. It looked like he might have escaped an encounter with the hangman's noose. Jackie was uncomfortable at the thought of that kind of man driving her around a foreign city.

She decided to try again, not to make conversation this time, but to point him in the right direction.

"I'm staying at..." She gave the name of her hotel and its address. The driver ignored this too. His silence was unnerving. Maybe he resented being treated like an ordinary taxi driver or a chauffeur. But one thing was clear—he had absolutely no intention of taking her back to her hotel.

With a growing sense of panic, Jackie lunged at the door and tried to open it, yanking at the door handle several times but unable to get it unlocked. Apparently, the driver was in control of the locking mechanism on the rear doors. Did all Silver Wraiths come with this feature? Jackie doubted it. Or did Rolls-Royce make a special kidnap vehicle for wealthy abductors? She doubted that too. All Jackie knew was that she was stuck here in the back of this mysterious, custom-made Silver Wraith until she reached the end of her journey, no matter where that might be.

Unless she pulled rank. Maybe she could deter the taciturn driver by waving her family's prominence in his face...or in this case, at the back of his head. It was worth a try.

"I'm very rich," she told him in French, the words suddenly coming back to her. "My parents have close ties with powerful men in government. My absence will be noted. If you don't want to feel the wrath of the gendarmes, you will release me at once."

That last remark must have done it. The driver slowly turned his head and said to Jackie with contempt, "The *flics*. They are like your Keystone Kops. They catch no one. All they are good for is taking bribes from *poules* and their *macs*."

Jackie understood the reference to prostitutes and their pimps, although these weren't the kind of terms one picked up while studying at the Sorbonne. What really surprised her was the fact that the driver chose to address her in English. How did he know she was American? She hadn't spoken ten words of English since arriving in Paris.

At least this explained one thing. The driver's surprise appearance was no accident. It had to have been planned. But what did he want with her? Where was he taking her? Jackie could do nothing but sit back and try to rein in her runaway fears until the car arrived at their unstated destination, where those questions would, she hoped, be answered.

As agitated as she was, Jackie dozed off. The Rolls-Royce was designed so that the interior could be constructed with all the comfort of a living room housed within a boxy-looking body, its parlor-perfect luxury lulling her asleep. Her nap was abetted by the steady, gentle thrum of the Silver Wraith's engine vibrating throughout the hushed cocoon of the car's relaxing confines.

The sudden cessation of the engine's hum caused Jackie to wake up. She fluttered her eyes and tried to blink away the fog of her disorientation. Through the car window, she could see a large and imposing three-story stone structure surrounded by lushly landscaped grounds, obviously someone's country estate. Her first impression was one of traditional nobility. Judging by the high sloped roof, medieval corner turrets, stacks of mullioned windows, and dignified front columns, she surmised that the chateau was from the same neoclassical period as Versailles—a little smaller, but only a little. It was still dark out, but few lights were on in the mansion, one on the first floor and one on the second. Jackie wondered who was in those rooms and whether those lights had stayed on because of her expected arrival.

The driver opened the door to the backseat and motioned for Jackie to come. She pulled herself together and stepped out of the vehicle. She could feel the crushed stone of the driveway beneath her stockinged feet and looked at the daunting distance between the Rolls-Royce and the steps leading up to the entrance to the house. The driver noticed too. Without a word, he swooped up Jackie in his massive arms and carried her across the driveway, up the steps, and through the main doors of the chateau. Jackie couldn't remember the last time she had been carried in this manner—she must have been a small child—and felt completely vulnerable in the arms of this strange man. But she got the sense that he was a man astutely aware of his own strength, because he carried her as delicately as if he were conveying an armful of fine Dresden china.

The driver set Jackie on her feet in the domed entry foyer, and she stood there for a moment struck by the opulence and elegance of the décor. As they walked down a hallway that seemed to stretch to infinity, her eyes played over the stucco detailing on the walls, the fluted pilasters on high bases, the museum-quality paintings and sculptures, the carvings in exotic woods, and the lacquered mother-of-pearl and ivory chinoiserie with Asian motifs.

Finally, they came to a carved, oak-paneled door. The driver opened it and led Jackie into one of the largest and most sumptuous rooms she had ever seen. It was filled with graceful Louis XV–style upholstered chairs and sofas, curvilinear walnut and fruitwood antique desks inlaid with rococo scrolls and flowers, a massive marble fireplace, and vivid paintings, alive with brilliant splashes of orange, yellow, and red, the colors of the sun-drenched flowers of Southern France.

The driver offered Jackie a seat on a pillowy scarlet divan. It was too dark at night to see much through the lace-curtained bay windows, but she had romantic visions of gardens and terraces, flowerbeds and jasmine-covered bowers, fountains and vineyards. This was the lighted room on the first floor that Jackie had observed from the outside, although in here, the lighting was so subdued and the far corners of the room so swathed in shadow that it was difficult to ascertain the true dimensions of the *salle*. Perhaps it only looked large enough to house the *Hindenburg*.

"You will wait here," the driver said to her, then disappeared through an oversized door embedded in a wall. He seemed to be gone a long time. Jackie wondered if she should fear for her life. But that seemed totally at odds with the way she had just been treated. Nevertheless, she suspected that she hadn't been brought to such a secluded place in the middle of the night, with no one to know her whereabouts, just to be the guest at a retreat in the countryside.

Jackie remained on the divan, but her gaze was drawn to an arresting ancient frieze that lined the entire length of one wall. It seemed to tell one unbroken story. Curious, Jackie rose from the divan and approached the frieze, slowly following it from one end to the other. Although she had a difficult time deciphering its precise details, she intuitively understood that the frieze depicted allegories of tragic events and scenes of heroic exploits taken from the ancient past—wars, famines, floods, revolutions, invasions, conquests—a whole litany of epic incidents and age-old strife. But through it all ran something else: an inspiring history of a country surviving all such hardships, both God and man-made, and ultimately prevailing triumphantly above these defining tests of man's courage and grace. In many ways, Jackie thought, it was an American story too.

"That is the history of my people," someone called from the far end of the room. The voice seemed to belong to a mature woman. But when Jackie turned and caught her first sight of the speaker, she was shocked to see that the person she thought was a middle-aged woman was younger than she was—twenty at the most. And although she was wearing a dress that might have come out of Jackie's own closet, there was something distinctly Middle Eastern in her looks and manner.

For some reason, this girl seemed familiar to Jackie. She thought that she had seen her before. But where?

"I am Princess Nureen of the House of Mansour," the

young woman said to Jackie with an utter solemnity that seemed incongruous in someone who was hardly more than a teenager.

Speaking French, Jackie introduced herself, using the name of the journalist she was impersonating.

"Is this true?" the princess asked. "I thought your name was Jacqueline Lee Bouvier."

And with that, Jackie knew the curtain had come down on her play-acting.

"You have me at a disadvantage. You seem to know more about me than I know about you," Jackie told her, trying not to sound as abashed as she felt.

And then it struck her. She did know where she had seen the princess. As an art-lover who stored pictures in her memory bank with the acquisitiveness of a collector, Jackie could never forget that remarkable award-winning photograph that resonated with her so emotionally.

"You're the little girl, aren't you?" she asked. "The one from the cover of *Life* magazine." She couldn't stop her voice from rising in excitement.

The princess shyly lowered her eyes. "That was many years ago."

Jackie could hardly believe it. She was having an audience with Princess Nureen, of the exiled House of Mansour. The same princess who had captivated the world with her display of bravery in the face of overwhelming cruelty. Her parents were brutally murdered before they could escape from their native Balazistan to France. Princess Nureen, as a young orphan girl, was also the leader of her country's government in exile. Her sole companion was the giant bodyguard who, Jackie realized, had shaved his head and grown a mustache since the day that famous picture had been snapped. This was all a bit overwhelming, and Jackie felt the need to return to the divan and sit down before her legs collapsed from under her.

"Are you all right?" the princess asked solicitously, joining her on the divan.

"Yes, it's been a long night."

"So I have been told."

Jackie studied her. Here was this girl, barely twenty, and she conducted herself with the gravity of someone three times her age. It was almost as if she believed the entire fate of the world rested on her shoulders. But then again, given her country of origin and its geopolitical place in the world, maybe that was true. Based on what little she remembered from the newspapers, Jackie recalled that Balazistan was not only rich in oil but was situated in a region that gave it strategic importance in the Cold War between the West and the East. The military junta that had murdered the princess's parents and was still in power had allied itself with neither side, which made the country sought after by its neighbors as a buffer zone. The princess's return to Balazistan could influence the balance of power one way or the other. But in her speeches and press statements, she said that all she wanted was for her people to be free from the yoke of oppression that the junta had forced on them twelve years ago. The princess's heartfelt goal was to return the country to the benign rule Balazistan had known under her late parents.

The driver appeared, carrying a silver tray with a pair of women's shoes on it. He deposited the tray on the floor in front of Jackie and wordlessly retreated back toward the doorway. Jackie looked from him to the princess.

"I think we're about the same size," the princess told Jackie. "They should fit."

"Thank you," said Jackie as she slid her feet into a pair of colorfully embroidered ballet slippers, no match for her hastily discarded satin peep-toed stilettos, but far more serviceable. At first, the new shoes pinched a little, but they gradually gave way enough for Jackie to feel a semblance of comfort.

"It is an old Balazistan custom," the princess explained, "that no guest be allowed to leave one's home barefoot."

"Well, that's good," Jackie said, "because I'm not exactly the barefoot type." She hoped to lighten the atmosphere slightly, but the princess failed to crack a smile.

"Miss Bouvier, I imagine you must wonder the reason you have been brought here."

"I didn't think it was because you needed a fourth hand for bridge," said Jackie in a martini-dry tone of voice.

She winced inwardly as her second attempt to alleviate the tension also landed with a resounding thud, and the princess continued as though she hadn't heard a thing.

"I have sources that tell me of your relationship with Mikhail Petrov."

"Your sources were misinformed," Jackie said coolly, dispensing with any further attempt at warmth. "We only met last evening." She didn't like the idea of this stranger knowing any of her business.

Undeterred, the princess continued. "We have reason to believe this Petrov planned to defect to your country with important information relevant to Balazistan."

Could this be true, Jackie wondered. Was this the "gift" Petrov was bringing as a walk-in? If so, what form did this information take?

"I'm sorry, but I don't know anything about that." Jackie shrugged, employing her best poker face.

"Yes, I'm sure you don't," said the princess, showing that she could bluff as well as Jackie.

"Miss Bouvier," she continued peremptorily, "this information Petrov carried could vastly affect the future of my country. It is of extreme importance that I get my hands on it. I will pay you handsomely if you give that information to me."

She snapped her fingers, loudly enough for the driver waiting by the door to hear her. Once again, he appeared with a silver tray. But this one was bearing a leather briefcase. He placed the briefcase before Jackie and snapped it open. To her surprise, she looked down on sheaf after bundled sheaf of hundred-dollar bills.

Jackie had heard of things being served on a silver platter, but this was getting ridiculous.

"One hundred thousand dollars," the princess elaborated. "Yours in exchange for the information."

"I'm sorry, but I just don't have it."

Jackie hoped the princess knew that she was telling the truth, but her impassive face gave no clue. She motioned summarily to the driver, who picked up the silver tray holding the briefcase and backed out of the room.

"And even if I did," Jackie continued, "I couldn't in all good conscience hand over something that was meant for my government."

"I understand," said the princess, disappointment casting a somber shadow on her face. "But you must understand that I will do whatever I have to do to acquire that information."

Jackie was shocked. Had she just been threatened by this twenty-year-old girl?

She rose from the divan and faced the princess. "Your Highness, already this evening, I've stumbled across a dead body, been attacked by an assassin, fallen from a six-story window, been chased barefoot through the streets of Paris, been almost run over by your driver, brought against my will to this place, and now threatened by you." Jackie fixed the princess with a look of all-American steadfastness. "So you must understand that I will do anything *I* have to not to betray my country's interests."

"I do," the princess said simply. In her eyes, Jackie saw a heartbreaking combination of long-remembered pain and hard-fought hope for the future.

Jackie began to take off the shoes.

"Keep them," the princess said. "Consider them a gift."

"That's so kind of you, but I'll just borrow them and have them returned when I'm back at my hotel," Jackie promised, assuming she would get there if the princess didn't have other, more ominous plans for her.

The princess clapped her hands, and the driver once more appeared. "Dexter, please take Miss Bouvier back to her hotel."

"Yes, your Highness." He bowed his way out of the room.

The two women waited in awkward silence while Dexter went to bring around the car.

In the back of the Rolls-Royce, Jackie idly watched the breathtaking French countryside roll past the car windows, a palette of green olive trees, bluish purple fields of lavender, mustard-colored broom grass and wheat, and red and ocher bauxite hills. It was now light enough to see where they were going—down a country road lined on both sides intermittently with soldier-straight cypresses. In her mind, Jackie replayed the scene with the princess and worried that Dulles's assignment was getting more complicated by the hour.

The scene in Jackie's mind switched to Petrov's final minutes in the garret. Almost from beyond the grave, he had tried to force that opera ticket on her. Why? What was its significance? Maybe the ticket had something to do with the information the princess wanted so desperately. Perhaps it would provide a clue.

Jackie went to check the ticket in her purse. And her purse was...in all the excitement, she hadn't noticed until now that she no longer had the purse on her. With a sinking feeling, she remembered that she had dropped it when she went to squeeze the atomizer in the assassin's face. With any luck, it was still there. But in order to retrieve the purse, she would have to go back to the garret. And risk a possible return bout with the killer.

Maybe she should go to the police and dump the whole thing in their laps. But then she remembered that she was in France on a false passport and was afraid that having a fake identity would raise too many uncomfortable questions.

Maybe she should just abandon the whole thing and return home to Washington. She could call Dulles and tell him the assignment had been one big bust. But she knew she would never do this. Dulles was depending on her. The CIA was depending on her. Her country was depending on her. And Jackie had not been raised to be a quitter.

She knew that she would return to the garret. Too much was at stake for her to drop the ball now. But one thing was for sure: she wasn't going back there alone. What, she asked herself, was the French equivalent of the U.S. Seventh Cavalry?

VI

When the phone in his apartment rang, Jacques Rivage was dreaming about the Liberation...again. It was a recurring dream that took him back to a watershed moment in his life like a favorite song that one never tires of listening to because it triggers a fond remembrance of things past.

Once again, he was a teenager living in Paris during the war years. His father was dead, arrested during a Gestapo roll-up of his Resistance cell. And his mother, who was foreign born, was reduced to making a living as a charwoman on the night shift at the Hotel Meurice, where the German Army of Occupation had its headquarters. Jacques wanted to join the Resistance, but his mother told him that he was too young to give his life for his country. In truth, if there had been an army, he would have been called up in another year anyhow. But to his mother, the Resistance was something else again, with so many more chances to be betrayed or killed. So to quiet his restlessness, Jacques began taking pictures with an old box camera that he had found among his late father's possessions.

It occurred to Jacques that he could use his box camera to document the effect of the German Occupation on the ordinary citizens of Paris. He took pictures of people lining up to buy food and going through piles of used clothes at the Bourse.

He photographed German soldiers playing tourist at the Eiffel Tower and browsing the colorful stalls in the rue de Rivoli. His lens captured children playing in front of parked German tanks and old women feeding pigeons against a background of deployed artillery pieces. His great hope was that, after the war was over and the occupiers were booted back to Germany, he would publish a book of these photographs as a testament to the resolute nature of the people of Paris.

As the war progressed, the nature of the outcome emerged, growing ever more distinct like a developing photograph taking recognizable shape. By July 1944, only a month after the Allied landing took the Germans by surprise at Normandy, it became obvious to Parisians that the occupiers were planning to pull up stakes. Liberation could now be counted in mere days, no longer months or years. And Jacques planned to be there, camera at the ready, when the first Allied tanks entered the city.

August 25. Liberation Day. The Allies were rolling through the outskirts of Paris. Some parts of the city were deserted, like ghost towns in an American western movie. Others were filled with throngs of citizens waiting to greet their Allied liberators with handshakes, kisses, hugs, confetti, and opened bottles of *vin ordinaire.* And still other areas held last-ditch pockets of German resistance.

Jacques waited, camera in hand, at a deserted intersection for the Allies to arrive. He heard them before he saw them. Or rather, he felt them, because the pavement beneath him suddenly began to rumble up through the worn-out soles of his shoes. And then he saw them coming up the *rue*—a column of ten Sherman tanks belonging to the Second Armored Division. This was a French unit. He could tell because each tank had the Cross of Lorraine stenciled on its sides. Jacques watched with pride swelling in his chest as the lead tank stopped and a captain poked his head out of the commander's cupola in the turret. Jacques tried to take a picture, but the camera's view-finder suddenly turned blurry. He put his hand to his eyes and realized that he was crying.

"Do you know where the Germans are?" the tanker captain asked Jacques.

"*Oui*," said Jacques, drying his eyes on his sleeve. "There is a manned pillbox back there." He pointed behind him to a *place* several streets away.

"Where?" asked the captain, holding up a street map, a well-worn Michelin guide instead of an army ordnance map, for Jacques to give him the exact location. He was from Nice, he explained a little sheepishly, and this was his first time in Paris.

"It's easier if I show you." Jacques was amused to see him ask for directions like any ordinary tourist.

The tanker captain held out his hand, and Jacques scrambled up over the hull and clambered on board. Ducking behind some sandbags piled up on the rear of the turret, Jacques directed the lead Sherman to the *place* where the pillbox was hidden. Right here, left there, down one narrow *rue* after another. Jacques looked back and was amazed to see the entire column of tanks following his lead. The war that had seemed so far away for so long was now in his neighborhood. And he was a part of it.

Arriving at the *place*, the tank opened fire on the pillbox installation with its 50-caliber Browning machine gun. At the risk of getting shot and possibly killed, the captain removed his helmet and put on his kepi to show the Germans who they were fighting. It didn't take long for the Germans to give up their position and wave a white flag. They came out of the pillbox slowly, their hands up, their bodies somehow markedly dimin-ished, and Jacques was surprised to find that he no longer felt intimidated by them. In defeat, they had ceased being Hitler's supersoldiers. They were mere men, ordinary and nakedly vulnerable. He watched as the Germans were taken away by the French soldiers of the Second Armored. Jacques was so excited at having a ringside seat for the assault on the *place* that he forgot to snap any pictures.

He was silently cursing himself for missing a fantastic shot for the book that he hoped to have published one day when he heard the captain asking him, "What's your name?"

"Jacques Rivage."

"Well, Jacques, I want to thank you for your help," the captain said, offering his hand for a man-to-man shake. "And this is Stevens," he added, introducing him to an American who had ridden with the column. Stevens, Jacques learned, was an OSS officer assigned to the Second Armored as an intelligence liaison.

"You did a first-rate job, Jacques, and we appreciate it," Stevens said in imperfect French, shaking hands too. He nodded at the camera Jacques was clutching in his other hand. "Mind if I take a look at that?"

Sevens examined the camera with a wistful smile. "I had one of these when I was a boy," he mused. Then he cocked his head at Jacques, scrunching his eyebrows inquisitively. "So tell me, what do you want to do after the war?"

"Be a photographer." The answer popped out of his mouth instantly although it was the first time that he had articulated his dream to anyone.

"In that case, I think I may be able to help you," the OSS officer said. He asked Jacques for his name and address and wrote it down in a notebook that he carried with him.

Jacques thought Stevens would forget about him as soon as he left Paris—after all, he was only a seventeen-year-old son of a charwoman who happened to be in the right place at the right time—but he didn't. A few months after the war ended, a former *Stars and Stripes* reporter named McGrew contacted Jacques. He said that he and some buddies from *Stars and Stripes* were starting a wire service here in Paris called the Allied Press Service and asked Jacques if he wanted to work as a stringer. Stevens had recommended him.

"We can't afford to pay much," McGrew said, "but the opportunity is priceless. All you have to do is wander around the city and take pictures that you think might be interesting for publication."

Jacques jumped at the offer. He graduated to a Speed Graphic but held on to the box camera for sentimental reasons. It reminded him of his father and also of the greatest day of his life—the day he played a small part in the liberation of his city.

Then, two years ago, came the surprise phone call from Stevens himself. He said he was in Paris on business and wanted to see him. Sitting outdoors and sipping espresso at the Café de la Paix, Stevens explained to Jacques that he was no longer with the OSS. He was now with the CIA, the postwar outgrowth of the OSS. He remembered Jacques for the grace under pressure he displayed on Liberation Day and said that he had a proposition for him....

Ring, ring, ring. The ringing of the telephone, Jacques realized, was not part of his dream. It was real. And persistent. Groggily, he reached for the phone and picked it up.

"Allo," he croaked, wondering who was calling him at this godforsaken hour.

It was only nine o'clock in the morning, but already the puppet show in the Tuileries was crowded with children laughing in unfettered delight as Punch and Judy hit each other with extravagant zeal. Their mothers and nannies stood behind the children so their view of the stage would be unobstructed. And just beyond these adults stood Jackie, waiting for Jacques Rivage to arrive. Jackie felt terrible about waking him up so early in the morning. Dulles had told her to use the second phone number only in case of an emergency, but this was one. And unlike the secure number he had given her, this one was working.

A lone single woman, Jackie felt slightly self-conscious standing here among all the mothers and their children. But she was getting wiser in the ways of tradecraft with each passing turn of events. She knew that the photographer picked this spot for the same reason Petrov had located his apartment in the *quartier Chinois*—to make anyone tailing them stand out from the rest of the crowd.

The laughter of the children drifted back to Jackie as she scanned the park beyond the puppet theater for any sign of the photographer. Not that she knew what he looked like. For security reasons, Jacques had neglected to provide a description of himself. He did say that he would be carrying a copy of the current *Paris Match*, turned to a picture on page 32 of the latest French heartthrob, Yves Montand, and asked her to do the same. So there Jackie stood, modeling her latest purchase, a striking Balmain prêt-à-porter sundress she had found the previous day at Le Bon Marché, magazine under her arm, waiting for the man who would help her out of this predicament.

Jackie liked to picture her rescuer as a latter-day swashbuckler à la *The Charge of the Light Brigade*, where Errol Flynn saved the life of, and fell in love with, Olivia de Havilland. In her mind's eye, Jacques Rivage was a suave, debonair rogue: handsome, authoritative, radiating strength, and with a can-do attitude that would immediately put her at ease. Yet she knew that this image derived more from her penchant for artistic panache than from any basis in reality. If Dulles was any example of a typical CIA man, she expected Jacques Rivage to be middle-aged, balding, paunchy, and about as captivating as a fallen soufflé.

Her mental vision of the photographer was broken by an unkempt-looking young man who was standing entirely too close to her. Jackie refused to acknowledge him as she continued to keep her eye out for Jacques Rivage. But the scruffy young man—she thought he might be an impoverished student or worse, a pickpocket—couldn't take a hint and failed to go away. Just to get rid of him, Jackie reached into her handbag, pulled out a few coins, and dropped them into his hand.

"Merci beaucoup," he said, before switching over into English. "You are too kind, Miss Bouvier." He held up a previously hidden copy of *Paris Match*, turned to page 32 and Yves Montand flashing his killer smile.

Jackie's mouth dropped open. This was Jacques Rivage? This was her swashbuckling chevalier? He was as dark skinned as a street Arab and looked like he hadn't shaved in two or three days. His hair was dark and wavy and hung down below his ears like a cocker spaniel's, so he needed a haircut even more than he needed a shave. He was only about her age, maybe a couple of years older. It was high summer, and he was wearing torn jeans with his knees poking out of them like round faces peering through portholes and a frayed pistachio-colored T-shirt that must have been a dark green before it faded. If his reason for dressing that way was to conceal his identity as a CIA stringer, it certainly had her fooled. Still, she reluctantly had to admit to herself that there was something attractive about him in a Rive Gauche, bohemian, I-only-wash-every-other-day-because-I-bathe-in-despair kind of way.

"You are Jacques Rivage?" she asked him.

"Oui," he replied.

"The photographer?"

"Oui."

"The person whose phone number I was given?"

"Oui."

Well, that seemed to eliminate any chance of making a mistake, Jackie thought.

"You *are* Jacques Rivage?" she asked one more time, just to make sure.

"Oui," Jacques said in an increasingly irritated tone of voice. "I am Jacques Rivage. The photographer. The person whose number you were given."

"I'm sorry," Jackie sighed, "I'm new at this."

"Really? I thought you must be an old hand."

Jackie chose to ignore the teasing sarcasm and move on.

"Can I get rid of this now?" she asked, referring to her copy of *Paris Match*.

"You don't like it?"

"I prefer *Life.*"

"That's okay, I don't have any pictures in this issue anyhow."

While Jackie dumped the magazine in the nearest wire trash bin, Jacques took a good, long look at her. "You know, you're pretty enough to be on the cover of *Life.*"

"I can't see that happening," Jackie demurred. More likely the *Police Gazette*, she thought, if things keep on this way. Why did he have to say she was pretty? It made her even more nervous than she already was. There was something so frankly sexy about him—the carelessly unconventional way he dressed, the devil-may-care attitude, the smoldering look in his eyes— that gave him the piquant aura of a foreign lust object for visiting American women. She might have found it alluring if her guard hadn't been up. Watch out, she told herself, he's a young

Black Jack, an audacious flirt who's used to getting his way with women. Don't give him an inch. He could be dangerous if you're not careful.

"So I gather you have an emergency," Jacques reminded her.

"Yes."

"Would you like to tell me about it?"

"Maybe we should find a place to sit first," Jackie suggested. "It's a long story."

They wandered over to a nearby empty park bench and sat down. Some hungry pigeons gathered around their feet. Jacques reached into a pocket, pulled out a handful of bread crumbs, and threw them to the birds, who pecked enthusiastically at them as Jackie launched into her story.

It took her a while to get the whole thing out. The meeting with Dulles. The flight to Paris. The dinner with Petrov. The agreement to help him walk in. Stumbling over his dead body in the apartment. The flight from the killer. The kidnapping and the conversation with the princess. The realization that the opera ticket must be some sort of clue.

Through it all, Jacques sat there silently and listened to her with a neutral expression on his face. It was difficult to tell what he was thinking, if anything. It added to Jackie's growing fear that Jacques, despite Dulles's recommendation, did not fit the job description of valiant hero.

At the end of her narrative, Jackie looked at Jacques and said, "Well, what do you think?"

"That is one strange story," he said noncommittally.

"*Strange* is an apt description. Thank you." Jackie almost rolled her eyes. Minute by minute, her estimation of Jacques was speedily going down while her anxiety rose.

"Based on what you told me, everything seems to hinge on that opera ticket."

"Yes, that's what I said." She tried to keep the exasperation out of her voice.

"And you put the ticket in your purse?"

"Yes, I did."

"And you left the purse back at the apartment?"

"Yes."

"That was rather careless of you, wasn't it?"

"I told you—I was running for my life at the time." God, but this Frenchman was thick.

"Right. Then I think we should return to that apartment and retrieve your purse."

"But what about the killer?"

Jacques thought about it for a moment, then curled his mouth in an ironic shape and said, "Let him get his own opera ticket."

And with that, he rose and held out his hand in a gallant manner to Jackie. She was glad to see that good manners weren't entirely lost on him. Together, the two of them walked across the Tuileries in the direction of the nearest exit.

Jacques stopped for a moment and reached into a pocket to retrieve something.

"I guess you'll want this back," he said, withdrawing his hand and opening his palm. Jackie could see the handful of coins that she had given him when she mistook him for an impoverished student or a pickpocket. His snide tone implied that he had Jackie pegged as a rich, empty-headed American girl who didn't know which end was up.

Smart aleck, she said to herself. Trying to show him that his attempt to embarrass her hadn't succeeded, she pretended to be pleased. "My, how generous of you, Monsieur Rivage," she said with exaggerated sincerity as she took the coins and deposited them back in her handbag. *"Merci beaucoup."*

"Pas de quoi." Jacques smiled and led her out of the park.

To anyone looking at them, they made an unusual combination—this sunny American beauty in her chic strapless sundress and this swarthy French bohemian in torn, flea market jeans and faded T-shirt. But to two middle-aged onlookers in particular, carefully camouflaged in the middle of the summer crowd, this just made the pair that much easier to follow at a distance... until the perfect time to execute their plan.

VII

Where was Jacques off to? Jackie wondered. As soon as they had walked out of the Tuileries and were on the rue de Rivoli on La Rive Droite, he told her that he had to leave. He said he would meet her later that evening and take her back to the garret to retrieve her purse with the opera ticket, hopefully, still in it.

"*À bientôt*," he said, waving good-bye. He looked around first as though trying to make sure that no knife-wielding thug was anywhere in sight. Then he took off at a brisk pace, glancing back at her over his shoulder with a smile that said he was reluctant to leave.

Business before pleasure, Jackie thought, even for someone as seemingly nonchalant as Jacques. He was probably hurrying to get his camera for a magazine shoot or heading to the CIA office to make a report and let Dulles know that he had met up with Miss Bouvier and had everything under control.

Sitting next to each other on the park bench, she had caught him gazing at her bare shoulders and swanlike neck—her mother said it was more like a giraffe's—the way someone looking in the window of Angélina's tea salon might ogle a mouthwatering gâteau. When she'd shifted her position to get more comfortable on the hard-backed bench and their thighs touched, she felt him tense up. She'd moved away quickly, letting him know that it was entirely unintentional and shouldn't give him any wrong ideas. If he thinks I'm a dimwit, why does he find me attractive? she wondered, or would he have had the same reaction to any young woman sitting next to him as long as she was warm and breathing? Not that it mattered, but she enjoyed the admiration she evoked in men, even a scamp like him. Wouldn't it be fun, she mused, to have a fling with someone so outrageously unsuitable? His ultra-confident manners were so irritating that she'd love to take him down a peg. Or maybe, to be honest, hubris had nothing to do with it, and she just wanted to be with a man who made her stomach do little flip-flops when he flashed his charming smile at her.

All right, that's enough, stop daydreaming about him, he's not your type, she reprimanded herself. This was no time for her to be acting like a silly schoolgirl developing a crush on the class bad boy. It was just as well that she'd have the afternoon to herself. She needed to relax, enjoy the delights of a sunny Paris afternoon, and get prepared for the terrifying task of going back into that dreadful garret where—was it only yesterday?—she'd stumbled upon the death-rattling corpse of the would-be Soviet defector, Mikhail Petrov. She shuddered to think what his mistress's house of horrors might have in store for Jacques and her tonight. At least she would not be alone this time if Petrov's killer suddenly reappeared brandishing his wicked knife.

The rue de Rivoli was crowded with pedestrians surging along elbow to elbow with the alert purposefulness of an advancing army. Jackie could tell from the cameras slung around their necks that many of them were tourists who'd been drawn to this famous street by the shops bearing the most fashionable designer names in the world. But today she was in no mood to join the bevy of shoppers seeking the perfect ensemble or the most exquisite piece of jewelry. No, what she wanted was to calm her nerves the way she often had after her morning classes at the Sorbonne—sitting quietly by herself in a café, nursing an aperitif, and making good use of her art lessons by sketching the scene around her.

Braving the traffic and the toots and waves of taxi drivers in their yellow Citroën 2CVs, Jackie made her way to WH Smith and picked up some art supplies. When she was near the Louvre, she came to an inviting café with dozens of patrons seated outside at tables under white scalloped parasols with blue trim. The blue-and-white motif reminded Jackie of the Café de Flore and Les Deux Magots in Saint-Germain-des-Prés, the twin cafés that were the Left Bank meccas of literary and artistic life. All the students at the Sorbonne knew those were the haunts where Jean-Paul Sartre and Simone de Beauvoir spent long hours formulating new ideas and writing their novels, rubbing shoulders with Hemingway, Camus, Picasso, and Brecht. Jackie didn't expect to find any of those intellectual elites here, but all she wanted was some solitude, so she went inside.

"*Bonjour, mademoiselle,*" the amiable headwaiter greeted her, "*voulez-vous une table pour deux?*"

"*Non, je suis seule,*" Jackie told him and pointed to her sketch pad, indicating that she came there to paint.

The headwaiter nodded, used to artists and their need for privacy, and led her to a small table in a secluded spot beside an opaque latticed window. A row of flowerpots sat on a ledge above the window like a line of miniature sentinels. The perfect little haven.

Jackie ordered Lillet on ice with a slice of orange and settled in. All around her, the café was pulsating with the kinetic exchange of ideas. She caught snatches of conversation with names like André Malraux, René Magritte, Maurice Bejart, and Jean Cocteau being bandied about. Yes, I've come to the right place, Jackie thought, where people are as excited about books and art and creativity and individualism as I am. She felt as far away from the life of stifling conformity that her mother devoutly wished for her as if she had ventured onto another planet.

The lunch crowd started to arrive, and Jackie began sketching—the pale, ascetic-looking man with soulful eyes staring into space, obviously a poet; the goateed man with a lopsided beret and graceful hands in constant motion, an artist no doubt; and anyone else who caught her eye. She had a style all her own, colorful and elaborate, that seemed to capture the essence of her subjects with a caricaturist's whimsical exaggeration.

When the waiter came by with another Lillet, he stole a look at her drawings, and his face broke into a wide smile.

"Merveilleux, vous êtes très douée, mademoiselle," he exclaimed, pressing his hands together with delight. Jackie laughed, pleased to be told that she was talented, even by a waiter who was probably just looking for a big tip. Still, the compliment seemed genuine, and waiters in cafés in Paris were like cab-drivers in New York—connoisseurs about everything. Her art teachers would be proud.

The time passed so quickly that she decided to eat a late lunch and skip dinner. She had a delicious *Salade Périgourdine*—mixed greens, French beans, foie gras, and smoked duck fillet—washed down with a glass of Côtes du Rhône and finished off with a demitasse of *café allongé*. Grateful for letting her while away the whole afternoon in what served as her private atelier, Jackie left the waiter a generous tip, equal to the bill itself, and hurried out of the café. It would be close to five o'clock by the time she reached her hotel—just enough time to take a nap, shower, and get dressed for her appointment with Jacques at seven in the evening, an appointment that filled her with renewed apprehension.

"I know this is not going to be pleasant for you, Jacque-LEEN"—she loved the Gallic way Jacques pronounced her full name—"but there's no other way for us to get that opera ticket Petrov wanted you to have. I doubt his murderer was chasing after you with a knife just to give your purse back."

She had to smile. There were few people who looked as cute as Jacques did when he was being sarcastic. The slight pucker of his lips and the impish glint in his chocolate eyes eased some of the tension.

"*Unpleasant* is hardly the word for it. A nightmare is more like it. I'm not used to walking into someone's apartment and finding a dead body there, not to mention a homicidal maniac who would have made medallions of beef out of me if I hadn't escaped by my fingernails."

"Then you must know God is on your side, Jacque-LEEN." He took her hand in his and gave it a light squeeze. "And so am I."

His warm, firm hand wrapped around her ice cold one felt reassuring, but she was still queasy with fear.

"It might be a good idea for us to act like lovers as a cover in case anyone's watching us," he explained as he continued to hold her hand.

She wondered if this was his idea of tradecraft or just a sneaky way for him to get romantic. But it still felt good. It was a balmy evening, and there were other couples strolling hand in hand along the quaint cobblestone street, sauntering in and out of restaurants and cafés. She would have enjoyed taking in the mild air too, if she hadn't been going to the apartment where Petrov was supposed to rendezvous with his mistress but met his death instead.

"Oh, no, we can't be here already." She looked at the door-step to the dilapidated brick building that she had fallen six stories from the night before and felt goose bumps rising like a small mountain range on her arms.

Inside, the musty odor of cigarette smoke and stale cooking grease assailed Jackie's nose, and she noticed the paint peel-ing from the grimy mustard-colored ceiling and walls. The place certainly hadn't improved any since she was last here. But would it be any worse?

"I'll go first, and you follow me," Jacques said, starting up the narrow flights of rickety wooden stairs to the sixth floor.

Jackie stared straight ahead, scarcely noticing the broad shoulders and well-rounded male derriere ascending before her, and felt her trepidation mounting with each stair she climbed.

Finally, they were at the sixth floor. When they came to the apartment at the end of the hall, they found the door slightly ajar. Jackie looked at Jacques questioningly, her eyes wide with fear, her heart racing. What now?

With a blasé nothing-ventured, nothing-gained tilt of his head, Jacques pushed open the door, and the hot jazzy tones of Josephine Baker singing "J'ai Deux Amours" at top volume poured into the hallway.

Jackie was stunned. What was Josephine Baker doing here? Wasn't she starring at the Folies-Bergère? It took her a second to realize that it was only a Victrola playing the entertainer's signature song, more popular than ever with her comeback. But why was it blasting away like that?

Cautiously following Jacques into the apartment, Jackie was astonished to discover the answer—a party was in full swing and someone had turned up the music so it could be heard over the loud chatter and boisterous laughter of the guests. Jackie looked around the room and couldn't believe what she saw. The garret was totally different. The dingy colorless walls were now a fresh blue and covered with paintings. Lacy white curtains hung on the windows of the lamp-lit room, and on the floor, the old threadbare Algerian rug has been replaced with a bright, new floral-patterned carpet. The bed with the lumpy mattress had disappeared. Gone, too, were the broken-down desk and chair. In the middle of the room, a handsome table had materialized and was stacked with hors d'oeuvres—cheeses, vol-au-vents, terrines, crudités, oysters, crêpes, and pâtés on toasted French rounds. There was no sign that any kind of a struggle had taken place here, much less a murder.

Jackie shook her head, trying to clear it of an eerie sense of seeing this place for the first time. She was familiar with *déjà vu*, the illusion of having already experienced something, but this opposite, *jamais vu*—the illusion of having never seen something she had encountered before—was entirely new to her. And it was weird, weird, weird.

The air was heavy with the burning tar smell of Gauloises and clouds of smoke swirling around the heads of an eclectic bunch of guests. A tall, thin man who wore his auburn hair in a page boy and held his wineglass aloft with balletic grace struck her as royalty, a prince or a count perhaps. Several men, well into their cups, were carousing loudly and pounding each other on the back like a polo team in the clubhouse after a winning game. A stylish, worldly-looking man in a form-fitting silk shirt and crisp linen slacks skimming suntanned bare ankles—the archetypal Riviera roué—was surrounded by a cluster of women who kept throwing their heads back and laughing uproariously at each bon mot he uttered. A few of the women in the crowd seemed to be Jackie's age, but most were older and dressed conservatively. The one standout was a stocky blonde in a long red dress decorated across the bodice in a herringbone pattern of green, white, and yellow threads that reminded Jackie of a Russian peasant costume.

And then, with a catch in her breath and a shiver running down her spine, Jackie spotted a thick-set man standing near the hors d'oeuvres table, looking up from the crêpe on his plate and glancing at her with hooded eyes. *Argh!* He was standing right on the same spot where Petrov's corpse had lain with rats scurrying around him. She shuddered uncontrollably, beset by the fear, irrational but all too real, that he was the killer, blending in with the partygoers, ready to draw out a knife concealed in his napkin and spring at her.

"Bon soir, mes amis, bievenue." A heavyset, sixtyish woman with a helmet of red hair, obviously the hostess, sailed up to Jackie and Jacques, her bosom approaching like the prow of an ocean liner, and greeted them warmly.

Could this be Petrov's mistress? No, more like his mother, Jackie thought, although the woman welcoming them to the party was in much too jovial a mood to have just lost a son to a murderer in this very room the night before.

Jackie looked at Jacques to see if he knew this woman, but he gave no indication that he did. Speaking in French, Jackie explained to the hostess that she had left her purse in the apartment the previous night and had come to get it back.

The woman looked baffled. *"C'est impossible. J'étais ici toute la nuit dernière et personne n'est venu pour visiter."*

"Quoi?" Jackie was dumbfounded. The woman was telling her that she had been there all last night and no one had come to visit.

Jackie saw the bemused expression on Jacques's face. Had she brought him to the wrong apartment? She shook her head.

No, this was the same garret all right, the last one down the hall on the sixth floor.

Why was the woman lying to them, and what was she doing there anyway?

Jackie tried questioning the hostess politely. Did anyone share the apartment with her?

The woman shook her head no.

Was it possible that someone could have come into the apartment while she was asleep?

"*Non.*"

Did she know a man by the name of Mikhail Petrov?

"*Non.*"

Had the police been to the apartment lately?

The woman laughed and shook her head again, as if to say don't be ridiculous.

Jackie was growing increasingly disconcerted, each "no" landing a fresh blow to her wobbly composure. The more the hostess maintained her impenetrably calm façade, smiling pleasantly while lying through her teeth, the more frustrated and infuriated Jackie became. Now Jacques was looking at her as if he thought she were crazy and had made the whole thing up. What was she to do? The woman was as intractable as Joan of Arc. Jackie could imagine her leading an army to victory in the Hundred Years War, then as a proud and tight-lipped martyr lashed to the stake, with flames leaping up her body and her red hair on fire, yet refusing to cough up a morsel of information.

Predictably, when she inquired again, Jackie was told that no lost evening bag had turned up in the garret. Now she was too agitated for words.

She turned to Jacques. "Why don't you do something?" she beseeched him. "Ask her if we can look around for the purse ourselves."

He shook his head, apparently unwilling to intercede. Instead, he turned to the hostess and asked politely, *"Puis-j'avoir votre permission pour utiliser les toilettes?"*

The hostess nodded in the direction of the bathroom, and Jacques excused himself, leaving Jackie stranded in tongue-tied misery, watching helplessly as he disappeared and the hostess returned to her guests.

When Jacques came back, he seemed in a hurry to get out of there. He grabbed Jackie by the arm and made a beeline for the hostess.

"Veuillez nous excuser pour l'interromption de votre soirée, Madame," he said, apologizing for interrupting her party, then said good-bye and ushered Jackie out the door.

Back on the street, Jackie exploded in anger at Jacques. "Why didn't you help me? I was never so humiliated in my life. You just stood there like one of the wooden Chinese statues at Les Deux Magots and said nothing. You could at least have asked that old battle-ax if we could have searched the place for my purse."

He gave her an indulgent smile. "But I did search for it and look what I found." Coolly, he reached inside his shirt, pulled out her black beaded evening bag, and handed it to her. *"Voilà."*

Jackie was wide-eyed with amazement. It seemed like a magician's trick. "Where did you get it?"

"It was stuffed behind the toilet tank where no one could see it. That's an old spy's ploy. The assassin didn't see it when he took off after you, and whoever found it didn't have time to search it. They figured you'd be coming back to get it, and they stashed it there so you wouldn't find it."

"But who was that woman and all those people?"

"Out-of-work French actors, probably. That wasn't a real party. It was an obvious 'Potemkin Village.'"

She stared at him. "What's that?"

"It's something created to look real, like a stage or movie set, but is fake."

Jackie was intrigued. "Why is it named after Potemkin?"

"He was the Russian minister who supposedly had mock villages built along the Dnieper River to impress Catherine II when she came to visit after the Crimean War." Jacques was amused. "After all these years, the Soviets are still up to their old tricks. They construct fictitious things to fool foreign visitors or hide a potentially damaging situation. That's why SMERSH created this party charade tonight. They wanted to cover up for the murder of one of their own agents before the Paris police could find out."

Jackie looked at him with new respect. He was no fool, this Jacques, although, like her, he seemed to take pains to hide how smart he was.

"Aren't you going to open it?" he asked, pointing to the beaded bag he'd handed over to her.

Good heavens, what was wrong with her? The evening had been so strange, so maddening, that she'd forgotten all about the opera ticket. Was it still there? Or was this even her real handbag and not some phony one SMERSH put there to fool them? She didn't know what to expect anymore.

With trembling fingers, Jackie flicked open the purse and looked inside. There, nestled within the contents like a toy surprise in a Cracker Jack box, was the lone ticket for the opera.

She held it up for Jacques to see and smiled. "Looks like we're ending this evening on a high note."

VIII

Standing at the gateway to the ancient Church of Saint Julien le Pauvre, Jackie looked down rue Galande at the old houses and the steeples of Saint Séverin rising across the way and thought a time warp had flung her back into medieval Paris. She half expected Saint Thomas Aquinas to come walking through the doors of the church into the courtyard.

"No wonder this is one of the scenes on the Left Bank that artists love to paint so much," she said to Jacques, standing beside her.

"It's a favorite of mine too," he said, peering into the viewfinder of his camera. *Click!* That was all it took for him to capture the crazy geometry of the rooftops and the pastiche of smoky gray stone, redbrick, and beige stucco dwellings; golden sunlit church spires; and cornflower blue sky.

Jackie was surprised when Jacques had called her that morning and asked her to spend the day with him in the Latin Quarter before going to the opera that night. Surprised, suspicious...and all right, admit it, more than a little pleased. His arrogance annoyed her at times, but when he wasn't condescending, she enjoyed being with him, his playfulness and the feeling of protection he offered. Even the whiff of mystery that hovered about him like a spicy cologne was part of his charm.

But the edgy uncertainty of never quite knowing what Jacques was thinking or what his intentions were, while exciting, made her suspicious. She could only guess what he was really up to. Had the CIA asked him to keep an eye on her and make sure she stayed out of harm's way? Or was his invitation to revisit the Left Bank, where she lived when she was a student at the Sorbonne, prompted by some ulterior motive? Was he hoping that an afternoon in the city's hotbed of avant-garde experimentation would strike a chord in her and lead to something more intimate between them than a working relationship? Yes, that was a distinct possibility, but she tucked it away in a remote corner of her mind when she agreed to meet him in the Square René Viviani. It would be fun returning to her old neighborhood with a bohemian like Jacques, who would fit right in among the writers, artists, musicians, and students living in the small, low-priced hotels in the maze of narrow streets.

"Ah, Jacque-LEEN, you look pretty as a picture," he said, snapping a shot of her as she walked up to meet him in the square. "Lovelier each time I see you."

"In slacks and sandals? I'm hardly dressed in the height of fashion today."

"You would look beautiful in anything. A potato sack even."

Or in nothing, he was saying with his eyes. He was so openly flirtatious that she had to laugh, but with him, it was more a celebration of feminine beauty and sensuality, something like Renoir's, than plain old prurience. At least that's what she told herself.

They left the area around the rue Saint Séverin, which was becoming a center for clochards—homeless people wrapped in rags who made Jackie feel guilty when she saw them—and started walking down boulevard Saint-Michel. Randomly, from among the hundreds of crooked streets leading off the boulevard like a bundle of nerve endings, they picked some to explore, sauntering into art galleries, antiques shops, and dusty used bookshops featuring titles on esoteric subjects like the occult, alchemy, and Eastern mysticism.

At rue de Buci, they meandered past the open-air markets with huge stalls displaying cheeses, poultry stuffed with foie gras, charcuterie, wine, and herbs. They passed by, inhaling the pungent aromas but completely unaware that the market was a hiding place for two people who were keeping Jackie and Jacques in their sights.

Mingling with the French housewives buying ingredients for the day's meals, wearing wide-brimmed sun hats and dark glasses to conceal their faces, were the same middle-aged man and woman who had followed them out of the Tuileries. As Jackie and Jacques walked by, the couple waited until there was enough distance between them not to be detected, then surreptitiously resumed tailing them.

"This is where student riots were always happening when I was here," Jackie remembered as she and Jacques stopped at the baroque fountain sculpture of Saint-Michel slaying a dragon.

"Yes, it's a place for protesters," he said, his lighthearted mood suddenly turning serious. "The Resistance fought the Nazis here many times. The biggest battle was in the summer of 'forty-four."

He took her by the hand and led her over to one of the plaques around the square engraved with the names of those who died there. With his forefinger, he traced the name François Rivage. "That's my father."

Jackie was aghast. "He was killed here?"

"No, he survived the battle but the Nazis arrested him afterward in a roll-up of his Resistance cell and shot him."

She flinched, struck by the monstrously brutal image his

words conjured up. "Oh, Jacques, I'm so sorry. How old were you when that happened?"

"Seventeen."

Jackie could see the pain flickering in his eyes, and her own eyes filled with tears. What would she have done had Black Jack been taken from her like that? She reached out to Jacques and patted his arm wordlessly, unable to think of anything more to say.

Strolling along the Seine, they passed artists at their easels, anglers casting lines, and *bouquinistes*—secondhand-book dealers peddling postcards, tattered prints, decades-old pornography, and well-thumbed books in crates that were hung on the wall fronting the river and locked up overnight.

"Here's one you might like," Jacques said, picking up a book of wartime photographs taken during the Nazi Occupation of France. He opened it and slowly flipped through the pages for Jackie.

She was aware of him looking at her, waiting for her response to the pictures of Parisians going through their daily activities—once-proud people standing in food lines and searching through used clothes on the street; children playing; old women feeding pigeons—all against a jarring background of armed German soldiers, parked tanks, artillery, or other disturbing reminders of the Nazi Occupation.

"These are wonderful, so sensitive and powerful, and they show a sense of humor too," Jackie said, genuinely moved. "Who's the photographer?"

He shut the book and let her see the name on the cover—Jacques Rivage.

"That's amazing! You're so talented! I didn't know you were published." She had to stop herself from squealing like a bobbysoxer at a Frank Sinatra concert.

"There's a lot about me you don't know," he said cryptically. She couldn't be sure whether he wanted her to learn more or would rather she didn't. That tantalizing air of mystery again.

"Yes, you're full of surprises, aren't you? And this one is impressive." She asked the *bouquiniste* the price and paid him before Jacques could stop her. "No, no, let me buy this myself. It's worth so much more."

"You're very kind."

"I'm not flattering you. I really love your pictures," Jackie said as she tucked the book under her arm and resumed strolling with him along the Seine. "They remind me of some of the things I saw when I spent my junior year here. I wanted to improve my French, so instead of living with the others in student lodgings, I lived with an impoverished noblewoman and her family."

"Oh, all the families who take on boarders say they're 'impoverished aristocrats,'" he told her. "If that were true, most of France would be royalty."

"I don't think she was lying," Jackie insisted. She didn't blame Jacques for being cynical, considering what he'd been through, but she wanted him to know she was no naïf either. "Her name was the Comtesse de Renty, and she'd been widowed when the Nazis took her husband off to a concentration camp. She had a daughter, Claude, my age, who made a trip with me across Europe. We saw what Vienna was like with Russians and their Tommy guns everywhere. We saw Salzburg and Berchtesgaden, where Hitler lived, and Munich and the Dachau concentration camp." She shuddered, remembering.

Jacques looked surprised. "And my photographs brought all of that back to you?"

"Yes, because they told the stories of everyday people's lives. And those are the stories I heard when I traveled with Claude.

We went second and third class, sitting up all night on trains, getting to know people and listening to them talking about the losses they suffered, the courage it took to go on, the love that kept them going. It was something I'll never forget."

He smiled and shook his head. "I think I underestimated you, Jackie. Someone in your position could shut their eyes to the suffering around them, but you pry yours open to it. You're quite a woman."

"Spoken like a true Frenchman," she teased. "I bet you say that to all the girls."

"Only the ones I really like."

"And how many of those are there? I hate to think."

"You're in a class by yourself."

"What a charmer you are," Jackie said, laughing. The trouble was, it might have been a game with him, yet she had the feeling that he understood her, even appreciated her, more than any of her beaux back home.

Jacques glanced at his watch. "I don't want to get you back too late, not with the opera tonight. Would you like to get something to eat?"

"I'm starved."

"How about Café des Arts? It's right around here."

"Perfect." It was one of her favorites, where art students sat on benches, and liter flagons of red wine stood on the bare wooden refectory tables.

When they walked into the restaurant, Jackie thought, what's this? Jacques was getting admiring stares from the men as well as the women. She hadn't realized it before, but the dark sexual magnetism he projected was so potent that it blurred gender lines.

Over a meal of tender fillet of veal with fresh asparagus and more glasses of wine than she'd ever consumed before at one sitting, she took Jacques into her confidence. She told him about her determination not to let her family's social position take over her whole identity and the fierce battle she was having with her mother over wanting to break up with John Husted.

"It's so frustrating because I know she's looking out for me, wants to protect me, and I can't be angry at her for that. She wants me to marry into money so I'll be taken care of the rest of my life. My boyfriend doesn't have any *real* money, as my mother likes to put it, but he's distantly related to the fabulously wealthy Harknesses of Standard Oil, and I think my mother is hoping that he'll inherit a fortune someday. Marrying for love—the kind of all-consuming love she had for my father—didn't turn out well for her, and she doesn't want me to make the same mistake."

Jacques nodded. "She thinks she's the voice of experience."

Jackie shook her head, her eyes glinting with defiance as she crumpled her napkin into a ball. "She can't raise me like a hothouse flower, Jacques. She's got to let me make my own mistakes and learn from them. How else can I grow into someone I can be proud of? I don't want to settle just to avoid sticking my neck out and taking my lumps on occasion. I'm not afraid of getting hurt by life. I want to earn the joy that comes from meeting life head on and triumphing over whatever it throws at me."

Jackie took a breath and explained almost shyly, as if confessing a secret, "I read Simone de Beauvoir's *Le Deuxième Sexe,* and it gave me a whole new way of thinking about who I am or might become. It made me realize that women are as capable of making choices about their lives and taking responsibility for themselves as men. We can choose our freedom. My mother doesn't understand that. Her generation thinks a woman is supposed to be taken care of by a man and shouldn't even think about making her own way in the world. She means well, but I can't let her good intentions break my spirit."

Jacques listened intently, gazing deep into her eyes, making her feel like she was the only person in the world. Was this an act, she wondered, feigning interest in her emotional turmoil when all he wanted was to get her into bed? She gave him the benefit of the doubt when he took her hand and held it in his. The warm pressure of his fingers against her palm seemed more a gesture of reassurance than an act of seduction.

"My mother was very protective of me too," he told her, "but it worked to my advantage. If she hadn't discouraged me from joining the Resistance, I never would have become a photographer. I know your mother is making you miserable right now by being so bossy, but maybe having her to rebel against will be good for you in the long run."

"Really? How so?"

"Just think." His eyes twinkled at her. "You're here in Paris, doing something brave and noble for your country, facing challenges and growing in a way I can't imagine any other young woman of your station in life would even attempt. All because you got into a fight with your mother."

She had to laugh. "It's funny how our parents sometimes encourage us to find our own direction in life in spite of themselves," she mused. "They push us to end up being authentic although I'm sure that thought never crossed their minds. All they wanted was for us to be safe."

Jacques shrugged. "This is a dangerous world. To think you can be safe in it only adds to the danger."

An image of the assassin's gleaming knife flashed into Jackie's mind, setting off a shiver that made her hug her chest. She gave Jacques a sober look and nodded. "I'll remember that."

"Yes, you need to be cautious always." He sounded almost

parental himself, but then his face softened in a smile. "Don't worry. I'll be keeping an eye out, and I won't let any harm come to you. You're in good hands with me."

She wanted to believe that, but the thought kept nagging at her that for all his brave words, he might not be up to the task of rescuing her if she ever found herself face to face with the assassin again. Would Jacques be willing to risk his own life to save hers? That was a tall order to put on him, no matter how seriously he took his role as her protector, and she didn't want to think what would happen to her if he failed to come through.

They went back to discussing her decision to break up with John Husted, and Jacques surprised her when he asked, "Do you love him?"

She wouldn't have thought love was a major concern in relationships for a roué like him, but then again, hadn't she seen the sensitivity in his photographs? Only someone capable of deep feeling could create art like that. She shook her head no. "Not in the way I think you should love a man you're about to get engaged to. I'm a romantic at heart. I believe in passionate love, the kind that leaps and dances like a roaring fire. But what I have with him is more like a warm blanket—comfortable to have in bed on a cold night but unexciting."

He looked sympathetic. "Ah, that's too bad. A beautiful young woman like you shouldn't settle for someone who doesn't excite her."

"And there's something else that's just as bad. I don't like the way of life I would have with him. It's too boring and restrictive, too *small*. I think it would drive me crazy after a while. Maybe I'm being grandiose, but I want to be significant in some way." She quickly corrected herself. "I mean, I want to *do* something significant. Not in politics—I like my privacy too much for that—but something in the arts as a painter or a writer or an impresario like Diaghilev, who seemed like a wizard to me, magically blending the talents of geniuses like Rimsky-Korsakov and Nijinksy into masterpieces."

She smiled at this last thought and closed her eyes, dreamily imagining herself in this role. "Yes, an impresario, combining the cultures of the East and West and taking the best works from different periods in art history and music and dance and applying them to our time and making them come alive for the public, the way a conductor leads a symphonic orchestra." She opened her eyes and shook her head, her mouth drawn into a firm line, her voice vehement. "One thing I know for sure. I'm not going to fritter away the rest of my life pouring tea."

Jacques regarded the intense look on her face like someone who had opened a wallet expecting it to be empty and had found a thick wad of bills inside. Then he reached over and patted her cheek, not to placate her but as a gesture of affirmation. "You're right not to want to sell yourself short, Jacque-LEEN, when you have such a highly developed artistic sense and so much to offer the world. You won't do anyone any good by pretending to be less than what you are."

They were standard words of encouragement but somehow comforting to Jackie. He's smooth, smooth as silk, she thought, as he kept his eyes fixed on hers with that you're-the-only-person-in-the-world look, but he made her feel understood and at peace with herself all the same, and she was grateful for that.

The way he kept savoring her with his eyes made her want to confide even more in him, trusting him with a family secret that explained her mother's obsession with marrying Jackie off to a man with money. "You know, Jacques, I'm not the rich girl everyone thinks I am. It's all a beautiful façade my mother keeps up, but she's worried about her children's future. Yes, Mr. Auchincloss, my stepfather, is very generous to me and my sister, Lee, and we enjoy a grand life at his Merrywood estate. But our only inheritance was the three thousand dollars we each received a few years ago when my paternal grandfather died. And we're not going to inherit anything from my stepfather."

Jacques raised his eyebrows in surprise. "Why not?"

"Because he has five children of his own, and only his direct descendants have trust funds from his mother, Grandmother Auchincloss, the family matriarch. My sister and I are the 'poor Bouviers'—we're just hangers-on, the proverbial stepchildren, you might say."

He looked a bit puzzled. "The 'poor Bouviers'?" he asked. "Isn't your father..."

She cut him off quickly. "My father gives me an allowance of fifty dollars a month." She said it in a way that let him know the subject was closed. As loose-tongued as the wine and her feeling of comfort with Jacques had made her, Jackie was still too loyal to her father to let anyone know how close to penury his alcoholism and profligate spending had brought him. Although meager by her friends' standards, the fifty-dollar-a-month allowance was almost more than Black Jack could afford, and she appreciated it as much as if it were ten times that.

"You don't have to inherit money or marry into it," Jacques assured her, surprising her with his acceptance of the brass she had exposed beneath her golden-girl image. "You have talent, Jacque-LEEN. And taste and breeding. You're capable of achieving success on your own in whatever you decide to do."

She smiled gratefully. "Thank you, Jacques."

Even more than the compliment, she appreciated his complete lack of snobbery. It was a welcome breath of fresh air compared to the judgmental pretentiousness she was surrounded by at home. She had taken a chance revealing herself to Jacques, something she rarely did with her dates, and was relieved to find that instead of being laughed at or looked down on, she had gone up in his estimation.

The afterglow of vulnerability rewarded was completely intoxicating—or maybe it was the wine—and by the time they left the restaurant arm in arm, Jackie felt herself sliding into something that was starting to feel like intimacy. She was so caught up in the moment that she didn't even notice—nor did Jacques, apparently—the middle-aged couple in large sun hats and dark glasses watching them from across the street.

Outside the door to her hotel room, Jackie felt woozy from all the wine and a simmering sexual attraction to Jacques that was threatening to boil over at any moment. To steady herself, she put her hand on his chest. The rhythmic *ba-bump, ba-bump, ba-bump* of his heart beating loudly beneath her palm made her start to sway in time with it.

"Are you all right?" he asked. He held her lightly by the shoulders and looked at her with concern.

She nodded and locked eyes with him, stopped moving, waited. She was so still, she could hear herself breathing.

He brought his face down to hers and inched closer and closer until their lips were touching. When he brushed his lips over hers, it felt like a whispered invitation, and her mouth gave in and opened. I shouldn't want this, she thought, but I do.

So she let the kiss draw out, igniting sparks of passion that caught fire and spread down to the deepest part of herself, and she pressed closer.

Suddenly, a loud, explosive sneeze and another person's perturbed "Shush!" coming from somewhere around a corner shattered the mood like a cannonball.

Jacques let go of Jackie and whirled around. "We're being

spied on," he told her. He began to give chase, calling back to her, "I'll find out what they're up to, and I'll see you tonight after the opera."

She was left staring at his back as he ran down the hall, all of the passion draining out of her like air from a punctured tire. That was a close call, she thought, in more ways than one.

"Saved by a sneeze," she muttered to herself, thankful for that unexpected deus ex machina, but fairly certain that even without its intrusion, she would have summoned the willpower to resist venturing beyond that deliciously seductive kiss. Jacques was turning out to be more of a genuine friend than she first thought he could be, a good listener and supportive, but after all, how well did she know him?

With a resigned sigh, she turned the corner to watch Jacques continue the chase after a middle-aged man and woman in ridiculously oversized hats. But they were surprisingly fast and leaped into an open elevator—the only one in the building—before he could catch them.

"Merde," he cursed as he watched the elevator doors clang shut.

Even from this distance, Jackie could sense his frustration at having too many flights of stairs to run down before the strange couple would be on the street and beyond his reach.

But it didn't matter. She couldn't shake the inkling that they were sure, all too sure, to turn up again.

Jackie paused outside the green copper-domed Opéra de Paris to marvel at the ornate Beaux Arts façade—the lavish cherubim and nymphs; the elaborate multicolored marble friezes and statuesque columns; and the bronze busts of Mozart, Rossini, Beethoven, and other great composers. Inside, she joined the bejeweled women and elegantly dressed men climbing the monumental white marble staircase and walked with them down the luxurious foyer lit with rows of crystal chandeliers under a mosaic-covered ceiling. This is like a fairy tale, she said to herself.

The auditorium was even more sumptuous. Red velvet and gold leaf were everywhere. And a massive chandelier—Jackie had been told it weighed six tons—glittered with a brilliance that could light up the sky. She wished Jacques could have been here with her, especially since the performance tonight was *La Bohème*, the perfect one for him. But she had only one ticket, so they had arranged to meet afterward at the Grand Café Capucines, a Paris institution that never closed its doors.

"This way, mademoiselle," a smartly uniformed usher said, glancing at her ticket and leading her to a loge. She was reminded once again that for a Communist, Petrov had class.

"Good evening, so pleased to have you join us," said a distinguished-looking gentleman in an upper-crust British accent. In his early forties, he had a long, thin face, an aquiline nose, a rugged jaw, and a manner that combined foreign intrigue and sophisticated refinement. In his beautifully tailored tuxedo, he looked as if he should have had a monocle in his eye, a martini in one hand, and a cigarette in an ivory holder in the other.

"Roger Latham here," he said, extending his hand. He introduced the middle-aged woman seated beside him as his fiancée, Miranda. Although expensively dressed, she struck Jackie as the kind of hearty Englishwoman who hiked around the countryside in sensible shoes and would make her grand entrance on a Raleigh three-speed bicycle. A divorcée or a widow, judging by her age, and by her jewelry, a woman who knew how to attract wealthy husbands and outlive them.

"My, what a lovely outfit you have on," she said to Jackie. "Is that a Givenchy?"

Jackie nodded, neglecting to say that the last place she'd worn her Givenchy was a garret where she'd discovered the dead man whose ticket she had. (Luckily, the concierge was able to have it cleaned for her overnight.) She took her seat and looked at the program. "Ah, I see Maria Callas is playing Mimi tonight. Have you heard her sing before?"

"No, we haven't, but she made quite an impression in Venice two years ago when she sang Brünnhilde in *Die Walküre*," the man said.

"That's not why she made the impression," the woman corrected him. "It was when she replaced Margherita Carosio as Elvira in Puccini's *I Puritani*. The critics couldn't get over how she was able to take on two such divergent roles in so short a time."

"It's not Puccini's *I Puritani*; it's Bellini's," the man said, determined to give his fiancée tit for tat.

The couple went on bickering like this until Jackie couldn't wait for the opera to begin. She was starting to wonder whether they would stay engaged long enough to get married or would kill each other first. Yet when they weren't fighting with each other, they were exceedingly gracious to Jackie, and she found them oddly endearing.

Finally, the curtain went up, and as soon as Maria Callas made her entrance at Rodolfo's door, filling the auditorium with her incomparably lyrical voice and atmospheric high notes, Jackie knew that she was in the presence of an astonishing talent. The velvet-toned tenor playing Rodolfo had dark Sicilian good looks that reminded her of Jacques. And when Callas sang the *O soave fanciulla* duet with him, declaring their newfound love in Act I, the sheer depth of Callas's emotion made Jackie certain that she would never want to go up against this woman in a fight over a man.

Jackie sat entranced through Acts II and III, thrilled by the exquisite singing of the arias, but she was at a complete loss trying to figure out why Petrov wanted her to have this seat. Then in Act IV, when Rodolfo and the dying Mimi were recalling their first days together, Jackie slipped her hand under her chair to move it slightly so she could get a better view and felt something. A hard wad of chewing gum held something in place on the underside of the seat. A small thrill ran through her as she realized that this must have been placed here by Petrov. Surreptitiously, so as not to arouse the undue attention of the English couple, Jackie pried loose the piece of chewing gum and removed the object. Based on feel alone, it seemed to be some kind of small metal key. Without looking at it, she palmed the object and slipped it into her purse. So this is what Petrov had so desperately wanted her to have.

As soon as the opera was over, Jackie said good-bye to her loge companions, politely telling them she hoped she would see them again soon, and hurried to meet Jacques. She found him standing outside the Grand Café Capucines, humming *"Che gelida manina,"* the aria from Act I of *La Bohème* when Rodolfo first meets Mimi. And to her surprise, he actually could quote the words for her.

"'What a frozen little hand, let me warm it for you,'" he said, holding his hand out to her and flashing his mischievous, ingratiating grin at her.

Then he got down to business. "So, Jacque-LEEN, what deep dark secret did you discover at the opera?"

"It was deep and dark, all right, stuck under my seat with chewing gum." She took the key out of her purse and handed it to him.

He turned it over in his hand, examining the lettering on a tag attached to the key—a three-digit number followed by the initials GdL.

"Hmmm, G-d-L... G-d-L." He pondered for a moment, lips pursed. Then he smiled. He had it. "Of course, what else? The Gare de Lyon."

He raised his arm, summoning a taxi to take them to the train station and the next stop on a journey to... where?

IX

D amn!" Jacques cursed when the taxi drew nearer, and he noticed that it was occupied. So was the next one...and the next one...and the next one.

"Come on," Jacques said, taking Jackie's arm. "Let's try another street. Maybe we'll have better luck."

They walked a block, and after another long wait, finally hailed an empty cab and got in.

"Gare de Lyon, *tout de suite,*" Jacques told the driver. But his directive to hurry was useless. Traffic was heavy, and the ride grindingly slow.

The cab had barely pulled to a stop when Jackie and Jacques flew out and entered the brightly lit Gare de Lyon at its main entrance on the boulevard Diderot. As she always did, Jackie paused for a moment before going down the stairs to take in the awesome beauty of this early-twentieth-century cathedral of railway travel. She loved the station and its ornate Belle Epoque architecture, especially the splendid statues that embellished the main concourse and brought to life technological achieve-ments of navigation, steam, electricity, and mechanics from a now quaint turn-of-the-century point of view. To embrace the eternal magnificence of the Gare de Lyon, Jackie believed, was to be swept up and returned to a time when rail travel was glamorous and filled with the promise of adventure.

By day, the bustling station was filled with the bittersweet romance of lovers parting and the unbound joy of lovers reuniting. It was the stuff of more nineteenth-century novels than Jackie could name. But now, in the very late evening, the *gare* took on a different ambience entirely, one that she had seldom experienced. The travelers seemed dispirited, mostly lonely salesmen carrying their overnight bags and sample cases with slumping shoulders. The tourists, sprawled across the benches with luggage strewn about, seemed frazzled and worn out. And the clochards, who considered the nocturnal station their home, moved furtively from one dark corner of the station to another in search of a place to spend the night. The large space was filled with the kind of loneliness that arises like a miasma from the collective weariness of travelers anxious to return home.

At the bottom of the steps, Jackie darted to the island of luggage lockers off to the left side of the *gare*'s main concourse. Without warning, Jacques seized her by her right elbow and rudely yanked her back.

Jackie glared at him. "Hey, don't push me around like that. Maybe the women you're familiar with like being manhandled. I don't."

"I'll remember that when we're on a date. Right now we're on an assignment, and you need to know what you're doing." He pointed to the island of lockers. "That's a dead drop. A cutout. It's where an agent is most vulnerable. If anyone wants to take him, it'll be here. There could be spies all around here just waiting for us to make our move." He moved his head to indicate the entire main concourse, and Jackie became acutely aware of the homeless who thronged the *gare* at night.

From the corner of one eye, she caught sight of a suspicious-looking clochard. Even though it was high summer, he was wearing at least three cast-off winter coats, one on top of another, giving him the appearance of an obese, threadbare character straight out of *Les Misérables*. Could he be a spy in disguise? Then she spotted a second man hiding behind a newspaper while surreptitiously sizing up every traveler who passed by him. He might have been a pickpocket looking for his next victim...or a spy. And then there was that woman encased like a sausage in skintight clothes with an overly made-up face, strutting around the concourse in black fishnet stockings and staggeringly high heels. She didn't need to be leaning up against a lamppost for Jackie to understand how she made her living. Perhaps she was one of those transvestites who promenaded ostentatiously in the nearby 13th arrondissement late at night, or she could be the incognito spy Jacques warned her about. With a sigh, Jackie conceded that Jacques had a point, and that maybe, although somewhat roughly, he had stopped her from doing something extremely stupid and *très dangereuse*.

Jacques picked out a bench with a good view of the island of lockers and motioned for her to have a seat. He followed and sat down next to her.

Jackie turned to him. "What are we doing?"

"We're waiting here. Checking out the lockers for anything suspicious. We wait. And then we make our move."

"And how long will that be?" Spending the night waiting for something to happen, that might never happen, seemed insufferably boring.

"Until I say so."

"Yes, your Highness," she said, affecting the kind of bow a

commoner gives to a royal. *Damn, he's arrogant*, she thought, and hoped her sarcastic gesture wouldn't be lost on him.

Jacques was too busy scanning the lockers to respond, but his brusque remark had slammed the lid shut on any further conversation. So Jackie sat on the bench, squirming until she found a position that would be comfortable until Jacques gave the command for action. Up until now, it hadn't occurred to her that a good part of being an espionage agent consisted of exposure to conditions of brain-numbing boredom for hours at a time.

Oh, well, Jackie grudgingly admitted to herself, there were far worse ways of passing the time than sitting on a bench at the Gare de Lyon next to a handsome young Frenchman, even one who was sometimes a little too domineering for comfort.

As she continued to sit next to him in separate parallel universes, Jackie came to the realization that there were two Jacques. One was Charming Jacques of the afternoon and evening who escorted her around Paris, flirted with her, and made her feel giddy as a schoolgirl at the scent of sexual danger he gave off as natural as musk. The other was Secret Agent Jacques who was all stone-cold business and deadly serious and made her feel like a hopelessly gauche simpleton in this arcane world of espionage. The problem was, with so many unknown hazards waiting to spring up and pounce on them like wild beasts in a forest, she wasn't sure which Jacques was going to react to her at any given moment of the day.

About a half hour later, Jacques finally gave Jackie the signal. He tapped her on the wrist and said, "Go. But be careful. Go slow. I'll watch you from here. At the first sign of trouble, come right back to me. *Comprends-tu?*"

"*Oui.*"

Jackie rose from the bench and began to walk across the

main concourse of the Gare de Lyon. She moved slowly to avoid bumping into the travelers who were making their way to or from the station's many platforms. As she went, she looked back to see if Jacques was watching her. He was. He gave the merest nod of his head as a sign of affirmation, and she continued walking.

Approaching the island of lockers, Jackie could quickly see that the number of the locker that matched the one on the key from the opera wasn't on this side. She would have to walk around to the other side, where she would momentarily be out of sight of Jacques. She moved slowly around the near corner of the island and was startled to be confronted by a tall and imposing gendarme, looking very crisp in his uniform and kepi, standing in front of the lockers on the other side. Jackie quickly tried to regain her composure so the gendarme wouldn't think that anything was amiss.

"May I help you, mademoiselle?" he asked.

"I need to get to my locker." She tried to suppress the quaver in her voice and convey a sense of quiet urgency.

"Vous ne pouvez pas venir ici." The gendarme held up his hand to prevent her from coming any farther. "This is a crime scene." With his other hand, he pointed down to a chalk outline in front of the lockers. Jackie knew what this meant. Someone had been murdered here. A woman, judging from the curves of the dead body outline. The area around the ghostly silhouette was splattered with dollops of blood, as though a butcher had tried his hand at being Jackson Pollock.

Jackie gazed down at the outline and felt dizzy, her head spinning like the carousel in the Tuileries. This was the second murder scene that she had run across in almost as many days. What was going on here? She had come to Paris to have dinner with a man, albeit a Russian spy and would-be defector, and now it seemed like she couldn't go anywhere in the city without stumbling across a fresh murder scene. She shut her eyes, blocking out the gruesome outline, and prayed that she wouldn't faint.

Slowly, as her dizziness began to subside, she opened her eyes and noticed that the gendarme was staring at her. Staring hard. Thunderstruck.

"Mon Dieu," he exclaimed. "You look just like her!"

"Like who?" Why was he looking at her like that, and what was he talking about?

"The woman who was killed. You look just like her. I saw her as she was being taken away. Same hair color and style. Same general build. Even a Givenchy dress, *le même chose.*" He kept staring at her as if he had just seen a ghost . . . as indeed, he thought he had.

Jackie smiled inwardly. Only in Paris, the fashion capital of the world, would a police officer be able to identify the designer of a homicide victim's clothes. But at the same time, this was very troubling. The murder victim resembled her? Was this a coincidence? Or could it be that the assassin from the garret had staked out this locker, waiting for her to show up in order to finish the job he had botched the other night? The blood splatters seemed to indicate that the killer had used a knife on his victim, the weapon of choice of the man from the garret, or that's how it appeared to Jackie's admittedly less than forensically trained eyes.

Flustered, Jackie looked up at the gendarme and said simply, "I'm sorry. Thank you." Then she slowly turned on her heel, rounded the corner of the island of lockers, and returned to Jacques, who was keeping a lookout near the bench where she'd left him.

He looked at her inquisitively. "Well, did you get it?"

Not trusting herself to speak, her heartbeat pounding loudly in her ears from her disconcerting conversation with the gendarme, Jackie could only shake her head no.

"You didn't? Why not?"

When she could talk again, she told Jacques what the gendarme had said.

"What do you think happened?" she asked him.

Jacques thought a moment before answering. "Let's save that for later. The first thing we have to do is figure out a way to get to that locker."

"He's standing guard there, and he won't let anyone near the lockers."

"So you said." Abruptly, Jacques stood.

"Where are you going?" Jackie asked.

"I want to take a look for myself. I'll be right back. Don't talk to anyone."

He left her on the bench and began casually strolling around the main concourse, taking his time as though he was in no hurry to get wherever he might be going. But from where she sat and waited, Jackie could see that Jacques had a definite destination in mind. Hands in pockets, he lackadaisically circumnavigated the island of lockers several times, making increasingly smaller circles until he rounded the corner and was lost from Jackie's sight.

In a few minutes, Jacques reappeared and returned to the bench with his appraisal of the situation. "This is not going to be easy."

"What are we going to do?"

"I think we need a diversion."

"What kind of diversion?"

"Maybe we could start a fire. A small one, nearby. When the gendarme goes to investigate, we could race to the locker, open it, take whatever's inside and, voilà, we take off."

"We could also get arrested for arson."

"Yes, there's always that."

Jackie had to smile at Jacques's display of typically European sangfroid.

Then it hit her. "Wait, I have an idea."

He looked at her expectantly.

"I could go up to him. Engage him in conversation. Flirt with him a little. Draw him away from the locker. Then, while I continue to chat him up, you could get in there and open the locker."

She could tell that he was impressed by her improvised plan.

"That's a brilliant idea... but there's just one problem," he said thoughtfully.

"What's that?" She was a little disappointed to have her idea die such a quick death.

"I spent some time watching the gendarme. Every time a woman passed him, his eyes remained forward at all times. But whenever a man walked by, he followed each one with his glance. I'm afraid our gendarme prefers *les hommes* to *les femmes.*"

Jackie had a momentary flashback to the way Jacques had been ogled by the men at the Café des Arts earlier in the day and brightened, knowing that her plan was not dead after all.

"My plan can still work," she told him. "All we have to do is switch roles."

"What?"

"You flirt with the gendarme, and I'll open the locker."

He looked at her open-mouthed, the old sangfroid vanishing like a mirage.

"C'est impossible!"

"Qu'est-que c'est impossible?"

"Because...," Jacques spluttered. "Because..." He couldn't bring himself to finish the sentence.

"Are you afraid to talk to a man?"

"No, of course not."

"Then what's the problem?"

"I don't know."

"Good. Then it's settled. You distract the gendarme. And I'll open the locker. Then we can meet back here."

Not allowing him any time to protest, Jackie sprang off the bench, opened up her evening bag, and rooted around in it until she came up with the key that would open the locker. I like being in charge for a change, she thought, as she walked in the direction of the island of lockers and shot a quick side-long glance at Jacques trailing behind her reluctantly, having no choice left to him.

When he caught up to her, he asked, "Are you ready?"

She nodded and held up the key for him to see.

"Good. Stand back and wait for me to get him away from the lockers. Then you go in. But be quick, don't fumble. I don't know how long I can maintain his attention."

Jackie watched as he headed off to the island of lockers and rounded the corner, then followed, waiting several beats for him to engage the gendarme. She arrived in time to watch Jacques approach the gendarme, an unusual lilt in his walk. Careful, Jacques, she mentally cautioned him. Don't overdo it. She saw Jacques step up to the crime scene and boldly begin to address the gendarme. With his flamboyantly gesticulating hands and arms, Jackie was afraid the gendarme might well mistake Jacques for an overzealous refugee from the commedia dell'arte.

As she continued observing the exchange, she saw Jacques

bring his over-the-top movements under control. For his part, the gendarme seemed to be answering politely but not indicating any sustained interest. Then Jacques took out a cigarette and asked the gendarme for a light. As he pulled out a lighter, Jacques took several small steps back, forcing the gendarme to take two or three steps away from the crime scene so he could bring the lighter to the tip of the cigarette. Jacques took the hand holding the lighter in order to steady it and puffed slowly on the cigarette, his eyes forthrightly meeting the gendarme's over the flame. That seemed to do the trick, Jackie could see. Jacques took several more steps away and pointed to something farther down the main concourse. The gendarme took an equal number of steps away from the crime scene in order to see what Jacques was pointing out.

Jackie knew this was her chance. As the two continued their conversation, she raced over to the island of lockers, key in hand. She matched up the number engraved on the key with the correct locker—fortunately for her it was one that was at chest height—and tried inserting the key in the lock. But her hand was shaking so badly that she couldn't get the key in. Come on, Jackie, she admonished herself, don't make Jacques sacrifice his manhood for nothing. It took her three tries before her hand was steady enough to insert the key in the lock and turn it to the right. To her relief, the locker door popped open instantly.

With bated breath, she opened the locker door all the way, wondering what she would find there. Would it be a briefcase stuffed with top-secret documents? A lockbox filled with rare coins and stamps? A sack containing damning evidence of a crime? Or, given the Grand Guignol discoveries of the past few days, perhaps a severed head in a hatbox, like in that movie with Robert Montgomery that had frightened her so when she was younger? With the locker door fully open, Jackie peered inside and was relieved—and puzzled—to find only a single business envelope taking up the interior space.

Quickly, she snagged the envelope and stashed it in her evening bag. No time to see what was in it right now. Then, just as quickly, she closed the locker door, left the key in the lock to be used by the next patron, and fled the lockers. She retreated to the bench and, with her heartbeat once again hammering in her ears, collapsed on the seat and waited for Jacques to return from his impromptu rendezvous with the gendarme.

And then, there he was, rounding the corner of the island of lockers and headed right toward her. He was walking at a fast clip and trying to compensate for it with an overly nonchalant attitude. As he arrived at the bench, he didn't break his stride, but whispered to her as he passed, "Meet me by the main entrance."

Jackie waited for him to pass her entirely, then followed him across the main concourse, up the stairs, out through the main entrance, and back onto the avenue Diderot. Once there, she joined Jacques, who was busy hailing the next cab at the taxi rank. The cab moved forward and stopped for them. Jacques opened the door and ushered her inside. He gave their destination, but, maddeningly, just sat there without saying anything further.

Finally, Jackie couldn't take it any longer and blurted out, "So what happened?"

He gave her a long look before responding. "It went very well. I'm meeting him when he gets off duty, at De Trop."

Jackie knew of De Trop, an infamous club in the 13th where audiences were entertained by performers in drag. "I'm glad the two of you were able to hit it off."

"I'm joking. Actually, all I did was ask for directions to De

Trop. He just assumed we were two of a kind, and I did nothing to disabuse him of the notion."

"So you see, it wasn't so difficult," Jackie said lightly, without trying to rub it in.

Jacques turned to her, a serious look on his face.

"Jaque-LEEN, please do me a favor?"

"What?"

"For the rest of your time here, please don't ask me to do anything like that again."

"All right."

"Now, please," he said, unable to contain himself any longer, "what was in the locker?"

She reached into her evening bag, took out the envelope, and handed it to him.

"This? Just this?"

She nodded.

"Shall I open it?"

"Go ahead. Or we'll never know what's in it."

He opened the envelope and removed from it a single piece of foolscap paper on which someone, presumably the dead Russian, had written something in a neat schoolboy hand.

"What does it say?"

"Longchamp. Third race. And tomorrow's date."

Jackie looked confused. "But what does it mean?"

Jacques shrugged. "I don't know." He folded up the piece of paper and put it back in the envelope. "But it figures. A night at the opera and a day at the races. Your Russian was obviously a devotee of Marx."

"Karl?" asked Jackie.

"No," replied Jacques with a straight face, "Groucho."

She laughed and squeezed his hand. The Charming Jacques was back, the one whose teasing sense of humor tickled her inside and kicked up delicious little flurries of desire as she remembered their first kiss.

When they got back to her hotel and were saying good night at the door to her room, they both moved in for a kiss at the same time. Gently, he took her face in his hands, and she was overcome with a feeling of tenderness for him. There was something so compelling about him, the combination of darkness and light, the coolness and, when she least expected it, the warmth.

She let the kiss draw out, savoring the taste of his lips on hers and the embrace of his arms. It was comforting to have him for her helpmate, an ally in a mission that was proving to be more dangerous and complicated than she had ever imagined it would be. She felt like a landlubber who'd been thrown into the deep end of the ocean and was expected to know how to swim. Jacques was her water wings, buoying her up and keeping her afloat while she was getting the hang of it. They were an unlikely pair, but still a team.

Maybe it was her imagination, but when they looked in each other's eyes, she thought he was also aware of a closeness developing between them, a we're-in-this-together bond. It was too strong to miss.

When his lips moved down to her neck and skipped across her bare chest, his kisses aroused flutters of excitement that made her gasp. Then his hands slid down her shoulders to her waist, and he drew her closer to him. Mouths and tongues moved together, deep thrusts, rising waves of passion swirling around inside. No more thinking. She was lost to sensation, weak-kneed and overwhelmed, as the kiss stretched on, igniting new sparks in her body, discovering new places to bring alive.

Jackie hovered on the verge of saying, "Do you want to come in?" but was fighting the temptation as hard as she could. She knew he was too dangerous and exotic, too calculating and cavalier for a lasting relationship. Yet she was still powerfully drawn to him, wanting to experience someone so different from the safe, proper, schoolboy beaux of her past. This was Paris, the most romantic city in the world. And if she dared to go all the way with someone so far outside the parameters of her narrow social circle, who would know?

Just as she thought she might surrender to the magnetic pull of sexual curiosity and invite Jacques into her room, they heard footsteps pounding down the hall like hoofbeats and a man shouting *"Arrêt! Arrêt!"* at the top of his lungs.

They drew apart and saw a gendarme—thankfully, not the one from the Gare de Lyon—chasing a bedraggled-looking man lurching toward them in an obviously inebriated state, but still moving quickly. The gendarme caught up with him and tackled him to the ground inches away from Jackie and Jacques's feet.

"Qu'est-ce que c'est?" Jacques asked the policeman.

"Il est un voleur," he said, hauling the man who reeked of alcohol to his feet and saying that he was a thief. *"Il est sorti en courant d'un restaurant sans payer l'addition."*

Explaining that the handcuffed drunk had run out of a restaurant without paying the bill, the officer held the man's arms behind his back, clapped handcuffs around his wrists with a no-nonsense finality, and led him away.

"Happens all the time around here," Jacques muttered, clearly irritated by this unwanted interruption of his amorous hopes.

Now Jackie was too shaken to even think about inviting Jacques into her room that night. She was beginning to wonder whether she and Jacques were destined to be star-crossed lovers. She only hoped they would come to a better ending than Romeo and Juliet.

Gallantly, Jacques took her hand and kissed it. "Good night, Jacque-LEEN. Thank you for an . . . interesting . . . day and evening. Let's see what the third race at Longchamp brings tomorrow."

Jackie nodded, wondering which was stronger—her curiosity about what tomorrow would bring or how much she looked forward to spending it with Jacques.

X

Y ou're right on time, and I must say, this is a step up from the
Metro," Jackie quipped, eyeing the bright red sports car with
an eggshell white convertible top—a Renault 4CV *décapotable*—
that Jacques pulled up in to take her to Longchamp.

"I'd have preferred a Rolls-Royce for you, but that's a little
hors-de-prix for me."

A Rolls? No, thank you, she said to herself, shaking her head
at the thought of her harrowing ride in the Silver Wraith with
Dexter.

"This'll do just fine," Jackie said, sliding in beside him on
the glove-soft leather seats. To tell the truth, she thought, photography must be paying pretty well for him to afford a car as
luxe as this. Or the CIA was.

He started the car and breezed down avenue de Choisy, the
high street of Chinatown, taking his eye off the road long enough
to look at her so appreciatively that she felt embarrassed.

"I like your dress. It looks like the one Marlene Dietrich
wore in *Stage Fright*."

"It's by the same designer, Dior." Her outsized sunglasses hid
her look of surprise, something that was getting to be a habit
when she was with him. She wouldn't have picked him for the
type who would remember what movie he saw a dress in and

who was wearing it—not after his consternation over having to dally with the gendarme in the Gare de Lyon. "How did you know that? Are you a Hitchcock fan?"

"I am. That was a great line she said when she tried the dress on: 'Can't you make it plunge a little in the front?'" He was weaving through traffic and navigating boulevards with the smooth, effortless skill of someone who knew the city like his own backyard.

Jackie was impressed. This was something else that she had in common with her French cohort—they were both Hitchcock lovers. "It was a good line," she said, watching the large shopping mall on Place d'Italie zip by, "but I didn't like the movie. The flashback in the beginning made you think Jonathan Cooper was innocent, but it was a lie. When you found out at the end that he really did murder his mistress's husband, it was a letdown."

"That's because you weren't thinking like an agent." Jacques shot her a meaningful glance as they passed a tollgate to the Périphérique Extérieur. "An agent always expects the unexpected. You would do well to remember that."

She wondered what he was trying to tell her with that suggestive look—was it a warning of some kind?—but decided he was probably just referring to the false starts they'd had in moving their relationship to a more intimate plane. Her lips turned up at the corners in a wry smile. "From the way things have been going, I'd say that's good advice."

As they tooled westward along the exterior ring road toward the Bois de Boulogne, Jackie breathed in the fragrance of the lilacs growing copiously in suburban gardens and savored the view of the chestnut trees in full blossom, the swallows gliding in the sky, and the apartment buildings with gardens sprouting on the balconies.

"Mmmm, this is delightful," Jackie said, feeling the breeze rippling the sleeves of her pale blue, gauzy silk dress. Lucky for her, she'd picked up a dusty blue-and-gold Dupioni silk hat to go with the dress when she went shopping on Place Vendôme or she hated to think what her hair would look like now.

"Here we are," Jacques said, pulling into the main parking lot in the Longchamp infield. He found a space for the car on the lot, got out, and went around to open the door for Jackie.

"What a perfect place for a picnic," Jackie said as they walked past families enjoying their lunch under shady trees on the grassy field; a children's play area with pony rides, food and beverage stands; souvenir kiosks; hospitality tents; and handsome statues of championship horses from past years. Her eyes swept over the manicured lawns and hedges, the white-painted concrete-and-glass grandstands, and the blue-and-gold banners with the racetrack emblem hanging all around.

The paddock was shaded by large trees and had high, concrete terraced viewing stands. "This paddock is as big as Belmont's," Jackie said, her mind flashing back to those girlhood Sundays when her father would take Jackie and Lee to the races and always visit the paddock, where he would introduce his daughters to the jockeys.

"Paddock?" Jacques asked, unfamiliar with the name.

She pointed. "You know, the walking ring."

"Ah, here we call it the *'rond de présentation'* for people who like to get a good look at the horses before they place their bets. But for our purposes, we should get a racing program too."

The "our purposes" brought Jackie back quickly to the present and their reason for being at Longchamp. What clue would they find here? Where should they look? A racing program couldn't hurt. "Okay, let's get one," she said.

They stopped at a newsstand outside the admission gates to

buy *Paris Turf,* and there—of all people—stood the eccentric British couple from the loge at the opera last night.

The man, wearing a pinstriped suit set off with an ascot and a bowler hat, turned when he saw Jackie and greeted her warmly. "Why, hello, Miss Bouvier, we meet again. A most pleasant coincidence, to be sure."

The woman took Jackie's hands in both of hers and was even more effusive. "My dear, what a lovely, lovely surprise! You look absolutely ravishing."

There was something about the way she stressed the word *surprise*—a touch of "methinks the lady doth protest too much" overemphasis—that aroused a fleeting suspicion in Jackie's mind. Were they actually following her? But Jackie dismissed the thought quickly, attributing it to the paranoia that she assumed was an occupational hazard of the espionage game.

She noticed that the two of them were both eyeing Jacques with curiosity. "This is Jacques Rivage," she said, "a photographer friend of mine, the one who did that wonderful book called *The Faces of War?*" They nodded, assuming this was a work they should know and not wanting to admit they didn't. "I've never been to Longchamp before, and Jacques wanted me to see it."

The couple seemed mollified. "Oh, I know you'll find it lovely," the woman said. She grasped Jackie's arm. "Do let's sit together."

Jacques looked uncomfortable, but Jackie slipped him a glance that said they're dotty but harmless; let's not be impolite. "Of course, we'd love to," she told the woman.

They were starting to walk toward the grandstand when the woman suddenly pointed and said, "Oh, look, there's Yves Montand."

Jackie turned her head to see the ruggedly handsome, dark-haired man whose picture was on the page of the *Paris Match* Jacques had been holding as a sign for her when they first met in the Tuileries. Now the real Montand was surrounded by a gaggle of autograph-seekers as he tried to make his way to a private section of the clubhouse.

"I heard he's wonderful in his new movie, *Paris Will Always Be Paris*," the woman said.

"It's *Paris* Is *Always Paris*," her fiancé corrected her.

Ignoring that, the woman said to Jackie, "He must be here to see Tantième run. That's the three-year-old who won the Prix de l'Arc de Triomphe."

"Tantième is a four-year-old," the British man said.

"How exciting," Jackie gushed, wondering, is this what I'm in for, a whole afternoon of these two playing tit-for-tat?

Inside the grandstand, the four of them found seats near the front row. The British couple went off to place their bets, and Jackie sat with Jacques while he studied *Paris Turf* and waited for the first race to begin.

Jackie could see why Longchamp was considered one of the premier racecourses in the world. "I've never seen a track as large as this," she said, "or as pretty." Her eyes took in the lush expanse of grass, the windmill at the clubhouse turn, the leafy trees overhanging the backstretch, and the large, blue arch with the sponsor and race name at the finish line. The crowd in the stands was as fashionably dressed as any she had seen at a debutantes ball, with an array of hats bobbing like boats in a vast marina—women's in all shapes and sizes, and round British bowlers and angular French trilbys on the men.

Jacques tugged on her sleeve. "The race is going to start. Pay attention." He handed her *Paris Turf* to read.

Uh-oh, Secret Agent Jacques again. All business. Why did she have to follow the first race? It wasn't until the third that they were supposed to find some clue. To appease him, she scanned the first-race information anyway, then paid close attention as the jockeys finished the warm-up run around the track and returned to the gate where the horses were being loaded into the stalls one at a time.

The gate opened, and the horses broke when the bell went off. She listened to the announcer calling the positions until after the wide, far turn when another announcer took over for the back-stretch and the finish. As the horses came around the last turn, the crowd noise swelled to a roar of shouting voices urging on their favorites. After the horses crossed the finish line, an electric chime sounded and a third announcer, a woman, called the names of the winners.

Had the top seven finishing positions not been posted on a board, Jackie wouldn't have known the winners. Their names would've been drowned out by the British couple squabbling over their bets.

"If you'd have put your fifteen francs on Samsarra to win, as I told you to," the man admonished his fiancée, "you'd have got back seventy-five. But no, you insisted on wasting your money on Magiche, a German colt who has yet to win a race."

"You're a fine one to talk," she shot back. "If I had all the money you've lost betting ridiculous Trios the way you do, I could buy Longchamp."

Oh, dear, Jackie thought, they'll surely come to blows before this day is over.

After the second race was run, Jackie decided that she needed to get away for a bit before the British couple returned from placing their bets, partly to escape their endless bickering and partly to prepare for the next race.

"I'm going down to the *rond de présentation*," she told Jacques. "Maybe if I get a closer look at the horses, I can pick up something that will help us with the clue."

He nodded, engrossed in his *Paris Turf.*

By the time Jackie got to the paddock, the grooms had already started parading the horses around the ring. As she entered the paddock, she was greeted—some would say assailed—by an odor of wet hay, dried sweat, and fresh manure. Many would find these commingled smells objectionable, but to Jackie, they were as welcome as an old friend because they were a reminder of a world in which she always felt at home. Paradoxically, these odors were to Jackie what the lemony-sweet madeleine was to Proust—something that set off only the fondest of memories in her mind.

She walked closer to the horses to get a better look at an approaching chestnut thoroughbred who reminded her of Danseuse. As the colt came nearer, she stood there admiring his glossy, dark reddish brown coat, the color of English toffee; brawny shoulders; sassy, alert ears; muscular hindquarters; and sinewy, graceful legs that she could imagine flying down the racecourse with meteoric speed. Ah, would I love to ride him, she thought, picturing herself astride that marvelous mount, carrying her wherever she wanted to go.

Jackie had been so engrossed in her inspection of the horse that she didn't notice a big hulk of a man making his way down from the viewing stand and approaching her. He looked like Oliver Hardy in an ill-fitting suit with an open jacket and a shirt stretched too tightly over his bulging midsection. A bowler hat sat askew on his massive head, and an incongruous little black mustache dotted his fleshy face. It wasn't until he was up to her and jostled her arm that Jackie became aware of him.

She turned her head with a smile on her face, thinking that Jacques had decided to come down and join her. Instead, she was shocked to come face to face with someone it took her a second to recognize—the assassin disguised as a cartoonish proper English gentleman. The only thing neither comical nor proper about him was the familiar-looking knife in his hand.

Was this a dream, some persistent nightmare she couldn't shake loose? No, it was the assassin in the flesh—she could tell by the way his chest was heaving up and down—and this time he had a furious look on his face. It wasn't his usual steely gaze of a cold-blooded hit man, but the angry snarl of a killer hell-bent on vengeance. Jackie knew in an instant what that expression meant. She'd been right about the murder in the Gare de Lyon. The assassin had been tipped off that she and Jacques were headed to the station, and he beat them to it—not too surprising, considering how long it took them to get there. Then the killer murdered an innocent woman whose only crime was that she too closely resembled Jacqueline Lee Bouvier, even down to her fondness for Givenchy clothes. Somehow the assassin had realized his mistake, and nothing was going to stop him from correcting it once and for all. Now. This very moment.

He was so close to her that Jackie could see the spidery red veins in the whites of his bulging eyes. *Run, run for your life,* she heard herself screaming inside. With not a second to spare, she whirled around, vaulted over the low railing, and entered the ring. She was sure that the railing would give the portly assassin some pause, but to her surprise, he vaulted it as easily as a trained gymnast. For a big man, she noted to her immense distress, he was quite nimble.

Jackie ran from him, threading her way in and out of the horses being led around the ring by their grooms. Every now and then, she would look behind, and there he was, the bowler-hatted assassin. Panic set in when she noticed that he had palmed his knife so no one in the ring would discern his intentions and stop him. She desperately wanted to cry out to the grooms to help her, but it was useless. Annoyed at this unwarranted game of tag in their midst, the grooms shouted and cursed at Jackie and her pursuer, their four-legged charges chiming in with nervous whinnying and whickering of their own.

Racing around the ring in high heels was a strain on Jackie's legs, and it was beginning to show. The implacable assassin, on the other hand, betrayed no sign of slowing down. In fact, he was almost about to catch up to her. Her gut knotted with fear, and she could feel a trail of sweat coursing down her back. Jackie knew that she had to do something extreme to escape being stabbed to death.

She reached the gap between the Danseuse look-alike and the horse immediately behind him, a brooding coal black Arabian, turned to the groom, and abruptly elbowed him in the midriff, knocking him sideways into the horse. The already high-strung Arabian reared up on his hind legs and began to paw the air with his front hooves, neighing indignantly. The assassin was knocked down by his flailing hooves and fell to the ground.

Jackie raced forward to the Danseuse look-alike, pushed aside his startled groom, and with the skill of an expert equestrian, quickly mounted the colt. She looked back and caught sight of the assassin rolling from side to side on the ground to avoid being trampled by the still irate horse. The Arabian's tantrum was infectious, and now the other horses in the ring were reacting in the same tempestuous mode, their grooms hard-pressed to get them under control.

This was the chance for her getaway. Leaving the mayhem behind her, Jackie bolted out of the walking ring, down a path and—yes!—onto the racetrack itself. With a final backward glance, she watched as the assassin disappeared in a cloud of dust kicked up by the ringful of spooked horses.

This is easier than riding the hills in Merrywood, Jackie thought, facing ahead again, as the well-trained horse took off at a brisk gallop, sensitive to the pressing need of his rider. Crouching forward, her eyes straight ahead, the horse's hooves thundering in her ears, Jackie was unaware of the sensation she was causing among the crowd in the grandstand. She was oblivious to the cries of "Do you see that?" "Look at her!" and the gawkers pointing at the woman in the diaphanous blue dress billowing out around her, a fancy hat with the tails of a large bow streaming behind, arms sheathed in long white gloves up to her elbows, and her stiletto heels expertly prodding the horse to higher speeds.

In her own world, Jackie had no idea of the mesmerizing effect her ride was having on Jacques and the English couple. As she rounded the clubhouse turn where the windmill stood, Jacques rose from his seat and stared in disbelief. Beside him, the British man said in an awed tone, "I say, old stick, your Miss Bouvier bloody well looks like Lady Godiva."

"No, she doesn't," his fiancée disagreed. "Lady Godiva was naked. Miss Bouvier is fully clothed."

"Pity," said the man.

Jackie sat astride the horse in perfect union with the rhythm of his swift legs pumping up and down like pistons. She exulted in the feeling of power it gave her to be moving like the wind over this silken grassy field. Now she was in the home stretch, racing toward the finish line, but when she crossed it, she didn't stop. She was not about to dismount and walk back to the paddock where the assassin could be waiting to take another crack at her.

Instead, she masterfully directed the horse around to the back of the grandstand and onto the infield. She tightened the horse's reins and relaxed the pressure of her thighs against his sides, trying to bring him to a trot, but he cantered across the field, scattering alarmed picnickers, sideswiping refreshment stands, and overturning souvenir kiosks.

"Whoa, boy, whoa!" Jackie shouted. She stood in the stirrups, lifted herself out of the saddle, and pulled on the reins some more. The horse raised his head and reared up, whinnying loudly, but Jackie managed not to get thrown. She sat back down and crouched over him again. Coaxing him with her voice and body, she slowly brought him into a trot and then a standstill.

When she dismounted, a crowd gathered around her, applauding and praising her horsemanship.

"Merci, merci," Jackie murmured, feeling like a rodeo performer. She led the horse over to the children's play area with the pony rides, tethered him there temporarily, and hurried to the parking lot. She knew Jacques had seen her gallop around to the infield, so she waited for him alongside his red convertible, looking to make sure there was no sign of the assassin anywhere. Hurry, Jacques, please come out, she said to herself, glancing anxiously at the gate to the grandstand.

She heard the applause of the crowd, signifying that the grooms had restored order, and the third race had begun. A few minutes later, to her great relief, Jacques came running out of the grandstand. He rushed over and embraced her, then stepped back and looked at her solicitously. "Are you all right?"

"I'll be better when we're out of here," Jackie said, sliding into the car as soon as he opened the door.

On the ride back to the city, after hearing about her encounter with the assassin in the paddock, Jacques seemed in awe of her skills as an equestrian. "You were amazing, Jacque-LEEN, absolutely *formidable*. Where did you learn to ride like that?"

"I was less than a year old when I was first put on a horse," she told him. "At five, I entered a horse show at Smithtown, Long Island, and at six, I was jumping horses in the Southampton Horse Show—that's the Southampton in New York, not the one in England." She didn't want to brag, but he seemed keenly interested in her history as an equestrian child prodigy, so she continued. "When I was eleven, I won two trophies offered to horse show exhibitors: one for horsemanship and another called the Good Hands award. The *New York Times* said I achieved a rare distinction winning both contests in the same show. I could go on, but I don't want to bore you."

"You're not boring me at all. I wanted to know." He smiled, thinking about her narrow escape. "Our assassin friend must have been dumbfounded."

Jackie shrugged. Then she shared the conclusions she'd drawn from the assassin's wrath. "Don't ask me how he knows every move I'm going to make, but the way I see it, he was waiting for me to come to the Gare de Lyon and open that locker, murdered that woman in the train station thinking she was me, and was furious when he opened her locker and realized that he had the wrong person."

"Or he could have learned of his mistake when he read the paper today. It was all over the front page. Didn't you read *Le Figaro* this morning?"

"No, I didn't get a chance. What did it say?"

He motioned to the backseat. "It's back there. See for yourself."

Jackie reached over for the paper, brought it to the front seat, and spread it open on her lap. She shuddered as the big, bold news item leaped out at her, and she mentally translated from the French.

SLASHER KILLS WOMAN IN GARE DE LYON

Marcelle LaCroix, a 24-year-old assistant to Hubert de Givenchy, a rising star in the fashion world, was killed last night by an unknown assailant who attacked her with a knife in the Gare de Lyon. Mademoiselle LaCroix's father, Gerard LaCroix, said his daughter made frequent business trips and stored items in a locker in the station when she was traveling. Her body with multiple wounds was discovered...

Jackie stopped reading and pushed aside the paper. She felt sick to her stomach, gripped by a wave of remorse so powerful that it clenched her belly. Poor Marcelle LaCroix, her life cut short at twenty-four for no reason other than her resemblance to a woman she didn't even know. It all seemed so senseless and unforgivably cruel.

She looked at Jacques, tears in her eyes, her voice trembling. "It's so unfair. What did she do to deserve that? And to think, all that was in that locker was a slip of paper with the number of a horserace on it."

Jackie began to weep quietly, and Jacques reached for her hand. "It's not your fault," he consoled her. "She was in the wrong place at the wrong time. Accidents like that happen all the time. It's sad, but *c'est la vie.*"

He did not say it blithely, but with a sigh of resignation that reminded her that Jacques had come by this stoic philosophy honestly as a seventeen-year-old boy whose father was murdered by the Nazis. How did someone that young deal with the enormity of such a loss? As Jackie grappled with the tragedy of innocent Marcelle LaCroix's horrifying and untimely death, she thought about the courage it took for Jacques to accept so brutal a fate for his own father. Even though the young woman was a total stranger to Jackie, the guilt she felt for having unknowingly caused her death was overwhelming.

They rode in silence for a while, Jackie's anguish precluding any conversation. When the heavy cloud of her sadness slowly began to lift, she remembered why they had come to Long-champ in the first place. She turned to Jacques, curious. "You waited for the third race to finish. Did it give you any clue?"

He shook his head. "None whatsoever. There was nothing unusual about the race at all. I can't imagine what was so special..." Suddenly, he let out a little snort and said, "The clue must be the name of one of the horses running in the race."

Jackie chuckled. "That was right in front of us, wasn't it?" she said. "Of course, if it's only a name of one of the horses, then all we needed to do was pick up a copy of *Paris Turf* and leave."

"What, and miss your spectacular ride? Never," Jacques said with a grin. Then he grew serious. "There were seven horses running in that race," he remembered. "Now we have to figure out, which one is it?" He motioned to his *Paris Turf* on the seat beside him. "Take a look and see what you think."

Jackie picked up the racing program, found the third race, and pored over the names of the horses. Then she picked up the copy of *Le Figaro* she had put aside and turned to the society page. She scanned it and began nodding her head vigorously.

"Aha, I've got it," she said, pointing to an item on the society page. "One of the horses that ran in the third race was Windsor Knot, an English horse. And here's an item in the paper about a party the Duke and Duchess of Windsor are having tonight at their Paris estate in honor of Andrei Vyshinsky, the visiting Soviet foreign minister. Maybe one of the guests has the information Petrov told me about."

Jacques gave her a big smile. With an appreciative look in his eye, he took her hand again and pressed it warmly. "Good thinking, Jacque-LEEN. I can see that your education was not wasted on you. The Windsor connection, yes. You need to go to that party tonight and mingle with all the guests."

The party idea appealed to her. She could imagine the kind of friends that real royalty like the Duke and Duchess of Windsor had—counts, ambassadors, princes, heads of state, and women with diamond necklaces as long as jumping ropes—and wouldn't mind being in their company. "I'd love to go to the party," she said, "but I don't have an invitation. How do you suggest that I crash it?"

Jacques came up with an idea only natural for someone in his profession. "You can pose as a society photographer for one of the newspapers. That'll get you in. After all, you read about the party in *Le Figaro*."

"But I don't know how to use a camera."

"Oh, you don't have to worry about that. I'll show you how. It'll be fun teaching you something new."

"We're talking about photography, right?"

"Yes . . . for now."

That sounded enticing, Jackie thought, but whatever else he had in mind—and from the way he kissed, it wasn't hard to guess what that was—it would have to wait. All she could think of right now was the elusive Petrov Puzzle and preparing herself to find someone at the Duke and Duchess of Windsor's party who would help them solve it.

She couldn't wait to find out who that might be.

XI

This is heavy," Jackie said, holding up the Speed Graphic that Jacques had just handed her. It was big and boxy, with a bellows making it look like a cross between a camera and a squeezebox.

"Weighs five pounds. You can get quite a workout from using it."

Jackie made a face. "I've got all the muscles I need, thank you very much."

"And in all the right places." It was the kind of line Jacques threw out basically as an automatic reflex, but Jackie took it as a compliment anyway.

They were nestled inside his apartment now, safe, for the moment, from the assassin. She looked around and couldn't decide whether his home was an apartment that doubled as a darkroom or a darkroom furnished like a home. His darkroom equipment—shelves of chemicals, sinks for developing and fixing photographs, a printer, and a clothesline with drying prints hanging like laundry flapping in the breeze—seemed to be at odds with the room's various pieces of furniture. None of Jacques's photographs hung on the walls. In fact, the sole concession to decoration was a vintage Campari poster, the apparent escutcheon of every European bachelor.

The furnishings themselves were unprepossessing—an unmade bed, a cluttered dining room table overflowing with photography books and magazines, several mismatched flea market antique chairs that looked cruelly uncomfortable, and a lumpen mud-colored brown couch, sagging in a way that suggested that many a seduction had taken place there.

Now it was Jackie who was seated on this veteran couch as Jacques gave her a personal tutorial on how to work the Speed Graphic camera. And seated she was determined to stay, rather than becoming just one more of what she imagined to be his long list of conquests.

"Have you ever used a camera before?" Jacques asked her.

"Sure, you know, a Brownie, when I was a kid. I took a class for it."

"That's what I used, during the war. It was my father's. I managed to take some great pics with it."

"I know," Jackie said, thinking of the haunting photographs in his book. They spoke to her with an emotional directness even the most eloquent of writers would find hard to match and revealed an artistic sensitivity that she valued as one of his most irresistible qualities.

Jacques took back the Speed Graphic. "Well, this is the camera favored by practically every press photographer throughout the world. In fact, it's called a press camera. If you look like you know how to use it, no one will question your journalistic credentials."

As she looked on, Jacques demonstrated how to load the film sheet, pop a flashbulb into the flash attachment, look through the viewfinder, cock the shutter, take the picture, then replace the film sheet and expended flashbulb and prepare to take the next picture.

"Okay, now it's your turn."

He handed the camera to Jackie. Clumsily, she tried to fit the film sheet into the camera.

"Don't try to jam it. If it jams, you're not doing it right."

Jackie tried again. This time, she slid the film sheet home, popped out the used flashbulb, popped in a new one, and looked through the viewfinder, but had a difficult time locating the button that cocked the shutter. Jacques took her hand and guided her to it. Jackie felt a tingle go up her arm from Jacques's touch and wondered if she was blushing.

"Now take the picture," he urged her. "The dining-room table. Pretend it's a still life."

She pointed the camera in the general direction of her subject and looked through the viewfinder. The dining-room table swam in and out of focus before she finally had a clear image. She clicked the shutter, and the room was momentarily flooded with light from the flash.

"Good, now what do you do?"

Without saying a word, Jackie removed the film sheet and popped out the bulb, picked up a new film sheet and flashbulb, and started the whole process all over again. She felt like a soldier in basic training with Jacques as her hard-nosed drill sergeant forcing her to practice many more times for hours on end—film, flashbulb, shutter, snap, repeat. Finally, when she was beginning to regard the Speed Graphic as a sadistic enemy, Jacques pronounced her ready for her big night. No longer the clumsy novice, she could at least do a reasonable impression of someone hired to snap the pictures of international celebrities and dignitaries used to having their photographs taken all the time.

"Would you like some coffee?" Jacques asked when the lesson was over.

"Love some."

While he was at the sink removing some photographic trays

from it so he could run the water, Jackie looked around the room and spotted a photograph of a young girl of about thirteen or fourteen. She had short brown hair that gave her a gamine look, an oval-shaped face, and doelike Bambi eyes. There was a heart-stopping loveliness to her, and for a moment, Jackie felt a characteristic—and unwarranted—pang of jealousy. Besides, there was something slightly haunting and desperate about the picture that made her want to know more.

"Jacques, who's this picture of?" she called to him.

He finished rinsing out two empty cups as large as bowls, which Jackie hoped hadn't been previously used to store a fixative agent, and turned to face her.

She pointed to the photograph on the stand next to her.

"Oh, that," he said in a dismissive tone of voice. "I don't know."

"You don't know, but you have her picture here?"

He didn't answer and busied himself making the coffee. This was obviously something he would rather not talk about, so Jackie decided to drop the subject—for now.

The crave-inducing aroma of fresh-roasted coffee filled the room, and Jacques brought the two big steaming cups to the dining-room table, cleared a space for them, and held out a chair for Jackie to join him.

"Ahhh," she said, savoring her first taste of the rich, full-bodied flavor of the coffee. "You're a man of many talents, I see."

"And I like to practice all of them," he said with a half smile, leaving his other unmentioned aptitudes up to her imagination.

They sat quietly drinking their coffee for a while, until Jackie got up the nerve and said, "Why don't you tell me about her?"

He had to know that she meant the girl in the photograph. "It's a long story."

"We have the time."

"And a sad one."

"I already figured that. Now please go ahead. I want to hear it."

Jacques led her over to the couch and sat down beside her.

"During the Occupation, I fell in love for the first time," he began. "Her name was Aurélie. We went to school together. The *école*. I was fifteen. She was thirteen. We were young, but we knew that we were in love and that it was the real thing, not some kind of adolescent infatuation. We wanted to make love, but never did anything about it. I guess we were two scared virgins."

He paused, and Jackie said nothing, allowing him to continue at his own pace. "Then, one day, I went to school, but Aurélie wasn't there," he went on. "Days passed and still she didn't return. I wondered where she was and when she would come back. Then came an announcement: Jewish students would no longer be able to attend the *école*. Aurélie, you see, was Jewish. Her last name was Spielvogel."

Jackie had suspected as much but remained quiet. She knew this was hard for Jacques and wanted to make it easier for him by simply being there, just listening.

He stared straight ahead, replaying some old movie in his mind. "For many weeks, I didn't hear from Aurélie. Or see her. Then, through a mutual friend, we were suddenly able to communicate with one another. We made plans to meet in out-of-the-way places, where there would be no one around to see us. We saw each other as much as we could. And I was relieved to find that despite everything that was happening to her family and all the other Jews, Aurélie still loved me. And she still wanted us to make love."

"But something happened. I can tell by your voice," Jackie said.

He looked at her, sadness darkening his face. "We made arrangements to meet and spend the night together at an apartment that Aurélie had access to. I would tell my parents—my father was still alive then—that I would be staying overnight at a friend's. I went to the apartment and waited outside. But Aurélie never showed. I waited and waited, but still she didn't come."

He stared at the dregs in the bottom of his coffee cup. "The next day I rode my bicycle past Aurélie's apartment house, but it was obvious that no one was home. I asked some of her neighbors where she was, but none of them wanted to talk to me. I found out later that Aurélie and her entire family, along with many other Jewish families, had been taken by the Nazis that day to Drancy, the transit camp outside the city. Several times I rode out there and tried to peer through the fence, hoping to catch sight of her. But nothing, never so much as a glimpse. From Drancy, they were eventually put onto cattle cars and removed by train to Auschwitz. I never found out what happened to her."

Jackie felt a wrenching sorrow for the young couple torn apart by the horror of war. "Your first love, that's heartbreaking," she murmured, touching his cheek. She tried to imagine what that pain was like. Her parents' divorce when she was only eleven was a different kind of loss, but she knew how it felt to have your world torn apart in childhood, a supposed age of innocence, and her heart went out to him. They were kindred souls.

She looked at the photograph on the stand. "But the picture of her? How did you get that?"

"That was my one big regret," he said. "I had no picture of Aurélie. This was before I took up my father's Brownie. I wanted a picture to remember her by, and one day—this was after the Allies liberated Paris and the Germans fled—I was riding around on my bicycle, looking for interesting subjects to photograph. I came across a pile of belongings of the transported that the Nazis had no use for. They only took things that would line their pockets—jewelry, cash, paintings, statues, silverware—and the rest they threw out.

"The pile I came across on the street was made up of books, records, family scrapbooks, and photo albums. Out of curiosity, I began to look through some of them. The photos leaped out at me. I saw Jewish families in happier times. At weddings and bar mitzvahs. At play and in the park. Getting dressed up for nights on the town. And then one picture in particular caught my eye. That one."

He pointed to the framed photograph of the young girl.

"It wasn't Aurélie. But the girl looked like her. Same hairstyle. Same beautiful eyes. So I removed it from the album and brought it home. I framed it and put it on a stand. I knew it wasn't her, but it was close enough. So now, whenever I look at that girl whose name I don't know, I think of Aurélie, and I remember my first love."

"Jacques, it's so beautiful that you can keep her memory alive that way," Jackie said softly. She was moved to tears by how the girl in the photograph, condemned to die in a Nazi extermination camp, would defy her persecutors and live on—if only in the memory of a man who never knew her.

Jackie brushed aside a teardrop from the corner of her eye and looked intently at Jacques, studying his face. She felt a wave of compassion surge inside her when she saw the sadness in his eyes and realized that her attraction to Jacques was undergoing a sea change. For the first time, she understood that the sexual pull he exerted as the seasoned Parisian photojournalist and charmingly louche man about town was only a cover. It was charming in its superficial way, but this hidden film noir hero that he rarely allowed anyone to see—sensitive, brooding, and haunted—aroused feelings of tenderness in her that were stronger than passion.

Without being able to stop herself—and frankly not wanting to—Jackie leaned in and kissed Jacques full on the lips, not sensuously but more like the kiss a mother plants on her young child's hurt to make it go away.

She could tell Jacques understood the meaning of the kiss and was comforted by it. But he was an agent first and foremost, and he knew Jackie had work to do.

"It's getting late," he said. "And you're going to need to have all your wits about you tonight if you want to pull off your impersonation."

He stood up and began to put together the camera bag that she would need to carry out her ruse. Jackie just sat there on the couch, watching him and wondering what, after this extraordinary afternoon, the evening ahead would bring.

"I'm sorry, mademoiselle," the security guard said in a huffy tone that indicated he was anything but sorry, "but your name is not on the invitation list."

"But I gave you a *Herald de Paris* press pass," Jackie told him in her flawless French, failing to mention that the press pass belonged to one Jacques Rivage and holding the boxy Speed Graphic out to him like a peace offering. "I'm their new society photographer, and they sent me to cover this party." She gave him one of her wide-eyed, damsel-in-distress looks that she hoped would melt his stone-faced mien. "You wouldn't want me to lose my job on my first assignment, would you?"

The uniformed guard, a tall, thin man with graying hair and an imperious manner, handed the press pass back to Jackie, unmoved. He pointed to the typewritten names on sheets of paper in his hand. "The name Jacqueline Bouvier is not on the list of guests invited to this soirée." He pressed his lips into an austere straight line. "I am under strict orders from the Duke and Duchess of Windsor to allow no one who is not on this list to attend this event tonight."

Small wonder, Jackie thought. The duchess's jewelry collection had more diamonds in it than a Congolese mine. No one could blame her for insisting on tight security, especially after a thief notoriously made off with some of her jewels when the duke and duchess were staying at the Earl of Dudley's estate in London some years ago. Now that they were living in Nuilly, the Paris municipal authorities were taking no such chances.

"Look, there's nothing in here but photographic equipment," Jackie said, opening her camera bag for the security guard to see that she wasn't concealing a blowtorch so she could crack open a safe.

The security guard was intransigent. *"Je regrette, Mademoiselle Bouvier, mais je ne peux pas vous laisser entrer,"* he said, repeating that he was sorry, but he couldn't let her go in.

What would it take to get this one-man Maginot Line to budge? Jackie wondered. She briefly considered making a transatlantic phone call to her stepfather back home, where it was only two in the afternoon, asking him to have one of his newspaper pals intercede for her with this stickler of a bureaucrat. His friend Arthur Krock, dean of the *New York Times* Washington correspondents, could call *his* friend Frank Waldrop, editor of the *Times-Herald* in Washington. But she dismissed the idea, preferring to save that connection for her return to the States where she might be able to get a job as an Inquiring Camera Girl now that she knew how to use a Speed Graphic.

"Good evening, Miss Bouvier. Are you having a problem?"

a vaguely familiar voice asked, cutting into her frantic ruminations.

Jackie turned away from the guard to see a young woman dressed in a dazzling Middle Eastern outfit—a long, pink chiffon shirt embroidered with beads, crystals, and sequins in geometrical patterns over red, raw-silk trousers. Although the last time Jackie had seen her, the young woman with the exotic features and regal bearing had been dressed in Western clothes, there was no mistaking who she was.

"Why, hello, Princess Nureen, it's so nice to see you again," Jackie said, trying to sound sincere and wondering how long the princess had been standing there listening to her contretemps with the inflexible security guard.

Jackie gave the guard a dirty look. "Actually, I *am* having a problem," she complained to Princess Nureen. "This gentleman refuses to let me into the party even though I presented a perfectly legitimate *Herald de Paris* press pass."

Speaking in a tone that Jackie remembered could eviscerate someone with a single sentence, the princess told the guard, "I am Princess Nureen, and Miss Bouvier is a friend of mine. Her credentials are impeccable. I'm certain the duke and duchess would be pleased to have her at their party. I insist that you allow her to go in without further delay."

"*Certainement, à votre demande,*" the guard said obsequiously to the princess, clearly in awe of her royal pedigree and bearing, and motioned for Jackie to go into the ballroom.

As they walked together down the long marble foyer, Princess Nureen glanced at the Speed Graphic and camera bag and asked out of the guard's earshot, "Who are you this time, Miss Bouvier? Margaret Bourke-White?"

Jackie laughed. "No, I just wanted to get into this party somehow, and this seemed the best way to do it."

"I won't give you away," the princess said when they were just outside the entrance to the ballroom, "but tell me, how is your search for Mikhail Petrov's information going?"

Jackie understood that the princess was expecting some quid pro quo in return, but she was determined not to give anything away—not that there was anything. "Not very well, I'm afraid. I seem to be on a wild goose chase." She thought of the assassin and added ruefully, "And I just hope it's not my goose that gets cooked."

The princess was about to enter the ballroom when Jackie said, "Oh, do you mind if I take your picture?" She could never hope to compete with the timeless Pulitzer prize–winning *Life* magazine cover photograph of the princess, but she needed the practice.

While the princess posed, Jackie silently repeated the film, flashbulb, shutter, snap mantra she'd spent hours that afternoon learning. She stood back for a full-length image of her subject and took the picture. That wasn't so hard, after all, she thought.

"Have a good evening, Miss Bouvier," the princess said before entering the ballroom. "And let me give you a piece of advice. Your pictures will come out much better if you remember to take the cover off the lens first."

Jackie's face turned red. Damn, would she never learn? She felt like a fool with no picture of the princess to show for her maiden effort, but there was no turning back now. Stuck in an unholy alliance with the Speed Graphic, she squared her shoulders, hoped for the best, and entered the ballroom.

Her first thought was that she had somehow found herself in a scene out of a Dumas novel, a voyeur among the crème de la crème of nineteenth-century London and Paris society. The lavish jewelry and garb; the décor of Louis XVI divans, floor-to-ceiling velvet drapes, ornate pedestals and sparkling crystal chandeliers; the Cézannes and Renoirs on the walls; the corps of liveried butlers balancing trays like jugglers; and the sedate chamber music quartet—it all seemed staged like a cotillion from an earlier, more gracious time.

To add to her awkward feeling of dislocation, she'd forgotten this was to be a costume ball. Now Jackie understood why Princess Nureen had shown up in her native Salwar Kameez outfit. It was funny how the disguises did little to prevent Jackie from spotting one celebrity after another. Even the lesser celebrities were identifiable to someone as familiar with the international social circuit as she was. Everywhere she looked she saw some personage she'd read about somewhere and couldn't believe she was seeing in real life.

The stunning blonde woman wearing a tuxedo and white silk shirt and tie, a cigarette held aloft in a world-weary manner, was—gasp!—Marlene Dietrich. Jackie would've known those high cheekbones and smoldering eyes—not to mention the legs that didn't stop—anywhere.

The debonair man Dietrich was talking to, who had a thin mustache and was dressed as a swashbuckler from one of his earlier films, Jackie surmised, was David Niven.

The lean, distinguished-looking man in his early forties, wearing the uniform of a French Army company commander with the square-cross Croix de Guerre medal hanging from a ribbon around his neck, was Baron Guy de Rothschild. Jackie couldn't pick up a newspaper or magazine in Paris without coming across the baron's legendary story. She'd read all about his heroism on the beaches at Dunkirk and how he was rebuilding the French branch of his family's banking dynasty after the Nazis seized its Paris bank during the war. And she saw the headlines when his thoroughbred racehorse, Vieux Manoir, won the Grand Prix de Paris at Longchamp last year—a feat that was especially impressive to her after running the race-course herself earlier that day.

The solidly built man in his late forties, standing off in a corner by himself watching everyone with a discerning eye, was, Jackie realized with a jolt, a world-renowned literary icon—Evelyn Waugh. She recognized his large square face from his photograph on the back of *Brideshead Revisited*, his satiric novel about aristocratic family life in vanished prewar England. Like many of the men there, he'd chosen not to wear a costume, but had come instead in custom-made, black-tie clothes. And it was clear that he was an observer rather than a participant in the festivities, no doubt taking mental notes for his next brilliant satire of upper-class society.

The balding man in his early forties whom she'd seen photos of in fashion magazines dressing women in his "New Look" creations—one of which Jackie had bought for herself during her Place Vendôme shopping spree—was none other than Christian Dior. His eyes kept flitting around the room, alighting like a bumblebee on this woman's gown and that one's, as if pollinating ideas for his next collection.

The glamorous young blonde, who Jackie had first thought was Marilyn Monroe, was actually Diana Dors, the British equivalent of Hollywood's sex-symbol bombshell. At twenty, Dors had already starred in a dozen movies—the one Jackie remembered most, because of its title, was *My Sister and I*. She also had the distinction, Jackie had read in the gossip columns with a touch of envy, of being the youngest registered owner of a Rolls-Royce in the United Kingdom.

Of course, it was the hosts of the party who most captured Jackie's attention. She thought it was exceedingly clever—and cheeky, to use the British expression—for the duchess to be dressed as Queen Elizabeth I in full regalia. The barbed joke was not lost on anyone. It was well known that the ambitious duchess had never forgiven the British establishment for forcing her husband to abdicate the throne when he was King Edward VIII in order to marry her, Wallis Simpson, a twice-divorced American commoner. As an outcast not permitted to share her husband's royal rank, she could at least poke fun at the British obsession with pure-blooded royalty by playing the part of a Queen of England at her parties. The mild-mannered duke, encased in a suit of armor as an Arthurian knight, was still acting as smitten with his chic, charismatic wife as he was fifteen years ago when he gave up the throne for "the woman I love."

Now Jackie had a decision to make. What was the best way to glean any tidbit of useful information from the people gathered here? She could randomly try to engage them in conversation while snapping their pictures, but they were not likely to tell her, a lowly newspaper photographer, anything important. She'd already tried that soon after entering the room and had been rebuffed.

"Hello, I'm the society photographer from the *Herald de Paris*, and I'd like to take your picture," she had said to a man dressed as a Russian cossack, thinking that if anyone had a connection to Petrov, he might be the one. "But first could you tell me a little about yourself? You know, who you are and how you know the duke and duchess."

"If you don't know who I am, you have no business taking my picture," the man had sneered at her over his shoulder as he walked away.

That brief encounter let Jackie know that these people might deign to have a society photographer snap a picture of them, but the privilege of speaking to them was reserved only for those occupying a notch above them in the social hierarchy.

Her best bet, she decided, was to eavesdrop. She would circulate around the room in her guise as a society photographer, not actually taking any pictures but keeping her ears open to any snatches of conversation that might lead her to something Petrov would have wanted her to know. She would use the camera only if forced to keep up the pretense, making sure to take off the lens cover first. By listening in on these people speaking confidentially to each other, unaware that anyone was snooping on them, she was more likely to snag a lead than by trying to talk to them herself.

Might as well go straight to the top, she thought, as she sidled up to the duchess, close enough to hear her conversation but not so close to call attention to herself.

"It was a breach of the worst kind, Diana, and we can't let it happen again," the duchess was saying to a beautiful woman who Jackie assumed was Diana Mosley, her closest friend, an infamous socialite who befriended Hitler before the war and married a British fascist at the home of Joseph Goebbels, Hitler's propaganda minister. It was no secret that the duke and duchess were both Nazi sympathizers too and believed Hitler should have been given a free hand to destroy communism. There was even a rumor that, after the war broke out, the duchess picked up details of the French and Belgian defenses from the duke and leaked them to the Nazi elite.

Jackie inched a little closer, anxious to find out what "breach" the duchess and the fascist's wife were discussing. The word had a counterintelligence ring to it. Given how the Mosleys and the Windsors hated the Communists but were none too fond of the British establishment either, did they have some plot afoot that Petrov wanted the CIA to know about?

Straining to hear, Jackie caught Diana Mosley's response. "You're absolutely right, Wallis. It was an appalling gaffe indeed.

Any fool knows that with tweeds you wear gold and with evening clothes you wear platinum."

Jackie tried to suppress a laugh, but the duchess heard her and gave her a stern look.

"Pardonnez-moi, Duchess, s'il vous plaît," Jackie said contritely, the blood rushing to her face. She quickly explained in French that the *Herald de Paris* had sent her to photograph the party.

The duchess nodded her assent and, with the ease of a quick-change artist, summoned a brilliant smile for the camera.

Jackie tried to control her shaking hands and remember all the steps Jacques had drilled into her as she focused on the face of a woman who was fifty-five but looked forty. She wanted to capture the vivacity in her eyes tinged with the sadness of living out a ruined romance and a life in exile spent in the vacuous, self-indulgent avoidance of boredom.

Snap. It was done. With a quick *"Merci beaucoup, Duchess,"* Jackie hurried away, half expecting to hear someone calling after her to stop, crying out that she was an imposter.

She breathed a deep sigh of relief when no one pursued her. Looking around, she saw that the other, legitimate photographers had quickly gotten the pictures they needed and left. *Circulate, circulate,* Jackie prodded herself, *but be careful.* She moved around the room as inconspicuously as possible, pausing to catch bits and pieces of conversation from whoever aroused the faintest implication of foreign intrigue. But it all seemed to be innocuous—mostly gossip-mongering and irrelevant braggadocio about the hosts and other guests.

"I heard she's having an affair with an American playboy, Jimmy Donahue, heir to the Woolworth fortune."

"Jimmy Donahue? Don't believe it. That bloke is a bigger poof than Noel Coward, gay as a pink hairnet."

"Poor bastard hasn't been able to get a job since he came back from the Bahamas."

"Might have gotten an appointment to Australia if he hadn't called the natives 'revolting' and 'the nearest thing to monkeys.'"

"I was doing swimmingly at Sunningdale yesterday, but the fifteenth hole was a disaster."

"Yes, Vieux Manoir did us proud in that race, and we also won the Grand Prix de Saint-Cloud with Ocarina and the Grand Prix de Deauville with Alizier."

"Have you heard about the Beístegui Ball in Venice in September? They say it's going to be sensational. I'm having my costume done by this new designer, Pierre Cardin."

After hours of listening in on this stream of inanities, Jackie's head was splitting. She had covered the entire ballroom, and nothing of any consequence had surfaced. Noticing that some of the guests had begun to take their leave, she was afraid to overstay her false welcome and be found out.

Resigned to defeat, she began packing up her camera equipment when a latecomer's theatrical entrance to the party captured her eye. A dandified-looking man with long hair, sideburns, and a thin mustache that curled up improbably at either end, he seemed like a visitor from a bygone era with his long coat, stockings, and knee breeches. Jackie assumed that this surreal creature could only be one individual—the renowned painter Salvador Dalí, whose flamboyant life was his own greatest work of art. She knew that he had once again made headlines with a new painting, *Raphaelesque Head Exploding*, which combined classical Christian imagery with the new mythology of the atomic age to shocking effect. She started to approach him, but Dalí waved her off when he saw what she had in mind. Odd, Jackie thought. From what she knew of

Dalí, the man was anything but publicity shy. Nevertheless she decided to honor his sense of privacy and turned her attention elsewhere.

Across the room, the Baron de Rothschild was deep in conversation with a younger man dressed as a nineteenth-century French hussar, complete with gold braid on his uniform, fur pelisse, and an incredibly tall, matching busby. The man cut quite an impressive figure, but that was not the reason Jackie was drawn to him. There was something slightly furtive about his movements around the baron. And it seemed to be catching, because now the baron was acting in an equally furtive manner.

Instinctively, Jackie sensed this was what she had been waiting for, the reason Petrov's convoluted trail of clues had sent her here—to spy on what these two men were up to. When the baron and the hussar casually walked off, Jackie decided to follow them, but at a discreet distance to avoid any undue attention to herself.

As she crossed the room, she was annoyed to find her way blocked by a strapping, luxuriously bearded man whose head was wrapped in a turban and whose flowing caftan did little to hide his corpulent body.

"Leaving so soon?" he asked pleasantly. His foreign-accented English was difficult to place.

"Just taking a little break. Tonight was my first assignment as a society photographer, and I didn't expect it to be so tiring," Jackie explained quickly, trying to be polite while still maintaining sight of her quarry.

"But you haven't taken my picture yet, and I'm the Pakistani ambassador to France." He sounded mildly reproving but not unkind, like a schoolteacher correcting the mistake of a slow student.

"I'm so sorry. That was purely an oversight," Jackie apologized fervently. She felt obliged to make up for her embarrassing snub. "If you like, I'll take it as soon as I return."

"That would be wonderful," the ambassador said enthusiastically.

Jackie excused herself and continued across the ballroom, but the baron and the hussar were nowhere to be found. She cursed the Pakastani ambassador for delaying her and deflecting her attention. But then she caught a glimpse of the hussar's busby bobbing above the crowd like a buoy in a rough sea. The body attached to the busby left the ballroom, together with the baron, and disappeared down a narrow service gallery, confirming Jackie's suspicion that these two were up to something.

She gave them a few minutes, then followed them down the hallway. There were any number of doors leading off, but only one was slightly ajar. That must be the one, Jackie assumed, and opened it slowly. She saw a set of ancient stone stairs leading down and followed them into the darkness beyond. Where is this going, she asked herself. And what was she getting into?

At the bottom of the stairs, Jackie found herself in a vast catacomb upon which the Windsor estate was apparently built. This part of the catacomb was devoted to the duke's extensive wine collection—aisle after aisle, rack after rack, shelf after shelf, bottle after bottle. There must be at least a thousand bottles collected here, Jackie estimated. She felt goose bumps rising on her arms from the chilly temperature of the wine cellar, kept in the low fifties to properly maintain the expensive rare vintages stored there. The airless quality of the atmosphere made Jackie feel slightly sleepy, as though her brain was oxygen deprived.

One section of the wine cellar was devoted to bottles from Philippe de Rothschild's estate in Pauillac. She saw row upon row of Château Lafite Rothschild, Mouton Rothschild, and

Mouton Cadet. In her social set, the name Philippe de Roth-schild, Guy's cousin, was synonymous with family-owned vine-yards that could rival any other in the Medoc region. Thanks to clever marketing—Jackie thought that commissioning famous artists like Georges Braque, Pablo Picasso, and even tonight's guest, Salvador Dalí, to create their signature labels was a par-ticularly brilliant stroke—the Rothschilds' wines were now among the most famous in the world, with individual bottles going for thousands of dollars at auction.

Jackie heard voices and hid behind the closest wooden wine rack. She peered around the corner and, at the far end of the row, caught sight of the baron and the hussar.

The hussar's voice was barely above a whisper. "If the duke knew what we were doing, he would kill us."

"Yes," agreed the baron softly, "that's why this has to be kept a secret."

Jackie was thankful that the lighting in the catacomb was so low—dim bare lightbulbs hanging from a wire in the rough stone ceiling—that she couldn't be seen by the two conspir-ators. She held her breath, waiting for the carefully guarded secret to be revealed.

As she looked on, the baron and the hussar began systemati-cally giving each bottle of Rothschild wine a good half turn in its place.

"He knows nothing about wines," said the hussar, shaking his head.

The baron nodded. "He is a fool. Philippe would never have sold to him had he known the duke would treat his wines so disrespectfully."

So this was the big secret? The dark conspiracy? Jackie felt like a complete idiot. These two men were up to nothing more nefarious than systematically turning each bottle of Rothschild wine so that the corks would remain moist and not dry out and shrink, allowing oxygen to enter the bottles and causing spoilage. The reverence these two men—the younger one was probably another Rothschild—showed their family wine was actually touching, she thought, and it was terrible that the Duke of Windsor was such a philistine that he would allow these valuable bottles to go to waste.

Fortunately for her, the men were so engrossed in rotating hundreds of bottles that they took no notice of Jackie. And to make sure they didn't, she decided to hightail it out of the wine cellar. She made a left and a right, thinking this would bring her back to the stone stairs that led up to the service gallery. But she must have miscalculated because she now found herself in a different part of the catacomb entirely.

Cursing the absence of any signposts to point her in the right direction, she turned around and tried to retrace her steps back to the wine cellar and start all over again. But she found her way blocked by a large figure whose bulk almost completely occluded the dim light coming from above. To her relief, it was the Pakistani ambassador.

"Hello again, Miss Bouvier. You appear to be lost."

"Yes, your Excellency, I'm afraid to say I am."

"Well, it's a good thing you bumped into me. Let me guide you out of here."

"Thank you very much."

The ambassador gallantly took hold of Jackie's arm and began to lead her through the catacomb. Nothing of her surroundings seemed familiar to her, and she hoped that the ambassador was taking her in the right direction.

"Are you a wine connoisseur?" she asked, wondering what the ambassador was doing down here.

"More of a catacomb fancier. I'm something of an amateur

archeologist, you see, and the catacombs under this structure are very old indeed. Perhaps among the oldest in all of Paris."

As he droned on about archeology and catacombs, Jackie realized that the ambassador's voice was lulling her into a false sense of security. Her instinct told her that this was not the way back to the stone stairs, that he was leading her deeper and deeper into the catacomb maze. Abruptly, she stopped.

"Something wrong, my dear?"

"I don't think this is the way back."

"Of course it is." The ambassador strengthened his hold on Jackie's arm and led her onward. Jackie tried to twist clear of his embrace, but found herself trapped in his iron grip.

"Your Excellency, you're hurting me," she exclaimed.

"I'm sorry about that," the ambassador said smoothly, while at the same time failing to relinquish his grip on her arm.

Then something else occurred to Jackie.

"How did you know my name?"

"I'm sorry?"

"I never told you my name. But you called me Miss Bouvier."

"I did? I must have heard it from another guest at the party."

His answer rang false. No longer afraid of being impolite, Jackie wrenched free of his viselike grasp. She looked around and found herself in a cul-de-sac inside the catacomb, with the ambassador strategically placed at the free end. No wonder he was finally willing to let go of her; she was trapped here. With a sinking feeling, Jackie knew she was in a perilous situation. Despite the relative coolness of the chamber, she could feel sweat begin to gather and bead down her sides.

Even though the light in the cul-de-sac was dim, Jackie could still see it glint off of something that suddenly appeared in the ambassador's hand. She had seen that glint before and knew, with a dreadful shock of recognition, that the Pakistani ambassador was really her assassin in disguise. Once again, to her utter chagrin and terror, he had managed to track her down. Her heart froze, and fear ran amok inside her. She tried to scream, but no sound came out of her throat. Who could hear her anyway in this tomb underground, isolated from the partygoers upstairs, merrily carousing and completely unaware of her plight? Tears of anguish welled in her eyes, glistening markers of a rising tide of despair and self-pity. Fury raged within her too. Why did she have to die this way? Cornered in a dank, dismal catacomb, alone and friendless, with her family on the other side of the ocean, and Jacques nowhere to be found. Didn't she deserve a kinder end than the one that awaited her at the hands of this butchering, cold-blooded killer?

A flash of movement from his hands signaled that the end was near. There was no time to flee and nowhere to go. As she watched helplessly, paralyzed by terror and unable to scream, the assassin's blade came down, and she could hear a swish as it sliced cleanly through her outfit. That was the last she knew as a merciful blackness enveloped her and erased all thoughts and fears from her mind.

XII

When Jackie came to, the first thing she saw was the Pakistani ambassador dancing with Salvador Dalí.

She was in some semidark place, and the ground under her felt rough. Where was she? Her first conscious thought was that she was dead, and this was hell, and that it featured stranger things than Dante had ever imagined. She looked up at the black ceiling, which seemed to undulate slightly. But this she chalked up to another function of her strained vision.

As her fogginess slowly began to dissipate, Jackie realized that she was still in the cul-de-sac in the catacomb beneath the Duke of Windsor's estate. And that the Pakistani ambassador was really the assassin who had already tried three times in as many days to kill her. But why was he dancing with Salvador Dalí?

And then it struck her: they weren't dancing. They were fighting for control of the knife that the assassin held in his hand. The knife that had sliced through Jackie's clothes before she lost consciousness.

Her hands instinctively went to her side and felt the long slice in the material of her dress. To her relief, she felt nothing wet. The knife had miraculously failed to puncture her skin. She was alive and unharmed—at least for the moment.

Mesmerized, she watched the deadly pas de deux between

the two men continue. In a moment, though, the assassin got the better of Dalí, catching him from behind. He yanked on his long hair and pulled back on his head, planning to expose his throat and slash across his windpipe with one efficient thrust of his knife.

Jackie saw a questioning look come over the assassin's face. He yanked again on Dalí's hair, and it inexplicably came loose in his hand. So powerful was the assassin's tug that he was thrown backward. Dali seized the opportunity to get out of the killer's range. He retreated to Jackie, and with his long hair gone and his trademark mustache askew, Jackie could see for the first time that Dalí was someone else in disguise.

"Jacques," she cried out to him in astonished relief.

"Are you all right? Did he hurt you?"

Jackie shook her head no. Then she called out a warning. "Jacques, look out!"

Jacques turned, and there was the assassin again, his menacing knife once more leading the way. Jacques tore off his long coat and used it as a flail to defend himself from the knife, which he attempted to knock out of the assassin's hand. The way they cautiously circled each other, the assassin thrusting forward with his knife and Jacques trying to ward it off with his coat, put Jackie in mind of two gladiators in ancient Rome fighting each other at the Circus Maximus.

Jackie had now completely regained her senses. She looked around, frantically trying to find something she could use as a weapon. She looked up at the black ceiling, hoping for inspiration to hit her, and noticed that it was still undulating. Jackie stared and realized the reason for the ceiling's movement. It was a solid mass of nesting bats! She shuddered at being in such close proximity to these disgusting creatures. Rats in the garret, bats in the catacomb—this was not the adventure she had envisioned when Allen Dulles first approached her. But it was also all the inspiration she needed. She reached into her camera bag and hauled out the Speed Graphic. Fortunately, as Jacques had taught her, she had already prepped the camera for her next shot, film sheet loaded and flashbulb in the flash attachment.

She rose to her feet, perhaps a little too quickly, and was assailed by an unexpected wave of dizziness. But it quickly passed as she gripped the camera in her two shaking hands. She didn't bother to look through the viewfinder or care that the lens cap was on. Instead, she pointed the camera up toward the ceiling, shouted out, "Jacques, duck!" and hit the shutter before throwing herself back to the ground.

Instantly, the cul-de-sac was filled with light, and the space was full of bats flying around the room in a flat-out panic from the sudden assault on their light-sensitive eyes. Jackie, back on the ground, and Jacques, squatting in place, were safe from the frantic flight of the bats. But the assassin was not so lucky. The panicked creatures were flying all around him, and he was protecting his eyes and mouth with a hand in front of his face.

Taking advantage of the assassin's plight, Jacques quickly rose to his feet, braving the flurry of sleek black projectiles winging through the air around him, and punched his assailant solidly on the jaw. Jackie watched the assassin fly across the room, hit the opposite wall, and carom off it like a well-placed billiard shot. To her amazement, the ancient wall crumbled around him, burying the man in an avalanche of rubble and sending up a plume of dust while the bats continued to circle around the room in a frenzied state.

"Do you think he's dead?" Jackie gasped.

"Looks that way, and we'll be too if we don't get out of here before the rest of this place falls down," Jacques said, taking Jackie by the hand.

She picked up her camera bag and followed him out the entrance to the cul-de-sac, holding her hands over her head to prevent any of the hysterical bats from crashing into her hair.

Hurriedly, Jacques put his coat and wig disguise back on and straightened his fake mustache. As he led her through the catacomb, Jackie said, "I hope you know your way out of here."

"Don't worry," he assured her. "I left a trail of bread crumbs behind. Just like in the storybook."

Jackie followed him back to the stone stairs to the service gallery—on a path that wisely skirted the Rothschild section of the wine cellar—up the stairs, down the service gallery, and through the door into the ballroom. Like a sycophantic art student keeping a respectful distance behind the great Dalí, she trailed after him as he strutted out of the ballroom, down the marble hall, and out of the estate.

Once outside, Jacques took off his Dalí disguise and hurried with her to his red convertible parked on an out-of-the way wooded side street. Jackie sank into the buttery soft leather passenger seat, leaned her head back, and closed her eyes, reeling from the events of the turbulent day.

She started to laugh giddily, on the verge of hysterics, thinking of the huge rush of relief she felt when she realized it was Jacques, and not Dalí, who had come to rescue her. It was the miracle that she had silently been praying for and never expected to happen.

Witnessing his face-to-face combat with the armed assassin erased any doubts she once had that Jacques would be willing to risk his life to save hers. And he wasn't just doing his duty. The fear she saw in his eyes when she came to and found him bending over her, asking if she was all right, revealed the depth of feeling he had developed for her. She wondered whether he had an instinctual sense that told him when her life was in danger and what to do to save her. "What made you come to the party?" she asked. "And where did you get that costume?"

"I had a feeling that the murderer might show up at the party in disguise," he explained, "so I decided at the last minute to check up on you and make sure you were safe. I had the Salvador Dalí costume around because I wore it to a costume party last year, and I knew Dalí was the one person who could get into any party in Paris without an invitation. It was a risk, but I figured Dalí is too busy working on his next show to run around to costume parties right now." He paused. "Interesting coincidence: Dalí lives at the Hôtel Meurice, and my mother worked there during the war, as a maid. It was German Occupation Headquarters." He was silent for a moment, then laughed. "You gave me a bad moment when you approached me, wanting to take my picture. I couldn't let you know it was me and blow my cover."

As he looked straight ahead at the road, Jackie gazed at his handsome profile and felt a surge of gratitude. "Thank God you were looking out for me," she said warmly. "You saved my life. I don't know how to thank you."

"We'll think of something," he said, "after I get you home."

"Are you taking me back to my hotel?"

"No, my place," he said matter-of-factly. "Your hotel has too much traffic. Spies. Drunks. You can't get a good night's sleep there."

"And that's what you think I'll get at your place?" she asked dryly. "A good night's sleep?"

"I think you'll be very happy with what you'll get at my place."

The smugness was a jarring note. "Aren't you being a little presumptuous?"

"I've never had any complaints."

"That's not what I meant." She didn't know whether it was because she was bone tired and her nerves were worn raw, but she felt a hesitancy about sleeping with him that went beyond any moral reservations. As close as they had grown, there was still something about him, something opaque and indefinable, that gave her pause. If only the feelings he aroused in her weren't so mixed—desire, fear, trust, suspicion, gratitude, vulnerability.

"Is something wrong?" he asked.

She tried to explain. "I'm so grateful to you, Jacques, and attracted to you—very attracted, as I'm sure you know—and you mean a lot to me... a *lot*... but you're different from anyone I've ever known. I... I'm just not sure I'm ready for this."

He pulled the car over to the side of the road. Here's trouble, she thought. She couldn't blame him if he was furious at her, thinking she'd been leading him on, only to back out now after he'd just saved her life. Was he insulted by what might have sounded like upper-class snobbery when she told him he was "different" from anyone she'd ever known? Did her timid explanation make her sound like a jejune schoolgirl compared to the worldly women he was probably used to? He cut off the engine, and she steeled herself, expecting him to unleash a tirade at her for rejecting him so awkwardly.

But Jacques didn't look angry. When he turned to her, the expression on his face was thoughtful rather than amorous, and he spoke to her in a sincere, heartfelt tone, choosing his words with care.

"Jacque-LEEN, you're a lovely woman—beautiful, smart, kind—and there's no denying that we've come to mean a great deal to each other. I want to make love to you. What's wrong with that? We have only a short time together and may never see each other again. Should we not make the most of the moments we have? Years from now, why should we look back on this time and wonder what might have been? Regrets are a waste." He took her hand in his, and she was reminded of how gentle his touch could be. "I'm a Frenchman. To me, making love is the highest form of art. I want to share it with you because I care for you. But I'm not going to push you into it. It has to be your choice, too, not mine alone. It's up to you."

Why fight it? she thought. The bond between them deserved to be acknowledged with more than words. She'd been through more with him already than she had with any of the men she'd dated for a long time. Yes, he was rougher than she liked occasionally, but those sharp edges made him all the more exciting and stirred up a white heat inside her. And he had proven himself beyond the call of duty as her protector—her savior, actually. She owed him. But there was no sense of duty in what she felt. It was the pull of her heart, a magnetic yearning that could not be denied.

"Your place," she said.

He started up the car again, and soon they were near his apartment in the foothills of Montmartre. She knew they'd come to Montmartre when she saw the red windmill on the roof of the Moulin Rouge cabaret in the red-light district of Pigalle. And on top of the hill, rising like an extravagant wedding cake, was the all-white Basilica of the Sacré Coeur with its onion dome and prominent towers.

Jacques drove down the narrow, winding streets of shabby-chic apartments with rows of balconies and shutters and turned into the Renault parking garage where he kept his car. Never forgetting his manners, he helped Jackie out of the car, and they walked around the corner to his apartment building on rue de Sofia, a quiet street away from the noisy nightlife of Montmartre. They went inside and climbed a flight of stairs to the second floor. Jackie waited while Jacques unlocked the door to his apartment.

When they were inside, it was exactly the same as before—cameras and photographic equipment strewn about the living room, the dining-room table cluttered with books and papers, and the small kitchen with half-eaten food on the counters and more photographic equipment in the sink.

Jackie cringed when she saw the sagging brown sofa where she imagined so many other seductions had taken place and wondered, is this where it's going to happen? But any misgivings she had were soon forgotten as Jacques locked the door behind them and gathered her in his arms. Fleetingly, she thought once again of resisting, but she cared for this man. His courage and compassion had touched her heart like no other man before him.

His mouth was on hers, and his tongue was probing inside with a raw insistence that made her whole body tremble. She raised her hands to slow him down, giving her some time to ease into this gracefully. But instead, as if they belonged to someone else, her arms wrapped around his neck, pulling him closer. She could feel his heart thumping against her chest, and she answered his kiss with one as deep and urgent as his own.

He moved her backward to the door and pressed her against it. She kissed his neck, drinking in his musky, male smell and delighting in the feel of his body, surprised at how firm and muscular it was for someone so slim. His hands cupped her face tenderly, and the last of her cool, iron-clad defenses melted away.

Then something inside her snapped, and her mind shifted like a fault line in an earthquake. Suddenly, she was back in the murky catacomb, back against the wall, terrified and defenseless. This wasn't Jacques stroking her face; it was the assassin pressing his cold, hard knife blade against her throat. Shaking and choking back sobs, her eyes glassy, her heart racing so fast that she could hardly breathe, she pushed Jacques away from her, and a choppy stream of words poured out of her, mostly unintelligible, but frantic with desperation.

"That knife...that awful knife...underground...no way out...so dark in there...all alone...couldn't scream...couldn't move...thought I was going to die...saw the knife come down...heard it slash my dress...knew I was going to die...oh, God, I didn't want to die...no, no, not like that..."

She broke off into uncontrollable sobbing and covered her eyes with her hands.

Jacques took her in his arms again, held her tightly, and spoke softly in her ear. "I didn't let you die. I would never let you die. I was there for you. I'll always be there for you, Jacque-LEEN. You're safe now."

Safe. I'm safe. She repeated that to herself like a mantra until the meaning of the words sank in and that's how she began to feel, enfolded in his arms.

When her shaking stopped and her sobs died down, he took her by the hand and led her into his bedroom. Slowly, carefully, as though he were unwrapping a fragile gift, he undid the buttons on her dress and slipped it over her head. Then he knelt down and slid her black garter belt and silk stockings down her legs and helped her step out of them.

Calm now, but weak and dazed and too exhausted to put up any resistance even if she had wanted to, Jackie stood in her bra and lace panties and waited for what Jacques would do next.

To her surprise, he went over to his closet, pulled a baggy long-sleeved cotton jersey shirt off a hanger, and brought it over to her. "Here, put this on. It's not very pretty, but it's comfortable and will keep you covered better than you are now. You were shivering before, and I don't want you to catch cold."

The old shirt, faded and frayed, fell to the middle of her thighs and the sleeves hung over her hands. Jackie looked down at herself and shook her head. This was hardly the kind of negligee she thought she'd be wearing on a night filled with romantic promise. What was Jacques thinking dressing her like this? Had there been a change in plans?

She gave him a questioning look. "But I thought you wanted to...I mean, I thought we came here because we were going to..."

He put his forefinger over her lips to shush her. Then he gently rolled the shirtsleeves up to her wrists and took her hands in his. He sounded contrite. "This is not a night for making love, *ma cherie*. I should have realized how badly shaken up you were by what that murderer put you through, but the way you helped me fight the fat *bâtard* fooled me. Neither one of us might have gotten out alive if you hadn't thought so quickly." He squeezed her hands, and she saw genuine admiration in his eyes. "Using the camera on the bats was such a clever idea. Believe me, you performed better under pressure than most agents would have who've been doing this for years."

"But why did I break down here when I wasn't in danger anymore?" She was proud that she had kept her wits about her in the catacomb but felt a twinge of embarrassment thinking of her sobbing outburst in the apartment. "Why did I become hysterical after it was all over?"

"You had a common reaction," he reassured her. "I've seen it happen with many agents. They survive a gunfight or escape from an explosion and only realize how close they came to dying when they're not in immediate danger anymore. After their adrenaline slows down and they stop being on alert, that's when the full impact of flirting with death hits them, and they fall apart."

She nodded, grateful for his understanding but feeling guilty for becoming so overwrought and ruining an evening of what she had imagined would be spectacular love-making. "Jacques, I'm sorry I spoiled the mood. I didn't mean to. It just happened. It's not like me." She felt she had to explain.

"I'm good at keeping my emotions under control...maybe too good. People don't know how deeply I feel things. They assume I'm stuck-up or aloof, but it's against my upbringing to show any sign of weakness or step out from behind the mask of composure we're supposed to wear all the time." Jackie shook her head, feeling uncertain and confused. "I thought that 'stiff upper lip' sort of thing, what you call sangfroid, was an asset in this line of work and would keep me from losing my nerve. It did for a while, but that changed when the girl in the Gare de Lyon was murdered just because she looked like me." She fought back tears and wiped her eyes with her fingers. "I know it wasn't my fault, but it's been eating away at me inside ever since. Now I'm afraid if I keep on letting things get to me, I won't last in this job. And I want so badly to do a good job. It's not just a matter of pride for me; I love my country, and I don't want to disappoint the people who put their faith in me."

Jacques cupped her face in his hand. "You're too hard on yourself, Jacque-LEEN," he said with compassion. "You've been very brave, going nonstop and not taking time to absorb the shocks that were thrown at you. You come from a sheltered world, and being an agent is like living in a war zone. The mental strain was bound to catch up with someone as sensitive as you are, but you have no reason to doubt yourself. You have what it takes to be a great agent. You've shown that. I have faith in you."

She smiled hopefully. "You mean that? You're not just saying that to make me feel better?"

"I mean it." He lifted strands of hair that had fallen on

her forehead. "You'll be yourself again after you've had some sleep."

I must look a mess, she thought. Matted, tangled hair; swollen, red; eyes, lipstick smeared. No wonder he doesn't want to make love. She yawned, suddenly so exhausted and drained that all she could think of was climbing into bed—alone—and sinking her head into a pillow.

Jacques caught her eying the bed longingly and smiled. "Go to bed, Jacque-LEEN. You're dead on your feet, so I'll sleep on the sofa. I'm letting you off the hook this time, but next time you won't be so lucky."

She was touched by his consideration. He could easily have taken advantage of her weakened condition, but he wanted the moment to be right—not just another score in his long string of casual sexual encounters, but something beautiful, something that mattered. *She* mattered to him, and that made all the difference. "Maybe next time I'll get really lucky," she said, smiling back at him with her eyes.

He drew her to him, and they kissed good night. It was a sweet kiss, tender and caring, so loving that it made her say to herself, I hope next time comes soon.

Jacques was right. She had the first good night's sleep she'd had in days, not at her disorderly hotel but at his quieter place. Her sleep was filled with dreams of them making love, dreams so real that she awakened with a contented feeling and luxuriated in it for a few moments like a purring cat. But when she felt around for him on the side of the bed where she thought he'd been sleeping, it was empty. Suddenly, memories of the night before came flooding back and she got out of bed quickly, drawing his baggy cotton jersey shirt around her, and went to find him.

When the intoxicating aroma of his divine coffee wafted toward her, she knew he was in the kitchen making two of those huge cups for them.

"Good morning, you're up early," she said.

"Yes, and I couldn't go back to sleep after thinking about my mistake."

Pow! That was a rude kick in the gut. She stared at him wide-eyed. Had the evening been such a disappointment to him that he was writing her off just like that? It suddenly occurred to her that he'd seen her in her bra and panties, and she glanced down at her body. Was that why he'd had a change of heart? Were her breasts too small, her hips too narrow to please him, and now he just wanted to be friends? How humiliating it would be if, after she agreed to go to bed with him, he was the one to do the rejecting in the end.

He brought the coffee to the dining-room table, and she followed him there, took a seat opposite from him, and waited. But he was quiet. He seemed to be mulling over something in his mind, probably trying to find the right words to say something that was never easy.

So Jackie began. "I'm sorry about last night," she said softly, avoiding his eyes. "It's all right if you just want us to be friends."

Jacques stared at her, uncomprehending. Then he understood what she was talking about and burst out laughing. "Oh, no, no, *ma cherie*, last night hasn't changed anything. You're still as beautiful to me as ever." His eyes took her in with the usual appreciation, and he shook his head as if he couldn't believe his good fortune. "You're even more desirable, if that's possible. Incredibly feminine—a princess on the outside and a gamine inside. I want us to be lovers, not just friends. *Je t'adore,* Jacque-LEEN."

That was a relief. He had seen her at her worst and now found her even more desirable? It was more than a relief—it was positively life affirming. She looked at him questioningly. "Then what mistake are you so upset about?"

"The wrong name of the horse," Jacques said. "Petrov wouldn't have wanted anything to do with Andrei Vyshinsky, even a party at the Windsor estate. I'd been briefed that what drove Petrov to defect was his outrage at the Soviet takeover of the Baltic states and Vyshinsky's role in it. I should have known better."

The *Paris Turf* racing form they'd gotten at Longchamp, a bit crumpled by now, was beside Jacques, and he handed it to Jackie. "I've looked at all the other horses that were running in the third race, and nothing jumps out at me. See if there's another one besides Windsor Knot that you think might be the clue."

Jackie studied the names and pointed to one with her finger. "Manet's Olympia," she said. "Manet's *Olympia* is one of my favorite paintings. When I was studying at the Sorbonne, I would always drop by the Jeu de Paume to commune with it. It's a long shot—actually, it *was* a long shot," she commented, glancing at the racing form, "but Petrov was very cultured. He knew all about the ballet, and he was an art-lover too." She smacked her forehead as she suddenly remembered something. "Come to think of it, when I first met Petrov, he mentioned how much he liked to visit the Jeu de Paume. It's a good bet that the painting is where we'll find the next clue."

"Tell me what you know about the painting."

"It's an oil painting of a nude high-class prostitute being attended to by her uniformed, dark-skinned servant as she lies on a bed waiting for a client," Jackie told him. She felt like a docent in a museum, glad to have a chance to talk about a subject she loved. "It caused a big uproar when it was first exhibited at the 1865 Paris Salon. It wasn't the nudity that was so shocking, but the way Manet's bold brushstrokes and harsh lighting made this nude a *real* woman, a self-assured sexual courtesan, not the usual idealized goddess or submissive concubine in a harem."

"How do you know she's a prostitute?"

"The black cat symbolizes prostitution, and all the other details—the orchid in her hair, her bracelet, the pearl earrings, and the expensive oriental shawl she's lying on—indicate a sensuous woman who uses sex to acquire wealth. The black ribbon around her neck against her pale skin evokes sensuality too. And the big bouquet of flowers her servant is presenting to her are probably from a client. The way she completely ignores them suggests they're not from someone she loves, but from just another man she's independent from and dominant over."

"You said you liked to commune with Manet's *Olympia* when you were a student at the Sorbonne. Why?"

"I liked her attitude," Jackie said. "She was proud of her sexuality, and she owned it. You could tell by the way she covered her pubic hair with her hand, not delicately, but like a 'keep off the grass' sign, if you'll pardon the crude analogy." She laughed at her unintentional bon mot. "I was hoping some of her earthiness would rub off on me."

"I think that's a distinct possibility."

"You're not encouraging me to go into her profession, are you?" she teased.

"Of course not, but I do think you're very sexy." He smiled at her, eyes twinkling. "Under the right circumstances, you could probably give Olympia a run for the money."

"I've had enough running the past few days to last me," Jackie said. "But if you like my idea, we can go to the Jeu de Paume today and check out the painting to see if it offers any clues to what Petrov's information might be."

"I like your idea very much. I think you're on to something," he told her enthusiastically. "There are so many details there—the black cat, the pearl earrings, the orchid in her hair, and all the rest—that might offer a clue."

"Good, but I need to go back to my hotel and get something else to wear besides your shirt or my dress that's practically in ribbons now, and I can meet you at the Jeu de Paume whenever you say."

Jacques eyed his dried black-and-white prints hanging on the clothesline in the living room and said, "I have some work to finish up here, so let's make it two this afternoon."

"Two it is." Jackie thought for a moment and asked, "Do you mind if I take the Speed Graphic? I think I'd like to walk to the Jeu de Paume and practice my photography along the way."

"Of course, take it, and keep my press pass too. It'll come in handy at the museum. You never know when someone's going to give you a hard time."

She knew he was just trying to be helpful, but for some reason she couldn't fathom, his words had an ominous ring.

XIII

Like the other passengers riding the Metro, Jackie was absorbed in her private thoughts. Her mind kept turning back to the party last night and the unexpectedly dramatic way the evening had ended. She saw herself getting rescued by Jacques and the outrageously sensuous kiss they shared back at his apartment. She blushed at the very thought of how his tongue felt inside her mouth, reliving every delicious flicker of excitement it aroused in her. Smiling inwardly, she hoped that no one on the crowded car was looking at her and could see the way her cheeks suddenly turned red.

Even though he had work to do, Jacques had insisted on driving her back to her hotel earlier that morning so she could shower and change into a fresh outfit. Now, as she sat in the crowded car and watched the different Metro stops pass by, she was hoping their elusive scavenger hunt would come to an end that afternoon when they inspected Manet's *Olympia* in the Jeu de Paume. With any luck, one final clue would emerge and bring them to the end of this rocky road that had begun with her discovery of Petrov's corpse. Yes, I could certainly use a bit of a breather, she thought.

As she sat there, Jackie got the uncomfortable feeling that she was being spied on. She looked around, but saw no one who seemed suspicious. The car was filled with the usual mix of casually dressed students and well-tailored businessmen, as well as a sprinkling of housewives in daytime dresses and a few shifty-eyed ne'er-do-wells who looked like they were up to no good. But whatever no good they were up to, Jackie was sure that it didn't involve her. Still, she felt uneasy. She kept trying to detect anyone who might pose a threat, but the crowd of passengers was too dense for her to see beyond the crush of people immediately around her.

She had plenty of time to kill before her meeting with Jacques and had already decided to get off the Metro several stops early so she could walk the streets and take pictures with the Speed Graphic. Good practice for what was shaping up to be a potentially rewarding career path. She wondered whether her repeated brushes with the assassin had made her paranoid, but getting off the Metro at the next station now seemed like a doubly good idea. If she did have a stalker, she stood a better chance of losing him aboveground, on the street.

The train came to a halt as it entered the station, and the doors opened onto the platform. Passengers exited and entered the car at a brisk pace. Jackie waited patiently for the last possible moment, then leaped off her seat and made for the exit, passing through the car doors a split second before they closed behind her. There, thought Jackie, that should stop anyone hoping to follow her off the Metro.

She quickly clambered up the station steps and out onto the street. It was a bright summer day, and Jackie worked up a light sweat walking briskly away from the Metro entrance, still lugging Jacques's camera bag with her. Although the equipment no longer felt as heavy as it once did, it was still somewhat cumbersome to tote along with her handbag. Jackie smiled to herself and wondered whether Dorothea Lange had ever encountered this problem while photographing the Dust Bowl.

She started looking around for someone to photograph, but the street was almost entirely empty of pedestrians. Ah, there's one, she thought, a big man who had obviously been badly beaten up in an accident. His head was heavily bandaged, and his arm was wrapped in a sling. Poor guy would be the kind of subject who would pull on viewers' heartstrings. She pointed the camera in his direction, looked through the viewfinder, and almost let out a scream when she recognized who it was.

The assassin! Miraculously, inexplicably, he had managed to survive being buried under a pile of rubble and had found her again. She hadn't been paranoid at all about someone stalking her on the Metro—she just hadn't been able to see him and couldn't elude him either. It was a small satisfaction knowing that those bandages were not part of any disguise, but the result of the damage Jacques had inflicted on him during their fight. Unfortunately, the sling was on the assassin's left arm, meaning that his knife-wielding arm was still in good shape.

Hurry, hurry, Jackie urged herself as she picked up her pace to put distance between herself and her seemingly omnipresent pursuer. At the same time, her eyes searched the street, looking for any convenient shop or business she could disappear inside. She was on the avenue Montaigne, a street of fashion houses and high-end jewelers and perfumeries; it was one of the most exclusive streets in the city. Something about the building coming up on her right seemed to call to her, and she saw a brass plaque next to the entrance that read:

30 AVENUE MONTAIGNE
LA MAISON DE DIOR

That sounded promising to Jackie. But instead of using the main entrance, she followed a narrow walkway that led to the back of the building, which had once been a private residence, and found the door to what must have originally been the servants' entrance. It was open, and she quickly passed through it. Inside, she found herself in a dimly lit corridor lined with naked dress dummies, so evenly spaced that they reminded her of a formation of soldiers standing at attention. The hallway led to the entrance of a long gallery. As Jackie passed through it, she was greeted by a scene of incredible chaos.

She saw slender young women standing still or running around in their scanties (or, in some cases, even less). Matronly-looking women had pins in their mouths. Harried men in suits gesticulated wildly as though they were conducting invisible symphony orchestras. Shirtsleeve-and-vested men had scissors in their hands, tape measures around their necks, and cigarettes dangling from their lips. And over it all reigned the sounds of extreme pandemonium. *Either I've wandered into an insane asylum,* Jackie thought, *or I'm backstage at a fashion show.* She decided it was the latter and searched around for someplace she could go to appear inconspicuous.

"Hello."

Jackie looked in front of her and saw that she was being addressed by a sylphlike young woman with pixieish short hair and one of the most strikingly beautiful faces she had ever seen. She was obviously a model. But she exhibited a vivacious quality far beyond the vacant glamour of the other models or mannequins, as they were called, in the gallery. At the same time, there was something slightly melancholy in her features that drew you in. "Are you here to take my picture?"

The woman standing in front of Jackie was wearing nothing but a taupe-colored slip and ballet slippers. Apparently, she was waiting to be dressed for the fashion show.

"Like that?" Jackie asked in surprise.

"I've posed in less," the young woman said with a sophisticated nonchalance that belied her years.

"Sure," said Jackie, intrigued by this enthrallingly stunning woman, "I'll take your picture." Jackie took out the Speed Graphic (already loaded, of course, as Jacques had so frequently drummed into her), remembered to remove the lens cover, and looked through the viewfinder. If anything, the young woman was even lovelier when eyed through the lens. The camera loved her.

Jackie hit the shutter release and took the picture. She noticed that the young woman had an unusual way of speaking. "Where are you from?" she asked as she changed film sheets and flashbulbs.

"I'm originally from Belgium," explained the young woman, "but raised in the Netherlands."

"Do you speak English too?"

"Yes. My first movie is coming out next month. It's a British production: *One Wild Oat*. It's just a small part—I play a desk clerk—but everybody has to start out somewhere, they say."

"Oh, so you're an actress too."

"Well, we'll see about that," said the model with an uncommon modesty that Jackie found quite becoming.

"I bet you're going to be a big star," Jackie blurted out, feeling foolish at making such a grandiose claim to someone she'd just met.

"Thank you," said the model, brightly and sincerely.

Jackie looked around and saw a large man in a black suit bearing down on her. It was time to wrap up this conversation.

"Well, I've enjoyed talking with you, Miss…"

"Hepburn," said the model. "Audrey Hepburn. *Le même chose*."

She stuck out her hand for Jackie to take.

"Sorry, no press allowed back here," a wide-shouldered, barrel-chested security guard informed her brusquely.

Jackie realized that with her Speed Graphic she was automatically mistaken now for a press photographer and looked around for an exit.

"This way," the man said as he led her firmly across the gallery and through a door that opened onto the salon where the fashion show was being held.

Jackie looked around and saw no sign of the bandaged assassin. Good. Her scan of the room took in a well-dressed crowd, and she was thankful that her outfit and diamond tennis bracelet, chosen for an afternoon of museum-going with Jacques, were up to snuff. She headed for the door in the rear of the salon that would hopefully lead to the foyer. But as she approached, a figure detached itself from the shadowed doorway. It was the assassin. Her heart sank, and her nerves began to scream. The man was everywhere!

With a feeling of growing panic, Jackie retreated back into the salon and tried to figure out her next move. As long as she sat in the audience, surrounded by witnesses, and with reporters and photographers everywhere, she was safe. In his condition, it would be too difficult for the assassin to get to her. But the fashion show would eventually end, and the guests would depart. And then the assassin would have Jackie right where he wanted her. She decided her best course of action was to find a seat, stay for the fashion show, and hope that something would occur to her before the last mannequin walked down the runway.

Jackie spotted an empty chair in the middle of the second row from the front, hurried to it, and quickly sat down, stowing her purse and camera bag in the narrow floor space between the chairs. The tall, thin man seated on her left was none too pleased with her alacrity. He had the dour look of a deposed prewar monarchist in exile, and Jackie recognized him and the woman sitting next to him, his wife, as Principe and Principessa de Something-or-other, wealthy but minor Italian royalty who were fixtures in the gossip columns. He gave Jackie a sniffy look as though she were something unpleasant he had found on the sole of his shoe, then retreated to a moue of deeply entrenched boredom. The *principessa* shared this expression. There are wax figures at Madame Tussauds who exhibit more joie de vivre than these two, Jackie thought. She hoped that they would let her be and not call for security.

She cased the room and noted that there were only two ways out—through the rear of the salon, where the imperturbable assassin was patiently waiting for her, and through the door to the gallery, where her exit was sure to be blocked by the security men guarding the room. As she waited, Jackie tried to focus her mind, concentrating on the story of the House of Dior as a way of trying to puzzle her way out of her plight.

She knew, for example, that Christian Dior had founded this house in 1946. His first collection for Spring-Summer 1947 was an instant success. Taking advantage of the postwar relaxation in restrictions on material for clothes, he extravagantly draped his models from ankle to throat in fabrics that emphasized their ultra-feminine silhouettes. Thanks, in part, to the success of his first collection, Dior and his New Look helped once again make Paris the epicenter of the fashion universe. And in the past four years, he had made his house one to rival any of the other great fashion houses in Paris, including Chanel, Balmain, and Balenciaga. Dior had recently branched out into the licensing of luxury goods, and today's fashion show was dedicated to the display of everything from his signature neckties and furs to handbags and lingerie, as well as his distinctive line of dresses.

There was something else about Dior that stuck in Jackie's

head, something she remembered from her conversation with Jacques about *Stage Fright*. She recalled telling Jacques, when he complimented her on the dress she was wearing, that Dior had designed both that dress and Marlene Dietrich's clothes for that movie. There was something about *Stage Fright* that held the key to getting out of this salon, Jackie thought, but what was it?

She looked back and saw the assassin still waiting in the doorway to the salon, his eyes as intimidatingly murderous as ever. Turning back to the runaway as the fashion show got underway, Jackie realized that her subconscious was signaling her that Hitchcock himself, and not *Stage Fright*, marked the path to her salvation. That made sense since, after all, Hitchcock was the great master of suspense, and his movies were filled with scenes of hairbreadth escapes. Mentally, she went over a checklist of his movies that she had seen—*Notorious, Suspicion, Shadow of a Doubt*—and one by one eliminated them as the source of any potential getaway scheme.

Finally, her mental movie inventory flashed on *The 39 Steps*. Jackie vividly recalled handsome Robert Donat and beautiful Madeline Carroll escaping across the Scottish Highlands, pursued by biplanes, and the haunting climax at the London Palladium. And then her movie memory displayed a scene from earlier in the film, and she knew exactly how to get herself out of this terrifying situation. She remembered Robert Donat's deliberate disruption of a political rally. Well, if it had been good enough for Robert Donat, it would more than suit her.

But what kind of disturbance could she cause? Jackie couldn't see standing up and giving an impromptu speech or heckling the mannequins as they came down the runway. Her upbringing just wouldn't allow her to do anything so vulgar. So what then? Her eye was suddenly caught by the diamond bracelet that dangled from her wrist. Thank you, she silently offered to her stepfather, who had purchased this lovely Tiffany bracelet for her as a recent graduation present. Without knowing it, he had given her a thoughtful gift that was going to save her life.

Jackie slipped the bracelet off her wrist, first making sure that those seated around her were too busy watching the parade of mannequins to pay any attention to what she was doing. Next, she waited for the *principe* to lean over and address the *principessa*, then took the bracelet and dropped it into his coat pocket, being sure that just the tiniest hint of the bracelet dangled down from the pocket flap, where it was barely visible. The *principe* seemed to notice nothing at all, and Jackie privately complimented herself for her reverse-pickpocket skills. The Artful Dodger had nothing on her.

Jackie sat there for a moment, screwing up her courage. Causing a scene was just not in her nature. But she had no choice if she wanted to survive to meet Jacques at the Jeu de Paume. Standing up before she could change her mind, Jackie took a deep breath and shouted, "My bracelet! It's missing!"

The mannequins continued to traipse up and down the runaway as though nothing was amiss. This was part of their training. But every head in the room was turned from the runway to Jackie as she continued to call out, "My diamond bracelet. It's gone. It was a gift from my father."

Only the *principe* and *principessa* refused to look in her direction. Jackie's cries quickly brought a florid-looking concierge to her side. "What seems to be the matter, mademoiselle?" he asked in a low tone of voice that he hoped she would emulate.

"My diamond bracelet is missing," said Jackie, plunging on. "Someone must've taken it."

"That's impossible, mademoiselle," protested the concierge, who was turning quickly apoplectic, his entire face a shade to rival the red of the boutonnière he wore in his lapel. "No one in this salon would dare to steal anything of yours. Or anyone else's, for that matter."

"Then can you explain what happened to it?" blustered Jackie, her voice once again rising.

"Perhaps you dropped it on the way here and failed to notice it."

"Impossible, I saw it on my wrist only a few minutes ago. I was sitting right there." She pointed to the seat next to the *principe*. She looked past her seat and pretended to "spot" the diamond bracelet sticking out of the *principe*'s coat pocket.

"There it is, in his pocket," Jackie announced to the concierge and to the rest of the room.

The concierge went over to the *principe*. "Your Highness," he said in as abject a manner as possible. "Would you mind turning out your pocket?"

"I certainly do," protested the *principe* huffily.

"The man's a thief," said Jackie. "He stole the diamond bracelet right off my wrist."

"I did no such thing." The *principe* was furious. He rose from his seat to confront the concierge and Jackie. His wife, though, continued to sit, as though complete indifference might make this whole terrible situation go away.

"Thief," Jackie reiterated.

The concierge turned to her. "Please, mademoiselle. Let me handle this." He turned back to the *principe*. "Your Highness, please, may I see what's inside your coat pocket?"

The *principe* said nothing, but just stood there as the concierge lifted the flap of his coat pocket and pulled out the diamond bracelet. The crowd inside the salon let out a collective gasp as the concierge held out the bracelet in front of the *principe*.

"Please, your Highness, can you tell me how this got in your pocket?"

"I have no idea," answered the *principe* with a chill in his voice that called to mind the remotest regions of Antarctica.

Jackie steadfastly maintained the charade. "You see," she told the concierge, "I told you he's a thief."

"Please, mademoiselle, that is something for the police to decide."

"Then call them. At once," Jackie said, in the most imperious tone she could muster.

The concierge caught the attention of a member of the security detail standing by the door to the gallery and used the international hand signal for making a telephone call.

A few minutes later, as the *principe* continued to fume in place and the mannequins maintained their seamless march down the runway, the wail of a siren could be heard outside, followed by a screech of car brakes. Three gendarmes strode purposefully into the salon and approached the concierge. He quickly explained the situation to them, and the gendarmes led Jackie and the *principe* out of the salon, through the foyer, and into the street, where their Fiat police car was waiting, driver behind the wheel and engine running. As she was escorted out, Jackie caught sight of the assassin out of the corner of her eye. He fixed her with a baleful glance that reluctantly ceded this round to her.

Once outside, Jackie coquettishly explained to the gendarmes that the situation must have been a misunderstanding. The *principe* was so reluctantly grateful to Jackie for not pressing charges that he failed to make more of a scene. All he wanted to do was return to his frozen-faced wife.

When Jackie said that this mix-up was going to make her late for an important date at the Jeu de Paume, the gallant gendarmes were only too happy to offer this beautiful young

American woman a ride in their police car. As they pulled away from the House of Dior, she looked through the rear window and saw the assassin standing in the entranceway, a look of soul-shriveling hatred on his face. He receded into the distance, and Jackie felt relief at having outsmarted him once again. But with his seemingly preternatural persistence, how much longer would her luck hold out?

Jacques was standing outside the entrance to the Jeu de Paume, the sun-splashed vaulted glass window rising high behind him, frowning impatiently at his watch as he waited for Jackie to arrive. She was twenty minutes late. He wondered what could be keeping her.

When he saw the police car pull up with Jackie in it, he was stunned. He watched, mouth agape, as she got out of the car, said "*Merci beaucoup*" to the gendarmes, and waved good-bye to them.

"For God's sake, what happened?" he asked her.

She didn't want to be overheard so she refrained from answering until she was close to him. "I would have been here on time but my friend—you know, the one with the knife who just can't let me out of his sight—showed up when I got off the Metro. I had to duck into a fashion show at the House of Dior to ditch him."

Jacques looked stricken. "If I hadn't thought he was dead or at least out of commission for a while, I would have made it my business to look out for you," he said apologetically. His brow furrowed. "But how did the gendarmes get into this?"

She filled him in on the scene she had created at the fashion show, and he shook his head, incredulous. "You're amazing" was all he could say.

"I amaze myself sometimes," Jackie admitted. She took his arm. "Come on, Mademoiselle Olympia is waiting for us. Let's go in."

They entered the building, a marvel of soaring height accentuated by the grandeur of a sweeping staircase and glacial white walls.

"It's hard to believe this was originally built to house two tennis courts for Napoleon," Jackie said.

"And sad to think that it was used as a 'concentration camp' for the thousands of art treasures the Nazis looted from the French Jews and stored here for transport to Germany during the Occupation," Jacques said.

Jackie caught the bitterness in his tone. She hadn't counted on the museum reminding him of the tragic fate of Aurélie, his first love. She wondered whether that teenage emotional wound would ever fully heal or if his relationships with women had been scarred for life by it.

Her musings were cut short when she heard someone calling her name and turned to see—oh, no, not those two again!— the eccentric British couple who were always fighting with each other but seemed enamored of Jackie. She expected them to pretend that this third meeting, after the ones at the opera and at Longchamp, was pure happenstance, but Jackie didn't believe it. Now she was convinced that her initial fleeting suspicion that they were following her, which she had thought might be paranoid, was spot on. Randomness had its limitations, especially when it came to bumping into the same people over and over again in a city as large and populous as Paris. Were they really just as dotty as they seemed or was that a pose? Who were they, and why were they tailing her? Was it her they were after, or Jacques too?

The woman cut into the questions bouncing around in

Jackie's head with her usual effusiveness. "Miss Bouvier, I can't believe it, we meet again. Oh my, this is indeed such a pleasant surprise," she gushed. She looked at Jacques and seemed to be struggling to remember who he was, but then her face lit up with recognition. "And Mr. Rivage, isn't it? The photographer who did that wonderful book...uh...*The Look of War.*"

"It's not *The Look of War*," her fiancé corrected her superciliously. "It's *The Faces of War.*"

Jacques smiled at him. "You have a good memory."

The man held his hand out to Jacques and shook it. "Good to see you again, old stick." He turned to Jackie. "And you as well, Miss Bouvier." He beamed at her, but she had the feeling that he thought something about her didn't quite add up. "Speaking of my memory, what I shan't forget is your impressive ride at Longchamp. I must say, you're quite the equestrienne." He gave her a searching look. "But that was most unusual, to say the least."

Jackie blushed and thought fast. "While I was at the paddock, the jockey saw how taken I was with that horse because he reminded me of my favorite mare when I was growing up. I told him I'd been riding horses since I was one year old and begged him to let me take the colt around the track for his warm-up, and he agreed." She batted her eyelashes demurely. "Longchamp is such a gracious place. I can't imagine that happening at any other track in the world."

"Quite," the man said, nodding. Apparently, he accepted her explanation.

"So, my dears, where are you headed?" the woman asked. "Is there any exhibition you're particularly interested in?"

Jackie was sure that no matter what she answered, this couple would cling to them the way a silk slip charged with static electricity stuck to her thighs. She gave Jacques a questioning look and from his impassive face surmised that they would just have to let the British couple follow them around until an opportunity presented itself to be alone with the Olympia painting.

"Actually, we didn't have any particular exhibit in mind," Jackie said. "We were just going to browse the entire museum."

"Oh, in that case then, why don't we start with the impressionist collection in the Musée?" the woman suggested.

Why don't we? Jackie thought. That's where Manet's *Olympia* was, along with the works of other famous impressionists like Renoir, Monet, Sisley, Degas, and Cézanne.

"Good idea," Jacques said. Apparently wanting to show some familiarity with the museum and not be left out of the conversation, he added, "It's a very inspiring collection. They moved it here after the war in the hopes that seeing these works would help people overcome the horrors of combat and celebrate the beauty of nature."

"Indeed," the man said. "Well, let's go take a look and celebrate, shall we?"

As they walked to the Musée part of the Galerie, the man elaborated on what Jacques had said about the Nazi confiscation of works of art that wealthy French Jews were forced to abandon before fleeing the German Occupation. With his detailed knowledge and upper-class British accent, he sounded like a curator, and his professorial manner reminded her, oddly enough, of Allen Dulles at his most pedantic.

"The story of this museum is a study in monumental rapacity," he began. "The Führer's Special Staff for Pictorial Art seized close to twenty-two thousand art objects of all types between 1940 and 1944 and stored them here temporarily. The Nazis found these objets d'art by conducting exhaustive investigations into the address lists of the French police, Jewish handbooks, warehouse inventories and order books of French shipping firms, and French art and collection catalogs. While the artworks were stored here, they were scientifically inventoried and photographed by Staff specialists. And by the end of the war, one hundred thirty-seven freight cars had shipped more than four thousand cases of artworks to six shelters in the Reich."

"Are you an art historian?" Jacques asked, sounding awestruck.

The man chuckled. "No, no, old stick, I'm simply fascinated by how bloody methodical those Nazi criminals were in tracking down what they wanted to get their greedy hands on. I'm an old Navy man and studying the means by which foreign governments acquire information, even for nefarious purposes, is a passion of mine."

"Now, dear, let's talk about something more pleasant, shall we?" his fiancée said as they arrived at the world-famous collection of impressionist paintings.

The four of them spent the next hour or so slowly walking through the gallery rooms, stopping to admire the radiant beauty and brilliant artistry of each of the treasured paintings. The woman proved to be as knowledgeable an art lover as Jackie and intelligently remarked on the techniques employed by Degas in *After the Bath, Woman Drying Her Nape*; Renoir in *Nude in the Sun*; Monet in *Seine Basin with Argenteuil*; and just about every other master impressionist's work in the large collection.

For once, the woman's fiancé seemed content not to question her statements, apparently conceding that her knowledge of art was superior to his. In fact, Jackie noticed with some relief that he was starting to glance at his watch more and more frequently, as if growing impatient with this tour. She caught

Jacques rolling his eyes a couple of times, desperately wanting the British couple to leave them alone so they could go about their business.

Fortunately, the woman had more to say about Cézanne's *A Modern Olympia* than she did about Manet's and passed by the latter painting with only a few cursory comments. Both Jackie and Jacques deliberately showed only moderate interest in it too, hiding how they were itching to get back to it when they were alone.

Jackie was thinking of pulling aside Jacques to figure out some creative way to get rid of the couple without having to leave the museum themselves, when the break she was looking for came of its own accord.

"Really, darling, we must be going or we'll be late for high tea at the Ritz," the man said to his fiancée after yet another impatient glance at his watch. "We mustn't keep our friends waiting."

Thank heaven they had other friends, Jackie thought.

But the woman still seemed reluctant to part company. "Would you and Mr. Rivage like to join us?" she asked Jackie. "I know our friends would be delighted to meet you both."

"Come now, dear," the man reproved her. "I'm sure these young people have more exciting things to do than muddle through high tea at the Ritz with folks twice their age."

"Nonsense, they'll have a grand time," she contradicted him, then turned to Jackie. "Wouldn't you like to join us, dear?"

Jackie looked pained, ostensibly because she had to turn down the invitation, but actually because she'd been asked. "Oh, that's so sweet of you," she said, "but Mr. Rivage and I are meeting up with some friends as well in a bit. Perhaps another time." Not if I can help it, she thought.

"Oh, I do hope so," the woman said. "We so enjoyed being with you."

"Cheerio," the man said, and they were gone.

After she was sure they'd given the couple enough time to leave the building, Jackie said in a confidential tone, "I don't trust them, Jacques. I think they're following us. Don't you think it's just a little too coincidental that we keep bumping into them everywhere?"

Jacques nodded, acknowledging how astute she was becoming at the spying game. "You could be right. They might have been the same couple who were spying on us that night in your hotel when I chased them to the elevator and they got away." He shrugged. "But if they are following us, we'll catch them at it sooner or later. Right now, we have an appointment with Mademoiselle Olympia."

"You're right, we'll worry about them later," Jackie said, hurrying with him to the room where Manet's *Olympia* hung on the wall. It was protected, as all of the priceless paintings were, Jackie noted, by motion detectors along the walls and guards stationed at either end of the room.

She knew they had to be discreet about their inspection of the painting or the guards' suspicions would be aroused. "Here, take this, Jacques," she said, handing him the Speed Graphic and the camera bag, which they couldn't use in the museum anyway. Then she took a notepad and artist's pencil out of her handbag and began sketching *Olympia* as she stood transfixed before it, resuming the role of the art student she'd been at the Sorbonne.

Jacques stood beside her, peering at the painting and comparing it with notes of his own that he'd brought along. Luckily, traffic in the gallery was very light, and they were able to conduct their investigation with only occasional interruptions by other viewers walking by.

"Do you see anything?" Jacques whispered to Jackie. "Anything about the black cat?"

She looked. "No."

"What about the bracelet?"

A long stare. "No."

"How about the pearl earrings?"

"Uh-uh."

"The orchid in her hair?"

"Nope."

"Anything in the basket of flowers?"

She looked closely. "Nothing."

"What about the maid? Do you see anything? Her uniform? The cap on her head?"

An intent examination. "No."

"How about the black ribbon around Olympia's neck? Could that be it?"

"Just a ribbon."

"Does the oriental shawl she's lying on have any writing on it?"

Jackie looked hard and shook her head no.

"She's wearing a slipper. Is anything there?"

"Uh-uh."

Jacques was starting to sound desperate. "How about the hand over her privates? Her nipples? Anything on her body?"

Jackie looked and shook her head no in answer to all his questions.

They went back over each of the items again and again, one by one, but nothing surfaced that could possibly be interpreted as a clue. The drapes in Olympia's room, the wall behind her, and the sheets and pillow she was lying on were similarly unproductive.

Jackie glanced at the guards, afraid they might be getting suspicious, but one was leaning back in his chair yawning and the other one looked bored silly. Apparently, they were used to students spending inordinate amounts of time studying this groundbreaking nude.

When she turned back to the painting, Jackie slanted her head this way and that, studying the face and figure of the nude from different angles. Then she stared straight ahead. Her eyes zoomed in like a telescope. Wait a minute. Hold on. She thought she saw something, but she couldn't be sure. She walked up closer to the painting, squinted, cocked her head, squinted some more, walked back from the painting, still staring at it, then turned to Jacques. "Wait here for me. I'll be right back."

"Where are you going?"

"To the gift shop."

"What for?"

"You'll see."

"Okay, but don't get in any trouble," he said lightly. "You have a knack for it."

She knew he was teasing. With all these guards around, there was little danger of the assassin cropping up anywhere in the museum to do her harm.

A short time later, Jackie returned with something in her hand and showed it to Jacques. It was a postcard with a large reproduction of Manet's *Olympia* on it. She walked up to the painting with the postcard in her hand and compared the two. Then she came back to Jacques and said, "At first I thought it was a speck of dust, but it isn't. Somebody added it to the painting."

"What are you talking about?"

She pointed to Olympia's neck on the reproduction of the painting on the postcard. "Do you see anything below the black ribbon?"

"No."

"Now go up to the painting and look at the space in the

crook of her neck, right above the clavicle. You'll see a tiny beauty mark there that was never in the original."

He went up to the painting and peered at it closely. When he came back, he said in a confidential tone, laced with admiration, "Good work, Jackie, you're a first-class sleuth. I'm proud of you."

"What is it?"

"I'll tell you when we're out of here," he said, taking her arm and walking out of the gallery with her.

They left the Jeu de Paume, walked across the street to the Tuileries, and sat down on a bench. This is where it all began, Jackie thought, a warm feeling of desire fluttering and beating its wings inside her as she remembered the day she first met him at the Punch and Judy show and sat on a park bench just like this.

"It's not a beauty mark," he was saying. "It's a microdot."

She perked up. "A microdot? What's that?"

"It's a photograph of a document made smaller so many times that it's been reduced to the size of a period," he explained. "It's an easy way for spies to deliver information in secret. The Germans invented it during World War II."

"I get it," Jackie exclaimed excitedly. "That microdot on the painting must contain the information Petrov was going to bring to the CIA."

"Exactly." Jacques shook his head in begrudging admiration. "How clever of Petrov to hide it in plain sight like that at the museum."

"And how equally impossible it is to get at," Jackie said with a rueful little laugh. "How do you propose that we remove the microdot from the painting with all those motion detectors along the walls and guards stationed at either end of the room?"

"That's the big question," Jacques said. "But Petrov got it on, so we should be able to get it out."

As they sat on the bench, their brows wrinkled in thought, a street vendor began to set up close by. He placed a suitcase on the pathway, opened it, and began to remove a regiment's worth of wind-up Napoleonic toy soldiers. One by one, he wound them up and let them march across the pathway, to the delight of the children who quickly gathered around him, begging their parents for money to buy his miniature mechanical marvels.

"Cute, aren't they?" Jackie remarked, idly watching the scene.

Jacques nodded, staring absently at the children and the toy soldiers too. Suddenly, his face lit up, and he turned to Jackie. "I think I have an idea," he said, an excited note in his voice, "that just might work."

XIV

In a flash, Jacques whisked Jackie away from the Tuileries to an apartment near the Montmartre Steps. There was no concierge for the building. Jacques simply pushed a button next to a warped and rusted iron door. The door buzzed open, and Jacques led Jackie through a shadowed courtyard to a moldering building that could have been an apartment or a factory, depending on how one viewed its ambiguous architectural design.

Once through the doorway, they climbed a cramped and curving set of stairs to the third floor. There was only one door on the landing, and it was slightly open. Jacques pushed through it, with Jackie right behind him. The room was so long and narrow that it could have easily been mistaken for a tunnel. But that wasn't the only unusual aspect of the room, which smelled musty, as though none of its begrimed windows had been open since the advent of Léon Blum and the Popular Front two decades ago. All the furniture had been lowered as if to accommodate someone of elflike stature. And a grouping of life-sized marionettes dangled by their strings from the room's high ceiling like a ghoulish aerial chorus line. Jackie counted eight of them before a voice came from the far reaches of the room, where an unmade camp bed and a hotplate-topped, deep blue–painted counter stood.

"Do you like them? They were commissioned by Jean Cocteau. For one of his experimental theater pieces."

Jackie looked closely at the outsized marionettes and thought that there was something freakish about them that fitted the twisted worldview of the author of *Les Enfants Terribles* and *Les Parents Terribles*. She heard the wooden floorboard creak and turned to see the man who had spoken approach in a wheelchair. He was thin and wiry and appeared to be about fifty years old. Jacques made the introductions with the formality befitting a diplomatic function instead of a visit to what looked like a room in a funhouse.

"Jackie, this is *mon ami*, Henri Blondel. Henri, *je te présente* Jacqueline Bouvier."

"*Bonjour*, Jacqueline. Any friend of Jacques's is welcome here," Henri said, wiping his grease-stained hands on a rag and emphasizing the word *friend* in a suggestive manner so that it took on another meaning entirely.

"*Merci beaucoup,*" Jackie responded graciously, ignoring the inference and taking Henri's hand in hers. His grip was powerful, and his work-roughened hand felt as if it had calluses piled on top of calluses.

Henri wheeled himself toward a workbench that his wheelchair fit under comfortably. Now Jackie understood why all the furniture in the room was set so low. The workbench, like the rest of the room, was littered with toys that seemed to be broken in one fashion or another: Plush animals with their seams open and their stuffing coming out. Dolls with missing limbs. Decapitated lead soldiers. And model cars and trucks that looked as if they had been in real-life accidents.

"How's business?" Jacques asked Henri.

"Can't complain. The children keep me busy." To Jackie, he explained, "I scour the city for discarded toys. I bring them back here and repair them. Then I distribute them to orphanages."

She didn't understand how one made a living in this fashion, but thought it would be less than polite to ask.

As though reading her mind, Henri explained, "I made enough in my lifetime. Now it's my turn to give back to this city that I love more than life itself." From the workbench he picked up a one-legged, cast-lead grenadier, then looked at it through a magnifying lens attached to a gooseneck extension.

"Lost his leg at Austerlitz," he said, handing the toy soldier to Jacques. "What do you think?"

Jacques looked over the toy soldier carefully. "Battle of Egypt is more like it." He returned the wounded grenadier to Henri, who put it back in its place on the workbench.

"And what brings you here?" Henri asked Jacques, picking up another stricken toy and peering at it through the magnifying lens.

"Henri, I have a favor to ask of you."

Henri put down the toy and looked up at Jacques. "Anything for the son of an old Resistance comrade."

Jacques took a long pause before answering. "I need to know how to break in to the Jeu de Paume."

Henri's response was unexpected, to say the least. He began to laugh. In fact, he laughed so hard that Jackie feared he was in danger of falling out of his wheelchair. "Break into the Jeu de Paume? Who do you think you are? Arsène Lupin? Fantômas?"

Jacques refused to take the bait and respond to Henri's flippant comparison of him to two of the most popular characters in the history of French crime fiction. "I'm serious, Henri. I need your help with this."

"*Non.*" Henri's answer was short but emphatic.

"Why not?"

"Because I don't want the son of an old Resistance comrade to wind up behind bars. Besides, you make a good living as a photographer. Why this swerve into a life of crime?"

"Oh, we don't want to steal anything, Monsieur Blondel," Jackie assured him.

"It's Henri, please," the man said, turning to her. "And if you don't want to steal anything, then why do you want to break into the Jeu de Paume?"

"It's complicated," Jacques tried to explain. "Let's just say it's a potential matter of national security and leave it at that."

"My answer is still no. You are amateurs. You are sure to be caught."

"Not if you showed us."

With an exasperated grunt, Henri propelled himself away from the workbench and screeched to a halt scant inches from Jacques's kneecaps. He looked up at him and said, "And how do you plan to break in? Through the main entrance? From a skylight in the roof? Or perhaps you plan to dig a tunnel underneath the museum?" He pushed forward, forcing Jacques to take a few steps back. "And when do you plan this break-in to take place?"

"Tomorrow night."

Henri reeled back as though physically struck. "*C'est ridicule!! Tu est fou!* There is not enough time."

"Henri, I wouldn't ask you if it wasn't important. Someone's life could be at stake."

"Whose?" asked Henri, looking dubious.

"Mine," responded Jackie, in a voice that was barely above a whisper.

Henri wheeled himself over to Jackie. "I'm sorry, mademoiselle, this is something I just cannot do. This is insanity. This is madness."

Jacques interposed himself between Henri and Jackie.

"Is that your final word, Henri?"

"Oui." Without a backward glance at the couple, he returned to his workbench and began to busy himself there.

"I'm sorry for bothering you then." Jacques turned to Jackie. "Let's go." To Henri, he said, "Don't worry. We'll see ourselves out."

But Henri wasn't listening. He was back at his workbench, sifting through a pile of tiny cast-lead limbs, hoping one might match the one-legged grenadier that he held in his hand. Jacques and Jackie closed the door on the way out and left him there, a broken man repairing broken toys to brighten his spirit and the lives of impoverished children.

Sitting outdoors on the cramped terrace of a small bistro near Henri's apartment, Jackie and Jacques ate a light dinner of *pan bagnats* and *frites* and shared an inexpensive bottle of white wine.

"What are we going to do now?" Jackie asked after a few mouthfuls of her sandwich.

"Wait," Jacques said, spearing a *frite* on his fork.

"For what?"

"For someone to make the next move."

Her thoughts returned to Henri. "Has your friend always been in a wheelchair?"

"No," said Jacques, taking a sip of wine and making a face at the off-vintage taste. "Henri was once the greatest second-story man in Paris. Whenever a crime had been committed, he would be the first person questioned by the police. Even if he had nothing to do with it. There was even a rumor that he was in on the theft of the *Mona Lisa* from the Louvre in 1911. Of course, he was only ten years old at the time."

"What happened to him?"

"You mean how did he wind up in a wheelchair?"

Jackie nodded.

"It's a long story," said Jacques, calling for the waiter and requesting another bottle of wine.

"Well, I'm not going anywhere."

"C'est vrai," said Jacques, adding with an arch smile on his face, "Actually, I was counting on that."

He paused while the waiter replaced the wine bottle and poured two fresh glasses, then relaxed in his chair, and began his story.

"I've told you about the Occupation. My father was killed for being in the Resistance. My mother worked as a housekeeper at the Hôtel Meurice. Henri was part of a different Resistance cell. Each cell was separate from every other cell, so if you were captured and tortured, you could only give up the members of your own small unit. Henri's cell capitalized on the fact that he was once the greatest second-story man in Paris. He pulled off incredible acts of espionage right under the noses of the Nazis, and Allied intelligence depended heavily on the information Henri provided when they planned the Liberation of Paris. That's how important he was to the war effort."

"I'm impressed," Jackie said, mentally adjusting her image of the wheelchair-bound toy repairman that she had met earlier to the daring action hero Jacques had just described.

"Henri had a lover, Marie-France," he went on. "She was a chanteuse. Not a very good one, but good enough to sing in a little boîte that just so happened to be frequented by German officers who either couldn't tell or didn't care about her lack of talent. Between sets, she would flirt with them. And occasionally, she would pick up a tidbit of information that she would pass on. You see, she too was a member of the Resistance, although in a different cell from Henri's."

He took a sip of his wine and made a face again, this time not from the wine, but from the bitter taste of what he was about to say. "One terrible day, Henri received word that Marie-France has been picked up by the Gestapo. Then Henri himself was taken right off the street and escorted to Gestapo headquarters where he was questioned by a colonel. But to his surprise, he wasn't interrogated about his Resistance contacts. Instead, the colonel explained that he had an offer to make him. He wanted Henri to crack a safe."

Jackie was intrigued. "A safe? What was in it?"

"It belonged to the biggest pornographer in Paris. He'd been arrested as part of a roundup of degenerates. When the Gestapo colonel got a look at this safe, his eyes lit up, imagining pictures inside of famous people caught in compromising positions. The possibilities for blackmail were unlimited—friends, enemies, anyone in need of a little coercion. The colonel became obsessed with the safe and its contents. He tried to torture its combination out of the pornographer, but he had a bad heart and died before he could give up the information. And this safe was an antique, so old that no one in the Gestapo knew how to open it."

"And this is where Henri comes in," Jackie guessed. "If he was the greatest second-story man in Paris, he probably had a reputation as a safecracker par excellence too, right?"

"Right. You're a quick study, *ma cherie,*" Jacques said, smiling at her in that way of his that made her pulse quicken and her viscera do little flip-flops. "The colonel assumed that Henri wouldn't voluntarily use his skills on his enemy's behalf. But he did know about his relationship with Marie-France. So he had her arrested and used her as leverage to force Henri to volunteer to crack the safe. And the colonel let him know, in no uncertain terms, that if he failed, not only would he be tortured to death, but that Marie-France would be killed too."

"How awful," Jackie said. "The pressure on Henri must have been terrible."

"It was," Jacques said. "The safe was so old it was like a sphinx to him. No blueprints could be found for it. And it was made in the days before safes were fireproofed, so he couldn't just blow it up with dynamite or nitroglycerine for fear of destroying its flammable contents. Henri once told me that safecracking is like seduction. You can't use brute force to get the safe to give up the valuables inside. You have to use your wiles. You have to speak softly to it. And you have to listen carefully to what it tells you."

"So you're saying a safe is like a woman," Jackie said with a smile.

"I didn't say that, Henri did," he reminded her, "but it's an apt comparison."

"Then I guess there's a good reason for making the safe difficult to open. The harder it is, the greater the pleasure when the safecracker finally succeeds."

"I'll drink to that," he said, smiling.

She clinked wineglasses with him, then settled back again. "So go on, what did Henri do?"

"For the first twenty-four hours, he just sat on a high-backed chair in a room in the basement of Gestapo headquarters, not far from the cells and the interrogation chambers, alone with the late pornographer's safe, communing with it. You would never know from his calm outward demeanor that inside he was sick to death that the fate of his beloved Marie-France hung on whether or not he could talk this antique safe into giving up its secrets."

"What was the colonel doing all this time?"

"He kept barging into the room, getting increasingly impatient, until at long last Henri asked for a drill, a soupçon of gelignite—that's a kind of dynamite—a detonator, a condom, chewing gum, and a typewriter."

"A condom and a typewriter?" Jackie asked incredulously. "Whatever for? It sounds more like he was planning to write a dirty novel than crack a safe."

"It was a trick he learned from an old English safecracker," Jacques explained. "His specialty was robbing theaters on the music-hall circuit. First, you drill a hole in the safe. Next, you put your gelignite and detonator in the condom. The condom goes in the hole in the safe. You cover up the hole with a wad of chewing gum to hold everything in place. Then you tie the typewriter to the safe's handle. When the gelignite goes off, it lifts the levers holding the handle in place, and the weight of the typewriter turns the handle and opens the safe. Simple, right? So simple that the colonel couldn't believe that's all it took to crack the pornographer's safe."

"Ingenious," Jackie exclaimed.

"Yes, and inside, there was only one object—a reel of sixteen-millimeter film. The colonel anxiously snatched it up and arranged for a viewing in front of the Gestapo's senior staff.

"Ah, that was where the colonel made his big mistake. Because if he had screened it first, he might have saved himself a lot of embarrassment. You see, the film was a Walt Disney cartoon."

"A cartoon?" Jackie could hardly believe her ears.

"Yes, but not the usual one. This one showed Mickey Mouse

and Donald Duck and even Goofy having sex with Adolf Hitler."

Jackie's mouth dropped open in shock.

"There were plenty of pornographic imitations of Disney cartoons in those days. Almost as many as the real things. But this one was totally unique. The colonel was completely humiliated. He almost lost his job over it. He worried that for penance he'd be sent to the Russian Front. But then came the Liberation, and the Gestapo had other worries."

"Did he keep his word to Henri?"

"Alas, no."

"What happened to Marie-France?"

"Unfortunately, the colonel executed her in a fit of pique over the cartoon."

"Oh, no!" Jackie was outraged.

Jacques sighed and shook his head sympathetically. "And poor Henri was tortured by the colonel to give up the names of his fellow Resistance members."

"And did he?"

"Of course he did. No one could stand up to such torture. They broke every bone in his legs. So in the end, he named the names. But by that time, his cell had gotten wind of Henri's capture, and they all had dispersed to the countryside, where they could evade capture. And that's why Henri is now con-fined to a wheelchair for the rest of his life."

They were both silent for a few minutes, contemplating Henri's cruel fate, when a voice broke into their thoughts.

"May I join you?"

It was Henri, rolling to a stop by their table. Jackie could tell from the knowing look on Jacques's face that this new develop-ment didn't come as a complete surprise to him.

"Of course," Jacques said, making room at the table to accommodate Henri's wheelchair. He signaled to the waiter to bring another glass and poured Henri some of the wine. Henri knocked back half the glass before speaking.

"I'll do it. I'll help you with your job. But only on one condition."

"What's that?" Jacques asked suspiciously.

"There's a small Brancusi horse. I want you to bring it out for me."

Both Jackie and Jacques looked aghast.

"It's just a joke," Henri said, and they all laughed before getting serious again.

"So how are we going to break in?" Jacques asked.

"You're not," Henri said.

Jacques looked confused. "But I thought you just said you were going to help us."

"I am," Henri said, "but I'm not going to help you break in to the museum. I'm going to help you break *out* of the museum."

Jackie could see that Henri's eyes seemed lit by the inner fire of a mastermind.

"You see, it's far easier breaking out of a museum than breaking in."

Jacques smiled and nodded in appreciation. "Break *out*—I like it."

"But how are we going to do that?" Jackie asked Henri, finding it hard to fathom that until a few days ago she'd been a completely law-abiding citizen, with not so much as a traffic ticket to her name, and now here she was plotting to gain illegal access to one of the most famous art museums in the world.

"It's very easy," Henri began to explain before being interrupted by Jacques.

"Excuse me, Henri. I don't mean to sound ungrateful, but I'm curious, what made you change your mind?"

Henri's face turned thoughtful. "Because you are the son of an old Resistance comrade."

Jacques raised his glass to Henri's and clicked it. "I'll drink to that," he said, "and to *nouveaux comrades de casse.*"

Jackie smiled, knowing that *casse* was French slang for "heist." Yes, she thought, it's *le mot juste.*

XV

They left the bistro and returned with Henri to his work-place. Jackie shivered when she saw those life-sized hang-ing marionettes again. They were almost too creepily real to suit her.

In deference to his guests' comfort, Henri turned on an industrial window fan to cool the room. It was thoughtful of him, but the loud scraping noise of the fan's bent blades offset any relief from the summer heat outside.

Jackie and Jacques were surprised to discover that, in their absence, Henri had cleared off his workbench. On it, he had constructed a scale model of the floor of the Jeu de Paume where Manet's *Olympia* could be found. The walls were made out of building blocks and pieces of forts from old play sets, and the miniature model was populated with cast-lead soldiers standing in for the museum's security guards. The pièce de résistance was a model of the *Olympia* itself—the picture cut out of a magazine and glued into a miniature picture frame that had once been part a child's dollhouse—mounted on the wall in the appropriate place.

Jackie and Jacques both looked at the model in amazement.

"You did this," Jacques asked, "while we were at the res-taurant?"

Henri nodded.

"But how were you able to re-create the interior so completely?" Jackie couldn't contain the wonder in her voice.

"I have blueprints to all the major structures in Paris," Henri answered simply.

Jacques looked askance. "But what do you need them for?"

Henri shrugged. "I like to keep my hand in. Every once in a while, someone comes to me and asks to have a job planned. I do it for a ten percent cut of the swag. I use the money to keep myself in tools and supplies for my toy-repair business."

Swag, Jackie liked that; meaning loot, obviously. With every new word she learned, she was moving further and further into a world of criminals and spies that paralleled her own previous life, but one she would never have encountered except for Allen Dulles's momentous invitation at her graduation party. It now seemed several lifetimes ago.

"So you are the Robin Hood of Montmartre," Jacques said with a grin.

Henri ignored Jacques's jibe and picked up a pointer. "Enough of this chitchat. We have a lot of work to do and a lot of ground to cover and not much time to do it in."

"There's one thing I don't understand," interrupted Jackie.

Henri looked up at her. "What's that?"

"How did the Russian manage to get the microdot onto the painting without setting off the alarms?"

Henri smiled at her as he put down the pointer. "That's a good question." He paused for dramatic effect and said, "I've given it some thought and I think I have the answer."

From his work surface he chose a paper drinking straw left in an empty glass and, from a little girl's makeup kit, a fake beauty mark. "Let's pretend," he said like a magician addressing an audience, "that this beauty mark represents your Russian spy's microdot. And that this piece of paper represents your painting." He picked up a blank sheet of construction paper and used tape to affix it to the wall a short distance away.

Returning to his place next to Jackie and Jacques, he placed the beauty mark against his tongue—"That's for adhesive purposes"—then inserted the microdot substitute in one end of the straw. "And when no one is looking," Henri continued, "all I have to do is—"

And he blew through the straw's other opening, propelling the beauty mark across the intervening space, where it attached itself to the piece of construction paper and stayed there firmly in place.

"*Et voilà,*" said Henri, "*très simple.*"

Jackie and Jacques stared at Henri in wonder. The best solutions were indeed often the simplest ones.

Henri exchanged the straw for the pointer and used it to show his pupils where all the motion detectors were located on the gallery in which the *Olympia* hung and throughout the floor in general. He spent the next several hours drilling them, taking them through the steps they would need to follow if they were to accomplish their task and get out of the museum without being apprehended by the security guards. At the end of that time, Jackie felt exhausted. Planning a major heist was no mere stroll through Sherwood Forest, she was learning. She looked at Jacques and was relieved to see that he was in an equal state of exhaustion.

Finally, Henri put down the pointer, and Jackie knew that the session was blessedly at an end. She yawned and gathered up their things, but he was not quite finished with them.

"Do you know how to pick a lock?" he asked Jacques.

"It was part of a CIA course I once took, but I've never actually had to put in practice anything I learned."

Henri rummaged in a cabinet, then wheeled himself over to

Jacques. As Jackie looked on, he picked up a small toolkit from his lap and handed it to Jacques.

"What's this?" Jacques asked.

"My burglar tools. Take them—just in case."

"Henri, I can't take these," he protested.

"Don't be silly. I fully expect you to bring them back to me when you're finished. Besides, they always brought me luck. Maybe they'll do the same for you."

"Thanks, Henri," Jacques said, obviously moved by his friend's offering.

Yes, a good idea, that charmed burglar toolkit, Jackie thought, because she had a feeling that she and Jacques were going to need all the luck they could get.

"Whew, that's better," Jackie said as she walked out the door of Henri's decrepit apartment building and drew the fresh evening air into her nostrils, the way a person about to faint inhales smelling salts. She felt as if she had emerged from a crypt and had come back to life. The griminess and dilapidation of Henri's apartment had been dreary enough, but it was those eight eerie life-sized marionettes dangling from the ceiling that had most unnerved her. Human-looking yet lifeless, they hung from the rafters like the newly dead suspended in limbo. Still, she couldn't help but be enthralled by the depth of Henri's expertise and his willingness to give so much of his time to help make the heist of the microdot a success.

"Henri is an amazing man," she said to Jacques as they walked through the courtyard to the street. "His knowledge of the Jeu de Paume down to the smallest detail is incredible. And his loyalty to your father's memory—I mean putting himself out like this for his son—that's remarkable too."

"Not really," Jacques said. "All of the comrades in the Resistance would die for each other—and many of them did. They were like family to each other, and their children were almost like their own." He looked around at the couples starting to fill the streets on their way to the cafés and racy cabarets for an evening out in the fabled "fleshpots" of Montmartre, as they were known, and his voice took on a lighter tone. "The night's still young. Would you like to go out on the town a bit?"

Jackie's face lit up. It had been a trying day, and Jacques's apartment was nearby, but she was grateful that he wasn't rushing her back there. She knew that his indulgence of her was intended ultimately as part of foreplay, but he had already shown that he had what it took to be an artful lover—his willingness to take his time. One of the most endearing things about him was how in sync he was with what she was feeling or needed. Now he sensed that she could use a little fun, some lighthearted entertainment that would take her mind off floor plans and microdots before the evening ended up where they both knew it would—in Jacques's bed. That's if they managed to get there before some malign unforeseen event reared its harrowing head.

"Yes, I'd love to get a drink somewhere. That would be great," she said appreciatively.

"How about the Moulin Rouge?"

"Wonderful! You couldn't have picked a better place."

Although Jackie had been to the Moulin Rouge only a few times during her student days at the Sorbonne, as a Francophile and lover of the arts, she was well-acquainted with the legendary cabaret's history as the birthplace of the modern cancan dance. She found it amusing that the cancan was originally performed there by Pigalle's high-class prostitutes as a seductive dance to entertain and seduce potential clients, lifting their skirts to reveal their legs, lingerie, and occasionally their private parts.

The Moulin Rouge arrived at a period in France—the late nineteenth century—that Jackie wished she had been living in herself. It was a time when the atmosphere was conducive to artistic creativity. Social barriers were collapsing, aristocrats mingled with the hoi polloi, and painters and writers were inspired by the spirit of jubilant rebellion. Gradually, the cabaret's explicit striptease-type dance review evolved into a respectable form of adult entertainment. Highly skilled dancers replaced the courtesans, and the Moulin Rouge became a legitimate nightclub that spawned musical entertainment cabarets throughout Europe. But Jackie revered it as an icon in the dance world immortalized in art nouveau posters by Toulouse-Lautrec. She brought home a print when she came back from the Sorbonne—an 1891 poster advertising the appearance at the Moulin Rouge of the famous cancan dancer La Goulue ("The Glutton"), Louise Weber's stage name. It was still hanging on the wall in her bedroom at Merrywood.

"Bonsoir, Monsieur Rivage et Mademoiselle," the maitre d' greeted them when they entered the cabaret. It did not escape Jackie that Jacques was greeted by name, an obvious indication that he was a Moulin Rouge regular. A little stab of jealousy pricked her ego, but it dissipated somewhat when she caught the wide-eyed look that the maitre d' gave Jacques, signaling his opinion that her competition paled in comparison.

The cabaret was starting to fill up with patrons, many of them tourists from around the world, judging by the cacophony of foreign languages sounding in the air. But the maitre d' escorted Jacques and Jackie to a ringside table close to the huge dance floor.

"Merci beaucoup, Monsieur Rivage," the maitre d' said to Jacques as he smoothly palmed a bill from him. He smiled at Jackie. *"Veuillez apprécier le divertissement,"* he said, telling her to enjoy the show and signaling a waiter over to their table.

Jacques ordered after-dinner drinks of Pernod and desserts of iced nougat with honey for the two of them. Jackie sipped her drink and felt the tension in her body evaporate as the anise-flavored liqueur slid down her throat and spread a soothing warmth in the pit of her stomach. It didn't matter to her that the elaborate turn-of-the-century décor overflowing with mirrors and ornate galleries was showing its age. It still seemed redolent with romance. She noticed that the atmosphere, or maybe it was the Pernod, was having an effect on Jacques too.

"You're so beautiful," he murmured, reaching for her hand. He raised it to his lips and kissed it, all the while gazing tenderly into her eyes.

Something other than the Pernod was making her feel warm and tingly inside. His adoring gaze traveled like an arrow down deep to her very core. She leaned toward him and felt a wave of desire steadily rising and gathering steam. If this keeps up, we'll have to leave before the show starts, she thought. But just then, the lights dimmed, and the orchestra started up with a loud flourish.

Soon a troupe of high-kicking, voluptuous, translucently dressed dancers filled the stage like a force of nature and commanded everyone's attention. The squealing, shrieking acrobatic dancers flashed breasts and thighs barely covered by frilly black bras and panties as they performed splits and cartwheels and hopped on one leg in formation while holding the other leg in the air. It wasn't vulgar, but it was provocative all the same, eliciting hoots and catcalls from the men in the audience and gasps from the women.

"They make the Rockettes in Radio City Music Hall look like a conga line at a Junior League dance," Jackie remarked.

Jacques said nothing. He was starting to fidget in his seat, and Jackie imagined that he was thinking, as she was, of their kiss the night before, a lightning bolt connection that flooded both of them with electrifying passion. When she recalled how safe she felt in the shelter of his arms and the loving feelings his protectiveness evoked in her, she started to fidget too. Locking eyes with him, she longed to feel his arms around her again, his lips on hers, and was glad when the show ended to rapturous applause from the audience.

Jacques motioned to her empty glass and dessert plate. "Would you like anything else?" he asked politely.

She shook her head no, then looked as if she had changed her mind. "Well, yes, I would like something else—very much, in fact—but not here." She didn't care how bold that sounded. It was the truth, and she wanted him to know it. Wanted him to know how strong her desire was, how deep her need.

"I think we can take care of that," he said with a smile and paid the bill.

When they were inside his apartment, Jackie quickly kicked off her shoes. She took one look at that ugly brown sofa in the living room and decided she wanted nothing to do with it and what she was sure was its sordid history. This was not going to be some clumsy coupling on a couch—purely physical and ultimately meaningless. No, they both wanted more than that. She started down the hallway, but it seemed too gauche to go marching into his bedroom first, so she stopped at the doorway and stood there uncertainly, waiting for him to make the next move.

And he did. He came up behind her, put his arms around her, and pulled her close to his chest. He began nuzzling her neck.

"Ah, Jacque-LEEN, Jacque-LEEN," he murmured in her ear.

She turned around, hungrily sought his lips, and whispered as she fell into his bed, "I think you can call me Jackie."

This time, it was the harsh ringing of the telephone that interrupted them just when their passion was about to cross the Rubicon.

"Oh, *no!*" Jacques groaned, looking utterly abashed as he turned away from Jackie to answer the phone. "It must be an emergency at this hour."

He picked up the receiver. "Hello...oh, hello." His voice dropped to a low tone that indicated both familiarity and embarrassment. Jacques glanced sideways at Jackie and turned back to the phone, cupping his mouth with his hand as he spoke. But Jackie heard and understood it all.

"Ce n'est pas un bon moment...parce que...je vous rappellerai....Bonsoir," Jacques murmured in a terse way that Jackie translated into a single word: *brush-off*. It didn't take a genius to surmise that the person on the other end of the line calling Jacques at this hour was a woman—a woman he knew intimately—who was being told that this wasn't a good time, and he would get back to her.

Jacques hung up the phone and turned to Jackie, looking apologetic and crestfallen. "I'm so sorry." He sighed. "It was... well, just a friend really...I mean..."

Jackie decided to put him out of his misery. Jacques hadn't even looked at another woman the whole time he'd been with her, and it was no surprise that an old girlfriend would try to find out what happened to him. Yes, the phone call had bruised Jackie's ego and irretrievably broken the mood for love, but Jacques wasn't responsible.

"These things happen," she said with a little shrug. *"C'est la vie,* remember?"

He nodded and got up from the bed. "I'll get some cigarettes," he said in a defeated tone, his shoulders slumped from crashing into this wall of frustration.

Jackie watched him retreat and thought, I guess I'll just have to settle for being *une demi-vierge*—a half-virgin, as the French called a woman who stopped short of going all the way.

Moments later, sitting up in bed next to this devilishly good-looking Frenchman, both of them half-clothed and smoking Galoises, Jackie felt incredibly French and sophisticated. The room was bathed in stillness except for the ticking of the clock on the nightstand and the soft whirring of an electric fan. What a far cry this was from the debutante dinner dances at the Clambake Club in Newport, she thought.

As allies on a dangerous mission, she had come to know the real Jacques, the brave, compassionate person he was essentially, but she wanted to know more. Even though he had the same need for privacy she had—the need to conceal his insecurities behind an intricate screen of defense mechanisms—she was eager for some details to fill in the empty spaces.

"You've told me about your father," Jackie began, trying to sound interested in his family but not too inquisitive, "but you haven't said much about your mother other than she was a chambermaid during the Occupation. Does she still work?"

"No, not any longer." He hesitated, and Jackie could see that he was struggling to control his emotions and was reluctant to say more. Finally, in a soft voice filled with sadness, he said, "My mother died of breast cancer two years ago. She battled hard against it, but there was nothing anyone could do to beat it. She was only forty-six when she passed away."

"Oh, Jacques, I'm so sorry," Jackie exclaimed, a catch in her throat. She reached for his hand and held it, and a tear slid down her cheek. "That had to be so terrible for you, to lose her like that so young." The pity she felt was mixed with anger. Why had life treated him so cruelly? Orphaned in his twenties, the people he loved—Aurélie, his father, his mother—all taken from him before their time.

Jacques drew deeply on his cigarette and stared ahead, completely lost in his thoughts.

Jackie visualized a deep well of loneliness inside him. She tried to form a picture of his mother in her mind and wanted to learn more about her and get a sense of this woman she would have loved to meet but never would. "Did your mother always live in Paris?" she asked.

"No, she was foreign born."

Jackie paused, waiting for him to elaborate, but he didn't seem to want to, so she went on, "What about the rest of your family? Do they live here?"

He shook his head. "There is no rest of my family, no brothers or sisters. I was an only child."

Only child. Jacques said the words without self-pity, as a simple statement of fact, but Jackie thought, what a lonely sound that has. She couldn't imagine what life would have been like growing up without her kid sister, Lee, to play with when they were young and to trade secrets about boys with as they got older. And what would Merrywood be like without the laughter and music and noisy shouts of toddlers and teenagers romping around the house on those family occasions when all the stepchildren got together?

"That's sad, but your mother and you must have been very close," she said, trying to find something positive in growing up without siblings.

"We were. She left her own family behind when she came here, and I was all she had." He spoke of his mother with a kind of reverence Jackie found touching. "My mother was a beautiful woman, inside and out. I was the world to her. She worked day and night to keep a roof over our heads and food on the table after my father died and never complained, not even when she got sick. Whenever she got a big tip, she bought something for me with it—film for my camera, a new pair of shoes to replace the ones with holes in them—nothing for herself." He smiled as he recalled, "She was so proud when my book came out. I gave her the first copy off the press, and she kept it on the night table beside her bed. It was the first thing she saw every morning when she woke up and the last thing she saw every night before she went to sleep."

Jackie was touched. "How wonderful for you, Jacques, that you had a mother who was so devoted to you, but it must have been very hard for you to become the man of the house at seventeen." She looked at him and tried to envision him at that age, a helpmate to his work-worn mother, the two of them alone in the world struggling to survive poverty and the threat of annihilation in Nazi-occupied Paris. To think of him finding out that his beloved mother was terminally ill and to be the only one at her bedside when she died made Jackie fight back tears.

She stroked his face and planted little kisses on it. "I wondered where you learned how to be a woman's guardian angel. Now I know."

"Yes, it is because of my mother," he said, "that I've always had a tender place in my heart for women."

Jackie had to smile. "Well, there are a lot of women out there who should be very grateful to her."

The pensive look on his face made her wonder what he was thinking. Were there things he wanted to tell her, words he knew she wanted to hear but couldn't bring himself to say?

"You don't fall in love easily, do you?" she asked gently.

She wanted him to know she understood the fears he was

grappling with, but as soon as she said it, she wished she could take it back. It sounded too much as if she were fishing for an admission from him.

He took a long drag on his cigarette, exhaled a stream of smoke in what Jackie thought was a very Gallic fashion, and looked at her with hooded eyes. She wasn't sure if it was from the smoke or from something he was trying to hide. When he answered her, it was with an enigmatic statement that she wasn't particularly thrilled to hear.

"When you're a spy for the CIA," he said, "falling in love can be dangerous."

XVI

Scrumptious," Jackie said as they walked into Le Coquelicot des Abbesses, an all-day breakfast bistro and bakery near Montmartre. The enticing smell of warm bread and baking croissants permeated the bistro with the charming country-kitsch décor—a hodgepodge of fanciful curios and old paintings in various genres that reminded Jackie of a quaint diner back home.

They stood at the counter, staring at the mouthwatering display of breads, rolls, madeleines, financiers, macaroons, petit fours, and cookies, trying to decide what to have.

"Oh, let's have a regular breakfast," Jackie said when she looked at the menu and saw how cheap the prices were. She knew Jacques would want to treat, and she didn't want him to go overboard on his CIA expense account, assuming he had one, or dip too far into his own wallet if he didn't.

It was a lovely summer morning, bright and sunny but not yet overly warm, so they decided to eat outside at a sidewalk table.

"That looks luscious," Jackie exclaimed when the waiter brought them their fluffy lightly browned omelets and a basket overflowing with breads and rolls.

"Mmmmmm," she said, as she tasted her omelet stuffed

with perfectly cooked onion, green pepper, zucchini, chopped tomato, and mild, creamy chèvre cheese and bit into the bistro's signature poppy roll slathered with homemade strawberry comfiture. She would have been embarrassed at how hungrily she was digging into her food if she hadn't noticed that Jacques was devouring his just as avidly.

"Isn't it nice that we're finally getting a chance to indulge our appetites?" Jacques said, laughing. He rolled his eyes at her, and she laughed too. His playfulness was so endearing.

It wasn't until they were drinking their last cup of coffee that Charming Jacques bid adieu, and Secret Agent Jacques took over. "Now, you have a list of all the items you need to purchase, right?" he asked crisply.

"Really, Jacques, there aren't that many. I think I can remember without a list," she chided him. It annoyed her that he kept telling her how smart she was yet at times he spoke to her as if she were still in first grade, and not at the head of the class either.

He caught her look and apologized instantly. "I'm sorry, *ma cherie*. I didn't mean to insult you. I know you're good at this game—surprisingly good for being new at it—but as agents we always have to keep checking for possible error."

"That's okay, I understand," she said with a little wave of her hand. She felt placated by the apology, a hopeful sign that he would treat her with more respect. She hoped her mother would do the same when she returned to Merrywood. One thing was certain—she was coming back a very different person from when she left. There was something to be said for facing your own mortality—fighting for your life put some steel in your spine. From now on, whoever tried to push her around would be in for a surprise.

"All right then, let's get going," Jacques said, motioning to the waiter for the bill. "I'll drive you back to your hotel so you can freshen up beforehand. I contacted a friend of mine who's helped me in the past with my CIA activities. He'll be following you, just in case the assassin shows up again. His name is Arnaud, and he's an experienced bodyguard."

Jacques showed her a photo of Arnaud. Jackie thought there was something faintly disreputable about him—the aspect of a gunrunner, she imagined—but he was a strapping Burt Lancaster look-alike any woman would be glad to have as a bodyguard.

"Good, then I'll buy everything and bring it back to your apartment." Shopping, Jackie thought. Finally, she'd been given something she actually liked to do.

After her shower, Jackie stood in front of the full-length mirror in her hotel room and took a good look at herself. Except for a small red bruise on her neck—what her classmates at Miss Porter's called a hickey and wore proudly as a trophy of frenzied necking with a boyfriend—her body appeared to be in fine shape.

As terrifying as being chased by the assassin had been, the exercise had proven to be a serendipitous calorie-burner. All the wine and liqueur she'd consumed, along with the rich food, hadn't added an ounce. She wondered if the sexual excitement Jacques had aroused in her made her look more sophisticated now, like trace evidence at a crime scene. There *was* something different about her face when she brought it closer to the mirror. Her eyes had a lambent glow, as if smiling at some private satisfaction. Bedroom eyes, she'd heard them called, but for her, they were the eyes of a woman in love.

Peering into the mirror, Jackie noticed something else new

in her eyes—the sadder-but-wiser look of a survivor. It said that her youthful illusions of a charmed existence had succumbed to the sense that life was stitched with an indelible thread of catastrophe. Jacques had made her feel that she could come through whatever calamities lay ahead unbowed and with her humanity intact. You're right to believe in me, Jacques, she thought, I won't let you down. She squared her shoulders, nodded at her image in the mirror, and gave it Churchill's famous *V* sign with her fingers.

Jackie dressed quickly, throwing on slacks and a shirt and slipping into a pair of sandals. She snatched up her handbag and an overnight case, put on her oversized sunglasses, and left the hotel. Making sure that Arnaud was following her, she headed to the Tuileries. She needed to get there before the street vendor with the mechanical toy soldiers arrived and drew a crowd.

Good. The park bench where she had last sat with Jacques was empty, and she could see the vendor approaching with his suitcase full of toy soldiers. She sat down and waited for him to reach the spot where he would begin setting up his display. He was an elderly man with a grizzled face and rumpled clothes who walked slowly, weighed down by the heavy suitcase.

Jackie rose from the bench and walked over to the vendor when she saw him come to a halt and put his suitcase down. She stopped him before he could open it.

"*Bonjour, monsieur, j'aime vos soldats, et je veux les acheter,*" she told him sweetly, informing him that she liked his soldiers and wanted to buy them.

"*Combien?*" How many, he wanted to know.

"*Tout.*"

"*Tout? Deux cents?*" His eyebrows shot up. He was clearly incredulous that she wanted all two hundred soldiers in his suitcase.

"Tout," she repeated firmly. *"Quel est le prix?"*

The man scratched his head, thinking about the price he should charge her. After a long pause, he said, *"Dix-sept mille."* He looked at Jackie questioningly, obviously expecting her to bargain with him.

"Très bon," she said agreeably, smiling at his look of pleased surprise. She reached into her handbag, counted out the money, and handed it to him. Seventeen thousand francs came to less than fifty dollars, so she figured it was a bargain.

The man took the money in his gnarled hand and thanked her profusely. *"Merci beaucoup, mademoiselle, merci beaucoup."*

He helped her unload the toy soldiers into her overnight case and was still calling out *"merci beaucoup"* after her when she left, her bodyguard following her at a discreet distance.

Next stop, Galeries Lafayette on boulevard Haussmann. Jackie's favorite department store in the world was not only a fashion trendsetter but also a superb example of Belle Epoque architecture. She never failed to feel a ripple of excitement when she walked into the huge store modeled after a Middle Eastern bazaar and gazed up at the glorious Neo-Byzantine glass dome, a historical monument that looked like a mammoth crystal umbrella.

At the Ladies Corner, Jackie resisted browsing through the glamorous designer collections and cutting-edge fashions and went immediately to the sportswear section. All she needed was a pair of black stretch pants and a black turtleneck. She picked these up quickly without needing to try them on—despite her five-foot, nine-inch height, a small size was all she ever wore—and proceeded to the shoe department.

Here the temptation was impossible to resist. She ogled the couture footwear by Balenciaga, Prada, Gucci, and Salvatore Ferragamo, admiring the seductive, elegant styles before forcing herself over to a table where a collection of mundane athletic shoes hung out like poor relatives. Reluctantly, she picked up a sample black crepe-soled shoe, something she never would have worn in her other life, brought it over to a salesgirl, and asked to try on a pair.

Still holding the dumpy sample crepe-soled shoe in her hand, she sat down on a chair, dropped her bulging overnight case and packages on the floor in front of her, and waited for the salesgirl to return. But instead of the salesgirl, who seemed to be taking her time, it was Princess Nureen she saw walking toward her in a chic designer dress and a pair of Gucci shoes similar to the ones Jackie had just been admiring covetously. Not again! What was it about her itinerary in the whole city of Paris, she wondered, that always seemed to put her on a collision course with the same people—the assassin, that oddball middle-aged British couple, and now Princess Nureen.

"Miss Bouvier, what a pleasant surprise meeting you here," Princess Nureen greeted her. That certainly had a familiar ring. Wasn't that what the British woman said when she and her fiancé "bumped into" Jackie and Jacques at the Jeu de Paume after "bumping into" them at Longchamp? She knew the assassin was deliberately following her and suspected the same of the British couple. Now she was beginning to think that Princess Nureen was tailing her too.

"Yes, it's a lovely surprise," Jackie said, going along with the pretense. Princess Nureen was not someone whose bluff she wanted to call. She let her eyes travel down to the princess's feet. "Those Guccis you have on are stunning. Did you get them here?"

"Yes, I just bought them and liked them so much I decided to wear them home." She nodded at the crepe-soled number in Jackie's hand. "Planning to do some hiking?"

Jackie blushed. It was embarrassing to be caught buying such cloddish footwear, like a Dior model waltzing down the runway at the fashion show in orthopedic shoes. She had to come up with some excuse fast. "Unfortunately, I'm not used to the cobblestone streets here, and I twisted my ankle a bit the other day. Nothing serious, but the doctor said I should wear something like this until it heals." Jackie looked anxiously at the entrance to the stockroom. Where in God's name was that salesgirl?

Princess Nureen took advantage of the fact that they were alone and sat down next to Jackie. She lowered her voice and spoke urgently. "Miss Bouvier, I need to know if you've had any success tracking down the information Mikhail Petrov wanted to give you. It's of the utmost importance to my country. You have my word that if you divulge that information to me, I would never reveal you as a source."

Jackie felt a stab of sympathy for the princess. The fervor in her voice and the look of grave concern in her eyes made her wonder what it had to be like for a twenty-year-old woman— an orphan at that—to carry the weight of a whole country's fate on her shoulders. But she had nothing to tell her. Nor would she compromise the trust that Dulles had invested in her as a CIA agent.

"I'm sorry, Princess Nureen," Jackie said, "but I haven't uncovered anything. I wish I could help you, but I can't."

The princess had just grabbed her arm insistently when the salesgirl came rushing toward them, waving a box of shoes. "I'm so sorry for taking so long," she apologized abjectly. "I had to search high and low for these. But you're lucky. They're the last pair left in your size."

My dear, you don't know how lucky I am, Jackie thought.

*   *   *

"Why do we need to make a microdot in the first place?" Jackie asked, watching Jacques go about setting up his equipment on the cleared-off kitchen table. She'd come back to his apartment with all her purchases as this whirlwind day wound down to its end before the even bigger night to come.

Jacques was giving her a quick tutorial on how to make a microdot, and as usual, Jackie found herself half charmed and half intimidated by his attempt to teach her any new skill in the photographic or espionage trade.

"We need to make one," he answered over his shoulder, "because we want to replace the microdot on the painting with one of our own so no one thinks the painting was tampered with."

"And why do we need to make two microdots?"

"In case we lose one, we still have another. That's just basic tradecraft."

At last, Jacques had a photographic stand set up on the kitchen table and his Nikon on a tripod at the opposite end. While he adjusted the camera's focal plane setting, he turned to Jackie and pointed to a pile of newspapers. "You see that? Go through it and pick out an article you think worthy of being copied."

She sifted through the pile of newspapers, opening them at random, before finally setting her sights on one article in particular. She picked up a nearby pair of scissors, cut out the article, and handed it to Jacques, who, without looking at its contents, mounted it on the stand. He walked over to the Nikon, looked through the viewfinder, and hit the cable release attached to the camera to take a photograph of the newspaper article on the stand.

"Now you will see how I reduce the image," he said as though he were a stage conjurer giving up the secret of one of his most prized illusions.

He turned out all the lights in the apartment except for a single red lightbulb over the sink. He removed the negative from the camera, developed it, then, lights back on, mounted it on the stand. With the stand now illuminated by a light from behind, he took a photograph of the negative.

As he worked, he said, "I've made a negative of a negative, which is a positive. So whoever finds this microdot will have no trouble reading what's on it."

After he had developed the second negative, he picked up a knife and cut out the miniaturized newspaper article, now reduced to the size of a typewritten period. He repeated this process a second time, then took both microdots and put them in a glassine envelope, the kind used to hold rare stamps.

"And that's how you make a microdot," Jacques exclaimed in his best trade-school-instructor voice. He took a deep breath and looked around the room. "I guess we should get ready to go."

Jackie excused herself to use the bathroom. When she came back, Jacques was removing the Nikon and photographic stand from the kitchen table. Jackie picked up her overnight case, but Jacques took it from her. "No, no, let me have that," he said. "You've been lugging it around long enough."

Ever the gentleman, she thought, even at a time like this.

He rummaged around in a closet, pulled out a battered old rucksack, and filled it with the toy soldiers from her overnight case, two flashlights he'd had the foresight to purchase that afternoon, and the other things they would need for the night ahead. Then he changed into his cat-burglar ensemble for the evening—a black turtleneck, black pants, and black crepe-soled shoes—a mirror image of Jackie's. Over this, he slipped on a lightweight summer sports jacket so his outfit wouldn't scream out BURGLAR! in neon letters to every passing security guard. Into a jacket pocket, he placed Henri's lucky toolkit. He checked out his appearance in a nearby mirror before turning to Jackie.

"I'm ready. Are you?"

She found her mouth suddenly dry. Unable to speak, she nodded wordlessly.

"Good, let's go," he said, heaving the rucksack over his shoulder.

On the way out the door, he stopped as a thought occurred to him. "I didn't even look. What was it I photographed for the microdot?"

Jackie smiled mischievously. "A recipe for Coquilles Saint Jacques."

He made a sour face.

"What's the matter?" she asked, disconcerted by his look of repugnance.

He closed the apartment door and locked it, turned to her, and said, "I hate Coquilles Saint Jacques."

Jacques thought it would be a good idea for them to get off the street, just in case the assassin was lurking nearby. He had an uncanny instinct for tracking them down so they decided to spend what was left of the day at the Cinémathèque Française, André Bazin's temple of film culture.

Inside the darkened theater, although keyed up about the coming evening, they tried to relax and enjoy a double feature by René Clair. The first one, Jackie had to admit, was a complete delight. *Le Million* was a musical romantic comedy about two friends vying to get their hands on a lottery ticket worth millions.

The movie began with a long, long tracking shot of the rooftops of Paris that reminded Jackie of the late Petrov's planned route of escape from the garret where she'd found his body. As the two friends in the movie chased the slippery ticket from one location to the next, Jackie was put in mind of the wild-goose chase Petrov had sent her and Jacques on. In the movie's most bravura scene, two lovers, a painter and a beautiful dancer on the outs with each other, find themselves backstage at a theater, trapped behind a piece of scenery on stage as the curtain rises on a musical production. The two musical actors sing a love duet that mirrors the way the two hidden lovers are secretly feeling about each other, and the song brings about their rapprochement to the joy of the enraptured movie audience. For an hour and a half, Jackie was transported to a place where the events of the last few days and the fateful night to come were far, far away.

Between features, Jackie excused herself to go to the ladies' room. In the lobby of the *cinémathèque*, amid the posters for Jean Vigo's *L'atalante* and Marcel Pagnol's *Fanny*, one for Hitchcock's *Stage Fright* caught her eye, and she smiled when she saw it. There was that movie again—the one that had led to her discovery on the ride to Longchamp that Jacques, like her, was a Hitchcock fan. As she stared at the poster, remembering, a voice broke into her thoughts.

"You like Hitchcock?"

Jackie looked up and found herself face to face with a young man in an army uniform. Its awkward fit made him look like a French version of Beetle Bailey from the comic strip. He was slightly built and had the restless energy of a dynamo and the most intense eyes she'd ever felt fixed on her.

"Yes, I do like Hitchcock," she said to the young soldier.

"I thought so. You look like you could be the heroine of one of his movies."

"Thank you. How kind of you to say." If you only knew, she thought.

"You're American, yes?"

"How could you tell?" Jackie asked in surprise.

"I watch a lot of American movies. John Ford. Howard Hawks. Buster Keaton," he said, naming three prominent Hollywood film directors.

He pointed to the *Stage Fright* poster. "Do you know the secret of Hitchcock's success?" he asked her, as though questioning a student in a film class he was teaching.

That was easy. "He's the master of suspense," she answered quickly.

"Ah, yes, but what makes him such a master?" he probed.

This was getting difficult. She shrugged.

"He teaches us something about the people we're familiar with—the lover who shares our bed or the co-worker we see every day."

Jackie was intrigued. "And what is that?"

"How unknowable they are. We can't be sure who they really are or what they'll do next, and that's what keeps us on the edge of our seats." He seemed proud of himself for having taught her this Hitchcockian lesson on human unpredictability.

It was worth pondering, but not now. Jacques would be wondering what happened to her.

"That's very interesting, *soldat*. I'll keep it in mind," she said, hoping to sound appreciative despite having to leave. She held out her hand to him. "Now if you'll excuse me, Corporal—"

"Private," corrected the young soldier as he took her hand, "Private François Truffaut, at your service."

"Au revoir, Private Truffaut. Thank you for the film lesson." Eager to return to Jacques, she turned away from the poster and the young soldier, went to the ladies' room, and then once again sought temporary refuge in the cocoon of the darkened theater.

XVII

Jackie tried stretching out her legs without making a sound, but it wasn't easy. For almost four hours now, she'd been perched on top of this toilet in the darkened ladies' room at the Jeu de Paume, and her legs were beginning to fall asleep. She moved them around to banish the pins-and-needles feeling and hoped that the next time she looked at her watch it would be midnight: the witching hour and time for this show to begin. She turned on the pen flashlight provided by Henri and pointed it at her wristwatch. It was a quarter to midnight. Fifteen minutes to go. And then she would be reunited with Jacques, and they could retrieve the microdot and get the hell out of here. The museum's vast silence was really beginning to wear on her nerves.

Midnight was when the cleaning crew would be finished and escorted out by the museum's security staff. It would be another half hour, according to the timetable given to them by Henri, before the guards made their rounds. They were probably in the guardroom, playing cards as a way to pass the time and get through their long night shift. Jackie knew how they felt. She had been here in the ladies' room since shortly before the museum closed at eight p.m. This was the only night the museum was open late, hence perfect for the plans that she and Jacques had made with Henri.

Twenty minutes before closing time, they had entered the museum and headed for the men's and ladies' rooms opposite each other on the first floor. Jackie found an OUT OF ORDER sign in the ladies' room utility closet and hung it on one of the stall doors. Then she entered the stall, locked herself inside, and remained hidden from view with her legs drawn up until the charwomen had finished cleaning the museum from top to bottom. She knew that in the men's room, Jacques was doing the exact same thing. She thought about his long legs, those marvelously muscular legs she loved to watch walking toward her, and wondered if he was as uncomfortable as she was.

When Jackie figured that enough time had elapsed, she once again flicked on the flashlight and looked at her wristwatch: midnight on the dot. The cleaning crew was through for the night. She climbed down from the toilet, unbolted the stall door, and walked across the ladies' room, stretching her legs as she went to make sure that the circulation had fully returned.

Very slowly and stealthily, Jackie opened the ladies' room door and peeked out. The corridor seemed to be empty. So far, so good. She stepped into the corridor. She was wearing her burglar ensemble and that was it. No handbag, no ID, nothing that could identify her in any way in case of her arrest. Her pants had two pockets in front: One was for the pen flashlight she held in her hand. The other nestled the lipstick tube she would use to transport the microdot from the painting.

And there Jacques was, emerging from the men's room and carrying the rucksack over his shoulder. He met her in the middle of the corridor and gave her a quick hug to boost her confidence. It worked. Feeling his body pressed manfully against hers was all the reassurance she needed that they could bring off this wickedly audacious heist.

Jacques put one finger up to his lips to indicate that silence was the order of the day—or rather, night—then hiked his thumb upward to say that they should climb the stairs to the top floor of the museum. Their crepe-soled shoes made not a sound, not a squeak, as they quickly went up the stairs, showing that Henri really had thought of everything when it came to planning this job.

When they reached the second floor, Jacques led Jackie into the first gallery they came to. Like all the others, it was filled with the impressionist overflow of the Louvre. A visitor could easily become distracted as the eye wandered from one glorious painting to the next. Landscapes and still lifes. Riots of color. Bold brushstrokes and intricate pointillist dots. But they were too fixated on their plans to pay much attention to the masterpieces that surrounded them. Instead, they each reached into the rucksack, lying open on the floor in the center of the room, and pulled out a handful of the mechanical toy soldiers. They wound them up, then stood them upright on the floor in the middle of the room, pointed them toward the walls, and watched as they began their slow but steady march toward the periphery of the gallery.

Earlier in the day, Jackie and Jacques had done some experimenting beforehand. They knew approximately how many minutes they had before these completely wound-up toys would reach the gallery walls and set off the motion detectors calibrated to emit a warning sound at the slightest trembling of air molecules in their vicinity. The alarm system for the motion detectors would then be set off in the guardroom, bringing the security staff running to whichever gallery had sounded the warning.

Jacques picked up the rucksack and they moved on to the next gallery, where they repeated the process: Open the rucksack. Take out a handful of toy soldiers. Wind them up. Place them on the floor so they would march outward from the center of the room to the far walls of the gallery.

In the third gallery, Jacques motioned that he and Jackie should split up to save time. He dumped a platoon's worth of toy soldiers on the floor for Jackie to wind up, then headed for the gallery across the corridor, where he would wind up an equal number of toy soldiers. By now, Jackie figured out that she and Jacques had wound up a full company of toy soldiers, and she hoped that this invasion of the museum would be a successful campaign on the order of D-day and not end in complete disaster like Dunkirk.

When they finished covering the second floor, they moved down the stairs to the first. Jackie looked at her watch. It was ten past midnight. They had twenty minutes until the guards would make their next rounds and interrupt them. If things worked out as planned, it would be the guards who were interrupted first. Before going down the stairs, Jackie had looked in the first gallery they had entered and noted that the toy soldiers had marched approximately halfway from the center of the room to the far walls. She and Jacques would have to hurry if they wanted to be in place when the first soldiers began setting off the motion detectors.

On the first floor, Jacques dropped the rucksack in the *Olympia* gallery. Jackie looked into the rucksack; there were only a few toy soldiers left. Impulsively, she reached in, removed one of them, and put it in her pocket—a souvenir of this evening. She knew it wasn't a good idea, but she couldn't help herself. Years from now, when the events of this evening grew dim, she wanted some kind of memento mori to remind herself that, yes, she had done something this recklessly illegal in the last days of her impetuous youth.

From Henri's lucky toolkit, Jacques removed a pair of tweezers and handed them to Jackie. She went over to the painting, careful not to lean in too close and set off the motion detector prematurely. Jacques took his flashlight out of the rucksack and held it at the ready. The ruckus would start any second now, as soon as the first wind-up toy soldier marched within range of the closest motion detector.

Even though she was expecting it, the sound of the first alarm going off still startled Jackie. The earsplitting metallic ring of a second and third motion detector followed, confirming that there was, indeed, an intruder in that gallery. Soon, motion detectors in other galleries on the second floor began to go off, not at evenly spaced intervals, but still within a respectable margin of error. Jackie heard frantic footsteps on the stairwell from the basement as the security staff raced up to the second floor to find out what was causing all the commotion.

The guards on the second floor could be heard shouting to one another, "Bien. Bien," as they checked out each gallery in turn, and calling out in astonishment as they saw what had been the source of the disturbances in the galleries. A practical joke, they would hopefully assume. If everything went according to Henri's plan, the guards, lulled into a false sense of security, would delay investigating the alarms in the *Olympia* gallery and give Jackie and Jacques time to escape.

Jacques pointed to his watch. What happened next had to be conducted within a two-minute window of opportunity: this was the time Henri figured it would take for the guards to get around to checking the ruckus in the *Olympia* gallery. Jacques waited until the sweeping secondhand of his watch hit the number 12 and motioned for Jackie to go. She saw what transpired next with strobelike flashes of clarity.

Jacques waved his arms to set off the motion detector and not allow it to surprise them with its sudden harsh clanging.

Jacques picked up the flashlight and pointed it at Manet's *Olympia*, illuminating the microdot-cum–beauty mark on her neck.

(In later years, Jackie would recall the events of these few moments with enhanced lucidity and remember that Jacques, the non-professional thief, held the flashlight with hands so still that one would have thought he did this kind of thing for a living.)

Jackie moved in with the tweezers, delicately plucking the microdot from the painting.

(Jackie would also later recall her hands shaking so profoundly that she had to make several stabs at the painting with the tweezers until she finally managed to grab hold of the tiny microdot.)

Jacques put the end of the flashlight in his mouth and used it to illuminate the empty glassine envelope he held in his hand.

Jackie used the tweezers to deposit the microdot from the painting in the glassine envelope.

Jacques produced the other glassine envelope, the one containing the two fake microdots, and handed it to her.

Jackie picked out one of the fake microdots with the tweezers and affixed it to the painting right where the real microdot had previously been installed. Then she put the envelope with the remaining fake microdot in one pants pocket.

Jackie turned back to Jacques, who handed the glassine envelope with the real microdot in it to her. She rolled up the envelope and carefully placed it inside her lipstick tube, which she then returned to her other pants pocket. (This was an excellent cover since what self-respecting Parisian woman leaves the house without her lipstick?)

Jacques packed up the rucksack, heaved it over his shoulder, and motioned to Jackie that the time had come to quit the gallery and, indeed, the museum. No use overstaying their welcome and hanging around for the security guards to find them.

They headed down the corridor to the main entrance door—and freedom. As they approached, Jackie fully expected someone to pop out of one of the intervening galleries and stop them. But no one did.

When they got to the main entrance, Jacques unbolted the door easily. As planned, he would go through the door, close it, make sure the coast was clear, and return to Jackie. They were still thirty seconds shy of the two-minute window of time Henri had estimated for them to take the microdot and make their getaway.

Jacques opened the door and disappeared through it. Acutely aware of her role of dutiful partner-in-crime, Jackie waited for Jacques to return. But as the seconds ticked by and he failed to reappear, she began to grow concerned. She was all set to defy Jacques's orders and go through the door herself—in fact, she had her hand on the door handle and was about to pull it—when she felt someone else's hand on her shoulder and a voice behind her said, "And what do you think you're doing?" Numbly, bereft of Jacques and hope, she turned slowly around to face a perverse and inescapable turn of fate.

The guard taking Jackie to the basement of the museum looked young and moved in a tentative manner, making her think that he was new to the job and had gotten lucky in spotting her.

As he walked her from the main entrance to the guardroom, Jackie made two resolutions in her mind. Number one: she would refuse to say anything that would implicate herself or Jacques. Or Henri either, for that matter. How she would do that she had no idea, but she was certain she would come up with something by the time they reached the guardroom. And two: she would do something to disguise her appearance so that she could go unrecognized and unidentifiable just in case she managed to get away later on. She had almost nothing to work with but when she put her hand in her pants pocket and felt the glassine envelope with the fake microdot in it, she knew exactly what she was going to do.

By the time they arrived at the guardroom, the microdot was out of the glassine envelope and was once again doing double duty as a beauty mark, not on Manet's *Olympia* this time, but on Jackie's face. She had wet her finger with her saliva and firmly pressed the microdot to her chin in such a prominent place that it seized the attention of every male eye in the room.

The guardroom stank of cigarette smoke and male bodies coming to the end of a shift and badly in need of a shower, making her feel that she was invading the men's locker room at the New York Racquet Club. She saw that the guards were in a state of extreme agitation at having had such havoc wreaked on their quiet evening by this unlikely intruder. Stay calm, Jackie kept saying to herself. Give Jacques the chance to rescue her.

Stall.

One guard looked older than the others, and Jackie assumed that he was in charge of the shift. She was right, because he pushed out a chair for her to sit in. But before he could ask any questions, another guard, this one with a cruel cast to his features, interposed himself and thrust his face right into Jackie's.

"Well, what do we have here," he asked with a sneer, "a creep-mouse? Did you fall into one of our traps, little creep-mouse? Is that how we captured you?"

The older guard shoved aside the nasty guard and took over for him with a more gentle tone in his voice. "You are in a lot of trouble, young lady. You know that, don't you?"

Jackie's mouth was too dry to speak. Instead, all she could do was look at the older guard with a quizzical expression on her face. The other guards gathered in a loose circle around her to hear what she was going to say.

The nasty guard interposed himself once more. "You heard him," he badgered her rudely. "He asked you if you know how much trouble you're in."

Now it was the young guard's turn to speak up. "Maybe she's deaf. Maybe that's why she's not answering."

Deaf, Jackie thought to herself. That was it. That was the answer. That was the role she would play.

She put an uncomprehending look on her face and shook her head.

"Are you deaf?" the older guard asked her.

She cupped an ear with her hand, hoping that was the universal sign for, "I can't hear a word you're saying."

"You see," the young guard said, "she's deaf. I told you so."

The nasty guard was adamant. "I don't believe it. I don't believe her." He leaned closer to Jackie and practically screamed into her ear, "Can you hear me?"

It took a monumental act of willpower to keep from flinching. If she wasn't deaf before, she was certain her eardrums were damaged now.

"That's enough, Bernard," the older guard said as he shouldered the nasty guard aside once again. "Call the police *préfecture*. Let them know that there's been a break-in here," he ordered the younger guard.

With a sinking feeling, Jackie watched the young guard go over to a red phone—one with no rotary dial—mounted on the wall. He picked it up and spoke into it. "This is the Jeu de Paume. We've had a break-in and have a suspect in custody. Please send someone at once."

He hung up the phone, and Jackie dreaded the next phone call that she knew was soon going to be made. A transatlantic one. She could just imagine her mother picking up the receiver at the other end in Virginia and hearing, "Hello, Mrs. Auchincloss. This is the Paris police. It's about your daughter, Mademoiselle Jacqueline Lee Bouvier. She's been arrested breaking into the Jeu de Paume museum. Yes, you heard me right: the Jeu de Paume. Can you please come here at once? To Paris? Her bail has been set at two million francs."

"What do we do now?" the young guard asked.

"We wait," the older guard told him.

"We question her," the nasty guard responded.

"We wait," repeated the older guard, ignoring the look of disappointment on the nasty one's face.

But after a few minutes of silence, the nasty guard decided to flout instructions and turned to Jackie, grilling her like an overzealous prosecutor. "What were you doing here in the museum?"

When she cupped her hand over her ear again and shrugged uncomprehendingly, he snatched a piece of paper, jotted the question down, and shoved it in front of her face.

Jackie had a flash of inspiration and began to mime pushing a broom. Her impromptu mute show made her feel like that new Paris performance sensation, Marcel Marceau.

"She says she's a member of the cleaning crew," the younger guard said brightly.

"Impossible," said the older guard, "I know every charwoman we've hired."

"Maybe she's new," the young guard hypothesized.

"Maybe she infiltrated the cleaning crew to steal one of our masterpieces," chimed in the nasty guard.

The older guard waved his hand dismissively. "All this

speculation is useless. It will be up to the police to find out what she was doing here."

A shrill ringing sound pierced the air and almost made Jackie jump out of her skin. A good thing she didn't, because that would have blown her cover as a deaf charwoman.

The older guard spoke into an intercom on his desk connected to the main entrance to the museum. "Who is it?"

"It's the police," responded the voice through the intercom's tinny speaker. "Please let us in."

The older guard motioned to the younger one, who charged out of the room and up the stairs to open the door for the police. He returned a minute later with a single gendarme in tow. Jackie couldn't even bring herself to look at this new arrival.

"I think you broke a world's record for getting here," the older guard remarked. It sounded like faint praise.

"I was in the neighborhood, on my patrol. I was told to come at once. So, as you can see, here I am."

"Where's Jean-Pierre?" asked the nasty guard suspiciously.

"Qui?"

"Jean-Pierre, the regular beat cop. Why isn't he on duty?"

"I'm afraid to say that he took sick at the last minute. I was asked to take his place."

"I think you're interrogating the wrong person," the older guard said to the nasty guard, hoping this would get him to *fermer la bouche.*

"Is this the suspect?" the gendarme asked, turning his attention to Jackie for the first time.

"Yes, this is her," answered the older guard.

Jackie could feel the gendarme giving her a cursory once-over. "She doesn't appear too dangerous," he said while she kept her eyes glued on the guard in front of her chair.

"We did a preliminary check, and so far nothing seems to

be missing. And none of the paintings appear to have been defaced," reported the older guard.

"Thank God for that," interjected the gendarme. He turned to Jackie. "Okay, mademoiselle, time to go."

Jackie didn't respond, trying to keep up the hearing-impaired charade for as long as possible.

"She's deaf," the young guard said to the gendarme.

"Or she's acting deaf," said the nasty guard.

"Well, we'll find that out when we get her to the *préfecture*," the gendarme said as he put his arm around Jackie and brought her to her feet. "We have ways of making our prisoners talk."

And with that ominous warning, the gendarme slipped handcuffs on Jackie, locked them, and pocketed the key. "Good night, gentlemen," he said, addressing the guards. "Your directors will have a transcript of our interrogation of this suspect in the morning. *À bientôt.*"

Then he took Jackie by the arm and led her out of the guardroom.

Once outside the museum and down the sidewalk leading away from it, the gendarme turned to Jackie and said, "Well, young lady, do you have anything to say for yourself?"

Jackie allowed herself to look into the familiar face of the gendarme. "Yes, Jacques," she said, giving him a grateful kiss on the cheek. "You can arrest me any time."

XVIII

Leave it to Henri when he planned the job, Jackie thought, to pick the right place for Jacques to park his Renault. The space was far enough away from the museum so it wouldn't raise any suspicions but close enough so they could get away quickly and, according to Jacques, with three different escape routes in case the police were called.

Going at a normal rate of speed that would not draw the attention of any police car cruising by, Jacques took the route that would lead them back to Henri's workshop in the abandoned building near the Montmarte Steps. He wanted to return Henri's lucky toolkit and let him know that they were all right and that the museum job had gone off as he had planned, except for the business where Jackie had been caught by the gendarme. At the first stoplight they came to, Jacques divested himself of the gendarme uniform he'd put on over his all-black cat burglar outfit and tossed it in the backseat, where he'd already stashed his rucksack and sports jacket.

"Where did that gendarme uniform come from?" Jackie couldn't wait to find out after her heartbeat had returned to its normal tempo.

"When I came back to the museum for you, I peeked in through the main entrance and saw you being led away by the guard," Jacques explained. "I knew I had to do something, but what? I looked around and, by good chance, saw a gendarme on his nightly patrol of the area. He was approaching his call box. I crouched in the bushes and waited for him to call in. As I suspected he would, he picked up the phone, received word of the museum intruder, and said that he would be there at once. But he never got the chance. Do you know why?"

"Because you knocked him out and took his uniform."

"Correct," he said magnanimously. "I caught him by surprise and knocked him out with one lucky punch, trussed him up with his own belt, and stashed his unconscious body in the same bushes I'd been hiding in. Fortunately, he and I were almost the same size, another piece of good luck." He laughed gleefully. "I'd love to see his face when he wakes up and finds himself in public in his underwear."

Jackie shook her head. "You have the guts of a cat burglar."

"But not the constitution for that career, I'm afraid."

"Me either."

"Really? I thought you handled yourself rather well with those guards. You gave nothing away and disguised yourself enough so they won't be able to identify you. That was quick thinking on your part. If I were you, though, I'd wait a while before venturing back to the Jeu de Paume."

Jackie beamed at his praise. She felt she'd really earned it that night.

"I hope that's the fake microdot you're wearing on your face."

"Of course it is, after all the trouble we went through to get the real one," she said huffily. "What do you take me for?"

"I'd be happy to show you, but I'm driving," he said with a sidelong suggestive glance.

She laughed, back in a good mood, still keyed up but feeling proud of herself.

They rode quietly the rest of the way, letting their adrenaline subside. When they reached the abandoned building that housed Henri's workshop, they parked nearby and went through the rusted doorway. As they crossed the courtyard, Jacques saw something that caused him to freeze in place.

"Jacques, what is it?" Jackie asked, alarmed.

She watched him approach something in the middle of the courtyard. It looked like a piece of contemporary sculpture that had incongruously been placed there. But as Jackie followed Jacques and got closer to it, she saw that it wasn't a piece of sculpture at all. It was Henri's wheelchair, and it had been twisted all out of shape until it barely resembled itself. Suddenly, she felt as though all the muscles in her legs had been replaced by floppy rubber bands, and she had a difficult time getting them to move.

"Jacques," she called out weakly, "what happened?"

"I don't know, but I don't like the looks of this. Stay here," he ordered as he continued across the courtyard. "I'm going upstairs to check on Henri."

"Wait, I'm going with you."

"No, you're not. You'll be safer here."

"Jacques, I'm not staying here by myself."

He shook his head with a bemused look as if to say, what am I going to do with this stubborn woman? "Okay." He shrugged. "You can come along. But try and stay out of my way."

They entered the building, and she followed him up the narrow, twisty stairs. It reminded her of returning with Jacques to the garret where she'd discovered Petrov dead, not knowing what they would find there and being surprised by the party going on in the place. With a dread Jackie could feel deep in her bones, she wondered what they would find when they arrived at Henri's workshop.

As before, the door was ajar. But this time, the open doorway hinted at some sinister implication. Jacques entered the room first, then waved in Jackie after he'd scoped out the space, lit as Jackie remembered it—poorly, with vast pools of shadow.

"Henri," Jacques called over the grinding sound of the window fan as he took out his penlight and used it to illuminate the shadows. No, Henri was not hiding anywhere inside the room.

"Where do you think he is?" Jackie asked, her voice quivering with fear.

"I don't know, but he was definitely here."

"How can you tell?"

"Look at his workbench." He aimed the penlight in that direction. Jackie could see a soldering iron on the counter, hissing from still being plugged in. Next to it was a ball of solder and a pile of cast-lead vehicles. Obviously, Henri had been interrupted while making repairs. But there didn't appear to be any signs that a struggle had taken place here.

"Then where is he?"

Jacques shook his head. "I have no idea."

He continued to search the room and call out Henri's name. But there was no response.

The air in the room was fetid with the smell of malevolence. It made Jackie want to escape and drew her eyes to the entranceway and the Grand Guignol chorus line of marionettes hanging from the ceiling there. For some reason, they seemed to be more crowded than usual. As though drawn magnetically to them, Jackie found herself walking toward the creepily lifelike marionette collection, counting them individually as she went. When she got to eight, she prepared to stop, but realized that she still had one more to go. Funny, she could have sworn that she had counted eight marionettes the first time she was here.

And then she knew why there was a ninth marionette.

"Jacques," Jackie cried out in a strangled voice that could barely be heard.

In a second, he was by her side. "Jackie, what is it?"

Her vocal cords frozen, Jackie could only look up and point. Jacques followed with his eyes and a look of pure horror passed over his features.

"Mon Dieu," he exclaimed. "Help me get him down."

The marionettes were all held up by ropes tied to a common batten set in the wall. Jacques found the one holding up the ninth "marionette" and slashed through it with a knife that he scooped up from Henri's workbench. Pocketing the knife, he quickly returned to Jackie's side, where the two of them helped lower the body to the floor.

They both leaned over it and realized with sinking hearts that the crippled toy repairman and Resistance hero who had taught them so much in the past day was dead. A deep stab wound in his chest was like a signature telegraphing to them the identity of the person responsible for this terrible deed.

Jackie got to her feet but doubled over, wracked by waves of nausea at the sight of Henri's face, a waxy death mask, immovable eyes staring out sightlessly and mouth twisted into a hideous howl of pain. Her legs buckled, and she clutched at the doorjamb to steady herself.

"Oh, God, oh, God, poor Henri," she sobbed brokenly. She shook her head in denial of so unthinkable an act. "Why... why?" was all she could say.

"After Arnaud left, that sick *bâtarde* went back on the hunt for you," Jacques said, "but you weren't here when he came. So he took it out on Henri and left him like a calling card."

Such vicious savagery was incomprehensible to Jackie. Like the girl at the Gare de Lyon, poor Henri was another of the assassin's innocent victims, murdered while he was searching for Jackie. "I can't believe he came here and killed Henri like this," she said, "just because he wasn't me. It's inhuman. How could anyone be so cruel?"

"He's gone," Jacques said when he finished exploring Henri's inert body for any signs of life. He clenched his fists. "The next time we meet, there will be one more murder. And it will be his." His face was twisted with anger, and there was a quaver in his voice that Jackie had never heard before.

Jackie had a sudden thought that pierced her outrage, sent shivers through her, and paralyzed her with dread. "Jacques, what if he's still here…"

"We'd have seen him by now."

"And what about Henri?"

"We'll call the police once we're back on the street and away from here. We'll do it anonymously."

Jacques slowly rose to his feet and embraced a trembling Jackie, holding on to her until her shaking subsided. Then he looked down at Henri's body. "Good-bye, *mon brave*," he said simply. "I will miss you. *Bon chance.*"

Jacques held Jackie's arm and propelled her toward the door. The sooner they were out of this place, the better. But as they reached the door, they found two figures blocking their way.

I knew it! Jackie thought. Her suspicions had been justified. The two people preventing them from entering the hallway were the middle-aged Englishman and his fiancée. Although it was no surprise that the couple had been tailing Jacques and her, showing up here was still an anomaly. After the opera, Longchamp, and the Jeu de Paume, this place was a little off the beaten path for them. What were they doing here? And what was it about their appearance that was different, something she couldn't quite put her finger on? Then Jackie realized what it was: the Englishman and his fiancée both held guns in their hands. And these guns were pointed right at her and Jacques.

What? A holdup by these two? Absurd, Jackie thought. She found it too incongruous for words and had no other choice but to backpedal with Jacques into the workshop. The English couple followed them, keeping their guns trained on their targets, and closed the door firmly behind them.

"Well, it looks like we meet again," the Englishman said too cheerily.

"What do you want with us?" asked Jacques.

"Just a conversation. Thought we'd have a bit of the old chin-wag."

"And you need guns for that?" Jackie asked sarcastically.

"For this kind of conversation—unfortunately, yes."

For the first time, the English couple took note of Henri's body.

"What happened to him?"

"I thought you could tell us," Jacques said.

"Haven't the foggiest, old stick."

Jackie shook her head. All this politeness under these circumstances was beginning to grate on her nerves. And there was something about the English couple that didn't jibe with her memory of them. They were no longer bickering with each other. They now seemed to be operating as two parts of a well-oiled machine. Their previous bouts of premarital disaffection, she now realized, were the same sort of cover that she had employed when posing as a dance journalist for her initial meeting with Petrov.

As though reading her mind, Jacques asked the couple, "Who are you, MI6?"

"High marks, old stick," said the Englishman in a fake, hearty tone of voice. "You go right to the head of the class."

"English was never my favorite subject," Jacques said drily.

"Well, then, this is the chance to redeem yourself, isn't it? Become the teacher's pet, so to speak."

As annoyed as Jackie was with all this bantering, at least it explained one thing—why wherever she and Jacques went, the English couple always seemed to be there too. They had deliberately targeted her in the hopes that she would eventually lead them to whatever it was Petrov had left behind. All they had to do was wait for Jackie to get her hands on it, then take it from her, which explained what they were doing here at Henri's workshop.

"What do you want from us?" Jacques repeated, apparently tired of the forced bantering too.

"The microdot," the Englishman responded simply.

"What microdot?" Jacques asked blandly.

"You know very well what microdot. The one from Manet's *Olympia*. The one you took when you broke into the Jeu de Paume this evening. The one this man"—he indicated Henri's body with a wave of the gun—"helped you to take. The one you even now must have on your person. That microdot."

Jackie understood that the English couple had allowed them to do the hard work of finding and retrieving the microdot, then simply moved in with guns drawn to take what they had waited so patiently to collect. In a way, you had to admire them for their cold-blooded calculation.

"I don't know what you're talking about," answered Jacques, in a voice even blander than before.

The Englishman sighed and shrugged his shoulders. "We can either do this the easy way or the hard way. The easy way:

you give us the microdot, and we vanish from your lives forever. The hard way: there will probably be some blood, sweat, and tears involved, as Winnie used to tell us. And let me assure you, old stick, those won't be coming from us." He waved his gun to include his partner in that threat.

Jackie didn't like this new English couple. She much preferred the old one, even if they had been somewhat trying. She wondered if the Englishman, with his voluble nature, was the mouthpiece here and the no-nonsense fiancée the muscle half of the team.

Jacques, meanwhile, was doing his own evaluation of the couple, Jackie could tell, and this reassured her that he, too, was trying to figure out a way for them to escape this potentially deadly encounter with the two English agents.

"Now, the first thing I want you to do is turn out your pockets. There," the Englishman said, indicating the workbench. Jackie and Jacques walked over to it and begin piling their personal possessions on the counter. Jacques removed the knife he had taken from the workbench, his car keys, and his penlight. Jackie placed her penlight, lipstick, and the toy wind-up soldier on the scarred surface, but when she felt the empty glassine envelope in her pocket, she remembered—the fake microdot was still stuck on her chin. That could be their deliverance, although, in the relative darkness of the workshop, it was unlikely that the two English spies would readily make it out.

The Englishman went through their possessions while his partner held her gun on Jackie and Jacques. Jackie breathed a silent sigh of relief when the Englishman picked up the lipstick tube and put it down just as quickly after a cursory examination. She guessed that he chalked it up to another foible of female vanity. When he was finished his inspection, the Englishman turned to Jacques and said, "So where is it?"

"We don't have it."

"Okay, then, you are forcing me to do things the hard way." He paused, then said, any trace of lightheartedness gone from his voice, "I'm now going to have my partner frisk you. Please don't make any unnecessary moves or I will be forced to shoot you."

As the English spy and his partner turned all their attention to Jacques, Jackie looked around for something that she could use as a weapon or diversion. She was learning from Jacques. You didn't need a knife or a gun to protect yourself. Often, some ordinary object lying around might do. She took a rapid inventory of the workshop, but saw nothing that could trump a gun, let alone two.

While the English agents continued to pat down Jacques, who wasn't making it easy, Jackie's eyes alighted on the soldering iron at the far end of the workbench. Henri had not unplugged it, and it was still sizzling away precariously next to a pile of sketches. Maybe there was something she could do with that, something inventive along the lines of the elaborate Rube Goldberg devices from the Sunday funny pages. As surreptitiously as she could, Jackie picked up the toy soldier she'd kept as a souvenir, wound it up fully, and sent it marching across the workbench counter. Fortunately, the noise of the fan covered any sound made by *le soldat*. She hoped that the countertop's scarred surface wouldn't prevent the wind-up toy from making its way straight and true to its destination.

"Is it my turn yet?" Jackie asked the English couple, hoping to distract them and keep their attention away from the workbench.

"It would be my pleasure to pat you down," said the Englishman smoothly, "but my partner will do the job so as not to offend your delicate sensibilities."

The fiancée checked to see if Jackie was concealing any weapons on her person. Her lingering touch made Jackie shiver with repulsion and think that, on balance, she might have been better off with the Englishman frisking her.

Finishing up, the woman shook her head no and the Englishman motioned with his gun for Jackie and Jacques to take seats in the chairs nearest them. While the woman held her gun on Jacques, the Englishman approached Jackie. On the way, though, he stopped off at the workbench, where he picked up the knife Jacques had deposited there. Jackie held her breath, fearing that he would spot the toy soldier marching steadfastly toward its destination, but the English spy was too intent on his new weapon to take note of anything else on the countertop.

"Do you know how sharp this is?" he asked Jackie nonchalantly, holding the knife in front of her after returning his gun to the quickdraw holster hidden by his jacket.

Jackie shook her head no.

"Should we find out?"

Jackie knew this was a rhetorical question and that the Englishman would do whatever he wanted regardless of how she answered.

"Unless you tell me where the microdot is, I'm going to have no choice but to test out this knife on your partner," the Englishman said to Jacques.

Oh, no, Jackie thought. But then she recalled what Jacques had told her about wresting information from someone. Threatening to torture a loved one, he'd said, was better than direct torture, since it was always easier to deal with one's own pain than with the imagined pain of that other person.

"I already told you," Jacques said, testing the Englishman's bluff, "we don't have it."

For the first time, the English spy looked closely at Jackie's face. "There's something different about you, but I can't put my finger on it." How typical for a man, Jackie couldn't help thinking; men were always so oblivious to any cosmetic changes a woman made, usually to attract one of them. He continued to stare. "Ah, I think I know what it is."

As Jackie looked on with fear pooling like a corrosive acid in her belly, the Englishman reached forward with the knife until she could feel its point poke lightly into her chin. But to her relief, he inserted it no deeper, just deftly twirled the blade around, then held it up to inspect it. "And what do we have here?" he asked, carefully removing something tiny and black from the point of the blade.

The Englishman's accomplice looked at the microdot, shrugged, and said, "How do we know it's the real thing? That was almost too easy."

"You're right," he said, and turned his attention back to Jacques.

"Well, is it?"

"Is it what?" Jacques asked in a tired voice, as though he were bored with the English spy's verbal joust. Meanwhile, Jackie glanced over to the workbench and saw that the toy wind-up soldier had reached its destination across the counter.

"Is it the correct microdot? Tell me the truth or this one"— he pointed the knife at Jackie—"will suffer the consequences."

"Yes, it's the real thing," Jacques said in a tone that indicated total capitulation.

"Then why don't I believe you?" asked the Englishman.

"Because you're a spy and you have a natural tendency not to believe anyone."

"Very good. I think you have captured the essence of my nature. That is why I regret what is going to happen next." He took the knife and placed it directly under Jackie's eye. She tried to shrink away from him, but the Englishman held her firmly in his embrace, preventing her from making any movement at all.

But before he could make good on his threat, the workbench was suddenly illuminated in a bright glow that spread to the rest of the room, and there was an accompanying WHOOMP! as the pile of sketches on the workbench went up in flames. Jackie had aimed the toy soldier on a collision course with the soldering iron. As she had hoped, the toy soldier's impact with it had been enough to cause the precariously placed soldering iron to roll into the pile of papers on the counter, its hot iron tip igniting them instantly. And there were enough flammable solvents and glues around to feed the flames, which were growing larger and brighter by the moment.

Instinctively, the Englishman released his hold on Jackie and went to put out the blaze. If the fire department was called, it could be a disaster for all of them.

In a flash, Jackie was off the chair and rounding the workbench to snag her lipstick tube and Jacques's car keys. Then she was out the door, not looking back, but hoping that Jacques was right behind her. He was, and she could hear him also clattering down the narrow, twisting stairway.

They went out of the building, through the courtyard, and out the rusted doorway without stopping. As they approached the Renault, Jackie threw Jacques his keys. Then they were inside the vehicle, and Jacques was turning the key in the ignition. But for some reason, the car refused to start.

"What's the matter?" Jackie asked urgently.

"I don't know. Damned engine won't turn over. I can't imagine why not."

The English spy, unfortunately, supplied the answer. He

stood calmly outside the car on the driver's side, his partner
on the other. In one hand, he held his familiar-looking gun. In
the other, he held the Renault's distributor cap. Without it, the
car wouldn't start. It seemed that no matter what they did, the
Englishman, like a chess grandmaster, was always several key
moves ahead of them. Jacques looked at the distributor cap and
turned to Jackie with a defeated expression on his face. He patted her on the knee and said, "Good try, *ma cherie*."

She watched as he got out of the car, shoulders slumping,
and at the Englishman's direction, lifted up the Renault's hood
to replace the distributor cap. When he was finished, the Englishman motioned for Jackie to get in the backseat along with
his partner. Jackie was forced to push aside the gendarme's
uniform and Jacques's rucksack and sports jacket he'd stashed
there earlier.

The Englishman sat in the passenger seat as Jacques once
again took his place behind the wheel. With the gun pointed
at him, the Englishman said, "Drive. Orly. Now. We're booked
on the first flight out of this godforsaken city."

As they drove away, Jackie turned and looked through the
rear window. She could see the top of the abandoned building
glowing red in the night and knew that the fire from the workshop was spreading—and quickly. She hoped that someone
was around to call the fire department.

Then she thought about poor Henri. His body would be
incinerated, immolated on a pyre like a Viking warrior, but the
fire was also going to incinerate all the evidence in the workshop, making his murder a difficult one for the police to solve.

As Jacques drove through the sparse late-night traffic on the
way to the airport, the Englishman turned to him and said,

"No funny business. I expect us to arrive at Orly in one piece, and I still expect to be told where the microdot is. And I think I know." He turned back to look at Jackie. "There were two items removed from the workbench when you and your partner left so quickly: a pair of keys and your lipstick tube. I could understand why you would want to take the keys, for your getaway. But the lipstick? Not even the vainest woman I know would stop to retrieve her lipstick if she felt her life was really in danger. Ergo, that lipstick tube must contain something of value. And what's the most valuable thing you could have in your possession small enough to be concealed in a lipstick tube? That microdot. And so, Miss Bouvier, if you could hand your lipstick to my confederate, I would be most grateful."

"You're a regular Sherlock Holmes, aren't you?" Jackie said, stalling for time.

"I'm more of a Bulldog Drummond type," the Englishman said coolly, "but thanks just the same for the compliment."

In the backseat, the fiancée prodded Jackie with her gun. "The lipstick, if you please."

Jackie did nothing. It was left to Jacques to have the final word. "Give it to them, Jackie. *Le jeu est fini.*"

Left with no other choice, Jackie reluctantly reached into her pants pocket, removed the lipstick tube, and handed it to the woman. The woman put down her gun momentarily, on the side away from Jackie, opened the lipstick tube, and withdrew the glassine envelope. Inside, the microdot could plainly be seen. "I have it," she said triumphantly.

"You see, that wasn't so hard, was it?" the Englishman said to Jacques, a gloating tone in his voice.

Jacques said nothing and kept his eyes on the road. When he passed the signpost for the airport, he eased into the right-hand lane. He followed the Englishman's directions and drove through the airport to the BOAC Departure Terminal, pulled up to the curb, and waited silently as the two English spies took their leave. To Jackie's surprise, they reverted back to their previous cover roles.

"Thanks, my good man," said the English agent to Jacques, clapping him on the shoulder in a display of complete affability. "Damned decent of you to bring us here."

Jacques remained steadfastly close-mouthed. In the backseat, the woman turned to Jackie. "It was such a pleasure to meet you, dear. If you're ever in London, please do look us up."

"Yes, do," reiterated the Englishman.

Jackie was thunderstruck. It was as if the events of the past hour had never happened. Like Jacques, she remained silent, not trusting herself to speak.

Numbly, she watched the two English agents take their leave. Arm in arm, they strolled across the sidewalk and entered the BOAC Departure Terminal, nattering away like any other normal English middle-aged couple returning home after an exhilarating vacation in Paris. No one would ever guess these two were ruthless spies who had played a rough game and just walked away with the prize.

In a daze, Jackie walked around the Renault and got in the passenger seat beside Jacques. Instead of driving away, though, he just sat there, a blank expression on his face. It was left to Jackie to fill the emotional vacuum with some kind of expression of frustration and loss: "I can't believe it. After all that trouble we went to, following that trail of clues, to the opera, to Longchamp, the Jeu de Paume, taking the microdot, losing Henri to the assassin, and then those two wind up taking Petrov's gift. It's not fair."

Jackie fully expected Jacques to respond by telling her that life isn't fair. But instead of the kind of pallid bromide people normally say in such circumstances, Jacques burst out laughing uproariously.

"You want to tell me what's so funny?" she asked, mystified. "I didn't know there was anything to laugh at."

Jacques stopped guffawing long enough to say, "Oh, there's always something to laugh at. Even in the worst circumstances. And believe me, you're talking to one who speaks from experience."

"So then, what are you laughing at?" she asked with mounting frustration.

As an answer, he reached into the backseat, dragged his sports jacket up front, and withdrew a small object from one of its pockets. As Jackie looked on in open-mouthed wonder, he held up a glassine envelope displaying a black microdot inside. "What's that?" Jackie asked in honest confusion.

"It's the microdot, the one we removed from Manet's *Olympia*."

"But how...? What...? What did those English spies take?"

"Well," Jacques whispered in an unnecessarily conspiratorial tone of voice, "I don't want to give away any secrets. But let's just say that I hope neither of them is allergic to *coquilles*."

Jackie was perplexed. "But how?"

"It's very simple. Back at my apartment, when you excused yourself, I made a third copy of the fake microdot—just in case we needed one. And at the museum, while you were getting the microdot out of the painting, it occurred to me that if we got caught in the act, and you had the real microdot, you would be the prime culprit. So I quickly switched envelopes, took the one with the real microdot and gave you the one with the fake. That's why you really had both fake microdots in your possession. *Comprends-tu?*"

Jackie nodded, moved that, as usual, he'd been looking out

for her. Still puzzled, she asked, "But how did you get the real one into your jacket pocket?"

"I was near the car when I spotted the gendarme on night patrol, so I put it there for safekeeping before I went back to the museum to get you."

Jackie began laughing hard too as she realized how lucky she was that Jacques was an even shrewder chess grandmaster than the English spy.

But then came the nagging thought, how long can my luck last?

XIX

D o you know what this is?" Jacques asked. He and Jackie were staring at the image of the microdot's contents cast onto a blank wall in his apartment from a slide projector. After carefully removing the microdot from its glassine envelope, he had placed it between two sheets of acetate, clamped them together, then set the encased microdot under the illuminated stage of the projector with the lens facing the wall. He sounded concerned.

Jackie stared at the image, trying to decipher it. "The minutes of some kind of meeting?" she guessed.

"Right. Between a representative of the Soviet Republic and a representative of the Pakistani government. These are the minutes of a secret meeting held last month."

"What was the meeting about?"

"It looks to me like Russia and Pakistan are making plans to carve up Balazistan so that each country takes approximately half of it. That way, both countries get a sort of buffer zone. Unfortunately, if they do this, Balazistan will cease to exist as a nation."

Jackie looked shocked. "Can they do that?"

"Countries can do anything they want. If history has taught us anything, it's that."

"But what will happen to the people of Balazistan?"

"Well, half of them will be under Soviet rule, and the other half will be under Pakistani rule."

"And they'll have no say in the matter."

"None whatsoever."

Now Jackie understood. "No wonder the princess wanted to get her hands on Petrov's gift," she said, sickened at the thought of ordinary people having their lives so drastically and unfairly changed. It was unthinkable that some high-handed foreign service types could partition a country as though it were nothing more than a birthday cake to be divided up among a group of greedy, lip-smacking children.

"Yes," Jacques agreed, "she must have somehow gotten wind of the meeting. She'll be turning twenty-one soon, the minimum age required to be head of state in Balazistan. She's returning to her country now, and this document will persuade her people that she needs to be in power and guide their fate."

Jackie nodded, but she was still puzzled. "But what's America's interest in this?"

He pointed to a name at the bottom of the minutes. "This is the name of the British agent who acted as middleman between the U.S.S.R and Pakistan. H.A.R. Philby. Harold Adrian Russell Philby. He's more commonly known as Kim Philby."

Jackie's look brightened. "I heard Mr. Dulles mention his name during our briefing. He works for MI6, but might have been mixed up in the defection of those other two English agents."

"High marks, Jackie," said Jacques. "Burgess and Maclean, that's who you're referring to." Jacques shook his head, as though in admiration of the audacity of this immoral scheme. "It all makes so much sense, Kim Philby acting as middleman. His father, St. John Philby, was a famous Arabist and explorer. There were rumors that he secretly worked for MI6. And during World War I, he was T.E. Lawrence's paymaster."

"T.E. who?" asked Jackie.

"You might know him better as Lawrence of Arabia. He led the Revolt in the Desert. He was made famous by your American journalist Lowell Thomas."

"But what does he have to do with this?"

"Nothing, except that Kim Philby has Middle Eastern nation-building as part of his family heritage. If he went rogue to broker this deal, the CIA definitely needs to know about this, since he's MI6's liaison to the agency."

"You think he's a double agent?"

"Yes, a mole. A deep-cover penetration agent. Probably recruited decades ago. People have been trying to prove it for years. But he's so slippery that he's always managed to squirm out of any accusations made against him. The information on this microdot could be all the proof Mother needs to have him arrested."

"Your mother?" Jackie asked in confusion. "I thought she passed away two years ago."

"No, sorry—Mother. That's the code name for James Jesus Angleton. He's the head of counterespionage at the CIA. The agency's chief spycatcher. He'll need to see what's on this microdot as quickly as possible."

"But I was told to stay away from the embassy no matter what," Jackie protested.

"This information is a real game changer. I'm going to call my embassy contact and tell him that I want you brought in at once. He'll make sure you're booked on the first available flight out."

Jackie's heart took a big thump. *The first available flight out? Had the time to leave him come so soon?*

Jacques was focused on the task at hand. He removed the acetate sheets from the stage of the slide projector, extracted the microdot, and placed it back in the glassine envelope. "Here, take this," he said, pressing the envelope on Jackie, "and go back to your hotel. Pack. And stay there until I call. I'll give you a location and time for a rendezvous. But don't leave your room under any circumstances. Not even if the place is on fire. I'll call you as soon as possible. Got that?"

His manner was so commanding that all she could do was nod.

Back in her hotel room, Jackie did as Jacques ordered and packed as quickly as possible. But the phone failed to ring. After this long night filled with dangerous adventures, breathless escapes, and deadly confrontations, she lay down on her bed as the first rays of the new day were starting to become visible through the window. Despite her valiant effort to stay awake, she sank into a dreamless slumber that lasted the next several hours. Finally, the insistent ringing of the room's telephone roused her from her sleep. She was relieved to hear Jacques's reassuring voice at the other end of the line.

"Okay, I made the call and everything's set. We're on for nine o'clock tonight. Meet me in front of Notre-Dame, the west entrance, between the bell towers. I'll be there with my embassy contact. He'll walk you in, and you'll be home and safe in your own bed by tomorrow night. How does that sound?"

Jackie couldn't answer. On the one hand, she was glad that her Paris sojourn would finally be over, and she wouldn't stumble upon any more brutally murdered dead bodies or have to worry about spies, counterspies, and assassins who popped up with ceaseless regularity. On the other hand, she was deeply sad because it would also mean saying good-bye to Jacques. And that she was not yet prepared to do.

If it weren't for the obvious dangers, she would like if her time in Paris could be stretched out to...well, to infinity, but that was obviously a pipe dream that would go up in smoke when exposed to the uncompromising light of day. Her only consolation—and it really wasn't one—was that Jacques would be as sad as she was that their time together had to end.

At eight o'clock, she took her bags, went down to the lobby, and checked out of the hotel. She left her luggage with the concierge to be picked up by the embassy later and put on the same plane that would fly her back home to the United States. As she waited for her bill to be prepared, she looked out and saw two Vespa motor scooters pull up in front of the hotel. Both riders wore the gray livery of a messenger service. One of them entered the lobby carrying a long white flower box tied with a red ribbon and waited to present it to the concierge.

Jackie paid her bill and walked out of the hotel. She had one hour before meeting Jacques, but she thought it best to allow time for delays—an elementary bit of spy business she had picked up from him. As she stepped outside, she caught sight of a familiar-looking figure in a white summer suit lurking in the shadows under the viaduct. She knew the assassin would be stalking her—wasn't he always?—so she'd arranged for Arnaud to pick her up in a taxi in front of the hotel and take her to meet Jacques and his embassy contact.

But the cab was nowhere in sight. Had she and Arnaud gotten their signals mixed? Well, she was on her way home and she'd be damned if she was going to let her nemesis stop her now. She didn't know when or if Arnaud would show up, and she didn't want to wait. So instead, Jackie did the next best thing. She went back inside and approached the messenger at the concierge desk as he was being handed a receipt for his flowers.

"Excuse me," she said.

The messenger turned inquiringly to her, and his face lit up as soon as she addressed him. "Yes, mademoiselle?"

"I'm late to meet someone, and I was wondering if you'd do me a favor and take me to Notre-Dame."

"I'm sorry, mademoiselle, I would love to be of service to you, but"—he looked at his watch—"I am due back at my office."

"What if I said there was fifty francs in it for you?" The messenger's scrunched eyebrows told Jackie that he was considering her offer seriously.

Finally, he said, "Okay, I'll do it, but on one more condition."

Jackie waited for it.

"A kiss."

"Excuse me?"

"A kiss. At the end of the ride, you give me a kiss."

Jackie had to smile. Only a true Frenchman would propose a conjoining of lips as a last condition to a business deal.

"Okay. A kiss it is."

"And the fifty francs."

"Yes, the fifty francs too."

"Good, then let's go."

"You go outside and start your motor scooter. I'll be there as soon as you do."

Jackie could tell that the messenger found this request unusual, but he weighed it against the fifty francs and the kiss, and that kept the scale tipped in her favor.

She watched as the messenger went outside, hopped on his Vespa, and kick-started the engine. As soon as she heard its roar, she was out the door and sitting behind him, pillion-style, as it was called. She put her feet behind his on the running boards, placed her arms around his waist, and with a burst of speed, they were off.

The messenger waved good-bye to his fellow messenger idling by his Vespa as they roared away, passing the assassin still skulking in the shadows of the viaduct, the look of lethal hatred he leveled in Jackie's direction illuminated by the streetlights. As he got smaller and smaller in the distance, Jackie hoped that look was the last she would ever see of him.

The messenger seemed to know where he was going and drove swiftly but nevertheless cautiously through the rush-hour traffic. In any other city, most commuters would be home by now. But in Paris, where businessmen took two- and three-hour lunches in the middle of the day (giving them more time to spend with their mistresses), seven o'clock was considered rush hour.

Jackie ducked her head behind the messenger's to keep the wind out of her eyes and her hair from getting completely mussed up. Luckily, she was wearing a wrap-around, silk paisley-print shirt that stayed snugly inside the belted waistband of her tapered slacks instead of billowing out like a parachute. And there was no danger of her toe-loop sandals—she'd wisely put them on in anticipation of doing some strolling around Notre-Dame—slipping off her feet, causing her to arrive shoeless at the cathedral.

The messenger transitioned neatly from boulevard Diderot to avenue Daumesnil. On her right, Jackie could see the Opéra Bastille rising above the more humble structures surrounding it. She heard an echo of the Vespa's engine and turned to look behind her. To her shock, there was a Vespa following them, but at a distance. And it wasn't the rider in the same messenger livery. It was an oversized person who looked as ridiculous on the motor scooter as a hippo would have, and his appearance might have been completely comic had Jackie not also known how deadly he could be. She could only hope that the assassin had acquired the Vespa by scaring off the rider with his knife instead of stabbing him with it, adding assault with a deadly weapon and possibly even murder to grand theft auto.

"Can you please speed it up?" Jackie said to the messenger, shouting to be heard over the Vespa's noisy slipstream of air. "I think there's someone following us."

The messenger looked back and saw the other motor scooter minus his friend. "Who's that?"

"Someone who's after me."

"If he's after you, then he's after me too." The messenger pushed the hand throttle forward, and Jackie could feel the Vespa accelerate *vitement*. She clenched her hands tighter around his waist to keep from falling off. And just in case speed wasn't enough, the messenger began veering right and left around the slower-moving traffic, hoping to put more distance between them and the other Vespa that was steadily creeping up behind them.

After several blocks of this quicksilver riding, Jackie looked back and was disappointed to see that they hadn't lost the Vespa-riding assassin. In fact, he seemed to be gaining on them. Jackie didn't know how he did it, but that assassin certainly had a knack for staying glued to her tail. Something was going to have to be done about it, she told herself—and fast.

Facing front, she saw a road sign coming up and knew what they had to do.

"At the next intersection, turn right," she shouted forward to the driver.

"What, are you crazy?" he asked, seeing the oncoming road sign too and figuring out what her intention was.

"It's our only hope of losing him."

"I won't do it!"

Jackie fished in her purse, pulled out a fifty-franc note, and passed it forward to the driver.

"What about now?"

The messenger looked at the money, then shrugged. "All right, I'll do it. But I also want two kisses."

"Don't push your luck."

The messenger knew when he was defeated and pocketed the additional cash. As the next street came up, he made an unexpected right turn—unexpected because this was a one-way street and he was entering it the wrong way. Fortunately, the cars were stopped for the light at the intersection so it was relatively easy for him to thread his way through the lanes of vehicles without much actual danger.

Unfortunately, they were only halfway down the long, seemingly unending street when the light changed, and the traffic started up again. Now the messenger and Jackie found themselves hurtling right into the path of oncoming cars. The frantic drivers were all flashing their lights, beeping their horns, and cursing out their windows to dissuade the reckless pair from their current lunatic course of action.

The messenger ignored them and continued to ram his way through the traffic, a suicide move for certain. He zigged, and he zagged, and he tempted fate with many a narrow miss, skillfully avoiding the careening vehicles that confronted them left, right, and center. He was such a good driver, with such a light touch on the throttle and brake, that he managed to maneuver in and out and around the cars that were headed right toward them and get into the proper lane for the next turn.

All Jackie could do was hold on as tenaciously as a barnacle and say a prayer that they would arrive at Notre-Dame in one piece. She promised herself that once there, she would go inside the cathedral and light a candle. In the meantime, she felt that she was getting more than her one hundred francs' worth for this ride.

But for the messenger, the ultimate challenge was coming up—a lumbering bus headed on a death trajectory right for them, its bulk so large that it seemed to take up both sides of the roadway. And the space on either side looked too narrow for the Vespa to pass.

"Hold tight to me," the messenger ordered Jackie, who didn't need to be told. She clutched his stomach in an iron grip as the messenger motioned for the bus driver to move his vehicle to the right, then pointed his scooter to the left. The incredulous driver didn't seem to understand what the messenger was asking for. But at the last possible second, it dawned on him and, not wanting to end up scraping the Vespa or its passengers off his bus's radiator grill, he yanked hard on the steering wheel and pulled the vehicle as far over to the right as possible. Luckily, there was just enough room for the Vespa to squeeze by the bus on the left without the messenger and Jackie being bounced into the gutter.

Jackie looked behind her. As expected, the second Vespa had performed the same bold maneuver of bucking oncoming traffic, but by now, the assassin was tailing far behind. As the messenger made a left turn onto the next street, the rue de Bercy—this time going in the same direction as the traffic—Jackie could see that the trailing Vespa was far enough behind to allow them to give the assassin the slip. It looked like her bold one-way-street gambit had worked!

Off to her left, Jackie could see the imposing twin bell towers of Notre-Dame. The messenger maneuvered his Vespa in their direction, taking the Quai de L'Hôtel de Ville along the Seine, and then going across the nearest bridge, the Pont d'Arcole, onto the Île de la Cité, the site of the city's earliest settlement and home of the most famous cathedral in Paris.

With a squeal of brakes, the messenger pulled up in front of the square, the gateway to this most formidable of Parisian architectural marvels. Jackie momentarily recalled the first time that she had gazed mouth-agape at this thirteenth-century wonder with its awe-inspiring, innovative flying buttresses. It was a timeless shrine dedicated not just to God but also to man's genius in building a towering ladder of stone and marble to reach the stratosphere of esthetic and spiritual creativity. Now this most enduring of Parisian monuments was undergoing repair and restoration work on the west-facing façade, and the twin bell towers of Notre-Dame were sheathed in steel scaffolding.

Jackie looked at her watch. Thanks to the messenger's speed in getting here, spurred on by the menacing potential of the Vespa-riding assassin, she was early for her rendezvous with Jacques and his embassy contact.

The square was not crowded at this time of night, and she and the messenger had the space almost to themselves. The workmen had stopped their restoration for the day, and the scaffolding stood empty. Jackie hopped off the Vespa, tried to pat her hair back in place, and turned to the messenger.

"Thank you," Jackie said simply, "I think you saved my life."

"It was nothing," he said with charming modesty. "I better go back to the hotel and make sure my friend is all right."

"Yes, I hope he is."

The messenger just stood there, his feet planted firmly on either side of his motor scooter. Jackie knew what he was waiting for. She leaned in and was all prepared to give him a kiss on the cheek when he craftily moved his face around so that his lips lightly rubbed up against hers. She let her lips linger there for the merest second, then pulled back slowly, leaving him with a faint, lopsided smile on his face. Without a word, he drove off.

Jackie watched him go. Now she had the square in front of the cathedral all to herself. She looked around. Jacques and his embassy contact were still nowhere in sight. From the far edge of the square, she heard the sound of the Vespa engine and assumed that it was the messenger, coming back to claim the second kiss he had asked for on the ride over. But to her shock, it was the Vespa with the overweight assassin astride it.

Oh, no, not him, not again, he just won't stop! Why can't I ever be free of him? a voice inside her wailed. She was beside herself that once again he had managed to stay on her tail despite her best efforts to lose him. The man was indefatigable, hell-bent on showing up over and over again to renew his deadly purpose, and she was terrified that her luck in eluding him might finally have run out.

She looked around for someplace to hide, but the square proved inhospitable to concealment or camouflage. There had to be somewhere that she could go to be safe from him. And wherever it was, she had to find it immediately, before he reached this part of the square and spotted her.

Jackie saw that she was standing next to the scaffolding covering the south bell tower. The ladder to the first stage of the scaffolding had already been withdrawn to prevent anybody with theft or mischief in mind from having access to the structure, but Jackie judged that the framework of the scaffolding could easily be scaled. So, before the assassin could spot her, Jackie began climbing up the trestles that held the scaffolding in place until she reached the first stage. There, she hid behind a large piece of construction equipment, some kind of huge bucket obviously made to haul heavy objects.

Jackie listened as the Vespa engine suddenly cut out. Then she heard footsteps echoing across the empty square and assumed that the assassin was attempting to search for her. After a few minutes of this clopping sound, she heard the Vespa motor start up again and grow softer and softer as the assassin apparently rode it out of the square. She decided to give it five minutes before coming down. By then, she hoped, Jacques would be here with his embassy contact, and she could put an end to this nightmare.

After waiting the additional time, Jackie lowered the ladder through the trapdoor set into the wood-planked deck of this stage and began to climb down. As she did, she caught sight of a figure crossing the square. It was the assassin, and he held his shoes in his hand and was moving stealthily toward the cathedral. He had obviously ridden off to trick her into thinking he had gone, then doubled back, shoes in hand so as not to make any noise, in the hope of catching her by surprise.

And it looked like his plan had worked, although not perfectly, because now Jackie reversed direction and started back up the ladder to the first stage. When she was safely there, she flexed her muscles and pulled the ladder back up, preventing the assassin from using it. But he doggedly began to climb the trestles that held the scaffolding together. Once again, Jackie was forced to see that despite his bulk, the assassin was preternaturally agile.

Up was the only direction she could take now. She spotted an open-cage elevator and got in. She pushed the button for the top stage and counted the seconds until she reached the top. But when she got there, she found there was no place to hide. The elevator began its descent, and Jackie felt stranded and utterly exposed.

Searching for cover, she saw that a wooden railing ran

around this top stage on three sides, the fourth being open to give workers access to the bell tower roof, which itself was bordered by a low stone balustrade. Jackie stepped over this balustrade as she made her way from the top of the scaffolding to the roof of the bell tower, almost 230 feet above the square. On the way, she spotted a toolbox that someone had left lying around, opened it, and, with no time left to lose, took out the first tool she came across—a claw hammer.

From the bell tower roof, she was able to look out over the entire Île de la Cité, the Seine flowing blackly between the Droite and Gauche banks, and the City of Light spread out beneath her in all its sparkling, bejeweled splendor. She could also dimly make out the gargoyles that made the eaves of the North Tower their home. But their appearance, frightening under most conditions, failed to faze her now, since she had an even more frightening apparition to face—one made not of stone, but of flesh that seemed almost as adamantine and invincible.

She could hear the elevator returning. She crouched down, trying to make herself as small as possible, and stayed still, hoping that she would be too indistinct a target for the assassin to see. But her hopes were dashed when he emerged from the elevator and almost immediately caught sight of her cowering on the roof of the adjacent bell tower.

As he crossed over to the bell tower roof, Jackie rose, thinking it better to meet her destiny on her feet instead of her knees. She stepped back until she was at the rear of the roof, her back to the cathedral's gardens and flying buttresses to the east. She brandished the hammer and warned, "I have a weapon."

Unfazed, the assassin continued to advance. When he was close enough, Jackie said, "I'm not afraid to use it. I'm warning you." That did nothing to deter the assassin, who kept right on coming. Left with no other choice, Jackie threw the hammer in his direction, but he managed to fend it off with one well-padded forearm.

As he got closer, he reached inside his jacket and removed his knife. Jackie's dread enfolded her like a shroud, black and impenetrable. Her eyes filled with tears at the thought that hers would be such an unfinished life, literally cut short far too soon. It was so unfair that this assassin, with his malignant stare and overstuffed body, was going to be the last thing she ever saw in this world.

With nothing left to lose, she decided to try another approach and stall for time. "If this is going to be the end," she called out to him, "there's one thing I want to know." There was no answer from the assassin, but she decided to forge ahead anyhow. "How come you want me dead?"

She was surprised when the assassin actually began to speak, in that same Middle Eastern–accented English he had used when he was pretending to be the Pakistani ambassador at the Windsor estate party. She had been expecting him to speak with a Slavic accent. "There are two rules in my profession," he said, as though speaking to a child. "Rule Number One: never leave any job half-done. And Rule Number Two: never leave any witnesses. You, I'm sorry to say, fall under Rule Number Two."

He kept on coming, like a monster in a nightmare from which she couldn't rouse herself. Jackie decided to ask another question, still hoping to stave off the inevitable for as long as possible. "But how did you always seem to know where I was going to be?"

"I bugged your friend's apartment. And his car."

She stared at him quizzically, wondering how insects were able to communicate her whereabouts to him.

"A bug is an electronic listening device," he explained. "The people I work with were using them to monitor you and your friend so I could follow you and put an end to you. I am sorry to say that your amateur status, your unpredictability, rendered you particularly difficult to neutralize."

"Neutralize?" The word sounded curiously clinical, but Jackie knew what this was a euphemism for—and that neutralization was the fate she was about to meet.

But she kept on talking, buying a few more minutes to stay alive. "You killed that woman in the Gare de Lyon, thinking she was me, didn't you?" she asked.

He nodded.

"But how did you know I was going there, and what locker I had the key to? My friend and I were standing outside when we decided to go to the station, and we took a taxi, so you couldn't have"—she almost wrinkled her nose when she said it—"'bugged' anything."

"You'd be surprised what you can do with opera glasses, an ability to read lips, and a fast car," he said with a smirk, drawing ever nearer.

When the distance between them closed to mere inches and Jackie was left with nowhere to go, the assassin grabbed her. With the same maneuver he'd used on Jacques in the catacomb, he spun Jackie around and prepared to slice open her windpipe from behind. She tried to say a quick prayer to ease her way into heaven when—

Emmanuel began to toll the hour!

Jackie, the art history student, knew all about Emmanuel. She knew that the giant bell in the South Tower was the oldest in Notre-Dame. She knew that it weighed thirteen metric tons. And she knew that it had been recast in 1631 when, according to legend, women threw their gold jewelry into the molten metal to give the bell its pure F-sharp tone. Emmanuel was rung hourly and on special occasions, such as the day Paris was liberated from its German conquerors, telling its citizens that they were once again free. What she didn't know, until now, was how ear-piercingly loud the bell would sound from here on top of the bell tower itself, like the sharp and shattering roar of a cannon.

As her hands went up to cover her ears, Jackie could feel the bell reverberating eight times in her head. Then she heard what sounded like ocean waves crashing into the shore as her eardrums reacted to the abuse. But she welcomed the tolling, because the first clang of Emmanuel was so shocking that it momentarily caused the assassin to loosen his grip on her. This was the break she'd been praying for. She wriggled out of his grasp and fled across the roof of the South Tower and back on to the top stage of the scaffolding. And the peal of the carillon had an added boon. The assassin, in instinctively putting his hands to his ears, had accidentally dropped his knife, which skittered to the edge of the roof and then over, hitting the ground far below.

Jackie made a dash for the elevator, but was yanked back by the assassin, who had quickly caught up with her. The tug caused her to overbalance and careen toward the wooden railing. Jackie and the assassin began a slow dance that led them perilously closer and closer to the edge of the platform. When they reached it, they found that the railing was not sturdy enough. With a piercing scream, Jackie went crashing through it, plummeting off the side of the scaffolding and taking the assassin with her.

But her fall was quickly arrested. Hanging precariously in midair, it took Jackie a moment or two to realize that she had her hands gripped in the assassin's belt. And that he was holding on, as best he could, to the last piece of railing on the scaffolding's top stage. Jackie was too afraid to look down. All she could do was clutch the assassin's belt with all her might, dangling 228 feet above the deserted cathedral square below.

The assassin twisted his body, trying to force Jackie to let go. But the more he writhed, the more the remaining piece of railing shook in his hands and squeaked in protest. So he decided to drop that tactic for his own good. And the two of them hung there, the assassin holding on desperately to the railing, Jackie holding on with equal desperation to the assassin's belt, for what seemed like hours, but could only have been minutes. Jackie felt like a gaffed fish, flopping helplessly on the end of a line that would inevitably lead her to a bad end.

Just when she was certain that her arms were about to give out and she would go hurtling to her death, she heard a familiar voice calling to her.

"Jackie!"

I must be imagining this, she thought.

"Jackie!" the voice called again, and this time she knew she was not hallucinating. Incredibly...no, miraculously...it was Jacques, and he had come to rescue her.

"Jackie, are you all right?"

Jacques's face appeared over the edge of the scaffolding.

Thank God, she breathed. As long as he was here, she knew everything was going to be fine. "Yes, but I don't know how much longer I can hold on."

"You have to," he encouraged her. "Don't let go, no matter what happens. I'll save you."

Of all the words Jacques had said to her, those were probably the three most meaningful, Jackie thought, as she clung even tighter to the assassin's belt. Jacques was here. She was going to be rescued. And that was all that mattered.

Through it all, the assassin had remained silent. As he watched, Jacques opened the overlooked toolbox and began rummaging through it. From it, he quickly withdrew a hammer and four heavy-duty nails.

"Don't try anything funny," Jacques said to the assassin as he kneeled down next to him. "Put one hand down on the platform."

The hapless killer gave him a blank look and did nothing.

"Do it," Jacques ordered in a voice that Jackie remembered wincingly from his Speed Graphic tutorial. "Now!"

This time, the assassin responded. He removed one hand from the railing and put it on the deck of the platform, reaching forward and gripping a gap in the planking about an arm's length away.

Quickly, Jacques took two nails and used the hammer to firmly nail the assassin's jacket sleeve to the deck. "Now your other hand," he said.

The assassin complied by lowering his free hand to the deck and gripping that same gap between the planks. Jacques took two more nails and hammered the other sleeve to the platform. Now, not only was the assassin effectively held in place, but he also presented a more stable platform for Jackie to hold on to.

"Is your suit made of good material?" Jacques asked the assassin.

He nodded.

"Good, then you shouldn't have anything to worry about—at least for a while."

Jacques leaned over the edge and called down to Jackie. "How are you doing?"

"I don't know how much longer I can hang on. My hands are getting cramped."

"Just a few minutes longer. I've nailed our friend here to the platform. He isn't going anywhere. I want you to climb up over him, and I'll get you."

"I don't think I can do that."

"Of course you can," Jacques said, making it sound as if he were asking her to tie her shoelaces. "Just don't look down. Concentrate on my voice. I'll guide you."

His calm manner made Jackie think that maybe she could do this. Her fear wanted to smother her will, but she fought back tenaciously, telling herself, *you can do this, you have to try.* So, with a final burst of adrenaline, she let go of the assassin's belt with her left hand, while still holding on to it with her right, reached up as far as she could, and grabbed on to the back of his summer-weight suit jacket in an attempt to find new purchase. The assassin made some sounds of protest, but was promptly silenced by Jacques, who threatened to use the hammer on him.

Jacques reached down over the assassin's shoulders and, with his right hand, got a firm grasp on Jackie's left wrist.

"Jacques, I'm afraid," she called up to him.

"You're doing fine," he reassured her. "Now do the same with your other hand."

Quaking, Jackie extended her right hand and seized hold of the back of the assassin's jacket. She could feel Jacques's left hand encircle her other wrist.

"I've got you. Now let me do all the work."

Slowly, inch by inch, Jacques pulled on Jackie's arms until her willowy frame was up and over the bulk of the assassin's dangling body. Jacques hauled her incrementally forward until the top half of her body was resting on the platform. Then he easily slid his hands under her armpits and dragged her fully to safety.

The two of them collapsed to the deck and lay there for a

moment, elated, exhausted, trying to catch their breath, before finally rising to their knees and embracing.

"Oh, Jacques, I was so frightened," Jackie sobbed in his arms.

"You're all right now," he whispered comfortingly. "Everything's going to be all right. Nothing will happen to you now."

They pulled apart and turned toward the assassin when they heard him whining plaintively to them, "But what about me? I can't stay like this forever."

Jacques looked up at him. "I think those nails should hold you until the police arrive."

"Could you consider releasing me? I served your purpose. One good turn deserves another..."

Jacques almost laughed. "Do you believe this?" he said to Jackie as he rose to his feet and swiped at his knees to clean them off. He turned back to the dangling assassin angrily. "And what good turn did you ever do us? Or that poor innocent woman at the Gare de Lyon? Or my friend Henri?"

Now the assassin sounded desperate, his voice a pitiful whine. "Please, if you let me go, you'll never see me again. I promise you. Just let me go."

Jacques looked disgusted at how craven this once terrifying murderer had become. He helped Jackie to her feet and said, "Let him twist in the wind."

As Jackie regained her breath, she asked, "Tell me, Jacques, how did you know I was up here?"

"You can thank your friend there," he said, pointing to the assassin. "When his knife hit the square, it made me look up. And I saw the two of you dangling from the edge of the tower."

At that moment, they heard a strange ripping sound. It was coming from the center seam in the back of the assassin's jacket, giving way from all the pressure it had been under. The assassin heard it and knew that the sound was his death knell. He looked up at Jacques with imploring eyes. "Help me, please," he begged in a small, scared voice, "I can't hold on any longer."

Jacques stood there for a moment, then looked at Jackie. She nodded her head in the briefest of affirmations. Quickly, he went to the edge of the platform and reached out to take the assassin's hand. But it was too late. The back seam split fully, leaving the jacket as two separate pieces flapping in the wind. His body no longer held in place, the assassin's numbed hands let go of the gap in the planks, his arms slid out of his sleeves, and he was launched into space. Destination: the cathedral square below.

XX

The assassin's blood-curdling scream and the sight of his wildly flailing arms as he plummeted to earth like a warplane shot out of the sky was horrifying. At the same time, Jackie heaved a sigh of relief that she was rid of him, *finally*, and that it was his body and not hers making that fatal descent.

She turned to Jacques and clung to him, trembling while he held her in his arms, the ghastly sight replaying itself behind her closed eyes.

"I know, I know, you think you'll never forget that, but you'll block it out of your mind," he murmured. "Maybe this was God's will. He was an evil man, a murderer who had no respect for human life, so in the end he brought it on himself."

Cradled in his arms and soothed by his consoling words, Jackie gradually stopped shaking. When he released her, she saw how troubled he looked. She sensed that something more than the assassin's death was eating away at him.

"Jacques, what is it?" she asked.

He spoke in a rush. "I'm sorry I was late. I should have gotten here sooner. You shouldn't have had to go through all that." The words kept tumbling out in a rapid stream. "Traffic was heavier than I thought it would be. When I got to the square and you weren't there, I kept looking around for you. I was getting really worried. But when I heard his knife, I knew where you were, and I went up after you as fast as I could."

Even in this pale moonlight, Jackie could see the tormented look on Jacques's face. She patted his arm reassuringly. "That's all right. Really. I'm okay now. I'm just glad you got here when you did." She took a deep breath and exhaled it slowly, feeling as if she'd been freed from some suffocating chokehold. "I can't believe he's really gone, and I won't have to look over my shoulder everywhere I go anymore."

She looked at the spot where the assassin had fallen, almost as if to make sure that he hadn't come rising up phoenixlike, and her eye fell on a small document case lying on the deck of the scaffolding. She had seen it drop out of the killer's pocket right before he fell.

"That's strange, I always thought he was Russian," she said when she picked up the document case and saw that it was a Pakistani passport. The assassin's name was Raheem Malik Maharraf, and his picture showed a full-faced man wearing a large turban with an oval gold ornament on it. She recognized the turban as the same one the killer had worn to the party at the Duke and Duchess of Windsor's estate when he came disguised as the Pakistani ambassador to France. He was obviously no ambassador, but he *was* Pakistani, which accounted for his costume's look of authenticity and the unfamiliar Middle Eastern accent she couldn't place, Jackie now realized.

"We know Pakistan is in on this too," Jacques said. "Why are you so surprised that he was Pakistani?"

"Because he killed Petrov," Jackie answered. "I assumed he was a fellow Soviet who assassinated a would-be defector before he could turn over information to the CIA. Of course, I never really got a good look at him. It was either too dark or he was in disguise or bandaged up, so he could have been from anywhere." She felt as if the pieces of the Petrov Puzzle were all starting to fall into place. "Okay, now we know who was working for the Pakistanis," she said and added lightly, "Any minute now I guess a spy from Balazistan will turn up."

"He's already here," Jacques said.

Jackie looked up from the passport, expecting to see a new man in their midst and another fight to the death begin, but only Jacques was standing there. She stared at him, confused. "What do you mean?"

He stared back at her, his face suddenly cold and hard, impassive. She'd never seen that detached expression on him before, and it made her feel uneasy. She thought he didn't seem like himself tonight. Nervous, edgy, guilty even. He had said that he felt bad about getting to Notre-Dame late, but now she thought the cause was much deeper than that. And she was right. The next words he spoke made her blood run cold.

"I'm the Balazistani spy. I'm a double agent."

Was this some kind of joke? She waited for him to erupt in laughter, slap his thigh, and shout, "Fooled you!" But he didn't. He just stood there like a stopped clock, staring at her with that steely, implacable look on his face.

Her heart began a loud drumbeat in her chest. Something was terribly wrong. She forced herself to stay calm and control the quivering in her voice. "Jacques, why don't you tell me what this is all about?"

"I told you. I'm a double agent," he said dispassionately. "I work for the CIA, but I'm also working for Balazistan."

She said nothing, her face frozen in shock, and he hurried to explain, dropping his detachment and sounding like the old Jacques. "Jackie, do you remember when I told you my mother was foreign-born? Well, she was born in Balazistan and emi-grated to Paris in the thirties. She became a French citizen when she married my father, but she kept in touch with her family back home and knew how volatile the situation was there. It was at her urging that I became a Balazistani agent, and I promised her on her deathbed that I would do whatever I could to help her native country survive."

Jackie couldn't help but be moved, but something didn't add up. "Then why did you become a CIA agent?" she demanded.

"I took the job with the CIA because I needed the money to help my mother when she got sick." His voice sounded defen-sive. "You know I was all she had in this world. My mother's medical bills kept mounting up, and I wasn't making enough money as a photographer and a Balazistani agent to pay for her treatment and have something left over for me too."

Now Jackie was beginning to understand how a struggling photographer could afford the snazzy red Renault convert-ible, repeated tips for the maitre d' at the Moulin Rouge, and the array of expensive cameras in his apartment. No wonder the British MI6 agents were suspicious of them—he was a dou-ble agent, only not for the country they thought. Wanting to take care of his sick mother's medical bills was commendable, but couldn't he have found some less duplicitous way to do it? As for the fast cars and women and nightclubbing, that was as much a sine qua non for a young, hot-blooded Frenchman as his passion for photography. But still, to sink so low as to be a double agent and to deceive her all along by pretending to be her ally? That was unforgivable.

Jackie went over to the edge of the rooftop to clear her mind as she looked out over the glittering lights of the Parisian night-scape.

"I wanted to tell you a dozen times before this, Jackie, but I couldn't," Jacques said. "My life was at stake. And my life isn't my own now. As an agent, I have to do what I have to do, regardless of my feelings. Can't you understand that?" The steeliness was gone, and his voice was filled with abject apology.

"I don't know what to think," she was starting to say as she turned around. "If you needed—"

But the words froze on her lips and she stopped dead in her tracks when she saw what he was holding in his hand.

A gun. And it was pointed straight at her.

He had a tortured look on his face, and he sounded desperate. "Jackie, you've got to give me the microdot. You can't take it back with you to the States. I would try to reason with you, but I don't have time. I need to have it now."

"What for? So you can cheat the CIA out of it?" she shouted vehemently. She stared at him, outraged and incredulous, as a voice inside her head kept insisting, *no, no, not Jacques, this can't be.* Suddenly, she thought of that young soldier she had bumped into at the Cinémathèque Française—Private Truffaut, wasn't it?—telling her that Hitchcock was such a master of suspense because he played up how unknowable the people we see every day are. Oh, was he ever right! Here was this man who'd been her partner and worked alongside her morning, noon, and night, the man she'd bared her soul to and had depended on for her very life—and now he was pointing a gun at her as coolly as if she were a dummy target in a shooting range.

It might have been a toy gun, for all that it mattered to her, so primal was her outrage. "Didn't I mean anything to you?" she screamed at him. "You're despicable. The lying! The treachery! I'm sorry I ever met you!"

His face softened, and she saw tears glistening in his eyes. "I can't do this," he said, dropping the gun to his side and slipping it in his pants pocket. "I never meant to hurt you, Jackie, please try to believe me," he implored her. "What we had meant more to me than I can tell you. I wouldn't have shot you. I didn't even shoot the assassin. I just brought the gun with me to intimidate you, but that was stupid of me. You're above that. I need to appeal to the goodness of your heart, because I know how good your heart is."

"Don't try to flatter me," Jackie said flatly, her guard up. "That's a cheap trick. There's nothing you can say or do that will make me give you the microdot that Petrov died for, trying to get it into Dulles's hands."

"But Princess Nureen needs it more than Dulles does," Jacques insisted, "and I'll have only myself to blame if she doesn't get it. And I can't live with that. You see, Jackie, I screwed up."

"What?" She looked at him, puzzled. "Screwed up in what way?"

Jacques passed a hand over his forehead wearily and sighed. "When I saw what was on the microdot—that Russia and Pakistan wanted to partition Balazistan out of existence—I wanted to make a copy of it for Princess Nureen, but I was afraid to take it from you and arouse your suspicion. So I went ahead with meeting you here, according to their plan, and had to lie to you and tell you I was bringing an embassy contact to arrange your flight home. It was rotten of me, I know, and I'm sorry. But I'm beyond that. All I want to do now is get the microdot into Princess Nureen's hands as fast as I can so she can go home and save my mother's homeland. Just let me make a copy of the microdot now and I'll give it back to you."

Jackie's head was reeling. This was so much to take in. First, her partner had pulled the wool over everyone's eyes—improbable as that was—and was actually working for Balazistan all along. And to top that off, this quintessential Frenchman, with whom she was having a passionate romance, was actually part Balazistani. The question was, what to do now? How could Jackie help him without compromising her loyalty to her own country?

"There's something else I need for you to know," Jacques said. The sadness in his eyes let Jackie know that what he was about to tell her pained him deeply. "I can't stay in Paris any longer. SMERSH is already suspicious of me as a covert Balazastani operative posing as a CIA agent. They could be coming after me this very minute. There's a price on my head as a double agent—doubly threatening to them—and I could wind up the same way Petrov did."

Jackie gasped. She couldn't bear to think of Jacques in a filthy garret somewhere, lying in a pool of blood with a gaping wound in his chest. She went to him, put her arms around him, and closed her eyes as she rested her head on his shoulder.

As she opened her eyes, Jackie saw a brief pinpoint of light coming from the cathedral's north bell tower. A second later, she felt something like a high-speed bumblebee whiz past her ear in a straight line. Simultaneously, the crisp sound of a gunshot echoed from a short distance away.

Reacting with lightning speed, Jacques pushed Jackie to the deck and put his body on top of hers. "There's a shooter on the other bell tower," he explained. "Probably SMERSH. We have to get out of here."

The shooter got off several more shots, harmlessly gouging holes in the wood planking nearby. Looking for something he could resort to as a diversion, Jacques grabbed the hammer he'd used to nail the assassin's suit to the scaffolding and flung it to the right, where it crashed into the toolbox, scattering implements and causing a loud racket. The shooter took the bait and poured more fire in that direction.

Taking advantage of the moment, Jacques rolled himself and Jackie across the wooden flooring to their left until they were at the entrance to the elevator, whose shaft gave them partial cover from the shooter. Lifting an arm and opening the door, he pushed Jackie inside, then crawled in himself. Raising his arm as high as it would go, he stabbed at the button that would take them down. The elevator was slow, but they would still beat the SMERSH shooter, who had to use the stairway in the North Tower.

As the elevator began its descent, Jackie handed Jacques the late assassin's document case that she had found lying on the deck and had clutched tightly to her chest while rolling with Jacques to the elevator.

Jacques quickly went through the rest of the papers.

"What are you looking for?" Jackie wanted to know.

"I think the assassin stole some information from the Russians that they don't want us to have." He riffled a few more pages and said, "Ah, here it is."

It appeared to be some sort of schematic. Jackie felt her stomach lurch, not from the motion of the elevator but from Jacques's face turning white at the sight of the drawing.

"Jacques, what is it?"

He held up the schematic for her to see, his hand shaking visibly. "This is a diagram of a bomb with a detonator preset to a certain altitude. When it reaches that altitude, the bomb will go off, killing everybody on board. It must have been planted on the princess's plane. To partition Balazistan easily, the Russians want the princess permanently out of the picture."

"Oh, my God, no!" Jackie stared at the terrifying schematic of a bomb, sickened to think that the proud princess's dream, along with the princess herself, was on the verge of being blown to pieces.

XXI

How do you know it's Russian?" Jackie asked, studying the strange-looking diagram of the bomb that had been planted on Princess Nureen's plane.

Jacques pointed to the lettering on the schematic. "It's written in Cyrillic."

Jackie nodded. Her concern for the young princess was mixed with a feeling of dread. "But what are we going to do?"

"We've got to prevent her plane from taking off," he said with simple conviction. He looked at his watch. "And we only have one hour to do it."

With those chilling words ringing in Jackie's ears, the elevator reached the second floor of the scaffolding. Jacques slowly opened the door and cautiously looked out.

"Let's run for it!" he said, grabbing Jackie's hand. "The shooter's not down from the tower yet." Together, they dashed out of the elevator, across the platform, and down the ladder to the Notre-Dame courtyard.

He led them to his Renault parked at the edge of the courtyard square. But before they could get in, Jacques cursed. Jackie followed his line of vision and saw that someone had slashed all four tires of his car. It looked like the SMERSH shooter, before climbing to the bell tower, had taken no chances on either of them making a getaway.

Angrily, Jacques kicked at one of the flattened tires. *"Merde."*

He looked around for another parked car, perhaps with the hope of stealing it, but the street beyond the courtyard was entirely deserted.

"Maybe we could call the airport," Jackie suggested.

Jacques looked around again. "Do you see any phone booths?"

She shook her head.

"We don't have the time to look for one, and who knows if we'd be able to get through to them if we tried to call?" He sounded desperate. "We have to get off this damned island. What are we supposed to do?"

"I guess we could swim," Jackie offered wryly, trying to calm him down.

To her surprise, Jacques looked at her as though her ironic comment was a flash of genius.

"Jackie, I could kiss you."

Then, without another word, he took her once more by the hand and led her in the direction of the Seine.

"I hope you know I wasn't serious," she said as they drew near the riverbank. "I'm not that good a swimmer."

"Neither am I. But it gave me an idea." They approached a small stone quay thrusting out into the river. "Look for a boat we can borrow. It's better than taking the car anyway. We can make better time. And let's be quick. That SMERSH shooter must be down from the tower by now."

At the quay, their choice was made simple. Only one vessel was tied up there. It seemed to be some kind of World War II–era surplus: a boat covered with armored plate, its cockpit open to the elements, with an open rear deck to carry troops or transport supplies. Right now, the rear deck was full of tied-down wooden crates of construction equipment obviously meant for the Notre-Dame restoration. Odd that it had been left here unattended for the night, but a lucky stroke for Jackie and Jacques.

"This is perfect," he proclaimed as they clambered into the front two seats of the boat's cockpit. Behind them were two more seats followed by a long open compartment. Jacques sat in the left-hand seat, familiarizing himself with the vessel's operation. Jackie was surprised to see that it looked just like the inside of a car, complete with dashboard, steering wheel, and clutch—only this dashboard had a few more gauges on it. Jacques stepped out momentarily to untie the boat from its mooring, then hopped back in behind the wheel, started up the boat, and slowly backed away from the quay.

"What's this thing called?" Jackie asked.

"DUCK," shouted Jacques over the roar of the boat's engine.

Jackie swiftly lowered her head below the boat's coaming. Suppressing a laugh, Jacques tapped her on the shoulder and motioned for her to lift her head.

"That's what this boat's called: a *Duck*."

"Oh." Jackie felt totally embarrassed. When Jacques had backed up far enough from the quay, he put the Duck into forward gear and started up the Seine, with the slowly disappearing bell towers of Notre-Dame on their left. Just then, a sudden sharp retort from the quay pierced the night air.

"Duck," Jacques commanded.

This time Jackie did nothing. She was startled when he put his hand on the back of her head and pushed her beneath the dashboard.

"Looks like the SMERSH shooter finally caught up with us."

Jackie stayed down until they had passed beyond the shooter's range, and Jacques gave her the all clear. She raised her head and looked back, hoping to catch sight of the SMERSH shooter receding in the distance. But instead, she watched as a fishing boat appeared from out of nowhere, slowed long enough to allow the SMERSH shooter to jump on board, then sped up as it started up the Seine after them. The Russians were intent on keeping them from warning the princess and preventing her plane from taking off.

Jackie turned to Jacques. "Don't look now, but I think we have company."

He glanced back and saw the fishing boat slowly gaining on them. "Double *merde,*" he cursed and switched gears.

Jackie could feel the Duck speed up and was jerked back in her seat from the acceleration. They were passing the northern tip of the Île de la Cité and sailing under the Pont Neuf, a hysterically funny name, Jackie thought, for one of the oldest bridges in Paris. Once past the island, Jacques steered the prow of the Duck several points to starboard, heading for a destination somewhere on the Right Bank.

Even though it was night, the river was crowded with traffic. They passed several *bateaux-mouches,* those romantic cruise boats much loved by the tourists, their interior lights warmly ablaze. These were interspersed with barges, fishing boats like the one following them, and the occasional houseboat and pleasure craft. Jacques tried to weave the Duck in and out of the water traffic in an attempt to lose the fishing boat. But whenever Jackie looked back, she could see the Russians doggedly pursuing them and narrowing the distance with each passing mile to get off a clean shot.

They finally reached a point of clear sailing, where there was no other river traffic in sight. Unobstructed, the fishing boat was closing the distance between the two vessels. Jackie hoped that Jacques had something in mind, some way to deal with this new threat, and was relieved when she heard him say, "I have an idea." It was what followed that unnerved her all over again.

"Jackie, take the wheel."

"What?" She was unable to keep the panic out of her voice.

"Take the wheel," Jacques ordered.

"But I can't drive this thing," she protested.

"Can you drive a car?"

Jackie nodded, too afraid to speak.

"Then you can drive this Duck."

He clambered into the backseat, then motioned for Jackie to get in the driver's seat. Her heart thumping wildly, Jackie slid over and put both her hands on the steering wheel. She looked down and saw that there was a brake pedal and an accelerator and a clutch with ten forward speeds and two reverse speeds.

"Just try to stay in the middle of the river," Jacques said. "And don't speed up suddenly or you might toss me overboard."

And with that, Jacques was gone, leaving Jackie all by herself in the cockpit. The running of the Duck was now up to her. She tried to get comfortable in her seat, which stubbornly wouldn't adjust the way a car seat would, and determined how much pressure her hands needed to steer the vessel. She experimented with brake pedal, accelerator, and clutch, being careful not to perform any maneuver that would land Jacques in the Seine. After a few wild gyrations to port and starboard, Jackie settled down and quickly got the hang of things, steering the Duck to follow the curves of the Seine as though she were an old river hand. Jacques was right: it was just like driving her 1947 Mercury convertible back home—with the top down.

Now that she had her confidence back, she dared to turn around and saw Jacques untying the netting holding down the construction equipment; one by one, he tossed the wooden crates overboard in the direction of the oncoming fishing boat. The crates bobbed up and down in the Duck's wake and created a virtual gymkhana of obstructions for the fishing boat to steer through. The Russian pilot must have been a skilled one, though, because he maneuvered his prow from port to starboard and back again, zigzagging to avoid all the bobbing crates. But there was a cost involved; he was forced to slow down his craft, and the fishing boat began to fall farther and farther astern of the Duck.

Jackie faced forward again and saw that there was more river traffic coming up, including a line of five barges being pulled by a tugboat, which was just coming into sight ahead of them. She heard a rustling beside her and found that Jacques was in the adjoining cockpit seat. Jackie began to get up, but Jacques put his hand on her shoulder and held her firmly in place. "You're doing a great job," he encouraged her.

Jackie brightened. She was always happy when she could please Secret Agent Jacques. Then she recalled that this secret agent was also a double agent working for a foreign country and found herself assailed by self-doubt all over again. But there was no time to sort out her confused feelings because Jacques tapped her on the arm, pointed to the barges, and said, "Make for the left of that barge train."

Jackie did as ordered, crossing the wake of the last barge in the train and moving up to the left. She looked at Jacques. "How are we doing on time?"

Jacques snatched a quick glance at his watch. "We have forty minutes to go. But don't worry. We're almost at our destination on the river."

A mist was slowly rolling in and covering the river in patches like a clochard's threadbare blanket, partially obscuring the

Grand Palais on the Right Bank and the lights of the Eiffel Tower just ahead on the Left Bank. Up ahead, the tugboat's foghorn sounded a warning to all oncoming river traffic. Jackie looked behind her and, through the mist, could clearly make out the running lights of the fishing boat. It was obvious that its pilot was so intent on catching up with them that he had failed to notice the slowly moving barge train. He was now in danger of smashing right into it. At the last possible second, the pilot was forced to head off to starboard, coming up on the right side of the barge train. Jackie hoped that between the slowly creeping fog and the intervening barge train, they could lose the Russian fishing boat once and for all.

But the combination of the fog and tricky maneuvering were taking their toll on Jackie and making her as skittish as a cat on a high wire. "This is worse than a traffic jam on l'avenue des Champs-Élysée," she muttered to Jacques.

His hand pressed down on her shoulder reassuringly. But Jackie shrieked in alarm when a long-range-rifle shot hit the glass windscreen in front of her, suddenly causing a spiderweb pattern that was impossible for her to see through.

"We're being fired on," Jacques warned. "It's coming from the barges. The SMERSH shooter got onto one from the fishing boat." He leaned down, found an oily rag wadded up in the bottom of the cockpit, wrapped it around his right hand and smashed his shrouded hand through the windscreen, allowing Jackie to see again. But without the glass, the wind rushed right through and created a hazard of its own. Jackie reached inside her handbag, pulled out her oversized sunglasses, and donned them to keep the wind out of her eyes.

"I'll be right back," Jacques said to Jackie lightly, as though excusing himself to go from one room to another.

"Wait, Jacques…" Jackie called to him, not wanting to

be alone while the SMERSH shooter was taking potshots at them.

But it was too late. Jacques was gone. While trying to steer at the same time, Jackie watched as Jacques jumped from the starboard side of the Duck to the port side of the nearest barge, where the SMERSH shooter was once again gunning for them. But the heaving deck of the barge was making it difficult to get off another shot in their direction. Before the shooter could aim his rifle again, Jacques was on him. Jackie couldn't believe what Jacques was doing, risking his life like this.

"Jacques, be careful!" she shouted to him. But he was too embroiled in stopping the SMERSH shooter to heed her warning.

Staying abreast of the barge, she saw Jacques grab hold of the shooter's weapon, and the two men begin to grapple over it. The rifle went off several times, but neither man seemed to be hurt. Finally, Jacques, who was clearly younger and stronger than the shooter, yanked the rifle out of his grasp and used its butt end to club the Russian into submission. Jacques left him there, slumped over on the deck of the barge, and jumped back onto the starboard coaming of the Duck. He threw the rifle in the stern and joined Jackie in the cockpit.

Jackie looked at Jacques and saw a red stain on the left shoulder of his jacket. "You're wounded!" she said in alarm.

He saw the stain for the first time and cursed, "Triple *merde.*"

"Jacques, we have to stop."

"It's nothing," he said, shrugging it off. "Probably just a scratch."

They were almost level with the tugboat and could see the glow of the Trocadéro high atop the Chaillot hill off to their right. "Head for those lights," Jacques directed her.

Jackie looked at him and could see that the red stain on his jacket was widening. "We've got to take a look at that," she said, unable to keep the apprehension out of her voice.

Jacques peered at his watch. "We only have thirty minutes to get to the airport. No time to waste. When the princess is safe, then we can see what the damage is."

Jackie didn't like this, but knew it was foolish to argue with Jacques when he was in this kind of mood. Instead, she concentrated on crossing in front of the tugboat.

Ignoring the wrath of the tugboat skipper—through the glass of the tug's pilothouse she could see him cursing and shaking his fist at her—she headed toward the lights of the Trocadero on the Right Bank. Unfortunately, this also meant crossing in front of the fishing boat, which was still shadowing the barge train from the starboard side.

As she cut diagonally across the river toward shore, she noted the Russian pilot copying the same maneuver. The fishing boat put on more speed, and Jackie knew that the race was on to see which boat would get to the Right Bank first. She was determined that it would be the Duck and changed gears, but the vessel was already going as fast as it could.

The site was a fortunate one. Although shut down for the night, this section of the embankment had repair work underway, making it easy to transition from the river to the Right Bank. "Just head for that gap in the embankment," he coached Jackie.

She looked at him and didn't like what she saw. He was sweating profusely, his breathing was labored, and his face was as white as a damask tablecloth.

She bit her lip. "I'm worried about you. Shouldn't we stop?"

"Just keep going."

To starboard, Jackie could see that the fishing boat was making for the same location, trying to cut them off before

they could reach it. The only thing she didn't understand was
what they were going to do when they got to the Right Bank.
How were they going to get from there to the airport? Was
Jacques planning on stealing a car? Hitching a ride? Taking
the Metro? There didn't seem to be enough time left. She was
frustrated because she had no idea what he was planning and
turned to ask him.

Jacques weakly waved away any questions with a limp hand
and grunted, "Just keep going." Then his eyes rolled up in his
head, and he passed out against her side.

"Jacques," Jackie cried out helplessly. This is too much for
me, she thought. Never had she felt so alone. She could feel
panic rising inside her, spiraling like a cyclone. She just wanted
to close her eyes and wake up from this bad dream back in her
bed at Merrywood, safe and snug. *Come on, Jackie, get a grip.*
She shook off that wishful fantasy, pushed down the panic
with an iron resolve, and concentrated on what she had to do
to survive.

She decided to trust Jacques and follow his instruction to
"just keep going" and aimed the bow of the Duck right for the
gap in the embankment. Changing gears once again, she could
feel the boat surge ahead. The fishing boat was still coming up
on her starboard side, but its pilot saw Jackie's suicidal maneuver and was content to watch her beach her craft against the
river's bank. The Duck hit the gap in the embankment, grinding its way out of the river. Instead of being beached, however,
the Duck was still moving. The boat seemed to rise up out of
the water and keep on going. Jackie looked down and couldn't
believe what she saw: the Duck's armored skirts had hidden
from view six tires, which the vessel was now riding on. Jackie
suddenly realized that she knew about this Duck from an article in *Life* magazine. The Duck was a U.S. Army amphibious

vehicle, unique for its ability to travel both on water and land, and had been used to ferry men and supplies to the beaches of Normandy during the D-day invasion. Now she understood why Jacques had declared this vessel "perfect" when he saw it moored in place at the quay.

Jackie drove past the repair site and up a conveniently located dirt ramp to the city street above, the sides of the Duck dripping water from the Seine like an alligator slinking onto dry land. She looked back and saw the pilot of the fishing boat shear off from his projected course in order to turn around and keep from crashing into the embankment. Even from this distance, she could see the resigned slope of the Russian's shoulders and knew that the pilot understood that he had lost the race.

Driving down the street with a feeling of triumph at having outwitted the Russians, Jackie could see pedestrians stopping to take note of the Duck, which took up more space and rode higher than the other vehicles surrounding it. To them, this symbol of the American military must have looked like Liberation Day all over again. She found it easy to drive the Duck on land and thought with pride, memo to self: add new skill to résumé—ability to drive amphibious military vehicle on both water and land.

This still didn't solve the problem of getting to the airport, though. She had no idea where it was located. While driving the Duck, Jackie turned to her right and tried to shake Jacques awake. After a few gentle but insistent prods, she was rewarded by the sight of Jacques opening his eyes.

In a daze, he looked around and asked, "Where are we?"

"Somewhere on the Right Bank," Jackie responded.

Jacques shook his head to clear it and looked around. He took note of the nearest street sign and said, "Make a right here. We're very close."

"I don't recall an airport around here," said Jackie as she followed Jacques's directions.

"It's a private airstrip. One runway only. Built by the Germans' Todt Organization during the war. Usually used for smaller aircraft, but can take a DC-3 in a pinch. We thought it would be the best place to sneak the princess out of France without anyone taking notice." He paused and said with chagrin, "I guess we were wrong." The words seemed to have exhausted him. He glanced at his watch and said, "Seven minutes. Better step on it."

Jackie put her foot on the accelerator and pushed the vehicle up to the Duck's top land speed. It seemed to eat up the roadway as it cruised down a deserted stretch of Paris highway where the apartment blocks had given way to an industrial zone of factories and warehouses. The large number of boarded-up windows and rubble-strewn lots signaled that many of the buildings were no longer in business, a sure early sign of urban decay. In the near distance, she could see the rotating light from the airstrip's control tower and knew they were getting close. She began to breathe a sigh of relief until she looked at Jacques and saw that the sleeve of his jacket was now saturated with blood.

"Jacques, your arm..."

"Just as soon as the princess is safe. Then we can take care of it."

Jackie shook her head. She was afraid that Jacques was going to sacrifice his life in order to save the princess. A noble cause, to be sure. An equally noble death. But Jackie couldn't imagine the world without Jacques in it.

The airstrip was surrounded on all four sides by a wire-mesh fence. Through it, they could see the princess's DC-3's propellers begin to spin in preparation for takeoff. Jackie had no idea where the entrance gate was and, apparently, neither did Jacques, who came up with the most expedient solution. "Just go through the fence."

"What?" Jackie asked, her voice rising on a note of incredulity.

"You heard me: go through the fence. This baby'll take it."

Jackie was dubious, but when in the past had Jacques ever been wrong about anything of a technical nature? So with a shrug of her shoulders, she turned the wheel to the left, gunned the accelerator, and pointed the Duck right at the fence. She shouted out "Brace yourself!" but was surprised when the armored prow of the Duck met little resistance and the wire-mesh fence simply collapsed around them.

She looked at Jacques, who wore a knowing look on his face. "Fortunately for us, the Todt Organization employed civilian contractors, many of whom were loyal to the Resistance. Substandard construction was their subtle way of sabotaging the Occupation."

The Duck's six tires ground over the fence and onto the air-field tarmac. In the near distance, they could see the princess's DC-3 beginning to taxi down the runway in their direction. Jackie's heart plummeted as she realized that they were too late to stop it from taking off. The princess was doomed. Jacques smashed the hand of his good arm against the dashboard in angry frustration. "We're too late. We've killed her."

"Maybe not," said Jackie, a sudden, crazy, suicidal idea popping into her head. She pressed hard on the accelerator and raced down the center of the runway, headed right for the oncoming DC-3.

Jacques stared at her in disbelief. "Jackie, what in God's name are you doing?"

"I'm going to stop that plane from taking off," she said simply.

"And kill us in the process?"

Jackie glanced at him. "You're not the only one who can risk his life for a good cause, you know."

The weak smile Jacques gave her was all the encouragement she needed. She didn't know from what deep well she had dredged up the courage—maybe it had something to do with her Roman Catholic upbringing and her deep-seated belief that good would triumph over evil—but she could not be stopped. She had the certainty of faith.

The unused runway tarmac was dimpled with ruts, and the Duck bounced up and down as Jackie poured on the speed and continued on her path of destruction. She knew that the pilot would have no choice but to bring the plane to a screeching halt to prevent it from crashing into the oncoming Duck.

But, there was not enough time for the pilot to put on the brakes now. He still came at them, twin engines roaring, waiting for Jackie to either stop the Duck or veer to the left or right. But Jackie, determined to see this through and force the pilot to abort his takeoff, maintained her direction and speed like a hot-rodder playing chicken with a rival driver.

As the distance between the Duck and plane steadily decreased, Jackie looked up and could see the pilot and copilot looking out through the DC-3's cockpit canopy. Her state of heightened sensory awareness made visual details pop out with crystalline clarity, and she noted that the copilot had a Clark Gable–like mustache and the pilot was clean shaven. They both seemed fiercely determined to get the plane into the air. Jackie wondered if they saw the same intense look of resolve on her face.

Jackie glanced to her right to check on Jacques and saw that he had used his injured left arm to wedge himself upright and brace his body against the open windscreen. Grimacing with pain, he was trying to wave off the plane, using his good right arm as a semaphore. But the princess's DC-3 just kept coming closer and closer until it seemed like a head-on collision was inevitable.

At the last possible second, though, when it seemed almost certain that the total annihilation of both plane and vehicle was imminent, Jackie's belief in a merciful God was rewarded—the pilot blinked first. He swerved the plane sharply to the left, running off the tarmac and onto the grass verge parallel to it. The plane's tail just missed the Duck altogether as Jackie swung the vehicle to the right to avoid being struck. It was impossible to tell whether she or Jacques breathed the bigger sigh of relief as the princess's takeoff was foiled.

Jackie slammed her foot on the brake, bringing the vehicle to a shuddering halt. "We did it! Jacques, we did it!" she screamed out, feeling as though a colossus had been lifted from her shoulders. She turned to him, expecting him to rejoice too, but his left shoulder was now completely saturated with blood and he had passed out once again. This time, though, his face was tinged with a deathly pallor that seemed like a harbinger of Jackie's most unthinkable fears.

There was a small wooden shack next to the control tower, and it was here that Jackie was taken by the princess's men and forced to spend the next several hours incommunicado while the bomb on board the DC-3 was defused (apparently another one of Dexter's many useful skills) and the plane was made ready for takeoff again. An ambulance arrived and whisked a wounded Jacques off to the hospital. She hadn't even been allowed to say good-bye to him.

There was a cot in the shack and a table with a bottle of

Vichy water, a drinking glass, and a plate of stale croissants. Jackie was locked in the shack with a guard outside and was left to her own devices. Occasionally she would shout out that what they were doing was illegal, that she wanted to see someone from her embassy, but her words seemed to fall on deaf ears. Anyway, Jackie had been told by Dulles to stay away from the American embassy, whose officials had no knowledge of her presence in Paris, so her words to her captors were only a bluff.

At one point, Jackie heard Dexter come over and talk with one of the guards. She put one ear to the thin plywood wall and couldn't believe what she was hearing. Jacques was dead. He had been rushed to the hospital, but apparently not in time to save his life. He had bled out in the emergency room before he could be operated on.

Jackie felt an icy cold wind suddenly blast through her, suffusing her whole body with a frozen heaviness. She had to lie down and barely made it over to the cot before collapsing on it. Jacques was dead. She couldn't believe it, couldn't conceive of it. And it was no consolation to know that he had gone out the way he wanted, having saved the life of his beloved princess and the country she represented.

As she lay there on the cot sobbing, her mind was crowded with images of Jacques over the past several days: sitting jauntily behind the wheel of his Renault convertible... teaching her photography in his Montmartre bachelor apartment... telling her the tragic story of his first love... looking so damned dashing in his cat burglar outfit... saving her from the Pakistani assassin on the rooftop of Notre-Dame... bravely wrestling with the SMERSH shooter on that barge. Then a welcome wave of black overtook her, and Jackie didn't have to think about Jacques or anything else for a while.

*   *   *

When she awoke and rose from the cot, everything was fine until Jackie remembered that Jacques was dead. It hit her with a palpable, rushing wave of emotion, like a blow to the gut, and she found herself forced to lie down all over again. She lay there, unable to move, until the door opened and Dexter appeared.

"The princess would like to see you," he said. "She wants to thank you, and she would like your permission for me to make a copy of the microdot for her to take home."

Dexter's words triggered a flashback in Jackie's mind of Jacques on the rooftop of Notre-Dame, pleading with her to give him the microdot so he could copy it. This is the least I can do to honor his memory, she thought.

Jackie spotted her purse on the table and motioned to Dexter to bring it to her. She removed the glassine envelope with the microdot inside, the one that Jacques had so cleverly made sure would stay out of the hands of the two English spies, and wordlessly handed it to Dexter.

"Thank you, Miss Bouvier," he said in a humble tone. "I'll be back as soon as I can."

When Dexter returned, he handed both microdots to Jackie and waited while she slipped the original one into her purse. Then he helped her off the cot and, holding her by the arm, brought her from the shack to the DC-3, apparently all ready for takeoff again.

The princess was standing by the door of the plane. Jackie had never seen her looking so happy before, almost like a young bride on her wedding day. Jackie wanted to go through the motions of greeting her, but felt empty inside.

"Bon soir, Mademoiselle Bouvier," Princess Nureen said warmly,

holding both her hands out to Jackie's. "I understand that I owe my life to you."

"Not just me, your Highness," Jackie said modestly, not wanting to take all the credit. "You also have Jacques to thank."

"Yes, Jacques," the princess said in what Jackie could swear was an oddly lighthearted tone of voice. She could not fathom the princess's attitude. Didn't she care that Jacques was dead, had given his life for her? Perhaps her sadness over Jacques's death was mitigated by the profound joy the princess felt to be returning to the country of her birth after so many years in exile.

"I have something for you," Jackie said, dutifully handing the copy of the microdot to the princess, half expecting a photographer to pop up from somewhere and capture this historic moment in perpetuity on a magazine cover.

As if reading her mind, the princess said, "There's someone on the plane waiting to say good-bye to you."

"There is?" Jackie's eyebrows shot up in surprise. She couldn't imagine who would have come to say good-bye. Other than Dexter and the princess and Jacques, there wasn't a soul on earth who knew that she was at this airstrip in the industrial outskirts of the city.

"*Bonjour*, Jacque-LEEN," she heard a familiar voice say from the doorway of the plane.

With a start, she turned to see who had greeted her like that and was now walking toward her. *It couldn't be.* But oh, my God, it was! Jacques!

She felt faint. But before she could fall, Jacques grabbed hold of her with his right arm, his left arm bandaged and held in place by a sling. His ever-present camera bag hung down from his right shoulder.

"I can't believe it!" Jackie exclaimed when she caught her breath. "Jacques, is that really you?"

"Yes, it's me."

"B...b...but...," Jackie stammered.

"I know," he interrupted her, "you heard I was dead. My death was faked at the hospital. The princess arranged it. She thought it was necessary to convince SMERSH that I was truly gone." He paused. "And maybe the Americans too. I have a feeling I'm not going to be asked to any more potluck dinners at the embassy."

When he saw that his little joke failed to provoke a laugh from Jackie, he said, "I'm sorry if I upset you."

"Upset me? You damn near killed me," she spat out, her cheeks flushed. But her flash of annoyance dissipated quickly. She was too thankful and incredulously glad that he was still alive to stay peeved for long. And she was curious. "What are you doing on the plane? Are you going to Balazistan with Princess Nureen?"

"Yes, I'm going to be the princess's personal photographer and help her lead her people to freedom." Then he corrected himself. "*Our* people."

"That's wonderful," Jackie said. She was happy that the princess was rescuing him from the murderous games that world powers play and was giving him a fresh start in his mother's homeland, doing what he loved most, although it pained Jackie to think that some new exotic beauty would soon be taking her place in his arms.

Jacques turned to Princess Nureen. "Would you mind if Jackie and I had a moment to ourselves?" he asked politely.

The princess nodded. "Dexter and I will be waiting on the plane." Again, she took Jackie's hands in both of hers. "Goodbye, Miss Bouvier, I'm very grateful to you for what you've done," she said, giving Jackie's hands a heartfelt squeeze. But she couldn't resist asking, "Tell me, what made you change your mind about sharing the microdot with me?"

A small smile tugged at the corners of Jackie's lips. "To put it simply," she said, "I'm a great admirer of the bravery of women in a man's world."

Princess Nureen smiled back. She appreciated how fraught with meaning that statement was, coming from a female CIA agent who had just risked her life to save her. "When things get settled, you must come to Balazistan for a visit," she said. "You'll be welcome there, and I'm sure you'll find it a very beautiful country."

"Thank you so much. I will come, and I know it will be lovely." She curtsied to the princess, who reciprocated with a low bow with hands steepled in front of her, the ultimate sign of respect in her country. Jackie watched her board the DC-3 with Dexter, holding hands as they did when they had first landed in Paris twelve years ago, and felt a lump in her throat. She knew that when the plane took off, her heart would soar along with the airborne princess going home at last.

When they were alone, Jacques told Jackie, "There's something I want to give you as a memento of our time together."

"You do? What is it?"

He opened his camera bag, removed his Speed Graphic, and held it out to her.

"Oh, Jacques, I can't take that. It's yours. You need it for your work."

"No, please keep it," he insisted. "I have other cameras, and I want you to have this one because you already know how to use it and you could make a nice career for yourself with it back in the States."

"That's so good of you." She took the camera from him and kissed him on the cheek. Even that light brush of her lips against his smooth skin sent little tremors of excitement dancing up her arms. She held the heavy camera with both hands and pressed it to her breast. "Whenever I take a picture with this, I'll think of you."

She looked in his eyes, saw the sadness there, and sighed. "You warned me," she said. "You told me that when you're a CIA agent, falling in love can be dangerous."

"*Oui*, and bittersweet too." He was quiet for a long beat, then his eyes brightened. "But we'll always have Paris," he told her.

Jackie smiled at the way he quoted Bogie's famous line to Ingrid Bergman. They were the ideal parting words, written, it seemed, for this very moment and especially, singularly, for the two of them. She was sure that Humphrey Bogart would forgive Jacques for stealing them. Jacques said them with the mischievous grin that she found so captivating, but she knew he was telling her that he would never forget her. And she also knew she would never forget him.

Although she imagined that parting lovers would be saying those words to each other for the next several decades, she couldn't resist coming back with another memorable line from that same wartime movie. Her delivery was pitch-perfect.

"Here's looking at you, kid," she said.

XXII

Yusha, it's so wonderful to see you!" Jackie cried when she deplaned at Washington National Airport and spotted her stepbrother waiting to drive her back to Merrywood.

"You too, Jackie, welcome home," he said, giving her a bear hug and a kiss on the cheek. His real name was Hugh D. Auchincloss III, but everyone called him Yusha, a nickname that was probably given to him by his mother, Maya de Chrapovitsky, the daughter of a White Russian émigré admiral and Hugh Auchincloss's first wife.

The Auchincloss brood was a large one, stemming from her stepfather's three marriages, the first to Nina S. Gore, an actress and socialite who was rumored to have had a long on-and-off affair with Clark Gable. Nina's son from a previous marriage, Gore Vidal, was a brilliant writer whom Jackie hoped to emulate some day as a novelist, although not necessarily so scandalous a one. Three years ago, at the age of twenty-three, Gore created a literary firestorm with *The City and the Pillar*, the first American novel featuring outright homosexuality. "Hughdie," Jackie's stepfather, and Nina had two children of their own, and he and Jackie's mother had another two, the youngest boy and girl in the family. Jackie was fond of all of her stepsiblings, but the one closest to her in age—only two years older—was Yusha, and he was the one with whom she had a special bond.

"Is this all the luggage you took?" Yusha asked her as he hauled her suitcase off the baggage claim carousel. "You usually don't travel that light."

"I wasn't there sightseeing," Jackie answered, not elaborating on the confidential nature of her visit to Paris. She smiled inwardly, remembering how the concierge at her hotel rescued her from having nothing to wear to the opera by getting her indispensable, basic black Givenchy dry-cleaned overnight.

"Well, as long as you had a good time," Yusha said agreeably. He eyed her appreciatively, taking stock, and seemed to be aware of something different about her. "You look great. You look...I don't know...more grown up somehow, I guess, although you weren't away very long." He laughed. "I guess Paris does that to you."

"Yes, Paris can make you grow up in a hurry," Jackie added to herself, especially if you run into a dead Russian spy, a Pakistani assassin out to kill you, an ardent French/ Middle Eastern partner, two English spies threatening to torture you, and the redoubtable Princess Nureen of Balazistan.

On the ride to Merrywood, her stepbrother made pleasant small talk with her, chatting about the family and filling her in on the latest news. Her younger sister, Lee, now eighteen, had a new boyfriend, Yusha told her. This development didn't surprise Jackie, knowing what an inveterate flirt Lee was. It was no secret that her younger sister's provocative wiles and postage stamp–sized skirts had the boys flocking to her through a revolving door.

"What's his name?" she asked.

"Michael Canfield."

"Is he nice?"

"He's okay. He's a booze hound but he has a good sense of humor, and his family is in the *Social Register*, which of course makes Janet happy."

At the mention of Janet, as Yusha always called his step-mother, Jackie felt a jolt of apprehension. Before boarding the plane to come home, she was starting to miss Merrywood. The ceaseless Sturm und Drang of her CIA mission had been enervating, and she longed for the tranquillity of the Virginia estate's lush greenery and the contentment of familial ties that made her feel anchored and safe.

But the closer she got to McLean, the more anxious she became about having to face her mother in another standoff about breaking up with John Husted. No matter how persistent her mother was—and God knows, her mother could be persistent—or how ugly it got, Jackie promised herself that she would not back down from her refusal to marry John. If her Paris adventure had taught her anything at all, it was that Jacqueline Lee Bouvier was not cut out to be just another society housewife.

Her mother was already standing in the mansion's doorway when Yusha pulled the car onto the circular flagstone driveway. As soon as she saw Jackie getting out of the car, she ran toward her, smiling broadly.

"Oh, Jacks, I'm so glad you're home safe," she said, embracing her and holding her close.

Jackie didn't know how much Dulles had told her parents about her mission in Paris, but she surmised that her mother had some inkling that it had proven to be far more dangerous than anyone had anticipated. She also knew that for all her mother's annoyingly controlling and peremptory qualities, her love for her children was boundless and well-intentioned.

She wanted only the best for them—the trouble was that her concept of what was best for them and theirs often had little in common.

"It's good to be home, Mummy," Jackie said. "I missed the family so much."

"Well, you go on up and rest for a while. We'll have dinner at seven when your stepfather gets home."

"Is Lee here?" Jackie couldn't wait to compare notes with her sister about Jacques and her sister's new beau.

"No, but she and Michael Canfield will be back for dinner. He's crazy about her. His real father is rumored to be Prince George, the Duke of Kent, and his mother is Kiki Preston, the American banking heiress. Michael was adopted as an infant by Cass Canfield, *the* Canfield who owns a publishing house."

Here we go, Jackie thought. The old status game. It wouldn't be long before the *Social Register* would come up and, with it, the hallowed place the Husteds occupied therein. Better get prepared, she warned herself. Dinner wasn't going to be easy.

All those things that so concerned people here at home—social standing, pricey acquisitions, party invitations—seemed inconsequential to Jackie now. Happy as she was to be back in the bosom of her family and safe in the sanctuary of Merry-wood, she couldn't help feeling a sense of dislocation after all the life-changing experiences she'd had in Paris. She'd looked death in the face, and she'd seen more evil than she ever thought human beings could be capable of. She'd witnessed firsthand the ruthless machinations of world powers, and when push came to shove, she'd discovered in herself a bedrock of courage and selflessness that made her proud. Next to all that, the *Social Register* didn't seem worth the paper it was written on.

Fortunately, dinner turned out to be far more enjoyable—and unexpectedly profitable—than Jackie would have imagined. As

Marie, the maid, trundled in and out with heaping serving platters of rib roast with horseradish sauce and Yorkshire pudding
and casseroles of ratatouille and scalloped potatoes, the large
family eagerly engaged Jackie in conversation. While no one at
the long, crowded table knew anything more than the sketchiest
details about her CIA assignment, they were all proud of her for
having carried off so daring and prestigious a venture. Hughdie,
her dignified but kindhearted stepfather, who presided at the
head of the table, was especially fulsome in his praise.

"Allen Dulles tells me you acquitted yourself with excep-
tional bravery and aplomb, Jackie," he said, beaming at her. "I
knew you could to it. That's my girl."

Nice of Dulles, Jackie thought, not to tell her parents how
she screwed up her assignment and to save whatever dressing
down he had in store for her until they met in private.

"I hope you had some fun too," her mother put in worriedly.
For some reason, she hadn't mentioned John Husted at all so
far, something Jackie gratefully attributed to her mother's new
respect for her spunky daughter's determination to call off the
engagement and lead a more adventurous life.

"Oh, yes, I certainly did enjoy myself." Jackie began recount-
ing the "fun" things she did. "Let's see, I saw *La Bohème* with
Maria Callas, a fantastic new Greek soprano, at the Paris
Opéra; I went to the races at Longchamp; a princess invited
me to a party at the Duke and Duchess of Windsor's estate; I
spent a lot of time at the Jeu de Paume museum; and I had a
neat boat ride on the Seine." If they ask me for any details, I'm
sunk, Jackie thought.

Luckily, no one did. They just nodded and made approving
noises.

Then Lee piped up. "Meet any interesting men?"

Naturally, what else would Lee be interested in? "Oh, I met

a nice young photographer who taught me how to use a Speed Graphic and took me to the Moulin Rouge one night," Jackie said offhandedly, "and we visited Notre-Dame together, but we went our separate ways after that." With her eyes, she signaled to Lee to let it go and discreetly pointed upstairs with a forefinger to indicate that they could discuss this in Jackie's bedroom after dinner.

It wasn't until dessert came—a towering strawberry shortcake that was the cook's specialty—that Hughdie surprised Jackie with a gracious and most welcome offer. "You say you've learned how to use a Speed Graphic, have you?" he asked.

Jackie nodded. "Yes, actually, I think I'm getting fairly good at it," she said, trying not to sound like a braggart, a gaucherie that was frowned upon among people in her stepfather's social class.

"In that case, I have a proposition that I think might interest you. I know what a talented writer you are, coming out first in that *Vogue* contest with 1,280 contestants"—how typical of Hughdie with his banker's mind to remember the exact number of entries—"and I thought you might want to go into journalism now that you're back from Paris. So I asked a friend you've met here on occasion—you know, Arthur Krock, the Washington correspondent for the *New York Times*—to put in a good word for you with Frank Waldrop, editor of the *Times-Herald*. It so happens that Waldrop is looking for a bright young woman to fill the Inquiring Camera Girl position he has open now. You have an appointment for an interview with him this Tuesday at eleven a.m."

"Oh, Hughdie, thank you! Thank you so much!" What a break! Jackie couldn't believe it. This was exactly the connection she was hoping her stepfather would make for her when she was posing as a society photographer at the Duke and Duchess of Windsor's party. She'd been tempted to call Hughdie then but was saving this favor from his wide network of Washington acquaintances to help her get an actual, full-time paying job.

She jumped up from the table, went around to her stepfather, and gave him a grateful kiss on the cheek.

"That's all right, Jackie. I know Waldrop will be impressed with you." He patted her arm affectionately. "If you have any pictures you took in Paris that you think he'd like, bring them to the meeting, okay?"

Noticing that everyone had finished eating dessert, Hughdie pushed himself back from the table and stood up. "I guess we're all finished here." He nodded at Yusha and then at Michael Canfield, who hadn't said much all evening but had consumed enough wine to put him in a stupor, and said, "Why don't you two join me in my study for a cigar and let the ladies have some time to themselves?"

Jackie and Lee raced upstairs, dying to have some frank, unadulterated girl talk. As soon as they were in her bedroom, Jackie locked the door and sank onto her bed while Lee sprawled in an armchair, waiting to hear all about the mysterious young photographer that her fascinating older sister met in Paris. Despite the usual sibling rivalry between them, their kinship was strong. Jackie felt that Lee was the only person close to her who wouldn't divulge to the rest of the world the passionate rebel living inside her carefully crafted aloof and reserved cover.

Louise Weber, or La Goulue, the famous Moulin Rouge can-can dancer looked down on them from Toulouse-Lautrec's souvenir poster hanging on the bedroom wall as Jackie launched into her tale of Parisian decadence.

"His name was Jacques Rivage, and Lee, he was so handsome and sexy and dashing and playful that he reminded me of Daddy," she gushed. "He was exactly like a young Black Jack Bouvier, even down to the dark skin. Only his didn't come from a suntan. He's part Balazistani."

"Balazis-whosis?" Lee asked, as if she thought the word was the name of some foreign disease.

"Balazistani. His mother was born in Balazistan, a Middle Eastern country, and his father was a Frenchman who joined the Resistance and was killed by the Nazis."

"Ooh, that's awful," Lee said, shuddering.

Jackie gave her sister a moment to compose herself. Then she turned back to the subject at hand and said, "It's funny, but when I first met Jacques, I didn't like him very much." She smiled, remembering that day in the Tuileries. "He came off like a know-it-all, arrogant and stuck on himself as a ladies' man. I don't think he liked me very much either. He thought I was this rich, dumb American girl who just wanted to gad about Europe and have a good time. I think he started to like me when he saw how dedicated I was and that I used my head to get out of some pretty bad scrapes. He was attracted to me physically and all that—but what really got to him is when he looked behind the debutante façade and saw a person he could respect."

"And what made you change your mind about him?"

"When I found out how much I could trust him." Jackie searched her sister's face. "Lee, how many guys do we know that we could really trust to be there for us if we got into trouble? I mean serious, life-threatening trouble—the knife-at-your-throat, do-or-die kind. If it came down to our lives or theirs, wouldn't most of them cut and run to save their own skins? Well, he was different. He looked out for me, came to my rescue, and put himself on the line for me time and again. I know it sounds corny, but the fact is, he was my hero."

Lee was fascinated. "Wow, that's so romantic. Your real live knight in shining armor."

"That's why I was so shocked when he pulled a gun on me. I couldn't believe he would do something like that after we became so close."

Now Lee almost fell out of her chair. "He pulled a *gun* on you?" The word *gun* came out in a screech of incredulity. "Why in the world would he do that?"

Jackie sighed, not knowing how to explain the situation without breaching CIA confidentiality. "It's complicated," she said finally, "but he said that he just wanted to scare me with the gun and never would have actually used it on me."

"That was decent of him."

"Oh, you don't know how decent he was," Jackie said with a catch in her throat as all her old feelings of tenderness for Jacques welled up inside her. "Life had been cruel to him, but he wasn't resentful. It just made him more sensitive to other people's pain."

Lee nodded, looking impressed. "Do you think you'll ever see him again?"

Jackie shook her head sadly. "No, I'm afraid not. He went back to Balazistan. The head of the country offered him a job as her personal photographer. He's a very talented photographer, actually. I've seen a book of his work, and it's quite good. He's an artist with a camera."

"An artist? Sounds like you had a lot in common with him. It's a shame he's a foreigner."

"Well, I knew at the outset that he was in a completely different league from me and wasn't someone I should let myself fall in love with, but I plunged in anyway. I felt kind of fatalistic about it—that it was part of some Grand Design for us to be together, that our connection was meant to be and I should make the most of it because it was also meant not to last." She added quickly, "Not because we didn't want it to, but for reasons beyond our control."

"That's a tough one," Lee commiserated. "Falling hard for someone but knowing from the first that it's going to be short-lived. You have to be very strong to handle that. It has to hurt."

"Oh, it hurts all right," Jackie said with a deep sigh. She thought about how the perfect world she and Lee grew up in was shattered by her parents' divorce, and she took her younger sibling under her wing. "You know what the problem with happiness is, Lee? It doesn't last. But transience is part of its beauty. Think about all the great love songs and poems that were written by someone with a broken heart. I guess when you fall in love with someone, you have to keep in mind that you can't have that person forever. Enjoy it while you can, because one way or another, you're going to lose the one you love in the end."

"That's so morbid," Lee said, frowning. "Divorce or death, not a whole lot to look forward to."

"Oh, Lee, I don't mean to be grim about it," Jackie said laughingly. "Love is the most wonderful thing in the world. All I'm saying is that falling in love is risky under any circumstances because ultimately, loss is inevitable. You just have to be thankful for the good times and treasure them." Jackie pursed her lips, reminiscing. "We had such a wild ride together in Paris. It was thrilling and crazy and funny and sad and terrifying and exhilarating all at the same time, and then it came to a screeching halt when..." She bit her lip, hesitating, and then said carefully, "All I can tell you is that it involved a promise he made to his mother on her deathbed."

Lee fanned her face with her hand. "Whew, Jackie, that's the kind of stuff you read about in novels. You should write a book about it someday. Where do you meet guys like Jacques?

Handsome, sexy, brave, talented, patriotic, *and* a wonderful son. No wonder you fell in love with him."

"I know, but he hurt me too," Jackie said, frowning. "He wasn't honest with me. His secrecy about himself should have made me suspicious, but I let it pass." She shook her head. "That's how women are in relationships," she mused. "The red flags are always there, but we choose to ignore them."

"Well, you know what they say, love is blind," Lee offered.

"Yes, but it's not really blindness; it's avoidance," Jackie said thoughtfully. "We see something, but we think if we ignore it, it'll go away." She paused for effect. "Maybe we'd all be better off if we trained ourselves to notice what's staring us in the face." She was thinking of Michael Canfield and his prodigious alcohol consumption, but decided to let the matter rest.

"Oh, Jackie, you can't be so intellectual about love," Lee remonstrated. "It's all about feelings and letting your heart lead the way, not your head."

"Then I'm in big trouble," she said with a rueful laugh. "Even though it irritated me that Jacques was such a Don Juan, that roguish quality drew me to him like a magnet."

"Why do you think that was?"

"Maybe it was the challenge—I thought I could be the one woman he'd be faithful to." She shrugged. "Or maybe it's just that a womanizer is familiar to me, and the familiar is hard to resist."

"I hope you get over it," Lee said. "We both love Daddy to pieces, but you know what lousy husbands skirt-chasers make."

"I do know," Jackie told her sister, "but I can't help it if I have a fatal attraction to a man with a roving eye." She shrugged. "I guess I'd rather suffer with an unfaithful man who makes me feel fully alive than be with a faithful one who bores me to death. As Bernard Berenson once said, there's a difference between living and existing. I choose living."

"Pick your poison," Lee said, tongue-in-cheek.

If there was one thing Allen Dulles hated worse than the Russians, it was the heat and humidity of a Washington, D.C., summer. Oh, the Russians were bad, all right, and the Chinese were climbing his list, but when it came to things he detested, spending the summer in Washington, D.C., certainly took the number one spot. As he sat in his office at the temporary headquarters of the Central Intelligence Agency on E Street in Foggy Bottom, Dulles cursed the Founding Fathers for deciding on the hellish lowlands of Virginia as the site of the nation's capital.

To make matters worse, air-conditioning in his temporary office was a hit-or-miss affair. And right now it was pretty much all miss. He made a mental note to have the air conditioner in the window behind him looked at, but since clearing janitors for security was considered low priority at the moment, it might take a while for the necessary repairs to be made. So Dulles did what, for a man of his breeding and background (Exeter, Princeton, Sullivan & Cromwell, OSS), was unthinkable: he took off his suit jacket, rolled up the sleeves of his oxford broadcloth shirt, and loosened his rep tie.

Seated across from the unaccustomedly informal Dulles was Jacqueline Bouvier, looking slightly nervous, as he could well imagine she would be under the circumstances. This was her first visit to the temporary offices of the Pickle Factory, the agency's private name for itself. (In Washington parlance, the more risible an agency's nickname, the more dangerous its function.) Well, he would soon have her at her ease.

Jackie, for her part, felt out of place in this unadorned room filled with battered furniture. The desk, the uncomfortable metal chair she sat in, the filing cabinets fitted with a special security bar and locking device, even the generic hunting and sailing prints on the wall, all appeared to have been ordered from the same federal furnishings catalog. The only object that seemed out of place in this anonymous setting was the comfortable-looking, old-fashioned leather executive chair Dulles sat in. It was an obvious antique, and Jackie felt sure that it was a holdover from the deputy director's days as a Wall Street litigator. The desk that stood between them was bare, except for a telephone to Dulles's right, an intercom to his left, and in between, a blotter on top of which rested a single top secret file—apparently hers—that he closed before looking up at her.

"Congratulations, Jacqueline, your mission was a smashing success," Dulles said, speaking around the ever-present Kaywoodie in his mouth, its pungent aroma filling the room.

Jackie looked flummoxed. How could he call her capitulation to Princess Nureen and Jacques a smashing success? If that was his idea of success, she wondered, what was the deputy director's definition of *failure*?

"But I don't understand," she blurted out. "Petrov is dead, and I shared his gift with someone else."

"It's very simple, Jacqueline." Dulles lapsed into his professorial mode. "Your mission was twofold. One was to get Petrov's gift into the right hands, which you did. You see, we already knew about the information contained on the microdot. You handed it over to Princess Nureen, something that we wanted to do, but couldn't, for fear of causing a serious rupture with our British cousins in MI6. So we did the next best thing: we had you deliver the information for us."

"But why didn't you just tell me that's what you wanted me to do?"

"Because we operate on a doctrine of plausible deniability. If you get caught, we simply deny any association with you. And you didn't need to know all that information to do the job we wanted. You just had to follow the dictates of your sense of decency, as I knew you would."

Jackie saw through the flattery and gave him a knowing look. "So you used me."

"In a word: yes. Look, Jacqueline, the English refer to spying as the Great Game. But since the end of the war, espionage is no longer a game. Not when it means preventing New York or Chicago from becoming the next Hiroshima or Nagasaki." Dulles pointed his Kaywoodie at Jackie to emphasize his point. "We may be gentlemen, but make no mistake about it, we play the game like a bunch of bare-knuckle brawlers. We have to come out on top against foe and friend alike—we don't share information even with our allies unless we have to. So I make no apologies for using people if it means protecting the security of this great nation."

Jackie was shocked to hear the usually sedate Dulles sound so passionate. Sufficiently cowed, she moved on. "You said there were two parts to my assignment. What was the second?"

"Unmasking the identity of the mole who was working out of our Paris station."

"Jacques?"

"Yes. We had our suspicions about him, but couldn't prove a damn thing. We knew you were just his type. So we unleashed your considerable charms on him and hoped that he would eventually crack."

Jackie had to laugh at that. Obviously Dulles didn't know Jacques all that well. Any woman with long legs and a pulse was "just his type."

"So you didn't know he was working for Princess Nureen?"

"No, that came as a complete surprise to us. We thought he might be a Russian spy." Dulles paused to fiddle with his Kaywoodie, which had unexpectedly gone out, and favored her with a small smile. "You see, Jacqueline, there are some things that even I don't know."

Just like those nasty British agents, Jackie thought. "And what about Kim Philby?" she asked. "His name was on the microdot document too."

"Yes, that was a considerably less pleasant surprise."

"Are you going to have him arrested?"

"Like the proverbial cat, our Mr. Philby seems to have nine lives. But I'm afraid that he's down to his last one or two. We might let him run awhile longer, just to see how many other operations he's compromised. But sooner or later, we'll get him. You mark my words."

"And what about the bomb on Princess Nureen's plane? Did you know about that?"

Dulles looked chagrined. "No, I must say, that one came out of left field. We didn't think the Russians would risk an international furor and go to such lengths to keep the princess out of Balazistan." He shook his head and chuckled. "Nor would we have expected you to go to such lengths to get her back there, but we're most appreciative that you did."

Jackie said nothing, her head spinning at this sudden burst of revelations. She did not like being used so gratuitously, even if for a higher purpose. If this was what the CIA was all about, then maybe this was not a career path she should seriously consider. She didn't want to end up like those two English spies, coldbloodedly duplicitous, cynical, and untrusting. From out of nowhere, she wondered what must have happened to them after they returned home to England with the wrong microdot.

*   *   *

The cabdriver with the lilting accent dropped the female British agent off at the front door of the villa called Goldeneye, owned by a man the locals referred to as "the Commander" in deference to his former naval rank. It was in Saint Mary Parish near the village of Oracabessa, and the air was fragrant with the scent of flowering hibiscus and African tulips. Despite being tired from the flight and the two-and-a-half-hour drive from Kingston, she had to admit to herself that the long journey here had been worth all the trouble; this villa along the north coast of Jamaica was one of the most heavenly places she had ever seen.

The house she approached was simplicity itself, a wide, white one-story affair. It was as if the architect had come up with the most austere design possible so it would not compete with Mother Nature at her most spectacular.

The male British agent, the owner of the villa, was waiting for her at the door. He leaned over and gave her a quick peck on the cheek.

"Is that any way to greet your fiancée?" she asked him. They both got a good laugh out of that.

"Come in, come in," the Englishman said as he picked up her bags and brought them into the house, which was spacious, furnished in a masculine style, and—best of all—cool after the suffocating heat of the Jamaican afternoon. The living room was all rattan and languorously turning ceiling fans, and the wide-open windows held no glass, erasing the distinction between indoors and outdoors. Spartan but comfortable, that's what you'd call it, the woman said to herself, defining the two poles of her former partner's personality.

"You're sure that Lady Ann won't mind my vacationing here?"

the woman asked, referring to his real fiancée, who was back in England awaiting her final divorce decree to come through.

"Oh, she trusts me implicitly."

"Thousands wouldn't," the woman retorted genially.

The Englishman set down his faux fiancée's bags in the living room and said in his distinctly upper-class accent, "Violet's out shopping. Says she can do anything for dinner. Any suggestions?"

"Yes," answered the woman without hesitation, "you can ask her to make anything but Coquilles Saint Jacques."

He winced just a bit.

"They were quite a pair, weren't they?" the woman said, breaking the uncomfortable silence that threatened to swallow them up.

"That frog photog and that American amateur? They got lucky," he responded dismissively, an arrogant look on his long, thin face.

"It was more than luck, and you know it. They were both good. They snookered us. That 'amateur,' as you call her, has the makings of a real agent."

The Englishman decided that the time had come to change the subject and cleared his throat loudly. "And how are you enjoying your forced retirement from MI6, Rosa?"

"Puttering around in my garden, mostly. And you?"

"Doing some puttering around of my own," he said as he led her through the house and out onto a picturesque terrace overlooking the villa's private beach. On the way they passed a piano atop which rested a framed, autographed picture of Noël Coward, one of the Englishman's many famous friends. On the terrace, the first thing the woman noticed was a typewriter on a glass table and a pile of manuscript pages held down by a large indigenous rock.

"Don't tell me," she said in a shocked voice, "you're writing your memoirs."

"A novel, actually. More to the point, a spy novel," he said in a slightly abashed tone.

"Who do you think you are, Somerset Maugham?"

"Well, with all due modesty, I don't think it'll turn out as well as *Ashenden*, but Willie's promised me a quote if it does."

"Willie. Listen to you. You are such an incorrigible name-dropper," she said teasingly.

"You know, Cyril pointed out the very same thing to me last week."

The woman knew that her former MI6 partner was referring to literary critic Cyril Connolly, another famous friend, but let the mention pass unremarked.

"And speaking of names, what do you plan to call your spy hero?" she asked instead.

"Don't have a name for him yet. But it's got to be just right. After all, good old Sapper has his Bulldog Drummond, and Buchan his Richard Haney."

"Can you use my name for the love interest? There will be a love interest, won't there?"

"Yes, but at the risk of hurting your feelings, I must say that Rosa Klebanoff sounds more like a villainess's name to me."

The woman sighed, and the Englishman gave her an apologetic look. "I'm sorry, I'm being a terrible host. Why don't you freshen up, and by the time you get back, I'll have drinks ready for us."

"That sounds lovely."

After showing Rosa where her bedroom was, the Englishman went to the bar and expertly mixed two extra-dry vodka martinis for himself and his guest. He took special care to ensure that both drinks were shaken, not stirred.

Drink in hand, the retired English spy returned to the terrace, sat down on a wicker chaise longue, and tried to concentrate on his most pressing matter at hand: what should the name of his secret agent hero be? He had tried so many combinations, but to no avail. The name had to be utterly bland and unmemorable as befitting a spy's secret identity. And as he turned over several more possibilities in his mind, Ian Fleming sat back and idly picked up the nearest book at hand—*Birds of the West Indies* by James Bond.

XXIII

W hy do I have to wear a suit?" Jackie asked her mother. "It's hot out. Why can't I wear a dress?"

"You're going to a job interview, not a tea party," her mother answered tartly. "You have to look professional."

"Yes, but I can still look feminine." She fixed her mother with a steely eye. Couldn't her mother see that she wasn't the old Jackie anymore, that after all the life-or-death decisions she'd had to make in Paris, this one was child's play? "Mummy, I appreciate your help, but I'm perfectly capable of finding the appropriate thing to wear for my job interview. Mr. Waldrop should be hiring me for what's inside my head, not what's on my back."

Her mother flinched at this retort, a response that gave Jackie no small satisfaction. Oh, what a joy it was to be getting the upper hand for once with the imperious Janet.

For a long moment, her mother said nothing, quietly taking the measure of her daughter. When she spoke, her tone was surprisingly conciliatory. "You're right, Jacks. I keep forgetting you're a woman now and how well you can take care of yourself. But that's how mothers are. We always want to look out for our children, no matter what their age." She gave Jackie's arm a little squeeze but couldn't resist a parting shot that she called over her shoulder as she walked out of the room. "Wait 'til you're a mother yourself. You'll see."

Jackie put on the dress that she wanted to wear—a tailored, form-fitting shirtwaist that hit just the right note between femininity and professionalism—and then left for her appointment.

The newsroom of the *Times-Herald* was everything Jackie expected it to be: a noisy warren of huddled desks spanning the entire floor, typewriters and telegraph machines clackety-clacking like the wheels of a train running at high speed, telephones ringing nonstop, papers and books strewn about everywhere, reporters and editors with shirt pockets full of pencils shouting to one another across the room, the smell of coffee and stale air, and the ongoing rise and fall of animated conversation broken by intermittent bursts of loud laughter. The atmosphere vibrated with the crazed, volatile energy of an asylum—and Jackie fell in love with it on the spot.

A girl typing furiously at her desk, without looking up or taking her hands off the keys, pointed Jackie in the direction of Frank Waldrop's office with a nod of her head. "It's over there," she said. "Third door on the right."

Jackie found the door ajar, but she stood outside for a moment, gathering her nerve before rapping lightly on its glass pane.

"Come in," a man's voice called. He sounded authoritative, but not unkind.

Stepping inside, she couldn't see what Waldrop looked like because he was seated behind his desk, engrossed in an open copy of *Life* magazine held up in front of him, obscuring his face. But what Jackie could see from that angle was the full-frontal cover of the magazine, and the riveting photograph on it gave her a start. There, standing proudly in front of the DC-3 in all her regal dignity, was a smiling Princess Nureen returning to her homeland with her giant bodyguard, Dexter, by her side.

"Hello, Mr. Waldrop, I'm Jacqueline Bouvier, and I know the photographer who did the cover of that magazine," she said.

Waldrop put his copy of *Life* down on his desk and looked up at her with a mixture of surprise and curiosity. "You do? And who might that be?"

"His name is Jacques Rivage. He's part French and part Balazistani and a very talented young photographer. I met him in Paris when I was there recently."

"Jacques Rivage, you say?" Waldrop thumbed to the credit page of the magazine, found the name of the photographer who did the front cover, nodded, and looked up at Jackie with an expression of approval on his face. "Recognizing a photographer's work is a good start for someone who wants to be an Inquiring Camera Girl," he said, a small smile playing about his lips.

"I'm familiar with your work too," Jackie said, surprised at her own boldness. But she had done her homework, asking Hughdie to tell her everything he knew about Waldrop, and she wanted her prospective employer to know it.

Waldrop's ears perked up. His face wore the typical newspaperman's expression of vigilant skepticism as if he were always sniffing the air for a scoop and distrusting it at the same time. "So tell me, what do you know about my work?"

"It was because of you that the *Washington Times-Herald* was the first newspaper in the country, certainly in Washington, to be out on the street with the news that Pearl Harbor was bombed," she answered quickly. As though reading a child his favorite bedtime story, Jackie went on to recount how he had managed this feat. "All of Washington was out at the Redskins football game that day, but you were at the office. When you got the news on the police radio, you called the Redskins office and told them to put on their loudspeaker at Griffith Stadium: 'All *Times-Herald* people report to their office on the double.' That's how you were able to round up your staff and beat the competition in reporting the attack. You're famous for that, Mr. Waldrop, and it would be my honor to work for someone like you."

Waldrop looked openly pleased, and Jackie had the feeling that she could have sat there dumb as a post for the rest of the interview, and he still would have hired her. But he stopped smiling and pursed his lips in a judicious way. "I'm flattered, Miss Bouvier," Waldrop said finally, "but I need to know a little more about you. Do you know how to use a camera?"

"Oh, yes, a Speed Graphic," Jackie said brightly. She pointed to a large leather folio she'd brought with her. "Would you like to see some of the photographs I've taken?"

"Yes, let's take a look."

She handed him the folio, and he put it on the desk and opened it. A look of amazement spread across his face as he turned the pages filled with photographs Jackie had taken of the famous guests at the Duke and Duchess of Windsor's party.

Jackie couldn't help smiling as she watched Waldrop's eyes pop open when he saw Marlene Dietrich, David Niven, the Duchess of Windsor, Christian Dior, Diana Dors, and Evelyn Waugh. "They were taken at a costume party, but I think the real people are recognizable anyway," she said helpfully.

"Oh, yes, they're recognizable all right," Waldrop said, unable to contain the slight note of astonishment in his voice at seeing this sample of her work.

He closed the folio and looked Jackie in the eye. "You've obviously had some experience photographing famous people, and some of the ones you'll be photographing on this job will be famous too, but they'll be Washington types—senators, congressmen, the first lady, and so on. And we'll be looking for some interesting human-interest angles. Do you have any thoughts about that?"

Jackie pursed her lips, trying to come up with something fresh to a hardened old newspaperman like him. She noticed some framed photographs on his desk of a young boy and a girl who were probably Waldrop's children, and she had an idea. "I think I'd like to do a column about how the young children of the president or his nieces and nephews feel about him and his job," she told Waldrop. "Are they proud of him? Do they worry about his safety? Do they wish he could spend more time with them? Children are refreshingly honest. They don't have the pretenses adults do, so what they have to say could be eye-opening. I'd photograph them coming out of school, but that's not all. I've studied art extensively, and I'd draw my own pictures of them too, capturing their personalities in a way photographs can't always do."

Waldrop nodded. "That's a good column. Readers will like it." He folded his hands on his desk, a sign that he was through questioning Jackie and was about to make an offer. "You know, Miss Bouvier, the Inquiring Camera Girl is not as high-paying a position as a correspondent," he began, sounding like a doctor giving bad news to a patient, but Jackie maintained the same pleasant expression she'd worn throughout the interview. "The most I can offer you is a starting salary of forty-two fifty a week."

Jackie smiled. It wasn't a windfall, but $42.50 a week at a nice steady job where her life wouldn't be in danger sounded good to her. Besides, added to the money she'd be making as a part-time CIA agent, it would be enough to keep her in an occasional Dior outfit or a pair of Gucci shoes.

"I'll take it, Mr. Waldrop," she said happily. "Thank you so much. I know you won't regret hiring me as the Inquiring Camera Girl." She rose and held out her hand to him.

"I have no doubt of that," he said, shaking her hand firmly. "If fact, if the truth be told, Miss Bouvier," he added with a broad smile, "I'd say you're ready to take on the world."

When she entered Allen Dulles's office, the receptionist greeted her warmly, apparently recognizing her from her last visit for her debriefing. Now she was here to get her second hush-hush assignment. "Good morning, Miss Bouvier, Mr. Dulles is expecting you. Go right on in."

Once again, Jackie was thankful that Hugh D. Auchincloss was her stepfather. Intelligence executives as highly placed as Allen Dulles usually kept their visitors waiting—unless, of course, the visitor was the president of the United States or someone of that ilk. But as an old family friend of Hughdie's, Dulles welcomed Jackie into his inner sanctum as readily as Hughdie had invited Dulles into Merrywood many times.

The aromatic smell of pipe tobacco wafted into Jackie's nostrils as she entered Dulles's office, and she saw his ubiquitous Kaywoodie in his mouth, smoke curling lazily to the ceiling. He was leaning back in his handsome antique leather executive chair, with his hands behind his head, chatting with a tall, thin man in his early thirties who stood beside him.

"Hello, Jacqueline. It's good to see you again," Dulles greeted her. He removed the pipe from his mouth and waved it toward the younger man wearing the same uniform that Dulles had on, a dark gray, three-piece suit and wire-rim eyeglasses, and made a perfunctory introduction. "This is Tod Henshaw, my assistant. Tod, meet Jacqueline Bouvier."

"Pleased to meet you," Tod said with a thin smile, coming forward and awkwardly sticking out his hand. Shy and studious-looking, with a pallor that suggested a life spent indoors poring over top secret documents, he was obviously unaccustomed to dealing with women CIA agents. But at least his handshake was firm, and his palm was not wet.

"A pleasure," Jackie murmured.

"Please have a seat, Jacqueline," Dulles said, motioning with the pipe toward an aging, mottled cognac-colored leather sofa. Jackie was beginning to think Dulles used the pipe more as a pointer than as an instrument for smoking tobacco.

Without being told, Tod joined Jackie on the sofa, keeping a respectable distance from her while Jackie folded her hands in her lap like an obedient schoolgirl waiting for class to begin.

"If you recall, when I approached you about your assignment in Paris at your graduation party at Merrywood last week"— my God, could it have been only a week ago? it seemed like a century, Jackie thought—" I told you that you would be undergoing intensive training until October when your next project would start," Dulles began. "Do you remember that?"

"Yes, I do remember," Jackie lied. Actually, she had no recollection of any intensive training or another three-month project starting in October or she wouldn't have taken the Inquiring Camera Girl job. But she'd wriggled her way out of the *Vogue* trainee position, so maybe she could get Waldrop to postpone her start until January. She'd have to cross that bridge when she came to it.

Dulles must have seen the wheels in her head spinning like a car's tires on a patch of ice because he asked, "Is anything wrong?"

"No, no," Jackie assured him quickly. "I was just wondering, will the October mission be in Paris again?"

"No, it'll be in Havana this time."

"Havana! Oh, how exciting! Can you tell me what I'll be doing there?"

Suddenly, Dulles found a use for his Kaywoodie besides pointing with it. He stuck the pipe in his mouth and drew on it, clearly stalling for time. After a long pause, he removed the pipe, blew out a puff of smoke that hung between them like a passing cloud, and said, "I'd rather not go into details at this time, but I can tell you that you'll be doing some highly important work for the CIA that is critical to our national security."

Jackie waited for further tidbits but realized none were forthcoming when she saw Dulles shove the Kaywoodie back in his mouth and clench on it hard enough to bite it in two. "Anything I can do to help," she offered lamely.

"Good. Now Tod here"—he motioned toward his assistant—"has another matter he wants to discuss with you that we think is 'up your alley,' to use a colloquial expression." Jackie was wondering whether Tod would ever get to say anything besides "Pleased to meet you" when Dulles finally turned the floor over to him. "Tod, why don't you tell Jacqueline what we have in mind."

Tod cleared his throat, plainly nervous about broaching this top secret subject, but he plunged in bravely. "As I've told Director Dulles, there's an ambitious young politician it would be advantageous for the agency to have on our side, and we think he would be very susceptible to your charms. He's a thirty-four-year-old Democratic congressman from Massachusetts, a war hero, and comes from a wealthy Boston family..."

"You don't mean John F. Kennedy, do you?" Jackie interrupted.

Tod and Dulles exchanged looks of surprise. "Why, yes... yes, I do," Tod stammered. "Do you know him?"

Jackie burst out laughing. "Friends of mine, Charles and Martha Bartlett—Charlie is the Washington correspondent for the *Chattanooga Times*—have been trying to match me up with Jack Kennedy like mad," she explained. "The Bartletts are very fond of both of us, and now that they're married, they think everyone else should be too. Every time Charlie sees me, he goes on and on about what a catch Jack Kennedy is—he's so handsome, he's so young to be a U.S. representative, he's a millionaire since his twenty-first birthday, he's a courageous war hero who was injured on a PT boat mission in the Pacific. Believe me, I know Jack Kennedy's curriculum vitae by heart."

Tod shot Dulles a look, silently pleading with him to intercede.

"All of those things about Jack Kennedy are true," Dulles said, picking up the ball, "but we're not asking you to marry him. We would just like you to go out with him a few times and use your considerable beauty and intelligence to persuade him to become a friend of the CIA. We need all the help we can get in Congress, especially from the Democrats." When Jackie didn't reply, Dulles pulled out his trump card. "You know, I happened to mention Jack Kennedy to your parents while you were in Paris, and your mother was very enthusiastic about your dating him."

Now Jackie threw back her head and burst out laughing a

second time. No wonder her mother had cooled off on John Husted and hadn't mentioned him once since she'd been home. Dulles had found a better match for her daughter—a handsome United States representative who became a millionaire at the age of twenty-one. What chance did poor, plodding $17,000-a-year stockbroker John Husted have against *that*?

Jackie felt as though a tag team of Dulles, the Bartletts, and her mother had converged on her and were twisting her arm to go out with Jack Kennedy. Still, if he was everything everyone said he was, what did she have to lose?

"So let me get this straight," she said. "All you want me to do is go on dates with the congressman a few times and talk up the CIA to him. Is that right?"

"Exactly, that's all there is to it," Dulles said. He could see she was wavering, so he added, "If you win him over, you'll score big points with the agency, and there's no danger involved in this at all."

Yeah, right, Jackie thought, that's what you said about Petrov.

Then Dulles felt morally obliged to impart some information to Jackie, even if it meant she would decline the mission. "As much as I want you to take on this project, Jacqueline, there's something I should warn you about." He paused as if trying to find the right words.

"Yes?" Jackie prompted him.

Dulles came out with it reluctantly. "Jack Kennedy has a reputation for being an incorrigible ladies' man."

Jackie's eyes widened in what Dulles mistook for disapproval. He knew that hearing a man was a womanizer would make most women run the other way. What he didn't know was that Jacqueline Lee Bouvier was not like most other women. It never would have occurred to him that for her, that familiar flaw was precisely what made John F. Kennedy impossible to resist, no matter how their meeting might test her mettle. After all, if the assassin hadn't done her in, who could?

"That's not going to stop me," she said, wiping the disappointed look off Dulles's face. "I can handle Jack Kennedy. He's about to meet his match."

Acknowledgments

These days, it takes a village to publish a novel. And these are the villagers I would like to thank for making this book possible:

To Kathrin King Segal, a talented writer and musician, who was a critical early reader of the book.

To Melissa Chinchillo, our indefatigable literary agent, for taking a chance on us.

To Tracy Martin, our first editor at Grand Central, for saying yes to us.

To Alex Logan, our second editor at Grand Central, for taking the baton and running with it all the way to the finish line.

To the staff at the Jefferson Market Library, for creating such a wonderful space for writers to work, inside a landmark Greenwich Village architectural treasure.

To Hy Bender and the writers and actors of his New York Screenwriters Workshop, for providing a creative environment for turning dreams into reality.

To Tim Hunkin, whose Web site on "Illegal Engineering" provided some details for Henri's exploits as a cracksman. Check it out if you want to learn the history of safecracking.

To the late Phyllis Levy, a publishing legend, who always encouraged me to write this type of novel.

To the memory of my mother, Gloria Salikof, for instilling in me a lifelong love of reading and writing.

And especially to Marilyn and Rachel, my two polestars, who make every new day a joy.

                                                    Ken Salikof

Special thanks are due Melissa Chinchillo, our agent at Fletcher & Company, and Tracy Martin, formerly an editor at Grand Central Publishing, both of whom championed this book from the beginning as the first in a Jackie spy novel series. Alex Logan, the Grand Central editor who "inherited" the book from Tracy, worked tirelessly to give us suggestions that were always astute and on point. We're also grateful to Beth deGuzman and all the other folks at Grand Central for their continuing support.

Thanks to Edward Klein's *All Too Human* (Pocket Books, 1996) for providing a detailed description of the dinner party scene in the preview of *Havana to Die For*.

Improbable as it may seem, it was my co-author's ad in Craigslist that brought us together as the writing team of Maxine Kenneth. So thank you, Craigslist, for giving me an opportunity to try my hand at a genre so different from anything I've done before.

And finally, I can never repay my husband, Lawrence Mitnick, and my daughters, Ilene Schnall and Rona Schnall, for their love and encouragement through all the travail that being an author involves. I'm incredibly lucky to have you in my corner. You've given my path its heart.

Maxine Schnall

Jackie's next mission, should she choose to accept it, will test her strength, her smarts—and her heart.

HAVANA TO DIE FOR

Please turn this page for a preview.

A Sneak Peek at

HAVANA TO DIE FOR

I'm as ready as I'll ever be, Jackie told herself as the front door clicked shut like an exclamation point. She drew in the early-evening air filled with the fragrance of gardens in bloom and the spice of a new adventure. This was the big night. A date that Jacqueline Lee Bouvier hoped would not live in infamy. She *had* to make a good impression on Jack Kennedy when the Bartletts introduced her at their supper party arranged for that very purpose.

What Charlie and Martha Bartlett didn't know was that Jackie had met Jack Kennedy once before. As she drove away from Merrywood, her stepfather Hugh Auchincloss's Virginia estate, and headed for the Bartletts' home in Georgetown, Jackie remembered that first random meeting with the young congressman from Massachusetts. She was on a train returning to her junior year at Vassar with a classmate when Jack and his assistant invited themselves into their compartment. Their conversation was all a blur now—mostly flirtatious bantering on Jack's part and tolerant amusement on Jackie's. But what stuck in her mind was Jack Kennedy's indisputable allure. He was matinee-idol handsome, wickedly funny, and fiercely ambitious, yet charmingly shy. Back at Vassar, she had dashed off a letter to a friend, describing what an insistent flirt the congressman had been, but that she felt an absolute attraction to him all the same.

Now, as Jackie crossed the Chain Bridge in the 1947 black Mercury convertible given to her by her father and took Reservoir Road into Georgetown, her pulse quickened at the thought of meeting Jack Kennedy again.

Within minutes she pulled up in front of 3419 Q Street, the typical mid-city narrow, brick row house where the Bartletts lived. Jackie had driven with the convertible's top up so her hair wouldn't get mussed, but she didn't bother locking the car. Georgetown, the oldest neighborhood in Washington, D.C., was a safe one. Besides, if the car did get stolen, her mother would be thrilled. She thought that a convertible was unsafe and had been badgering Jackie's stepfather to buy her a Buick sedan. The fact that the convertible belonged to "Black Jack"—her mother's philandering ex-husband who still made her blood boil more than a decade after their divorce—was an even bigger strike against it.

At the front door, Jackie smoothed out the Dior outfit that she'd bought in Paris, took a deep breath, and announced her arrival with the brass knocker.

"Hi, Jackie, we've been waiting for you," Charlie Bartlett said, smiling broadly as he opened the door and gave her a quick peck, appropriate for an old flame who was now a married man with a baby on the way.

"I'm not late, am I?" Jackie asked.

"No, no, you're right on time," Charlie said, squeezing her hand in a way that reminded her of their dates two and a half years ago. Jackie had been an impressionable nineteen-year-old college student then, and he was a twenty-seven-year-old wunderkind journalist who had opened the first Washington bureau for the *Chattanooga Times*, a sister paper of the *New*

York Times. Their romance fizzled when Charlie said that he could never give Jackie the exciting high life she coveted, but now he was determined to find a more appropriate suitor for her. Who better than Jack Kennedy, one of Charlie's closest friends and the most eligible bachelor in Washington?

A year had gone by since Charlie had married the perfect mate for himself—Martha Buck, the daughter of a wealthy steel mogul—and now he wanted to help Jackie find the same marital bliss with Jack Kennedy. Little did he know that Allen Dulles, deputy director of the CIA, was even more eager for the two to hit it off.

For a moment, Jackie saw herself back in Dulles's office receiving her assignment, and she again heard his cajoling voice speaking to her about Jack Kennedy. "We're not asking you to marry him," he'd said. "We would just like you to go out with him a few times and use your considerable beauty and intelligence to persuade him to become a friend of the CIA." Jackie felt a pang of conscience. *What would the Bartletts think if they knew the real reason why I'm here?*

"Let me introduce you to everyone," Charlie said, cutting into Jackie's thoughts and leading her into the living room. Guests were milling around in the small room that was modestly decorated with a pair of antique armchairs, some inexpensive furniture, and a few nondescript prints on the ivory-colored walls.

Jackie turned to Charlie and gave him an anxious look. "Is he here?" she whispered.

"No, Jack hasn't come yet," Charlie whispered back, "but he's always late."

Martha Bartlett, a striking redhead who appeared to be about five months' pregnant, emerged from the kitchen, cigarette aloft in one hand and cocktail in the other.

"Jackie, you look divine," she said, air kissing her on both cheeks, European-style. She turned to her husband. "Charlie, why don't you fix Jackie a drink, and I'll do the introductions."

A quick glance around the room told Jackie that Martha had invited the usual crowd of young, up-and-coming socialite couples who frequented the Clambake Club in Newport and wintered in Palm Beach. The only one who stood out was a beautiful, slim young woman who apparently had come to the party alone.

"And this is Loretta Sumers. She's an accessories editor at *Glamour* magazine and an old Long Island schoolmate of mine," Martha said, introducing Jackie.

"So nice to meet you, Loretta," Jackie said with a tight smile. *Uh-oh, I know who you are. You're the extra woman who's here in case Jack Kennedy doesn't think that I'm his cup of tea.* She couldn't help wondering, cattily, if *Glamour* paid for Loretta to get those fashionable blonde highlights in her light brown hair and where Jackie could get hers streaked the same way.

Martha prattled away about how Loretta's family had such fun socializing with the Kennedys every winter in Palm Beach. Jackie listened politely to all this, but when she heard that Loretta's nickname was Hickey, she almost laughed out loud. Then, imagining how Loretta might have come by that moniker and would be competing for Jack Kennedy's attention, Jackie fell victim to a sharp stab of self-doubt.

At that moment, the door burst open and John Fitzgerald Kennedy made his entrance.

He still looks so *young,* Jackie thought, more like a teenager than a three-term congressman about to be thirty-four in a couple of weeks. He couldn't have weighed more than 150 pounds and had to be at least six feet tall, so he looked as if he were still growing. His haystack of reddish brown hair, toothy smile, and twinkling periwinkle eyes added to the boyish impression. So did the careless way he dressed. Someone will have to do something about his clothes, Jackie mused, eyeing the shapeless, too-big sports jacket and skimpy, too-short trousers dangling gracelessly around his ankles. But his overall effect was that of a genial force of nature—a magnetic field of charisma that drew everyone to him irresistibly and captivated them with his charm.

Jack immediately began working the room, inquiring how this person's sailboat did in Nantucket's Figawi race and how that person's trip to Acapulco had gone and when another person's cousin who was serving in the Korean War was coming home. Jackie was amazed at the almost encyclopedic knowledge Jack had about each guest. Even more impressive was his satiric sense of humor and hilarious impersonations of people in the news (everyone from President Truman to a Mafia gangster) that had them all laughing.

Finally, Martha extricated Jackie from her perch on a love seat in a corner of the room from which she'd been quietly observing the scene at a distance like a bird-watcher with binoculars, and brought her over to the life-of-the-party congressman.

"Jack, I'd like you to meet Jacqueline Bouvier," Martha said, tapping him on the shoulder.

"The *lovely* Jacqueline Bouvier," he said, looking at Jackie with interest and flashing his intoxicating smile. "Pleased to meet you, Jacqueline."

"The pleasure is mine," Jackie said, batting her eyelids at him demurely and returning his smile. "Actually, we've met before."

"We have?"

His look of surprise told Jackie that, by this time, she had

probably disappeared into a faceless crowd of college girls, sec-
retaries, models, actresses, and other assorted females Jack had
flirted with instinctively.

"Yes, it was on a train..."

Suddenly, Loretta Sumers was tugging on Jack's sleeve. "Oh,
Jack, there's something I need to speak with you about," she
said, adding as she glanced at Jackie, "Do you mind?"

Without waiting for an answer, Loretta led Jack away. He
looked back at Jackie and shrugged, unable to get out from the
insistent "Hickey's" talonlike grasp.

Jackie retreated to her refuge on the love seat, feeling defeated
by a score of Loretta, 1; Jackie, 0.

But within moments, Jack was back. With athletic grace, he
slipped into the empty seat beside Jackie. "So tell me something
about yourself, Jacqueline," he said. Displaying the inquisitive-
ness that he was known for, he started asking her questions.
Where did she go to school? What was her degree in? Had she
done any traveling lately? Did she have a job?

Jackie answered all his questions without revealing anything about herself that she didn't want him to know: she had
a degree in French literature from Washington University;
yes, she'd just returned from Paris (on a pleasure trip, not a
CIA assignment); and she would soon be starting work as the
Inquiring Camera Girl for the *Times-Herald*.

This last piece of information seemed to pique Jack's interest. "Really? The *Times-Herald*? Have you been following their
coverage of the House Un-American Activities Committee?
And of Joe McCarthy in the Senate?"

Jackie wrinkled her nose at Jack's mention of this zealous
anti-Communist crusader. The blacklisting of writers, actors,
directors, and musicians whose work she loved was unconscio-
nable to her. "I think there's something creepy about a fanatic

like Senator McCarthy," she said. "Anyone who works with him has to be a malicious goon who enjoys persecuting the most talented people in the country."

Jack started as if blindsided, then quickly recovered his usual aplomb. "I'll tell my brother Bobby that," he said, his lips curled in an ironic half smile. "Bobby is a staff lawyer for Joe McCarthy's Permanent Subcommittee on Investigations."

"Oh." Jackie gulped and felt her cheeks grow flaming hot. She studied her drink, wishing she could take back her words and drown them there.

Once again, Martha Bartlett saved her, announcing that dinner was being served. "Take your places, everyone," she called out, pointing to the table set with place cards and china.

Naturally, Martha had arranged for Jackie to be seated next to Jack. This is going to be horrible, Jackie thought. He probably won't say another word to me all night.

But Jack surprised her. He gave her an admiring look as he pulled out her chair and said with a smile in his voice, "I like a woman who speaks her mind."

Whew! Jackie felt like a death row inmate whose sentence had been commuted, but she didn't know if Jack really meant the comment or was just being polite. Play it safe, she warned herself, and let him do the talking from now on.

While Jack tore into the chicken casserole that the cook had prepared, Jackie hardly ate. She was intent on following her father's expert mating game instructions to pay attention to everything a man says. "Fasten your eyes on him like you were staring into the sun," he had told her. But he had also warned her to be inaccessible and mysterious, claiming that once a man possesses a woman, he automatically loses interest in her.

So Jackie hung on every word that Jack said, fixing her large brown eyes on him as if mesmerized, her lips slightly parted, as she responded with an overawed "golly" or "gee" in a whispery, little-girl voice to Jack's monologue. He spoke about what a close-knit family the Kennedys were and how his father had tapped him to fill in the empty shoes left by his older brother Joe when he had been killed in the war. And although Jackie gave the impression that she found Jack utterly captivating, she remembered what Black Jack had told her about being untouchable. Whenever Jack leaned in too close or put his hand on hers, she politely pulled away.

Jackie's performance was so convincing that everyone else in the room seemed to have disappeared. She needn't have worried about competition from Hickey Sumers (she was the one who looked defeated now) or any other women there—Jack had eyes only for her. Jackie's intense adulation leavened with a pinch of coquettishness seemed to impel Jack to drop a politician's natural instinct for guarding his privacy. Over dessert and coffee, he confided in Jackie that he was bored being a congressman and was thinking of challenging Henry Cabot Lodge, the Republican junior senator from Massachusetts, in the coming election.

Jackie wasn't sure how she should respond to this revelation— somehow "golly" and "gee" didn't seem adequate—when Martha stood up from the table and said, "Come on, everyone, it's time for charades."

Oh no, I was doing so well, Jackie thought, when she discovered that she and Jack were on opposing teams. She knew from his history as a war hero and winner of tough political campaigns that Jack was a competitor to be feared. A little tremor of apprehension coursed through her when she imagined making such a complete fool of herself that he might never want to see her again.

"You *didn't*," she said to Jack when she unfolded the paper he'd handed her and saw the name scribbled on it: Henry Cabot Lodge. Was she a sparring partner for Jack's potential bout with the senator? She felt like slinking off to the powder room, but the teasing grin on Jack's face got her dander up, and an idea came to her that she had to try.

She put her arms out at her sides, began waving them, and mouthed the sounds of clucking. "Chicken," someone on her team shouted. Jackie shook her head and brought her hands toward each other in a shortening motion. "Hen," another team member shouted. Jackie nodded encouragingly, then made a stretching motion. "Henna…henpeck…Henry," someone else called out.

Jackie nodded an emphatic yes.

Then she depicted a big box with a line down the middle and a knob on each side. "Door," someone shouted. Jackie shook her head. "Closet," someone else called out. Again Jackie shook her head. "Armoire," said another, and they all laughed as Jackie rolled her eyes. Then Charlie Bartlett, who was on her team shouted, "Cabinet." Jackie nodded and brought her hands together as if squeezing something. And Charlie said, "Cab… cabin…" Jackie nodded hard, and Charlie finally shouted, "Cabot! Henry Cabot Lodge!"

"Oh, Charlie, yes, thank you!" Jackie said. She wanted to kiss him when she caught the admiring look that Jack gave her. But then she glanced at her watch and gasped. It was 9:30, almost time for her to be meeting John Husted for a nightcap at the Georgetown Inn. She desperately wanted to break up with John and was hoping that she'd have the courage to do it tonight.

"You're leaving so soon?" Jack asked with disappointment in his voice.

"I'm sorry, but I have to," Jackie said. She gave him an inviting look. "But if you'd like to walk me to my car, that would be wonderful."

"Of course," Jack said, leaping up from his chair and linking his arm in hers.

When they reached her black Mercury convertible parked in the middle of Q Street, Jack asked, "Would you like to go someplace for a drink, Jackie?"

He was smiling at her, but he had a predatory look in his silver-blue eyes. It was the same look that Jackie had seen her father give a woman when he was sizing her up to see how fast he could get her into bed.

The womanizer once-over, Jackie thought and looked away. "Uh...I don't know..." she stammered. Do I have a headache? Do I have to get up early? As she frantically searched for an excuse, she absentmindedly yanked the car door open.

And to her shock, a body fell half out of the car, like a corpse making its entrance in a mystery melodrama.

It was John Husted!

"Hey, Jacks," he said, to her complete and utter humiliation, "who's your friend?"

Allen Dulles sat behind his desk, puffing on his Kaywoodie, his face expressionless as he listened to Jackie's account of her meeting with Jack Kennedy the night before.

"Everything was going along swimmingly just as we had planned when out of the blue, there was my boyfriend," she said, "and I can tell you, Jack Kennedy didn't take it any too kindly." Slumped in a chair across from Dulles, she sounded like a dazed accident victim describing the catastrophe to the police.

Jackie shuddered as she recalled how badly the evening had ended. A rudely awakened Husted explained to her that he was walking along Q Street, saw her car parked there, decided to wait for her in it, and had fallen asleep. As for Jack, he hadn't bothered to hang around for an explanation. He merely gave

Jackie a withering look and slunk off into the night in a mist of bruised ego.

Jackie was beside herself. Leave it to good-old-dependable John Husted to show up at the most inopportune time and turn such an auspicious beginning into a fiasco. She sighed and looked at Dulles with a pained expression. "If only I had locked the car, that never would have happened."

Dulles nodded. "That's a good lesson learned," he said evenly.

Jackie stiffened, expecting him to reprimand her, but instead, Dulles smiled at her in an avuncular way and said, "Cheer up, Jacqueline. This may turn out to be a bit of serendipity."

"What do you mean?" Jackie asked.

"For a man like Jack Kennedy, nothing is a bigger aphrodisiac than competition," Dulles said with a chuckle. "You'll hear from him again. I guarantee it."